REALMS OF PEACE

A SOVEREIGN SISTERS NOVEL

Teanna Lynne

Cover design by: Delilah Cay

Printed in the United States of America

Authors Note: This edition of Realms of Peace was updated January 2025 and page numbers vary in previous editions.

To Ali, Delilah, and Kaitie, my chosen sisters.
This is for us.

Pronunciation Guide

Locations

Estarynn - (es-tare-rin)

Vulca - (vulh-ka)

Sena - (sen-uh)

Rayan - (ray-in)

Eteri- (eh-tare-ee)

Cansu - (con-su)

People

Eve- (eve)

Mar - (marr)

Rose- (rose)

Cay- (kay)

Oak - (oak)

Queen Elani - (queen el-on-e)

King Basc - (king bask)

High Lady Ayana - (high lady a-on-ah)

Terran - (tare-in)

Oliver - (ol-iv-er)

Reed - (reeed)

Queen Mira - (queen meer-ah)

King Callan - (king cal-in)

Finn - (fin)

Rian - (ree-in)

Nat- (nat)

Prologue

"Child, fetch the wine and bring it to the banquet hall immediately, the royals will be here any moment," my mother says to me with her usual bite.

"Yes, mother," I acknowledge with a nod of my head. I take off at a steady pace to the kitchen, letting my feet carry me there quickly and hoping to not make a scene.

There are hundreds of staff milling about the temple today in preparation. Priestesses and acolytes alike, all working together to ensure that everything is ready for their arrival. One royal would be reason enough to go to all this trouble but it's not just one of them, they're all coming. The most important figureheads of the five realms; Eteri, Vulca, Rayan, Sena, and Cansu. It is practically unheard of given how vulnerable they will be here in the mortal lands; yet here we are, preparing everything so that it is perfect for them.

The ruling families rarely leave their realms and kingdoms, choosing instead to remain within the safety of their respective elemental, and magical protections. At least when they travel to a different land they will feel some connection to their magic should they need it.

They will find no such protections here.

Use of magic is entirely off limits within the mortal lands and especially the temple. Whether it's used to harm, heal, or anything in between, all magic is strictly forbidden. The only magic found is that of the Goddess of Protection herself, Vana. Her guiding light shines down on all of us who call the temple home and guide us in our way of life.

One *without* magic.

The Goddess hasn't been seen in thousands of years but we who live in the temple still worship her. We feel her presence and love every day and continue to live as she had hoped for us, in peace. When the Goddess gave birth to our world she gifted her children with magic in the hopes that it would ensure they live a life of ease and happiness.

She never intended for us to use it against one another.

Which is exactly why those of us who choose to worship her have abandoned magic entirely. To free ourselves from its taint, the corruption of power.

I turn down a busy hallway cluttered with acolytes trying to prepare and nearly run straight into a table stacked with the fine porcelain plates.

"Be careful child, you break one of those and your mother will have your head," reprimands one of the older acolytes with a shake of her head.

I mutter my apologies and continue down the hall, slipping through the archway into the kitchen. It too is crowded. People cross back and forth in front of me as I search the room, spying the glass pitcher filled with wine on the counter. I weave through the chaos and snatch it up before anyone even notices I am here. I slip past a group of younger girls and into the back pathway, avoiding the mess of people back the way I came and heading back toward the banquet hall.

The narrow corridor is much less busy and as I pass a stone statue of Vana, I stop to pay my respects, taking a moment to bow my head and whisper the words of the Goddess, hoping to feel her blessings pass over me. Our devotion continues to protect the lands and guide those in death to eternal peace, even if they might not realize it. Although us acolytes don't use magic- at least not in the same way those outside the mortal lands do- we use prayer and offerings to help guide our path.

Still, we must never interfere with the Goddess's plans. Many acolytes choose to die an early death rather than rely on elemental magic to sustain them for so long as others do. We believe that Vana brought us into this world with a purpose, and when that purpose has been fulfilled she will call us back to her side. Some believe that using magic to sustain themselves is in itself an act that goes directly against the Goddess's wishes. People like my mother.

Once my prayer is complete I continue on my path. I'm a few feet from the door when I hear voices. A riot of people talking at once, all trying to be heard above everyone else. It takes me a moment to realize those voices do not belong to any of the others from the temple.

Muttering a curse under my breath, I slip through the small door that is hidden in the back of the banquet hall, although we rarely refer to it as anything other than the cafeteria. It's where the acolytes take their meals in the morning and at night, during the day we convert it into a prayer room where we can perform our daily blessings. It's nothing lavish, just a simple set of tables and chairs all in neat rows.

Now, a large round table takes up the majority of the space with candles placed at the center to cast a soft glow on the faces seated around it. I suck in a breath and hold it as I take in the rare sight of the royals all gathered together.

The king and queen of Rayan, the Kingdom of Water. The high lord and high lady of Sena, the Earth Realm. The king and queen of Vulca, the Kingdom of Fire. The chief and chieftess of Eteri, the Air Realm. And sitting at the farthest positions from where I stand, the king and queen of Cansu, the Land of Mist.

Or the Land of Darkness as many refer to it.

A chill washes over me as I take in the preternatural darkness that seems to gather around them as the king and queen speak in hushed tones to each other. Their dark heads bent together and cast in shadows.

I shuffle and side-step silently along the wall until I reach my mother and hand her the wine. She gives me a look that tells me she is not pleased with how long I was gone but won't make a scene until after our guests have left. I fight the urge to roll my eyes, knowing that I was barely gone a few minutes and that it is the royals who are early.

Still, my mother is the highest ranking acolyte in the entire temple due to her blessing from the Goddess herself. Visions of the future are sent so that she might protect us from whatever danger awaits, exactly as Vana desires.

As a young girl, she had a vision of a plague that would wipe out half the population. Thankfully, her mother was able to contact the top healers and prepare them so that we could save many lives. It was a miracle, a *true* blessing. The royals thanked my mother for her warnings and help in saving their people and she forever gained their respect. Her service to Estarynn, the home the Goddess created for us, is what fills me with overwhelming pride.

I stand there silently admiring my mother as she walks around the table and pours each glass of wine without so much as spilling a drop. She seems to float across the room, her steps graceful, elegant, almost like a dancer.

I can't help but envy that as I am notoriously clumsy, constantly dropping and breaking things. I am shocked that my mother dared to trust me with the wine at all. Still, even in all my many faults, my mother chose *me* to be the next Great Seer after her time has come to join the Goddess. I say a silent prayer that that time is not soon as I still have much to learn.

I watch as she circles the table, finishing pouring the wine and taking her place with a sweep of her robes.

The Cansu King's voice booms above all others, cutting off their conversations. "My fellow rulers, while it is lovely to see you all here today,

I have to wonder if anyone might share with me *why* this meeting is necessary?" His hand rests gently across his Queen's large, pregnant belly. His thumb moves in small circles, his eyes brimming with love for his mate and unborn child.

The Queen's eyes reflect a similar adoration as I take in the way her hand caresses and smoothes over her stomach in time with his. Wisps of darkness dance around them like smoke, beautiful and terrifying at the same time.

The King of Vulca speaks next, his voice deep and gravelly, "Yes, I do not enjoy traveling so far with all this daylight. My eyes have yet to adjust even after the long trip." He and his Queen squint their eyes, even in the dimly lit room, likely due to the fact their kingdom resides inside a cavern at the base of a volcano. One with very little sunlight if any at all.

I've never traveled outside of the mortal lands but we have an acolyte here who was originally born in the fire kingdom. She speaks of the river of lava and the glowing caverns in such a way that I feel that I have seen it all myself. It is said to be more beautiful than one could imagine.

More complaints file in from the various royals until the Chieftess of Eteri, the Air realm, cuts in, "We have all traveled a long way, far beyond the protection of our elements. I would like to return to my home as soon as possible. So, who is it that called this meeting?"

When nobody speaks up my mother clears her throat. They all turn to look at her where she stands just a few feet in front of me, at the head of the table. Their eyes brim with respect yet there is a hesitation there that I am not used to seeing. My mother's presence *always* inspires confidence.

"I did," she declares confidently, chin raised high. Her dark skin glows with the flicker of candle light, casting shadows under her sharp cheekbones.

I fight to hide the shock from my face. I didn't know that and my mother never keeps secrets from me. Why would she hide that she is the one who summoned the rulers here?

When she told us they would be coming we had all assumed they desired to use our lands since it is a place of peace, of neutrality, where they all are of equal power and status.

"The Goddess herself spoke to me and delivered a message. I asked you all here today to pass that message along. She gave me a vision of the future of all of your realms," my mother continues.

The royals shift in their seats and look to their partners, clearly uncomfortable with this twist. When my mother doesn't continue they all wave their hands as if to grant her permission.

She nods, "Months ago, I was awoken by a terrible vision. The lands, sky, and sea, all stained red with blood. Hundreds of thousands of bodies littered the ground, and screams could be heard from miles away. A great war had broken out and few survived. All of you included. It was unlike any vision I have had before, dark and utterly *terrifying*."

A soft gasp echoes around the table as they demand she continue, sitting on the very edge of their seats.

"What was the cause of this war?" asks the High Lord of Sena, squeezing his High Lady's hand. The couple exchanges a brief, concerned, glance.

"Power. Greed. *Fear*. It is not clear *who* was the cause of this war, but it is clear that one or more kingdoms sought to claim more power for their own and found that they could not take it so easily." My mother takes a deep breath. "Whoever that was led the world into a state of complete darkness and ruin."

"Darkness? What do you mean by darkness?" asked the Eteri Chief. His eyes cut to the Cansu rulers suspiciously.

"I cannot explain it in words. It is more a feeling. Hopelessness. Despair. Pain. Grief. The most unimaginable suffering for all of our people," my mother says with a shudder.

I ache to go to her, to soothe her worries and tell her that everything will be alright, just as she does when I am feeling overwhelmed.

The table is struck silent.

Looks are exchanged until finally the Eteri chief stands and points a finger directly at the King and Queen of Cansu. "You," he says, "you will be the cause of this darkness. This suffering. You are all blind if you think it could be anyone else. The Dark King and Queen have always sought more power; they are not content to rule over their small stretch of mist. We must not allow them to destroy us. We must end them now." His fist slams down on the table, startling me.

I hold back my gasp as the other royals all begin to point to one another and place blame, accusing each other of things that have yet to come to pass.

Until finally my mother holds up a hand, silencing them all.

"We must not allow this vision to happen. No matter what. We must form a blood oath that all those who hold power over an elemental land will never seek to claim another, and that should they attempt to do so, their entire line will perish."

The Rayan Queen laughs, her voice carries a lyrical sort of charm to it, "you can't possibly expect us to agree to such a thing?"

"I do," my mother states plainly, "I would like to perform the ceremony now. It is why I have gathered you all here. We mustn't wait another moment."

I wait for the royals to stand, to get into position and heed my mother's warnings. They don't. If anything, my mother's words only cause more fighting to break out.

Soon, so many people are talking that it is impossible to distinguish one from another, their words becoming an unintelligible scream. All of them are pointing and shouting until the King and Queen of Cansu stand from their seats.

"Where do you think you are going?" yells the King of Vulca. His face is a mix of concern and anger, his face as red as his auburn hair.

"My mate and I are leaving. This prophecy is utter nonsense and unless you are willing to do as the priestess has said, there is no reason for us to entertain this foolishness any longer." The pair turn to leave but suddenly his wife is clutching her throat, gasping for breath.

I turn and see the Eteri chief holding out his hand, controlling the very air in her lungs. He shouldn't be able to use magic here, there are wards in place to prevent it. Yet somehow, he does. The others turn to look at him as he continues to deprive the pregnant Queen of oxygen.

My heart races as the scene unfolds before me.

The King of Cansu screams to release his wife, his Queen, his mate, as he tries to desperately block the magic. But it's no use, her face turns blue as she claws at her throat, her eyes bulging as a trickle of blood leaks from her nose.

She drops, her entire body going limp as it hits the floor with an unceremonious thud.

A gut wrenching scream tears from her mate's chest and with a blast he releases his magic all at once.

Darkness consumes the room and my eyes go black. I raise my hand in front of me but I can't even make out an outline. There are shouts and screams as the royals all begin to attack. Magic is flying everywhere and the metallic scent of blood is thick in the air. A flash of fire passes just past my nose, leaving the stench of sulfur behind in its wake.

I stumble back and hit the wall, sliding down and curling into a tight ball. The entire room descends into chaos, the walls are on fire, casting the space in a red hue as the battle continues. Frantic voices seem to come from every direction, some I recognize as other acolytes.

My eyes peel open, watering from the smoke filling the air as I search the dim light for my mother. I can't find her anywhere so I start to crawl along the wall back towards where I know the door to the hall is. My hand slips in something hot and sticky and I almost smack my forehead against the floor.

I look down and find the concrete covered in sticky hot blood. Pools of it. Everywhere. At the center of the pool in front of me, my *mother*.

I cover my mouth as a scream threatens to tear from my lips, much like the Cansu King's. Her eyes are open and glossy but her chest still rises and falls. I gather her into my lap and try to find the source of the bleeding but it feels like it's coming from everywhere. Pouring her life out onto the floor as though it is nothing.

She looks me in the eyes and touches her hand to my temple. Her fingers are so cold that I'm momentarily distracted but then I see it. All of it. My mother leaves me with her vision and what needs to be done, even this very moment and every moment to come after it. Years and years. Many *centuries* into the future. Until the path is clear and I know what I need to do.

I see it all until it goes black and there is nothing else. I look down intending to ask my mother what it means but her eyes have gone vacant, her hand has fallen limp. The bitter taste of denial coats my tongue as I shake my head.

It's all too much, it's happening too soon. The vision showed me what would happen if I stayed here but I can't just leave my mother like this. She deserves better, she's earned it. Hot tears spill across my cheeks as I try to think of a way to fix this, fix everything, even what has yet to happen.

Cries of battle and bloodshed echo through the room. Flashes of light and flames break through the darkness around me as the royals continue to throw all of their magic at the Dark King. Wind whips my hair around me, the scorching heat in the room has sweat dripping down the back of my neck. Their magic is wild, most likely uncontrolled due to the wards that *should* be preventing them from casting any magic at all.

A rogue spell nearly catches me in the head and I realize it's hopeless. I swallow back a sob and kiss my mother's forehead.

There is only one way to fix things. I know what needs to happen next, and it's not possible if I stay here in this room.

I continue to crawl until I feel the outline of the door and I slip through, standing on shaking legs and sprint back down the hall towards the kitchen. I pass the statue of Vana as tears continue to roll down my cheeks.

I go to wipe them away but realize my hands are covered in my mother's blood.

I pull my collar up to wipe at my face but it still comes back red. I fight to ignore the smell of death that clings to me. Try to focus instead on the sound of my feet as I run through the hall, the wet smack of them against the stone floor. I don't bother to stop and explain to the other acolytes what has happened. Don't stop to grab my things. I just run. Run from the only home I have ever known.

I push through the final door that leads outside and continue to sprint away. For once, my feet carry me without hesitation, without fear of tumbling or falling. I race through the fields outside the temple with my heart breaking inside my chest. The forest line is far off in the distance, stretching out over an open field of wildflowers.

A large boom sounds from behind me followed by an agonized cry which I know from my vision belongs to the Dark King.

I don't look back. I already know what is about to happen.

My stomach turns as a mix of emotions clouds my mind. There is no time to stop and think about what any of this means, what I must do.

So I keep running, not truly knowing where I am going but I can hear something calling to me in the back of my mind. A voice, trying to get my attention. I ignore it and hope that I can do what my mother has set out for me to do. There is only one way to stop the chaos and destruction that awaits us.

1,000 Years Later

Chapter 1

Eve

The music is blaring so loud the walls shake. I'm on the dance floor in the center of the small room but I can see how they sway. If I didn't know better I would be concerned about the whole building caving in on itself. No, this building has been here for hundreds of years and no amount of jumping up and down is going to cause it to fall.

Hot flesh rubs against my bare skin on all sides and a mix of sweat and body glitter coats my skin. I sway along to the beat letting my hands roam over my exposed thighs and up my short dress. My hands tangle in the dark mess of hair falling down my back. The beat changes and people start jumping along. I throw my head back and stare up at the glowing ceiling as the magic changes it from one color to the next. Blues, then purples, then greens. All bright, vibrant and casting a multicolor glow on everyone crowded beneath them.

"Are you having a good time?" the musician calls from the platform at the front of the room. He casts an amplifying spell to make his voice loud enough to be heard over the music as cheers echo around me and I find myself joining in.

Excitement washes over my skin as it brushes against someone new, sending a buzz straight to my head as I drink it in. I grab on to their shoulder to steady myself before looking at the back towards the bar. Bodies are pressed together in a solid wall but it parts for me as I make my way through, pulling up a stool and laying my chest across the cold marble counter.

"What'll it be Eve?" asks Oz, the bartender. He raises his eyebrows at me while mixing someone's drink. He smiles at them as he hands it over, flashing the tips of his fangs and marking him as a vampire.

"You know me, the usual," I answer, looking around the room for other familiar faces. I spot a few phoenix girls I used to hook up with, huddled along the wall. One of them winks at me and I smile before turning my attention back to the bar.

"One day I'm gonna get you to try something that actually tastes *good*." Oz scoffs, walking to the other end of the bar.

Given that his idea of a good drink comes from someone's neck, I choose to ignore him, opting to bob my head along to the music instead. I let the beat drown everything else out as my drink appears in front of me. I hold the cold glass to my cheek, sighing. A bead of condensation drips from the glass and down my neck but a finger appears to catch it. I turn, ready to bite the finger off for touching me without permission but I stop, recognizing the owner of said finger.

"Hey Eve, I'm surprised to see you here," Sebastian asserts, letting his eyes roam over my body. A slow smirk spreads across his lips as his gaze gets caught on my chest.

I roll my eyes, "And why would you be surprised Sebastian? I come here almost every night." Sebastian and I dated for a few months. Nothing serious but he cried like a bitch when I dumped him a few weeks back.

"Don't go getting all angry, babe. I just thought you might have changed up the routine now that we're not together anymore."

I laugh. "First, don't call me babe. Second, if you thought for even a second that *you* have any impact on what I do with my life, you are sorely mistaken. Do I need to remind you who I am?" I don't often use my title against people but when those people are acting like creeps, I have no hesitation.

His jaw tics but he plasters an easy smile onto his face. He's not terrible to look at, the same pale eyes like most of Vulca. Good jawline and gorgeous blonde curls that he styles perfectly. I consider him for a second before adjusting my posture, pushing my breasts into clearer view. He might be a sleaze but there is one thing he can be good for.

"So, what can I do for you, *babe*," I say mockingly. It's been a few days since I truly fed and I might just be willing to stoop tonight. Not that I haven't gone longer. Still, the small hit I got from the dance floor has me more on edge than I like.

Sebastian reaches out and lets his greasy finger slide down my bare arm making goosebumps rise, not the good kind. "You know I can tell that you're hungry. You've got that look in your eyes. Maybe we can help each other out? You get what you need, I get what I want. Win-win."

I let my gaze travel over him, catching on his exposed chest where he 'forgot' a few buttons on his tunic. "And what is it that you want from me?" I ask. My eyes swirl with the lust I can taste rolling off of him, more intoxicating than any drink I can get at the bar.

He leans in close to whisper in my ear, "You and I both know that I've never tasted anything like you before and probably never will. Call me an addict but I've grown to crave that delicious blood of yours coursing down my throat."

I swallow, trying to hide the heat that his words shoot straight to my core. Vampire bites can be painful but when you have the right partner the pain can quickly turn to pleasure. The memory of his sharp bite against my delicate neck has me feeling reckless. I lean forward to whisper back but before I reach him a familiar voice cuts in.

14

"Back off Sebastian. Eve dumped you weeks ago and everyone here can smell the desperation oozing off of you."

I lean back as my sister steps up beside me. I glance up at Mar and ignore how Sebastian glares at the both of us before stalking away.

Mar replaces him in the stool beside me and a glass appears in front of her. She smiles at Oz and lifts the glass to her lips. "O Positive, my favorite." She groans, taking a sip. A small droplet of blood lingers on her lips which she greedily licks.

I stare at her with my eyebrows raised, waiting for an explanation.

She takes her time downing the glass before setting it back on the counter and turning to look at me, tossing her pale blonde hair over her shoulder. "Oh come on, you weren't seriously about to fuck him again were you?" she asks with a roll of her eyes.

"Don't give me that judgy tone. What, you're allowed to get fed but I'm not?"

"If you're that desperate to feed then I'm worried for you. Besides, you told me yourself that he was awful in bed and more times than not you left his place *starving*," she exaggerates.

I laugh at the truth in her words. As a succubus, I feed off of positive energies like happiness, excitement, and especially lust. Any positive emotion will keep my magic strong but sex, that carnal pleasure, tastes the best. It can be slow and sweet or fast and rich. Good or bad, sex tastes better than anything else.

"Still, it's been a few days since I have been able to feed and I'm getting hangry." I spare a glance back over my shoulder, hoping to catch the eye of that phoenix girl again.

Mar nods, looking around the room and narrowing her eyes at something in the corner. She groans, turning to look at me. "Well that might be the case but the biggest ass in all of Vulca just walked in, and I don't know about you but I'm not in the mood to fight with him tonight."

I turn to look at the door and sure enough, in walks a small horde of cyclops. It's not that I have anything against cyclops as a species, just these particular ones. A few months back one of them decided to get handsy on the dance floor and found themselves missing said hand in under a minute. Their friends didn't exactly appreciate that, but no one touches me unless I want them to.

Not anymore.

I nod to Mar, "Yeah let's just head home, not worth getting into it." A part of me knows that all it would take is one word to the owner and the whole lot of them would be gone in a second. Power in the name and all that. But the other part of me knows I'm not particularly supposed to be here so the less attention the better.

Mar throws a few coins on the counter for Oz and we wave goodbye as we sneak out the back. She falls into step beside me despite her longer legs. Her platinum hair is pushed back behind her ears and down her back, hanging in a sheet that brushes her waist. She wears a fitted tunic that dips into a deep V, showing off her collarbones and drawing attention to her full chest and long neck.

Mar is all angles and sharp features. Her blueish gray eyes are framed by full lashes and her cheekbones are perfectly bronzed. Mar is effortlessly beautiful, but when she tries, she's breathtaking. Most people probably assume she is a succubus with looks like hers. They wouldn't know any better till her teeth sunk deep into their carotid and they were being sucked dry.

She glances at me from the corner of her eyes and flashes me a grin before taking off. She shifts into her vampire form easily, taking off in a split second and racing down the narrow streets of the city. We weave through the alleys and rooftops using our enhanced speed.

I follow close behind her in my own shifted form. For half shifters like us the change is easy, heightened senses, slight physical changes, but for the most part we look the same as we do in our mortal forms.

We race like this all the way back to the palace. I find her leaning against the glass doors to the entrance as I come to a stop.

"Damn, I guess you really do need to feed, Eve, that was pitiful." She grimaces playfully.

"Well maybe if you hadn't scared Seb off I would have had enough energy to beat your cheating ass."

She gasps dramatically and moves her hand over her heart. "I would *never*. It's not my fault you catch on slow. Besides, us vamps can never be beat in a race." She winks at me as she walks through the revolving doors. I follow close behind her shaking my head.

The palace is less of a traditional castle and more of a tall tower nestled at the heart of the city. The top floor is a beautiful patio that overlooks the city and has a clear view to the flowing river of lava. Even though living inside a dormant volcano means no sunlight, there are more pros than cons.

The walls and ceilings of the city are covered in bioluminescent plants that light up the city day and night. Magic helps to change the brightness so we can keep some sense of time without the sun itself. The river flows through the center of the city and casts a beautiful red glow on everything, giving the city the look of a perpetual sunset. It is by far my favorite part of the kingdom I am to inherit, Vulca.

Mar and I only wait a few seconds before the lift arrives to take us up to the residence. Out of all the kingdoms ours is the most advanced. We found a way to use magic to power most of the city. I asked our father how once and he talked for hours, I zoned out after a few minutes. Mar on the other hand, seemed utterly captivated. I pull the level to indicate the 10th floor and try to ignore the questioning looks Mar is not so subtly casting my way.

"What?" I ask, feigning innocence.

She just laughs as the doors open to the large kitchen. A few years ago we worked with some water elementals to create ice boxes that never melt, even with how hot it is here. Being a part of the royal family has its perks afterall.

I walk straight to the box and grab an entire tub of flavored ice. A speciality that I grew to love after visiting Rayan so often. "I told you before, I'm hungry." Even though we both know what kind of hunger I truly feel, at least this will sate the kind that makes my stomach rumble.

Mar shrugs before grabbing a bag of potato crisps from off the counter. "No judgment here, just wondering if you were avoiding home for a reason or if I should just continue to pretend I didn't notice."

I ignore her and walk over to the service stairwell. Mar follows me up the two flights of stairs in silence, pausing behind me while I peek into the hallway and make sure it is empty before walking towards my bedroom door. Mar's room is directly across from mine but she walks in behind me anyways. We make our way to the large bed in the center of the room and get comfy. I offer her a spoon but she shakes her head.

"No, thank you. I'm gonna stick to these," she answers, holding up the bag.

I stick out my hand to grab a crisp but she snatches it away.

"No way, these are mine. If you want them you're going to have to fight me for them."

I raise my hands in surrender and pick up my flavored ice. "All good, I'll stick to this."

We sit in silence for a few minutes before Mar clears her throat. "So, are you going to tell me why you missed the meeting with the advisors tonight?"

I push my spoon around the bowl and shrug.

"That's it? A shrug? I'm going to need a better explanation than that, Eve."

I sigh. "What does it matter if I'm there or not? Besides, you were there to cover for me." I give her a broad smile.

Mar takes the bowl from me and leans over to set it on the nightstand. "Listen, you know I don't mind covering for you. But you're starting to worry father, and your mother keeps asking me where you are. I'm beginning to run out of answers."

Of course my mother is asking questions. The Queen has to know every*thing* about every*one*. Mar is lucky that we only share a father and she doesn't have to deal with my mother's snooping. I love her, but she has become extremely annoying as of late. Always in my business and asking me where I am and what I am doing. Nagging me about responsibilities and *taking care of myself*.

I turn to look at Mar and she is giving me her 'I'm not letting this go' look.

"I've just been feeling a bit antsy lately. Too much time at home and not enough time out in the city. You know me, I can't stay cooped up for long," I state simply, staring longingly at the glow just outside my window.

"Yeah not buying that, you go out every night and I know that you skip meetings at least once a week to hangout at the bar."

"I mean, yeah okay you got me there. But can you really blame me? You know that those meetings are boring, and it's not even like I'm really needed there anyways." I may be the heir but I'm not the queen. Yet.

Mar rolls her eyes. "What is this really about Eve? Is it about what father said?"

My mind takes me back to when father cornered me. *"It's time you start taking your responsibilities as heir seriously, Eve."* He even used his stern voice which tells me who this was all really coming from. It was the first time he had ever really pushed me to do anything more than enjoy my life.

Mar and I have always been given a lot of freedom, even encouraged to get up to trouble, not that he would ever admit it. Yet all of a sudden he wants to play the responsible father, use his *king* voice and make demands that are completely unreasonable. I won't do it.

"You and I both know that my mother is the one pushing for me to become more involved. But it makes no sense, why now? Father isn't even 250 years old and in perfect health. My mom, well she's basically fine too. Why the push for me to become responsible all of a sudden when I still have plenty of time left before I'm even considered mature."

The age of maturity for all people in Estarynn, regardless of species or realm, is 100. We age like mortals until 25 and then slow down to a tenth

19

of the speed. My father is around 200 yet he looks to only be in his fourth decade. I on the other hand, am only 23 which means I have a solid two more years before my body is even considered immortal, or at least the closest we can get to it. But for some reason two months ago my parents sat me down and told me that I need to start taking my role more seriously and start learning about what it takes to rule. It's complete bullshit.

Mar was always interested in learning about the throne. From the day she got here six years ago she has been eager to sit by our father's side and take it all in. Not that I blame her. She was raised by her mother on the outskirts of the city. Moving to the palace was a huge change for her, even if she did spend a lot of time here as a child. Even after all the years, her skin still has a natural golden hue to it from her time spent out in the sun.

"If you don't want to talk about it that's fine," Mar offers, pulling me from my thoughts.

"Sorry, Mar, just distracted. I promise it has nothing to do with you." I force a smile.

"Good," she says but I can hear the hesitation in her voice. "Anyways, I have to tell you what Keegan did this weekend."

I listen to Mar talk about her time with her brothers and laugh as she tells me about their latest mischief. Keegan is only six years younger than Mar but she loves to treat him like he's still a kid. I swear he lets her do it because he secretly loves to be babied. The twins on the other hand, Flint and Hagan, they're six going on 600.

Mar's mom died giving birth to the twins and it is clear in the way she talks about them that she is sad her mom never got the chance to know them. She was excited to come live with me and our father, but I can also tell that she still misses them. Seeing them every other weekend isn't enough and she worries about them every day that they are apart.

Our father offered to take the boys in along with Mar, but their father was adamant that he could raise them even without his wife. Father respected his wishes but still insisted that Mar and the boys spend as much time together as possible.

Mar continues to go on about her weekend, telling me about Hagan getting his foot stuck in a jar and Flint trying to use fire to get it out. The boys are still so young that they don't quite have a grasp on their magic yet but damn if they don't try.

I lay back, relaxing into the pillows as my sister paints a beautiful picture of her life. Laughing as they walk through the marketplace and pick out school supplies. Keegan will be in his first combat training class this year and it feels like just yesterday I was entering my own. Mar has endless stories that make me wish I had a life like that. Something simple and without responsibility. Even Mar has less to worry about since she is second in line. My eyes start to drift shut and I can't fight it as Mar's voice fades and sleep pulls me in.

~~~

I'm running through a cave. I hear Mar's laughter just ahead as we turn a corner. The sound of bare feet echo behind us, followed by Keegan's voice. "Wait! Don't leave me alone!" It's a few years before the twins were born. Keegan is around seven and I'm about to turn 14. Mar pulls me into a hidden alcove beside her while we both try to stifle our giggles.

Keegan is so easy to scare and it's one of our favorite things to do. We tricked him into following us so that we could hide and pop out. It's not the first time but he never learns. I hear his footsteps getting closer and Mar and I move into position, crouching low and getting ready to jump. A blur of movement comes around the corner and we pounce.

Keegan screams and Mar bursts out laughing.

I want to laugh too but I can't. I can't do anything.

My body is frozen and I can't control my arms or legs, can't even speak. All of a sudden my head is fuzzy and I can hardly hear Mar yell as I reach out and snatch Keegan by the shoulders. My nails dig into his arms as I draw him close.

He's crying and Mar is saying something, I think she's telling me to cut it out. But I can't. A weird feeling creeps over my skin and my whole body feels like it's on fire. I squeeze Keegan's shoulders tighter without meaning to, making him scream as my nails bite into his flesh.

Mar is shouting now but I can't make out the words. I lean forward until our faces are close together and I breathe in deep. Something happens when I do that and my body becomes tense. I can feel my grip tighten and the screams grow louder.

Who's screaming again?

I breathe in deep and feel heat move down my throat and into my stomach. Heady and sweet. Suddenly I am flying backwards. My back slams into the stone wall of the cave and the fog in my head clears.

Mar is cradling Keegan in her arms as tears cascade over her flushed cheeks. She's rocking back and forth and calling for help over and over again. I try to make sense of what is happening but everything is foggy. Something red is covering Mar's hands and Keegan's shirt. It takes a second but then I realize.

It's blood. But why is Keegan bleeding? Were we attacked?

The last thing I remember clearly is waiting to jump out and scare him. Wait. No. That's not right. Something happened to me. I shake my head to try and clear my thoughts further and then a figure becomes clear. My mother is staring at me from 10 feet away, next to Mar.

She leans down and touches Keegan before whispering to Mar. Mar nods her head and tries to pull her brother's small, limp, body into her arms. My mother helps her stand and then Mar runs away.

"Is... is Keegan dead?" I ask, my voice barely above a whisper. My throat is raw, overused, as if I had been the one screaming.

"No. He will be fine, he just fainted," she says straight faced, not even a hint of emotion in her eyes.

"But, there was blood. He was bleeding. What-what happened?" I say, vaguely aware that my entire body is trembling now.

"It doesn't matter what happened. All that does matter is that you never speak of it again. Not even with your sister," she says harshly.

"But why? Mother, I don't understand. Did I- did I hurt him?"

My mother sighs and walks to me, crouching down so she is eye level. "Yes. You did. But what really matters is that he will be fine and you'll learn to control yourself from now on. Understood?"

I nod my head.

"I need to hear you say it, Eve, you need to learn control or you will continue to hurt people that you care about. Do you understand?" she asks pointedly.

"Yes, mother, I understand."

She smiles. "Good. Now, let's get you back home and cleaned up."

I look down at my dress and find it covered in hot blood. I scream, and I don't stop screaming.

Chapter 2

Mar

Eve has been tossing and turning for hours. I glance over at the window and see only the faintest hint of light peeking through. We don't get any sunlight here but there are charms in place to light the kingdom in time with the world outside the volcano. I watch the dim light grow, longing for the sunrises that I grew up watching with my mother and brothers.

Easing out of bed I make my way slowly to the door and head across the hall into my own room. I quickly change into a set of training clothes, grab my bag, and head back out for the training rooms. It's not very often that I can get a full night's sleep so on nights like tonight, I find something to do. Some nights it's wandering the city, exploring every back alley and sloping rooftop, but most nights it's training.

My sister and I practically grew up in the training rooms. Every time I came to visit she would dare me to fight just to show off her new skills. She had an obvious advantage given that she trained almost every single day whereas I only ever got formal training while visiting her and our father.

Still, her skill with a dagger is unmatched. She uses her succubus charm to pull her opponents in and then right when they think they've gotten lucky she pulls a blade against their throat. Most would probably think that would turn a person away but for most it just makes them more excited, which is why I rarely stick around to watch Eve fight anymore. There are some things a sister should never see.

I enter the training room and cross the matted floor towards the back wall lined with weapons. I toss my bag down and quickly pick up a few things I want to work with. I'm pretty damn good with a dagger myself, but my real weapon of choice is something that gave me an edge against my sister. I weigh the bo staff in my hands, flipping it over and around my back a few times getting reacquainted with the feel of it in my hands.

I begin to speed up my movements until I've got some momentum behind it and start on my warmup forms. I learned pretty early on that if you want to beat someone with a dagger, give yourself a bit of distance. My father was the one to suggest a staff, and from the moment I first held the thin wooden rod in my hand, I knew it was mine. Now, I've upgraded to a metal staff that can collapse into a small cylinder so I can carry it around easier.

After a few minutes of getting myself warm I move over to the dummies and start with my combos. Solo training isn't the best for a staff but if you take the time you can learn a lot about your own movements and how to properly attack an opponent. I spin and hit the bo staff clean against the side of the dummy's head, knocking the heavy thing over and making a small bit of sand leak from the base.

"What did the dummy do this time?"

I turn at the sound of the familiar voice and spot one of the guards, Rian, standing by the door. A knowing smile is plastered across his handsome face, highlighting his elongated canines. The sight has my own pushing into my bottom lip.

"He snuck up on me while I was training. Oh wait, that was you. Maybe I should knock *you* on your ass." I raise my eyebrows.

I'm not particularly surprised to find him here. Rian likes to flirt. He likes to flash a smile and run a hand through his ashy blonde hair in a way that shows off his muscled biceps. Admittedly, I had a huge crush on him as a girl but recently learned he was already 100 which meant he was probably looking for someone to try and mate with. I am absolutely not that girl.

Rian laughs. "You sure can try princess but I've been training far longer than you have even drawn breath."

I tilt my head and give him a once over. He's strong. As a royal guard he has to be. But it's more than that. It's clear that he takes his training seriously and puts in the effort to build up all of his muscles, not just the ones that make a man nice to look at.

Still, I could totally kick his ass.

"Why don't you come over here and let this *princess* prove you wrong?" I counter.

He seems to consider it for a second before shaking his head, "Unlikely. Your father would have my head if I harmed you or the heir." He stalks around the room, watching me as I twirl my staff casually.

"Well then there we go, problem solved."

"And how exactly do you figure that?" he asks, eyes narrowing suspiciously.

"Simple, you won't even be able to touch me." It's my only warning before shifting and using my vampire speed to shoot towards him.

Not surprisingly, by the time I stop in the exact spot where Rian stood, he has already moved, using his own speed to outrun me. I turn and find him across the room, a smug smile tugging at his full lips. "You're gonna have to be quicker than that, little girl, if you hope to catch me." His eyes roam over me, a challenge lying in their icy blue depths. His teasing smile has my skin heating in anger, and maybe the slightest hint of something else too.

I shoot across the room in a blink of an eye until I am practically nose to nose with him. He could have moved, but he didn't. "I am no little girl. You'd do well to remember that."

He looks me up and down, taking in my cropped leather top and fitted shorts. "That you certainly are not," he says, licking his lips and drawing my attention to their fullness. He steps away from me and drops down, sweeping his leg out in an attempt to knock me on my ass.

I jump up, spinning around and delivering a wicked back side kick to his chest as he pops back up. He grunts and bares his fangs at me. I shoot off and the two of us begin racing around the room. I turn on my toes and catch him at his waist, tackling him to the floor.

He quickly flips me so I am under him and tries to pin my arms down. My heart beats wildly with the thought of it. I reach into the waistband of my pants and draw out the blade hidden there. Before he can get the upper hand I roll us both until I am straddling his waist with the dagger pressed to his throat.

"Well that wasn't very nice," he says with a grumble. His pupils are huge, almost erasing any sign of blue as he licks his lips, drawing my attention to his mouth yet again.

My body heats at the sight of his fangs peeking through. A wild idea flashes in my mind and I press the blade in a little until a thin line of blood appears from his neck. He hisses but doesn't move or try to stop me. I lower my mouth to the cut and lick away the blood, stifling a moan as my body presses against his hard chest and tenses with hunger. The thick scent of cedarwood invades my senses.

Rian groans and tilts his head back, exposing his neck further as I allow my fangs to slip free and move closer. His hands grab my waist and squeeze tightly. For a second I think he's going to pull me closer and my heart skips a beat, but then he pushes me back ever so slightly.

"As much as I love where this is going, princess, you should know that I came to find you for a reason," he says, causing me to pause.

I sit back and stare down at him, "And what would that reason be?"

He taps my thighs and I move to stand, reaching out a hand to help him up. He takes it, pressing a hand to his neck to heal the small cut. "Your father has asked that you see him before breakfast. Something about a meeting and the heir…" he trails off.

I nod, looking at the clock hanging above the door. It's barely been an hour since I've gotten here but my father will be expecting me soon. "Understood, thank you, Rian." I start to walk towards my bag but Rian has already run and grabbed it for me.

He holds it out to me with one hand and I take it, slinging it over my shoulder. "Next time you want a training buddy, come find me. Then we can have a real fight."

I let my gaze move over him, appreciating the view. His eyes heat as my gaze lingers on his neck and I know exactly where his mind is. Maybe there is time. I glance back at the clock and decide it won't be worth it, even if I am feeling a bit famished. Turning back to him I scoff, "Trust me, you against my staff, won't be much of a fight."

~~~

I wrap a fluffy towel around myself as I step out of the walk in shower. It's been years since I moved into the palace permanently but I don't think I'll ever truly get used to the luxury that this home provides. Back in my mother's home we all shared one bathroom with a small tub that required fire magic to heat the water. Here, I hardly have to lift a finger, everything is simply there for me when I need or want it. A true testament to just how advanced the city is compared to the rest of Estarynn. I use my hand to clear away the fog on the mirror and take in my reflection. My eyes are ringed with circles that show just how much I need to hunt.

I had planned on going out and finding someone to feed off of last night but then I heard some drunk girls giggling about the *dancing heir* and I figured I should make sure Eve wasn't getting into too much trouble. Anyone who doesn't know us would probably assume I'm older, since I'm pretty much always looking after my sister, but in fact she has exactly one year and three months on me. My father likes to say it's because I got so used to taking care of my brothers that it was only natural to take care of my sister too.

I throw on a pair of tight leather pants and a matching tunic, before making my way out of the bathroom. I'm not surprised to find Eve curled up on my bed reading from the book I had left on my nightstand.

"What do you think father would say if he found out you stay up reading these kinds of stories at night?" my sister asks, wiggling her eyebrows at me.

I shake my head and snatch the book from her, placing it in the bedside drawer, safe from prying eyes.

"Let's not find out," I say with a laugh. I look my sister over and find she is still in her dress from last night.

Her dark hair is a tangled mess and shadows have appeared under her dark gray eyes, making them appear even bigger and more round. Eve looks different from most succubi. Most of her kind have features that can only be described as sexy, but Eve is sort of softer. She still has the typical curves and full breasts but her face is more approachable. Her defined cheekbones can usually be found covered with a natural flush to them. Her small, straight nose, comes to a soft, rounded end that just makes you want to boop it. She's almost innocent looking, inviting.

Where most succubi draw people in with their lust, Eve makes people feel like they can trust her. Of course when she wants to she can fully embody what we call her 'sexy persona', but that is typically reserved for nights out or when she needs to feed. Here at home, most people will be used to this softer, more delicate side of my sister. In some ways we are the same but in others, the exact opposite. My features are sharp where hers are delicate. My features are light, hers dark. If not for our personalities one might not recognize us as sisters.

I sit down beside her and pinch the skin below her shoulder. She yelps and rubs at the spot but doesn't say anything. "Eve, what's up with you? You kept me up half the night with your tossing and turning, and now you look like someone raised you from the dead," I say, my voice laced with concern.

She shrugs and continues to rub at her shoulder. I roll my eyes at her and quickly heal the sore spot, something that she could have done just as easily.

I lower my voice to a whisper, "Is it the nightmares again? What is it this time?"

She sighs but answers with a nod, "The cave."

I pause. My breath catching in my throat at the traumatic memory. My brother was only seven years old when it happened. Eve's mother had found us in the cave and instructed me to carry Keegan back to the entrance where a healer would be waiting. I was terrified but did as she said and she later came to find me sitting outside his room in the medical wing.

"Mar, you must never speak of this to anyone. Not your brother nor your mother. Nobody," she said, a hint of fear in her voice.

"What about Eve, can't I talk to her? What happened?" I asked.

She shook her head, "No, Mar, not even Eve. It's for everyone's safety, especially Eve's. You must pretend as if nothing ever happened, do you understand me?"

When I said nothing she asked again and I nodded my head.

Two years later, Eve and I were having a sleepover together when she had a nightmare. She woke me up screaming and I begged her to tell me what was wrong. When she finally caved we stayed up for hours talking.

"Eve, it sounds like you fed off of his fear," I said as she shuddered. "But, how is that possible? Succubi can only feed off of positive emotions."

She shrugged her shoulders, "I don't know. My mother refuses to answer my questions and any time I bring it up she tells me to forget it ever happened and that it is 'for my own good.'"

"WAIT! I have an idea!" I yelled, "What if you are distantly related to a siren? It's possible right? Sometimes traits can be passed down dormantly from one generation to the next, maybe some long lost relative was actually a siren."

"I mean I guess it is a possibility, but if that was the case, why wouldn't my mother want to talk about it?" she asked.

"Well that's an easy one, your mother isn't royal by blood. She married into power. Maybe her family has some dark past and she has to keep it hidden to protect you? It's not exactly like everyone loves sirens to begin with," I offered.

Every time I came to visit since that night, Eve and I have tried to dig up some sort of explanation for what happened. After a few years we both just gave up and figured that the siren explanation made the most sense. But I can tell neither of us are really all that convinced. We once asked our friend Cay about sirens but she brushed us off saying something about not mentioning such wicked creatures.

"Mar?" Eve asks, bringing me back to the conversation.

"Yes, Eve, sorry. Go on. You said you were having nightmares about the cave again?"

She nods, pulling her legs up to her chest and resting her chin on her knees. "It was the same as always. We were playing, we jumped out, and then…." she trails off.

I nod, knowing exactly where this story goes. There are few things that keep me up at night but what happened that day is surely one of them. "What do you think is causing the nightmares to get bad again?"

"I don't know. But it's been happening for weeks now and I can hardly sleep. I wake up feeling like my throat is on fire and I can hardly breathe. It's like I am choking on something and sometimes it is so intense that I almost throw up. I usually calm down after a while but I don't know what's happening and it fucking sucks." My sister groans, throwing her head back and staring up at the ceiling.

"Is there anything that helps?" I ask. There is nothing I wouldn't do for my sister or brothers. They have been and always will be my first priority.

She seems to consider that for a second before she turns to face me, raising her eyebrows, "Are you sure you want the answer to that?"

I narrow my eyes before shaking my head, "Nevermind. As long as it works, I don't need to know more than that." My eyes catch the time on the clock and realize I should have found our father a while ago. He is a patient man but it isn't exactly wise to keep a king waiting.

Eve notices where I am looking and nods to the door. "Go. I'll be down in a bit. Just need to take a quick shower and try to look presentable." She stands and walks into *my* bathroom.

"Eve, I swear if you use my nice products again I am going to murder you," I call after her.

She pretends to not hear me, the little thief.

~~~

I enter the small room and find my father sitting at the table, his Queen to his right. This is one of my favorite rooms in the entire palace. Most royals would choose to eat inside their banquet halls or in large elaborate dining rooms but this room is the exact opposite of both of those things.

To start, the table is round. Meaning there is no "head seat" or position of power. We all sit together and enjoy our meals as equals. Of course the palace has larger spaces for entertaining guests but when it's just the four of us we take a far more casual approach.

"Ah, daughter, you've finally found your way back to me," my father says with mock surprise. His red hair is sticking up on all sides, his ruby crown forgotten where it is placed on the table beside him.

I laugh as I pull my chair out. "Yes, father. It was a daring journey filled with battles and bloodshed and betrayal." I pretend to clutch my stomach in pain, groaning and whimpering dramatically.

He slams his fist down on the table, knocking over the jar of sugar. "Tell me who would dare to harm a daughter of mine and I will bring them to their knees at once."

I circle around the table and stand behind him, crossing my arms around his neck like he used to when I was little. I let my chin rest on his head and breathe in his familiar cinnamon scent.

He reaches up and wraps his hand around my wrists comfortingly, "What kept you, little one?"

I groan but don't protest the nickname further. "Nothing you should worry about. I was training and needed to shower before coming down." I place a kiss on his head and hope he drops the subject.

He nods before releasing me, gesturing to the seat to his left which I take. "Am I going to have to ask then?" he asks, eyebrows raised in the same way Eve does. My sister might not look like our father but that personality? All his.

"No," I say, looking back towards the doorway, "she's just having some difficulties sleeping is all."

He gives me a look that says to go on, a look that does not give room for refusal. I sigh, leaning back in my chair and wishing I wasn't constantly put in the middle.

"I don't know, really, she said she's been having nightmares, that's all," I say, sneaking a look at the Queen.

She doesn't even raise her head from her book.

Eve's mother, Queen Elani, has always been kind to me. Kind to everyone really. Truly a beloved queen despite her status outside of her marriage. She seems to have this soothing nature about her that makes everyone around her want to please her. She never criticized her husband and his relationship with my mother. She even welcomed me into her home frequently as a child. She was the one who encouraged us to have a relationship and made sure that we got alone time together. After my mother died, I moved in permanently and she would treat me just like Eve. I always considered her like a second mother to me.

Over the last year she has become more… reserved. Rarely seen outside the palace walls, and inside she keeps to a few rooms. I asked Eve about it but she told me her mother refused to talk about it. Even our father tried to coax whatever was bothering her out but she would just smile and shake her head. Some rumors had spread in the beginning and people thought

33

she was sick or even possibly pregnant. She laughed at those and assured us that it was nothing like that, she just wants to rest.

I know better though. I once caught her wiping her nose with a rag and when she threw it away I saw it covered in blood. When I saw it I couldn't help but picture Eve's mother like my own, sprawled out on a bed, covered in blood, the light fading from her eyes. Her skin ice cold. I blink the image away and focus on the food in front of me instead.

"Look who decided to join us," my father says as Eve slumps into her chair. I hadn't even heard her enter.

Queen Elani looks up and gives her a once over. "Are you feeling well? You look a bit tired. Do you need to feed?"

Father's face turns fiercely red, the same shade it always does when anyone brings up Eve and feeding. You would think he would have become desensitized to it given that he is married to a succubus himself but I guess it doesn't work that way when it's your daughter people are talking about. Maybe it would be different if he was also a succubus and not a vampire like me.

"It's been a few days since I have had a real meal but I got a small hit last night when I was out," she answers nonchalantly.

Meanwhile our father has suddenly found his mug to be the most interesting thing in the world.

I suppress a chuckle as my sister rolls her eyes.

The Queen scoffs, "Well why is that? We've kept people on staff for just this thing since you were what, 14 years old? Are they no longer to your liking?"

Eve sighs, "No mother. They're fine. I just prefer to feed with people who *aren't* paid to bed me."

Father chokes on his water, spitting it out across the table and frantically trying to soak it up with a rag. His eyes meet mine as I try to fight back my laughter and I offer him my napkin.

Queen Elani sighs, using her magic to evaporate the water and casting her husband a bland look. "Suit yourself. Drink your tonic dear," she says

34

simply, returning to her book and not bothering to touch a single morsel of food on her plate.

She's become thin, too thin. Her skin is pulled tight over bones and her eyes have sunken back into her face, almost skeletal. Her usually shiny black hair has become dull, lifeless. It is difficult to look at what she has become, knowing the glowing person she used to be no more than a year ago. Her eyes flash to mine for a brief moment and my heart skips a beat as I catch a flash of red in the corner of her eyes before they drop back to her book.

I look over to Eve as she downs the same bluish tonic she drinks every morning. I asked her what it was for but even she wasn't sure exactly. She just knew that since she came into her powers and started feeding she needed it to help calm the urges. We thought she would grow out of it but her mother is insistent that she drink one every day.

Once, Eve joined me on a visit to my brother's and she argued that she wouldn't need it. Her mother threw her hands up and told her to deal with the consequences. Eve and I both laughed at the small victory, that is until Eve grew weak and could hardly get out of bed. We weren't laughing then.

I clear my throat, "Eve and I were thinking about heading to Sena a bit early. Rose's birthday party is coming up but we thought we might surprise her ahead of the crowds."

Eve sits up in her seat giving me a look of excitement and a promise of mischief. We aren't known as the *wild sisters* for nothing.

Father looks between the two of us. "There wouldn't happen to be any other reasons for this visit, would there? Any reason why you wouldn't wait for the rest of the travel party?" he questions, eyebrows raised. Each kingdom would be sending a handful of emissaries to show the support of their respective royal family. Still, there was no reason for Eve and I to travel with ours.

"Nope, no reason," Eve and I answer in unison, looking at each other with smiles plastered across our faces. Her foot brushes my ankle and I can see her skin begin to glow as she feeds off of my own excitement. I flash my fangs and she rolls her eyes, cutting off her powers and pulling back her foot.

Father sighs, "Fine. But you will take guards with you. No exception. We have been getting some odd reports lately of attacks and I'm not going to risk either of you getting caught up in something, the blood would be far too difficult to get out of your pretty dresses," he says with a wink.

Eve laughs and I just shake my head. Most of the time father allows us unlimited freedom from the guards. Knowing that we can handle our own and that, as he alluded to, the ones more likely to end up in a medical wing would be the attacker, not us. Still, anytime we travel outside of the safety of the kingdom he insists on sending us with guards. Usually of his own choosing.

"Speaking of reports, Eve, would you care to explain to me where you have been hiding during the last half dozen meetings? You know very well that you are expected to be there," the *King* asks, voice stern.

Eve jumps up from her chair and grabs my arm, pulling me from my seat and behind her as she races for the door. Our food is left untouched on the table. "Gotta go, love you! See you in a few weeks bye!" she calls behind us.

"We're not done talking about this!" our father shouts after us.

We both laugh and take off before he can catch us in another interrogation.

"Come on, we've got lots to do to get ready and we've gotta leave before father asks too many questions." Eve says with a wiggle of her eyebrows.

Chapter 3

Rose

The wind whips through my hair as I gather the reins tighter in my fist, my horse's hooves crunching dried leaves as he gallops at full speed beneath me. My thighs burn and my lower back aches from the strain of riding for hours. Still, I push harder until we are nothing but a blur in the woods.

Steadying myself I turn back and send a throwing knife flying. It hits the target in the dead center and I smile to myself. I call on my earth magic, bringing the blade soaring back to me until my hand wraps around the vines encasing the handle. I repeat these steps over and over again, weaving through the woods. I send my blades flying until they hit their mark and then summon them right back into my hand. It's a technique I have been trying to perfect for over a year now.

I lean forward and smooth a hand over my horse's silky mane as we slow to a walk. I reach into the saddlebag and pull out some sugar cubes which makes him slow to a stop with interest. I sling my leg over the saddle and hop down. Reaching out, I offer the cubes, which he takes greedily. "Good boy," I say, patting his neck and pressing my forehead to his snout.

I tie the reins off to a branch and walk towards a clearing. A few fauns are in their shifted forms laying together in the sun. Their goat-like legs are covered in a thick fur that looks like it is far too warm for the fading summer heat. I use my fae hearing to listen to the yells of a centaur hunting party in the distance, and can't help but smile. This is where I am meant to be.

It's different out here. Back on the castle grounds, hundreds of people are milling about, preparing for the celebration in a week. I can hardly walk through the halls without hearing excited whispers or giggling from the shadows. There is nothing quite like a royal party to get everyone in a tizzy. But here in the woods, far from the castle and away from my mother's fussing, here it is quiet. There is life in the forest and a sense of calm that I can't get anywhere else, but beyond that, here I can remain invisible.

At home I can hardly walk 10 feet without someone asking me if I need anything. Especially my mother or eldest brother. Growing up I adored the attention and being doted on. Being third in line to my realm's throne might not be all that special, but being my mother's only daughter, now that has its perks. My mother gave me everything that I could ask for and more as a child. The only thing she ever denied me, is the training that I so desperately craved.

My mother always insisted that I learn what my position means, even from an early age. I followed her around everywhere, even in places where a child certainly did not belong. Still, she never paid the whispers any mind. She would smile down at me and tell me *"people will always have something to say but it rarely makes any difference so pay them no mind"*. Her trust in me has only grown as I have gotten older and now, I hope she might finally let me in completely.

I walk to the center of the clearing and lay down, closing my eyes. The earth's energy sinks into my skin and a soft buzz builds inside my mind as I restore my magic. Feeling the warmth of the sun on my light bronze skin fills me with a sense of peace as I outstretch my arms and twine my fingers in the dewy grass.

This is what we are meant to do. To lay with the earth and feel the life inside the ground. I love my home but there is nothing like being out here, with my people and surrounded by the very thing that gives us life and magic. There is energy in the castle but it is different, channeled from my ancestors rather than the earth itself. It leaves something to be desired.

The sun suddenly disappears and the warmth is gone. I open one eye and find my second brother blocking the precious rays. Groaning, I sit up. "Yes, Oliver? Is there something I can do for you?" I ask with a bite of annoyance.

Oliver is second in line and 12 years older than me, although with the way immortals age he looks to be midway through his second decade. Anyone who looks at us would know we were related. His hair is the same shade of chestnut brown as mine and just as curly, but whereas my curls hang just past my shoulder, his are short on the sides and longer on the top, draping across his forehead haphazardly.

His skin is a shade darker than mine, a deep golden brown, and our wide eyes are the same shade of hazel. Even our physique is similar. He stands a head taller than me despite my own towering height. But where I have subtle curves he has defined muscles from years of training with our eldest brother, Terran. Something that I envy of him.

"Why yes, Rose, there is something you could do for me," he says with equal annoyance, "how about you stop running off to play in the woods while the entire staff loses their mind looking for you. Oh, and while you're at it, can you please talk to mother about this ridiculous party?"

I scoff, "You and I both know that once mother sets her mind to something there is no changing it. She's the one who wants to throw this party, not me."

"Really? Because last time I checked it was *your* birthday." he says, extending his hand for me.

I take it and pull myself to my feet. "It may very well be *my* birthday. But if I had it my way we would have a small festival here, in the woods. Not some stuffy ball."

Oliver rolls his eyes as we walk back to where our horses wait by the tree. "I can assure you, this will be no *stuffy ball*. Besides, you love the attention and any excuse to get all dressed up. You used to drag anyone you could find into those little tea parties of yours."

"Sure, when I was six. I turn 23 in less than a week." Besides, soon enough I will be 25 and no one will dare to treat me like a little girl anymore, not even mother.

Most creatures in the four realms and kingdoms are considered to be immortal. We age like a mortal would until we mature and then our aging slows. In 10 years we might age as much as a mortal does in one, allowing us to live well into the late hundreds, even sometimes over a thousand.

The only exception to this rule are the priestesses and acolytes who choose to live outside an elemental kingdom, in the mortal lands residing in the heart of Estarynn. Their connection to their magic is cut off there, causing them to be more fragile and to age like a mortal. They can still live to be around 200 but it comes with other difficulties as well. Like creating children.

Children are already rare, a blessing for many. It is near impossible to bear a child before reaching the age of maturity and even then, the window of opportunity is a mere 100 years. For those who choose to allow their aging to progress at a much more rapid pace, they are lucky to get even 10 years of fertility, if any at all. It is unimaginable to me why anyone would *choose* to limit their lifespan like that.

Oliver steps up beside his horse and mounts it easily. Not bothering to offer me help as he knows I would just refuse it anyways. "Give it another 75 years sister, maybe then everyone will stop treating you like a precious little princess."

I mount my own horse. "And then you would feel all better, wouldn't you? No more competition for mother's attention. Or is it Terran's you really want? Now, if you'll excuse me, I hear I am wanted back at the castle."

I take off like an arrow from a bow. We race through the woods, my horse easily maneuvering through the trees and over downed logs. I glance back over my shoulder to find Oliver right behind me. His horse easily avoiding the obstacles that took me weeks to memorize.

Irritation pricks my skin but I decide to keep my eyes forward and on the unofficial race. This is how it is with us, a competition in everything that we do. Even when unspoken. Something as simple as drinking a glass of water would turn into who can drink more and how fast. Terran used to get on the both of us for *acting like children*. I at least *was* a child, Oliver on the other hand, had no excuse.

I lean forward and give an encouraging pat as we shoot off again. A log is stuck in the path and without time to avoid it I make the split section decision to jump. I squeeze my legs and feel the horse's muscles contract before we are flying through the air. We land on the other side and I absorb the impact, feeling the burn in my legs even more than before. We take off again and I can see the castle in the distance.

I spare a glance back and see that Oliver is nowhere in sight. Smirking, I pick up the pace until the ground shifts from moss to stones and we are running up the entranceway. I allow my horse to slow to a walk, stopping in front of the guard standing outside the castle doors.

"Princess, the High Lady has been looking for you," he says, taking the reins as I hop down. His eyes skirt over my rumpled clothing with distaste but he quickly looks away.

"I know, my brother found me. He should be just behind me," I say, walking up the stone steps and ignoring the guard's disapproval.

Many of them think that I spend too much time in the woods, that I should be more focused on the more political side of things than fighting. What they don't realize is that I've read almost every book in the library a hundred times over. I've studied every law and history that I could get my hands on. All except the books from my parents' private collections in their chambers.

The castle is almost entirely stone on the outside although almost all of the exterior walls are covered in climbing vines and thick moss. The glass windows are set into wooden frames that were created by my ancestors' earth magic, carved into swirling designs. When I was a young girl my father used to take me through the halls and tell me about the history. How each high lord will allow a small drop of their power into the grounds to strengthen and protect them.

He died when I was six years old and I have very few memories of him left. Still, everytime I walk through the castle I feel like I can hear his voice. Feel him calling to me from hidden alcoves and secret passageways as I hide from staff.

My favorite memory of all is when he showed me the library. The large room has a beautiful glass ceiling that lets in all this natural light and casts a golden glow in the evenings. There are dozens of tables and benches to sit at but we always chose a couch in the center of the room so we were surrounded by books on all sides. I couldn't even read yet but he would sit with me and tell me the stories of the great high lords and ladies of Sena, our ancestors.

I stop for a moment and peek inside. The librarians are moving about returning books to shelves, taking time to dust off the more unloved sections as they go. One of them seems to sense my presence and smiles at me. She gestures toward our old couch but I shake my head. She gives me a sort of sad smile and a slight bow before returning to her work.

I used to spend every night in that room after my father died. Just laying there, staring up at the glass ceiling and wondering how someone like my father could be gone. He was trying to save a village near the north mountains where a fire had broken out. He rushed to the aid of his people without a moment's hesitation, but his earth magic alone couldn't calm the flames. The villagers called for help from Vulca, hoping their fire magic might help, but they were too far away and by the time their help came, he was already gone. His body returned to the earth and his magic released. My brother Terran inherited his power and has been preparing to take over as high lord ever since.

I continue walking towards my mother's bedchamber, and knock lightly on the door, a soft voice calls to me from the other side and I push the door open slowly.

My mother is standing on the far side of the room, bent over a table with a large map. She looks up and gives me one of her wide smiles. Dark waves frame her long delicate face. She wears a forest green gown that makes her look utterly ethereal. The dress is made of a sheer gossamer and clings to her curves, accentuating them. "My beautiful daughter. How was your ride?" she asks. Her voice is light but I can hear a twinge of something in it.

I cross the room and stand opposite her, running my hand over the map. "It was exactly what I needed. What's this all about?"

She points to a village on the southern border to Rayan, "do you see this village? There have been an increase of attacks over the past few weeks and I am trying to find out why and how."

"Attacks? What kind of attacks?"

She shakes her head, "It is unclear. Could be rogue sirens or it could just be a group of rowdy centaurs as we draw closer to the end of summer."

I taste bitter disgust on my tongue as I look up at my mother. "Do you really think the sirens would be so far inland? They would have to cross the border to reach this village."

My mother begins folding the map with a sigh,."It is impossible to know for sure without going out to investigate. I have already sent your brother to see if he can find out any information."

My eyes narrow, "which brother?"

"Oliver. Didn't he tell you when he found you?" she asks, placing the map into a stack on the table without looking back at me.

I grind my teeth together, the little sneak. "No, he failed to mention it. I would have liked to join him. If I leave now I might be able to catch up before dark." I'm already moving to the door when she stops me. Her magic pulling on the thread to my own and making me freeze in place, one foot halfway out the door.

My mother tsks, "You will do no such thing. Your birthday is just around the corner and you are needed here. Besides, you have a dress fitting tomorrow and I will not allow my only daughter to look anything less than astonishing."

I roll my eyes but drop it, turning back to my mother and giving her my full undivided attention. Like I told Oliver, there is no reasoning with her when she gets this way.

A small knock comes from the door and one of my mother's advisors stands waiting. "High Lady Ayana, I have just been informed that there was an issue with the banquet flowers that needs your immediate attention."

"How is it possible that we live in the earth realm and carry earth magic yet no one can seem to follow basic instructions when it comes to flowers of all things?" she says with a shake of her head. She walks over to me and places a soft kiss on my forehead before following her advisor from the room. She stops on the threshold and turns back to me, "Make sure that you are on time for your fitting. No running off again."

I give her a nod before she leaves. Walking back to the table I move my hand over the folded map, trying to make sense of things. The village is just outside the forest and miles from the Rayan border. It would take days on foot to reach the sea. What would sirens be doing so far from the water?

~~~

"You look beautiful, princess."

I've been standing on this podium for nearly six hours while the seamstress pokes me with needles and yells at me to *stand up straight, don't slouch*. My mother would be impressed by her earnest work. Although I fear the dress might not be as *astonishing* as she had in mind.

"I don't know, you look kind of like a big tree if you ask me," says my cousin, Oak, jokingly. She's laid out across a settee with her head dangling over the side.

The seamstress blanches and looks me up and down. "Oakley, while I do respect your opinion. I have to disagree wholeheartedly. The princess is going to look positively stunning in this gown."

My cousin tilts her head and narrows her eyes, "Hmmm. Nope, still looks like a tree to me." Oak flips back up with a shrug and crosses her legs under her.

I laugh as the seamstress begins unpinning the back of the gown and pulling it from my shoulders, all the while muttering under her breath. The dress is beautiful, that much is true, but I can also see where Oak is coming from.

The shape of the dress is one long column which does little to show off my own curves. My wide hips and the dip of my waist. The color is a warm brown which is beautiful but doesn't compliment my skin tone. It is also not quite my style. This dress is very simple, and where I would usually go for a soft and airy fabric, this one is dense.

"It's beautiful," I assure the seamstress, "but perhaps we could revisit the design? Something a bit more like gowns I have worn in the past?"

The seamstress sighs but nods. Walking to the back room and taking the dress with her.

As soon as she is gone Oak bursts into laughter, "Did you see her face? She looked ready to slit my throat."

I fix Oak with a stare, "you could have been a bit nicer about it."

Oak just shakes her head, "absolutely not. Your mother would have killed me had I not spoken up."

I slip back into my simple peach colored dress, and tighten a belt around my waist. I start towards the door and Oak follows beside me, her short legs doing double time to keep up with me. She barely stands to my shoulders even with her hair fluffed up atop her head.

"So, cousin, what's on the agenda for today?" she asks, running a hand through her short hair. It's worn in a layered pixie cut, the top spelled to look neon green and kept a bit longer, the bottom shaved. She runs her hand through it again, a habit she has had since we were children and usually means she is feeling anxious.

I smile at her and loop my arm through hers. "Well, now that my dress fitting is taken care of, the only thing left to do is check on the party setup. So, where to?"

Oak gestures towards the pathway that leads to the courtyard. I assumed we would be going towards the ballroom but know better than to question my cousin. Especially when she's doing her best to hide her facial expressions. She's not very good at it.

We walk through the halls together, arm in arm, nodding to the staff as we go. Many call out to us and offer us assistance but we move quickly. Usually I would gladly stop and spend time with my people but Oak is far more reserved, preferring to stay in the shadows where she can remain unnoticed.

I squeeze her arm and she looks up at me with a smile. Oak is a lot like the big sister I never had, despite the fact she is only two years older than me. When we celebrated her 25th birthday a few months back she refused a party despite my mother's protests. She groaned about how it's what her sister, Oak's mother, would have wanted.

Oak and her younger brother, my other cousin, Reed, moved in with us after their parents were killed. Reed was only a babe at the time and never knew anything different. Oak took it much harder. She would never admit it but losing her parents left her closed off and hesitant to really let anyone in. I remember what she was like before. Now it seems as though she keeps everyone at arms length so that she doesn't have to fear losing them.

All except me. Or at least she used to.

I glance down at her again as we move through the castle grounds. She looks to anyone else to be perfectly content. Just happy to walk by my side and listen to me talk about dresses and parties. If I look deeper there is a look behind her dark green eyes that makes me wonder where her mind is truly at. Her hand brushes through her hair again.

We turn a corner and the stone archways that lead to the courtyard come into view. People are working all around, hanging lights and using magic to make flowers bloom. The ground is a mix of stone and moss with paths cut out for people to walk. I am taken aback for a moment by how perfect everything looks. Oliver was right for once, this will be no stuffy ball.

I let go of Oak's arm and walk towards the center, spinning around to take it all in. I've begged my mother for years to allow me to throw parties in this space but she always said it would be too 'wild' for our foreign friends. This year I insisted that if it wasn't here I didn't want the party at all. Part of me thought she would call my bluff.

"So sister, what do you think?"

Turning I find Oak has vanished, replaced by my eldest brother. Terran is nearly identical to Oliver despite being nearly 15 years older. The only difference is that where Oliver shares the same bronzed skin as my own, Terran's is more similar to our mother's and cousins, a deep olive. Still, we all share the same splatter of freckles. This must be the surprise that had Oak so anxious.

"What are you doing here?" I ask, rushing over to give him a hug.

He wraps his arms around me and gathers me into his embrace. He lifts my feet off the ground and spins me around the same way he would do when I was a child. I breathe in his familiar scent of rosemary and pine. He sets me back down and grabs my shoulders to hold me steady. In many ways he is more like a father to me than our real father. He was the man who took care of me, taught me how to fight despite our mother's protests. He is the one who taught me how to use my magic like it was an extension of my soul, as it was meant to be.

"Like I would miss my darling sister's birthday? Absurd." he says with a smile.

Terran has been away visiting villages across the realm, as is expected of the heir. Unlike the other kingdoms, our people need their magic resorted by our blood. We must feed it back into the land so it may replenish their magic. Over the last year though we have been receiving reports of a lack of magic flowing from the land. Almost like it has been drained by something even our blood cannot fully replenish.

I hold my brother's hands between us and stare up into his kind eyes. "I've missed you. How was the north? Were you able to replenish the land?"

His smile falters but he quickly regains composure, "Of course. What kind of ruler would I be if I failed to help my people." He gives my hands a squeeze and leads me to a bench under a large willow tree. "Now, tell me about you. How has your training been going?"

I smile and with a subtle flick of my wrist, send a blade soaring into a nearby stump. My brother's eyes track the movement and look back at me with pride.

"I would ask where on earth you were hiding that blade but I fear I don't want to know," he says with a grin.

I laugh and lean into his shoulder. We sit like this for what feels like hours, with him telling me about his journey and all the villages he visited. How he ran with a pack of wolf shifters near the northern border and spotted gargoyles flying high overhead, a large group of them heading deep into the woods.

Our land is vast, covering the entire western end of Estarynn and bordering both Eteri to the north and Rayan in the south. My brothers have seen it all. I, however, have only seen small, carefully guarded areas. I spent some time in the south visiting Oak and Reed before they came to live with us. I have also traveled north almost every year to pay respects to my father's final resting place. Yet my mother's unwavering refusal to allow me anywhere farther east has ensured I have never seen Vulca, nor the stretch of mortal land between our realms.

I want to see it all, as my brothers have, but my mother insists it is not safe until I have fully developed my immortality. I keep telling myself only two more years although it feels like an eternity.

Terran nudges my shoulder, making me look up at him, "I have a surprise for you little sister."

My eyes light with excitement, "And what might that surprise be, brother?"

He looks to the door and a messenger quickly runs over to us, handing me a letter addressed to me. I flip it over and find a red wax seal with a flame in the center. Looking up at my brother with wide eyes he just laughs.

"Well, go on, open it." he says.

I rip the letter open and quickly read it. It's from Eve, she and Mar are on their way from Vulca. Based on the date they left they should be more than halfway here by now. "How did you know?" I ask my brother with surprise and excitement.

Eve and Mar have been my closest friends since we were babes. Our parents have been friends for hundreds of years and chose to raise us just as close. Eve and Mar have spent many summers in this castle, teaching me how to use daggers or use our heightened senses to hide from anyone, especially guards.

"I was hoping there would be two letters actually…" my brother says with a look of disappointment.

I give him a sad smile knowing exactly who that letter would be from.

"I reached out to the King and Queen but haven't heard back from them," he explains.

I nod, "You know how they can be. Since the incident, they rarely allow Cay out of the city, let alone the kingdom."

Cay is the heir to the Rayan throne and the remaining piece of our group. The five of us: Eve, Mar, Oak, Cay, and I, have been inseparable from the moment we were first introduced to one another all those years ago.

Terran nods and stands, offering me his arm, "Well, enough of that. Let's go track down that cousin of ours and prepare her for the terrors that are on their way. We can only hope that the castle survives Mar and Oak's next brawl. "

I laugh, "Oak loves Eve, *and* Mar."

Terran looks down at me with eyebrows raised, "Does she know that?"

I elbow him in his side but take his arm anyway.

Chapter 4

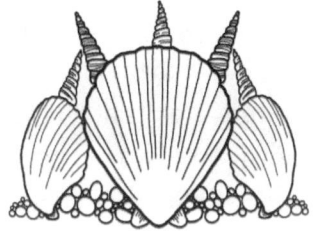

Cay

This is not turning out the way I had hoped. I tilt my head at the canvas in frustration. I've been sitting on the floor of my studio for hours. My hands are caked in paint and my dress is a wrinkled mess around me. When I came into this room and started picking out paint it was supposed to help me gather my thoughts. Now, I can't see past the spot in the corner that I accidentally smudged. I see stray bristles that have come out of the worn brush and dried beneath the latest layer of paint, adding unwelcomed texture.

I groan and lay back on the cool tile. The ceiling is covered in a mural depicting my mother and father's mating ceremony, a gift from a member of court for their 100th anniversary. My mother looks to be the staggering queen that she is. My father smiles at her with a love I hope I can one day find.

The mural depicts them as they were in the palace ballroom, near the heart of the city. Or at least we call it a city. In truth, Tepis is one giant palace with more than a dozen buildings surrounding the royal residence in the exact center, connected by long tunnels and stone archways.

Our home is beautiful. The exterior walls are made from multi-colored sea glass that creates ripples of light in every room and hall. It rests miles off shore on the bottom of the sea, where even the highest towers are deep beneath the surface. The tunnels take people in and out of the city, the *only* way in and out of the city. Guards roam the tunnels at all times, ensuring the barrier remains intact so the air stays where it should and our less aquatic friends and citizens aren't left floundering about.

My eyes continue to roam over the work of art, noting the way the artist used their magic to encase certain areas in bubbles of water. I've tried to replicate the technique hundreds of times but it never quite looks the same. More like someone dropped a glob of paint and let it dry. I sigh as I sit up, staring at my own work. The background is painted shades of green and brown. Outlines of trees have been sketched with a light charcoal as a guide. It's supposed to be a lush forest.

But not just any forest, Rose's forest. Her latest letter was nearly 10 pages long, half of which was spent describing the way the sun broke through the gaps in the trees and created this *"mystical glow"*. I wanted to capture that moment for her as a birthday gift. However, I am finding it is much harder to picture the forest for myself, never having seen it in person.

I gather my dress in my dirty hands and stand, moving about the room while collecting paint tins and brushes and carrying them over to the painting table. I pick up the canvas last, moving it and its stand to the corner where it is less likely to get knocked over when my little brother, Finn, inevitably comes bounding through the room.

Using a bit of water magic I rinse the paint from my body until I am pristine again. I can do nothing to ease the wrinkles from my gown but I need to change either way. Looking around and ensuring everything is back in its place I nod to myself. Even if I am not put together myself, there's no need for this space to reflect it. I pull the double doors closed behind me as I head back towards my chambers.

This part of the city is closest to the royal residence, connected by long hallways that cut through the east side of the courtyard. I look through the windows and see a couple of nymphs teaching their little one how to manipulate water to create air pockets. The child manages to hold the form for a few seconds before it collapses above him, drenching him from head to toe. He cries into his father's arms while his mother laughs.

The magic is similar to that used to protect the city. Walls surround the palace and cast a continuous stream of water into a dome covering the entire city. Being underwater allows the magic to remain strong at all times, never needing to pull much power and allowing our people to remain at peace at all times. The opposite of the portion of our kingdom that remains on land, Atran.

I enter my chamber and call for a maid to help me change into a new gown before supper. She gets to work unlacing the bodice while I begin combing through my tangled hair, focusing on the ends. My dark waves reach midway down my back but a few shorter strands curl around my face.

The maid finishes with the bodice and I step out of the plain dress. She helps me into a new gown, doing up the buttons along my spine, the fabric a deep shade of teal. It flows to the ground, pooling at my feet and cinching at my waist, drawing attention to my generous curves. The neckline sits just beneath my collarbones, drawing the eyes up to my round face. She finishes with the buttons and moves her hands to my hair but I stop her.

"Thank you, that will be all," I say, excusing the maid with a smile.

I sit in front of my vanity and continue fixing my hair. I start by gathering shorter pieces in the back with pearl pins, pushing them into the thick sections. The effect leaves my hair flowing like a waterfall down my back in layers. I move onto my face and pinch my pale cheeks. I let the blood flow into them, granting me the subtle blush I was going for. I add a light dusting of sparkles to my eyelids, accenting my sea green eyes. Satisfied with the look, I make my way to the dining hall, cutting through the servants' passage to avoid any lingering guards.

Tonight we will be joined by not only the entire court, but also a group of visiting dignitaries from Sena. A shiver of nervousness washes over me, leaving my skin feeling sensitive. I enter the large dining hall and find the long table nearly full. My father and mother are seated on the opposite end, an open seat is left beside my father's, waiting for me. I nod to the many smiling faces as I cross the room. I make a mental note that Finn is not among those gathered. Not that I am surprised, my younger brother rarely joins us for formal meals.

I am halfway across the room when I take in who sits beside my mother, talking intently. The familiar chestnut curls make my heart race and I nearly stumble. But then he turns. My heart beat returns to normal and my steps come with more ease. I take my seat across from Oliver, Rose's second brother, who gives me an odd smile and continues his conversation with my mother.

My father squeezes my hands where they are folded in my lap, and gives me a reassuring smile. "You look beautiful, minnow."

I am the last to arrive and the food has already been brought out on silver trays, servants wait to serve our hungry guests until my father allows it. My eyes roam over the Sena travel party but no familiar faces stand out aside from Rose's brother. Maybe one of the guards but I couldn't be sure, it has been so long. My father instructs the servants to bring forth the food and then the loud buzz of conversation starts up around the table.

"Princess Cay, you are looking as lovely as ever," says Oliver with a nod of his head.

"You are too kind," I say with a small smile, ignoring the nausea building in my gut at his mere presence.

His eyes narrow on me and a smirk graces his lips, "Although, it could be that it has been so long since I have seen you. Perhaps you have always looked so exquisite."

I can hear my father grumble but my mother places a silencing hand on his arm.

"Yes, well, we should hope not to make a habit of it," I say by way of response. Refusing to meet his stare.

He chuckles, "And what would that habit be exactly?"

I sip my wine and ignore him, turning to the advisor who sits on my left. "Sagal, tell me, have you made much progress on establishing a new line of trade with Eteri?" I ask, directing the subject away from Oliver.

Sagal looks taken aback for a moment before wiping wine from his upper lip and clearing his throat, "Um, yes, princess. We received word from them a few weeks ago stating that they might be willing to send a representative out to meet with us, a manticore, I believe."

My eyes widen. "A manticore? Truly?"

Sagal nods, his eyes shooting over my shoulder to where my father is undoubtedly listening in on our conversation.

"Manticores are not all that interesting, you know," chimes in Oliver.

I don't even spare him a glance. "Should they make the journey, would they stay here, in the city?" I ask Sagal.

He bursts out into a fit of laughter, turning my lips into a frown. He waves a hand in front of his face, "Pardon me, your highness. It is just, it would be unreasonable to allow a foreign stranger into the city upon our first meeting."

I consider that for a moment before responding. "So if not here, then where would negotiations happen?"

"Ah, you see, I have the answer for that," Oliver chimes in.

I turn to face him, "And why would you know the answer?" I can feel my magic stirring under my skin and I force it down, taking calming breaths. A melody plays low in the back of my mind but I shut it out.

He smirks, the annoying fool. "Well you see it has to do with part of my being here. The Eteri are very stubborn people. They prefer not to leave their home when possible, and as your advisor might suggest. They feel it is not in their best interest to travel into a foreign land where they have

55

made no friends," he says simply. His eyes are filled with mischief and arrogance unrivaled by anyone else I have ever met.

My face contorts in anger, "Are you suggesting that our land is not welcoming? Not safe for our foreign *friends*?"

Oliver raises his shoulders in a shrug, "I say no such thing, only that one must be careful when visiting any foreign land. Especially when surrounded by magic that one can't use. The air is a bit thin down here, don't you think?"

"Now, Oliver, don't be unkind. You as our guest know that we would never wish you to feel uncomfortable. We are perfectly capable of meeting outside of the city should that be what you or any other kingdom choose," my father says, putting a stop to that particular conversation. His eyes carry the smallest hint of fondness.

I look at my father with a hint of awe behind my eyes. He knows exactly what to say. How to be a leader for his people. I could spend my entire life watching him and never learn how to do that. It must be something you are born with.

I turn back to Oliver, channeling my father as best I can. "You said that was merely one part of the reason for your visit. What, pray tell, is the other part?"

Oliver's face turns more serious. "We have been receiving reports of attacks on the border between our lands. One of our villages, mere miles outside of Atran."

My face twists in confusion but before I can respond my mother jumps in. "Attacks? We have heard nothing of the sort. Our guards roam all borders, land and sea, they would have reported something if such a thing was happening close to our lands." My mother's face searches Oliver's, waiting for an explanation.

"Not if they were bewitched," Oliver responds, turning my body cold.

I down the remainder of my wine with numb fingers, hoping the alcohol brings my body some warmth. I notice my father's eyes glance my way but he doesn't say anything, just slips a hand under the table and squeezes my knee comfortingly.

"Bewitched? That is absurd. We would never allow such actions to go unchecked," assures my mother with annoyance. Her magic pools, calling to my own, a thread connecting our power to one another and allowing me to feel the swell of it in the air.

"I am not accusing, just stating facts. The reports of the attacks are consistent with…" Oliver's eyes dart to me for a moment.

My mother notices the movement and looks over at me, "Cay, my little minnow, why don't you turn in for the night. It is getting quite late." She shares a glance with my father and he gives me a reassuring nod.

Normally I would refuse, insist that I should be here, watching and learning as much as I can. But I know she is right. My body feels like ice is moving through my veins and my head has started to buzz from drinking too much wine, too quickly. I've barely touched my food, although whatever appetite I had, it has now evaporated.

Nodding, I fold my napkin and set it on the table, standing carefully. My father calls for a guard to escort me back and I barely hear him. I feel my body leave the room and hear the voices begin to fade, the music closing in on my mind again. I spare one glance back towards Oliver and his people before heading down the hall that will lead to my rooms. I can't help but be disappointed that Rose is not here. Oliver was right, it has been too long since I have seen her or allowed anyone to truly see me.

I follow the guards as they lead me through the halls, letting my mind wander as we walk. As an heir I have many responsibilities. I have tried to take them seriously, to learn from my parents and their advisors, but there is still so much to learn. Oliver's words are more than a little concerning. As heir, it is my job to keep the peace, how can I do that when I don't know that there is some kind of strife happening to begin with?

Aside from that, I am a mermaid, and mermaids are healers by nature. We seek to protect others, to keep everyone safe. Something that is much easier said than done when your kingdom is crawling with sirens whose very nature calls to chaos and mischief. The wicked creatures who leave nothing but trouble and destruction in their wake.

We turn the corner that leads to my doors and I excuse the guards. I enter my room and quickly make my way to the bathing chamber where my maid is waiting. Upon seeing me she starts the water for the bath then moves to help me undress. She starts on the buttons while I haphazardly pull out the pins, allowing my hair to fall freely down my back. Once I am undressed, she excuses herself and I slip into the water.

Bubbles form as I let myself shift and my tail sloshes over the edge of the tub. Blue and green scales shimmer beneath the water as I close my eyes. My mind goes back to a moment I have tried to ignore for a long time now. I let the water magic sink into my body, fighting the chill even as I hear a distant singing in my mind.

Sirens are banned from entering the city, but that doesn't stop them from terrorizing the citizens who live on the docks on Atran. Mermaids and sirens are a sort of 'cousin' species. Nearly the same in appearance once shifted, they both can use their voice to affect others. Sirens use their songs to manipulate people into doing whatever they want and often do. Mermaids can cultivate their voice to bring peace, even drown out the siren's songs. They can be extremely powerful if harnessed correctly.

I have had little experience with sirens, having spent the majority of my time within the safety of the city. Especially in the last few years. Even outside the city, mermaids are nearly impossible to bewitch, our own songs protect our minds like a shield. When I was younger I asked my mother why we allow the sirens to remain in our land but she just told me they were our people too, and we have to protect them as much as any other species. I argued that they were the monsters we were protecting people *from* but she just shook her head and told me I would understand when I was older. I have yet to reach that understanding.

It has been nearly a year and a half since Rose's last visit. We were walking through the dockside market together when we heard them. Their voices carried through the crowd directly into our ears. My mind protected

58

me from their bewitchment but fae like Rose are highly susceptible to their powers without proper training. Unfortunately, Rose had never had such training.

I watched in horror as Rose's eyes glassed over and a sort of mindless smile graced her lips. She walked towards them without any hesitation, nearly floating on air in her dreamstate. I called for guards but when none came I began to panic. I hadn't noticed we had become separated from them. I started demanding the sirens free her but they just laughed in my face.

It didn't matter that I was their princess, that I gave them a direct order, they just ignored me, like I was nothing. I tried to think of what my parents would do. How to channel my mother's tone that left no room for argument. How to mold my face like my father's when he lectures Finn. I failed to do either.

The leader of the group appeared beside me and whispered in my ear. She gave me a choice, do as she said and they would let Rose go. Or refuse and watch as they commanded Rose to jump from the pier and drown herself, for no reason other than to create chaos and strife. I could do nothing. Say nothing. This only made them laugh more. They turned, leading Rose to the water's edge, when Terran, Rose's eldest brother, appeared out of nowhere. He grabbed his sister and looked deep into her eyes.

It took him but a moment to understand the situation before he whirled on them. Only he didn't attack, didn't even raise a fist. No, he simply commanded them to release Rose at once. The sirens looked between themselves, seeming to consider their options but ultimately they did as he said. Jumping into the water and swimming away before they could be held accountable for their actions.

Released from her bewitchment, Rose collapsed. But again, Terran was there to catch her, to save her as I was unable to do myself. She was dazed and disoriented, asking what happened and why her head was pounding. Terran gave her soothing words before calling for guards and directing them to take her to the palace healers. Then he turned his gaze on me. I expected anger. I expected betrayal at what I had basically allowed my own citizens to do to his family. Instead I only saw concern.

He grabbed my face and looked into my eyes, sighing when he saw or didn't see whatever it was he was looking for. He asked me if I was okay and to explain what happened. I found it impossible to form any words. Instead, tears tracked down my cheeks. His face turned to stone as he called again for the guards, this time ordering them to escort me back to my rooms. I let them.

I spent the rest of the evening sobbing into my pillow. Warring with the guilt and anger that threatened to consume me from the inside out. Hours passed and eventually Rose came by the room. I turned her away, not being able to bear looking her in the eyes after what I allowed to happen to her within the so called *safety* of my own kingdom. I allowed months to go by without contacting her. She wrote me letters and sent messengers but I ignored them all. My throat burned with failure as I read each one.

Eventually, she sent Terran, hoping he could get through to me I guess. He was the last person I expected to come knocking at my door. When I opened it I wished I could slam it shut but that is hardly the polite thing to do to someone who has traveled nearly halfway across the world to see you. So I let him in. He stayed for a week. Many things happened during that week, things I have never put to words, but in the end he failed to convince me to return with him to Sena. He used Rose's birthday as an excuse but I refused nonetheless.

Now I have allowed more than a year to go by without seeing the person I consider to be my best friend. I started replying to her letters after she began threatening to send Eve and Mar to drag me ashore. But since that day I haven't set foot on land or allowed any of my friends to visit me. My father and mother continue to tell me that I need to see our people, show them that I am their heir, but the thought of leaving the city makes me feel ill. Thankfully, they haven't tried to force me.

I open my eyes and allow my mind to center and the thoughts float away. It's a sort of meditation I began practicing after the incident kept me awake for weeks. The healers tried to use their magic on my mind but they said it is a sickness not so easily fixed, and likely one I will work at for the rest of my life. Shifting back, I ease from the tub and wrap myself in a fluffy robe, making my way to the dressing room. I quickly dry myself and throw on a silk nightgown that barely reaches mid thigh. Walking to my bedroom desk I begin to flip through the piles of notes I have written over the last week.

One thing that I learned from the run in with the sirens is that I still have a lot to learn about my own people, let alone the world outside the water. I have spent nearly every day over the last year by my parent's side, listening and observing, learning all that I can from them. Sometimes it still doesn't feel like enough so I find other things to work on. I read up on the foreign courts and cultures. I practice my art, singing, dancing, everything that could make me appear to be half as graceful as my mother. The advisors were excited by my sudden increase in interest at first, but now I believe they have grown tired of my constant questions. And then there are the things they don't quite approve of, like my *other* training.

It started off easy at first, just some basic self defense techniques. My father and mother agreed that it was best I learn how to at least defend myself. But after a while I got bored of blocks and running away. I started spending more time in the training rooms until I built up some muscle and learned how to make my body move in the way I wanted, at least most of the time. Then I moved on to handling a weapon. I only had a short amount of instruction about how to use it before I was on my own and I'm still not entirely comfortable with the feel of it in my hand, but given the fact I am almost entirely self taught I'm not half bad.

I finish writing up some basic notes from the evening's dinner conversation and tuck them away in the desk drawer with a promise to myself to review them later. As I slide it shut something catches my eye. I reach inside and pull out the letter, bound in twine with a metal metal charm shaped like a leaf hanging from it. Flipping it over, the familiar green seal of Sena stares back at me. Not just the royal family's seal, Terran's personal seal. My finger glides over the hardened wax, contemplating my next decision. Sighing I reach for my letter opener and slide it into the edge. I pause for a moment longer before pushing it through the delicate paper and letting the letter slide out.

It's short. Only a single page inside. I unfold it gently and smooth out the creases. The scent of pine and rosemary wafts from the page as I allow my eyes to move over Terran's neat handwriting. I get to the bottom and read it again. I read it ten times before a single tear drops onto the page. Folding it again, I slip it back into the drawer and push it shut. I quickly cross to my bed, climb under the blankets and pull them up to my neck. It takes hours before sleep finally claims me, tears still hot on my cheeks.

Chapter 5

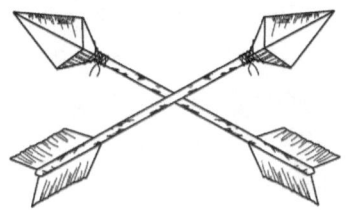

Oak

Terran and Rose find me in my room, bent over a pile of paperwork that the high lady asked me to complete. Thankfully, they don't stay long and I am able to get back to my work soon enough.

Eve and Mar are on their way here from Vulca and the moment they arrive I know I will be chasing after them, trying to keep chaos from ensuing. Mar is the calmer of the two sisters, Eve on the other hand practically breathes trouble. No matter how long we have known each other or how close we have grown, I will never be able to understand where she gets some of her ideas.

Once, when we were younger, she snuck out of the castle and went running through the forest at night. Apparently she wanted to see if she could take down a wolf shifter in their wolf form. To say the least it did not go well. She nearly ended up mauled to death and it took hours to calm the shifter down enough to get the full story. Eve was adamant that it wasn't her fault and that it was all some big misunderstanding. The shifter didn't agree.

Gathering up the paperwork into one neat stack, I head for the high lady's chambers. Walking through the halls, I watch the staff as they continue to work diligently on the party decorations, even well into the night.

A small group of fauns cast spells to create small orbs of light that will hang from the trees on the night of the party. Another group of fae, like me, are using their elemental magic to string long vines together, creating a sheet of greenery that will back the tables where the food will rest.

I'm so caught up in watching their work that I don't bother watching where I'm going as I turn the corner and end up slamming into someone.

"Woah, are you alright, Oak?"

I look up at my little brother's concerned gaze. His unruly curls fall across his forehead and into his green eyes, the color bright against his deep olive skin. He's nearly twice my size, his lithe frame towering over my own so I have to crane my head back.

"Reed, sorry, I was distracted," I apologize with a smile.

Two dimples appear in his cheeks as he smiles broadly. "That's okay. Where were you headed? I was just coming from the apothecary, he was showing me a new herb that can be used to treat nausea."

"Wow, that's... interesting. I take it everything is going well with your apprenticeship?"

Reed is seven years younger than me and infinitely kinder. He was so young when our parents were killed that he doesn't have many memories of them to begin with, but what he does remember is our mother's kindness and our father's generosity. Somehow, my little brother inherited both, where at times I feel as if I got none.

Where Reed sees someone wounded and in need of help, I can only see the danger they present, the weakness. A year ago, Reed practically begged the apothecary to take him in as an apprentice so he could study potions, healing, and everything in between. Now, his arms are stacked with a pile of books half as tall as I am.

"It's great! I've been learning about cures for different kinds of ailments that can't be treated with healing magic. There are some types of water that are even known to reduce the effects of poisons." He beams. Still so innocent, happy and carefree. He has no idea the danger that lurks in the shadows just outside these castle walls.

"That is truly incredible. Listen, I would love to catch up with you but the high lady asked me to get these to her and I really don't want to keep her waiting." I glance over his shoulder in the direction of her study and send a silent prayer to the Goddess that she is feeling patient.

"Oh, of course, I'm sorry to keep you. Go ahead, we can catch up later. Tell auntie Ayana that I said hello," Reed says with a wink. He moves past me, balancing his many books effortlessly on one hand while he squeezes my shoulder lovingly with the other.

Not wasting any more time, I hurry down the corridor until I am waiting outside the high lady's chambers. I raise my hand and hesitate for the briefest moment to take a deep breath. Even after years of working for my aunt, I can't seem to help the unease that fills me anytime I am in her presence. Rapping two short knocks on the carved wooden door, I wait to be summoned. When a voice calls from the other side I ease the ornate door open and step inside, searching the room for any sign of my aunt.

"Oakley, over here," She calls from behind her desk on the far side of the room, bent over a table littered with paper.

"I brought the paperwork that you asked for," I say, holding up the stack.

"Perfect, bring them here," she demands, not bothering to look up from her work.

I cross the room quickly and deposit the papers neatly in front of her. Turning on my heels I try to take my leave quickly.

"Actually, can you spare a moment? I would like to talk to you about an assignment that I may need your assistance with." Hey eyes continue to scour the maps strewn about before her, a singular crease is set deeply between her thick, manicured brows.

"Of course. What do you need?" I ask, standing at attention. I've come to realize that when it comes to my aunt, she is the high lady first, family second. Which means that when she has a task for me to do it is less of a request and more of a demand.

"Come take a look at this, will you? I have been puzzling over it for hours now and I can't seem to wrap my head around it," she says with a sigh.

Nodding my head I step forward and look at the maps. It shows the whole of Estarynn including each of the four realms and kingdoms as well as the mortal lands. Sena makes up nearly the entirety of the western land from the edge of Rayan, the Kingdom of Water, and up to the base of the mountains that border Eteri, the Air Realm. Vulca takes up the majority of the east, mirroring our realm. The Kingdom of Fire extends from the smallest peak of the mountains all the way to the far south, bordering the wastelands that used to be Cansu, the Land of Mist.

The mortal lands are nestled in the very center of our world, ringed by the forest and protected by miles and miles of open fields. I let my eyes roam over the forest and find a handful of red circles in seemingly random locations. A few places are marked with red x's, drawing my attention.

"What are these?" I say, pointing to a small cluster in the south.

"You don't need to worry about those, Oliver has it taken care of. What do you think about the areas that have been circled?" she presses.

I look over the map with more attention this time, focusing on the circles and searching for any sort of pattern. The only thing that stands out is that they are clustered in the areas of the forest that are the most dense.

"Well, they are all from regions where the trees are dense, especially here and here," I say, pointing to a large group of circles near the mountains. I can't help but notice it is on the path that Eve and Mar are most likely taking. Though I doubt the high lady would care about that small fact.

"Right, now why do you think that is?" she questions, her voice tinged with the smallest hint of annoyance.

Wracking my brain for any semblance of an explanation, only one thing comes to mind. Gargoyles. "These areas would be home to the gargoyles. They prefer to live up in the trees so they tend to pick areas where the trees are dense like these places." Gargoyles are one of the more elusive creatures in Sena. They're among the full shifters, transforming into beasts made entirely of stone with large wings that can carve through the air as they fly above the treetops.

"Precisely. Now, why would the gargoyles under my own protection be harming innocent bystanders? That is the true question." She begins to pace, her long gown trailing behind her as she walks the same length of carpet back and forth. It's unusual to see her so worked up. She is usually the perfect picture of poise and composure.

"Would you like me to find out? I could go out and search the forest, find out if there is a reason. Maybe there is more to the story..." I drone off when Ayana's head snaps in my direction.

"Really? You would do that for me, Oakley?" she beams, her eyes shining and her face looking more relaxed than it had when I first entered. A small smirk tugs at her lips.

There is a chance that I could miss Rose's party if I do this. That I might not get to see Mar or Eve at all. Still, I already know this is more than a request. "Of course. Tell me where you would like me to head first and I'll leave at once."

"Excellent, why don't you follow this pathway up towards the mountain and check the trees, see if you can find any information on what is going on," she says with a clap of her hands.

Nodding, I turn to leave when the sound of my name stops me.

"Oakley, please keep this between us. No need to go getting Rose all worked up before her big day, she has so been looking forward to it."

I force a smile, "of course, High Lady, I wouldn't dream of it."

"Please, I am your aunt, no need for such formality." Ayana's eyes soften and she appears so much like my mother, her sister, in that moment that I am momentarily frozen. Their eyes and nose are the same, the soft waves of her hair and the darker skin, each little feature is so much like her that it hurts.

Looking away, I stare out the window where a light drizzle has started up outside. I watch as the glass fogs and droplets slide down the panes until they splash against the stone windowsill outside. I remember sitting next to Reed when he was really little and watching them fall, waiting to see if the one we chose would win the 'race'. My brother's face flashes in my mind, all smiles and dimples, and I'm reminded of his request. "Reed says hello, I ran into him as he was leaving the apothecary."

"Right, of course, I remember he wanted to take up an apprenticeship, didn't he? How is that going? Well, I presume. As a member of this family I would expect no less." She gives me a pointed look.

I nod quickly, "He's doing great. Learning more and more every day. He will be a true asset to the healers should they require his assistance." He has no choice but to be.

"Let us hope that we never have need for it, even if the knowledge gives me a bit of added comfort," she says with a distant stare. Her eyes appear miles away, like she is locked in some sort of memory and she can't escape.

Silence stretches on between us until it becomes unbearable. Clearing my throat I say my goodbyes and quickly make my way from the room. I stop by my own briefly to gather a few necessities and then head straight to the stables. I consider stopping to say goodbye to Terran and Rose but decide against it, knowing that they would both have plenty of questions and Ayana asked me not to say anything anyways.

The stable hands immediately begin preparing my horse the moment I walk in. Meanwhile, I spend some time thinking over my plan. If I want to move quickly and unnoticed, I won't be able to ride this whole time. No, instead I will take the horse deep into the forest and then send her back while I continue on foot. That way, I'll be able to jump from tree to tree if needed without having to worry about leaving her behind.

As soon as she is ready, I mount up with only minimal difficulty, and take off for the forest.

Chapter 6

Eve

"How much longer until we arrive?" I whine to the guards, leaning out the carriage window. I hear a collective groan from where they're riding beside us on their horses. Father insisted that Mar and I ride in the carriage rather than on our own horses, something we both protested at first, but now I'm grateful for the added comfort. We left Vulca almost four days ago and I began to grow antsy only a few hours into the journey.

"We are almost to the northern border, princess. Another two days of riding *at least* until we reach the royal grounds. If you need to rest, we can take a break and water the horses," answers a female guard to the right of the carriage.

Prior to departing the city I had never seen her before. I spent the first day leaning out the window asking her a million questions, all of which she answered with a smile. Her name is Nat, she is a dragon, a small fact that got my blood heated and had nothing to do with my fire magic. She grew up in one of the towns on our southern border. Her parents were both guards themselves but they recently retired which is when she decided to follow in their footsteps.

She's only been a royal guard for a few weeks; she joined after her 25th birthday last month. Something about her draws my eye, it could be her coppery hair, or the way her entire body shows the evidence of her hard work in training. Her muscles are defined, cut in a way that is both strong and graceful at the same time. I saw the hint of toned abs when she lifted her shirt to wipe her face earlier and I think I actually drooled a bit.

But it's not just her body that has caught my attention. I've heard whispers under her breath that make me laugh. I've seen the smile that crosses her face when she talks about her family. Everything about her lights up when she talks about the things she loves. For a moment I consider bombarding her with more questions but the last time I did Mar almost kicked me out and made me walk.

"No, I'm fine," I say with a sigh, leaning back from the window and against the cushioned seat. I watch my sister in awe as she meticulously works on the puzzlebox father had given her before we left.

"Here," he said, handing her the wrapped present, "something to entertain you on your journey."

When I asked where my gift was he laughed and told me that nothing would keep me entertained long enough to be worth giving. He wasn't wrong. Although I would have liked to see him at least try. Mar offered to let me try out her puzzle but I quickly became frustrated with it and handed it back. She, on the other hand, has been entirely focused on the damned thing for the last four hours.

Mar has a tendency to disappear into her own mind sometimes, a habit we share. Although my mind tends to wander to fantasies of feeding or training. I watch her examine the box with intense focus, her hands glide gently over the edges as she looks for some sort of irregularity. She has barely put the thing down since we left and she has still only managed to move one tile. I snort to myself, wondering how long it will take before she becomes frustrated with it and chucks it out the window.

I lean forward to look closer when the carriage comes to a jolted stop. I am thrown forward and land across Mar's lap. Her light eyes blink as her mind clears and she takes in my new positioning. I push back into my seat and poke my head out the window. Nat isn't there which sends a small spike of anxiety shooting through my veins.

A few of the guards have jumped down from their horses and are walking ahead. I start to lean out further to watch where they're going but Nat appears in front of the window, having approached from behind.

"You should both stay inside. There are signs of some type of struggle on the road ahead," she says, nodding towards the other guards. Her freckled nose scrunches up as she places a hand on the sword strapped across her back.

I give Mar a mischievous look that she returns without any hesitation. Jumping to our feet, we quickly exit the carriage, following the guards who are now far enough ahead they are difficult to make out. There is a crisp breeze in the air that marks how far north we have traveled, sending chills over my exposed arms. My sleeveless tunic is thin, which was perfect for home but the farther we travel the more I wish I had brought a cloak.

We catch up to the guards quick enough and unsurprisingly they don't even bother to tell us to return to the carriage. One of our father's guards, Rian, is crouched down, inspecting what looks like a discarded dress. His ash blonde hair is perfectly styled despite the days of travel already under our belt.

"This dress is still warm, whoever it belongs to is close by," he says with a frown.

The other guards circle him and us, withdrawing their weapons and standing ready for a fight.

Nat approaches our group partially shifted. Her skin is covered in rough, stone-like scales, and her hands have become sharp, elongated claws. It's impressive, the control she has over her other form. Dragons are not known to be the most calm creatures, often losing control of their mortal form and fully shifting in the middle of crowded rooms. All it takes is pissing one of them off and bam, face full of fire breath. It's no wonder she was added to our personal guard so quickly. That level of control is unmatched and shows a great deal of magical power.

The strength of a person's magic is determined by three key factors, control, power, and status. Control comes down to how you wield magic whether it's spells, incantations, potions, or any other kind. The more control you have, the stronger you are. Elemental magic tends to be easier to control since it is something we are born with, determined by our creatures and where our ancestors originated. Some people can wield it like an extension of themselves, using the elements as easily as they breathe.

Power is more about the force of which you can use said elemental magic. There's not really much you can do to increase your power levels aside from acquiring more magic and there's really only two ways to do that. Either by inheriting the magic from your parents upon their deaths, or if someone offers the magic to you, a small kernel from their well of magic that gives you an extra little boost.

Status is solely determined by your creature and your blood. Each realm and kingdom is home to a menagerie of creatures each with their own place on the food chain. Ancestry is important for some as it grants them status, like the royals, but for many it's their creature that elevates them in the world.

In Vulca, the cyclops are on the bottom. Their creatures don't have a lot of elemental magic and they tend to be more rough around the edges. The phoenixes are next, they're known to be excellent healers and even better at spells, but on the other hand, their elemental magic is more or less just for show, not much power behind it.

In comparison, succubi and vampires are tied at the top. Centuries ago they established their spots at the top by using their manipulation to control the other species. Power is more than just brute strength after all. Dragons are smack in the middle, exceptionally strong but again, not very good at controlling their power. Or at least most aren't.

Nat seems to be the exception.

I watch her in awe as she allows her eyes to shift and her pupils become thin slits. She scans the forest edge and stops by a dense cluster of trees. "There," she says, pointing a sharpened claw.

The guards exchange a look before three break off and march forward.

Beside me, Mar pulls out a small dagger and holds it parallel to her arm, ready to attack. Her other hand rests against the small metal tube attached to her waist. We both shift, ready to attack if need be. I pull out my own daggers and twirl them in my hand, knowing that even without them, our magic is strong enough on its own.

Rian steps forward, putting himself in front of us while Nat guards our backs. I flash her a smile over my shoulder and throw in a quick wink which makes her laugh and the sound does something funny to my stomach.

One of the guards appears in the tree line, he takes up a light jog towards us and stops in front of Rian. "You better come see this," he says, his face grim.

We follow him back to where he left the other two guards standing, staring up into the trees. They both have their shirts pulled up over their mouths and a disgusted look on their faces. As we get closer the smell becomes pungent. Death and rot cling to the air.

I gag and notice Mar and Rian shift quickly, cutting off their heightened senses which is making it ten times worse, no doubt. I follow their lead and the smell instantly becomes a bit more bearable.

We stand in a semicircle at the base of a large tree. I squint my eyes as we look up but I can barely see anything aside from branches and leaves which is the downside of shifting back into my mortal form.

"Okay, someone with better eyesight tell me what I'm looking at please," I groan.

Nat steps forward in her mortal form again. "Is that what I think it is?" she asks.

One of the guards quickly ducks to the side as he throws up, the other patting his back sympathetically.

"It looks like some sort of… nest," Mar says in a nasally voice. My head whips to her at the sound and I find she has pinched the bridge of her nose. A snort escapes me and she cuts me a look of contempt.

I shrug my shoulders and stare up at the tree again. The vague outline of a nest is about 50 feet in the air but whether or not something else is up there is unclear. "Hello!" I yell into the air, "is anyone up there?"

The guards turn to stare at me, mouths agape.

"What, it's not like we were getting any answers just sitting here staring," I say pointedly.

Nat swallows a laugh while Mar tries to hide her smile. The rest of the guards don't seem too pleased with my completely reasonable explanation. Besides, if something really was up there I doubt my screaming would make it come down.

A large eagle head appears over the edge of the nest, followed by a very large lion's body and enormous wings. It's a fucking griffin. Which explains the smell. Unlike with other shifters, griffins completely shed their mortal form, sloshing off skin and fat as they transform into their larger beast-like form.

"Shit," Rian says under his breath. He grabs hold of the guard closest to him and pulls him back a step away from the tree.

A loud, bird-like screech blasts through the silent forest, causing all of us to cover our ears. The griffin stands upon its nest and a pile of gold shines proudly beneath its belly.

"If we have any desire to leave here alive we best move now. We just stumbled upon a griffin's stash and they are fiercely protective, almost as bad as a dragon. I do not want to stick around to find out if they feel like sharing today." Nat begins backing away slowly, never looking away from the nest.

Another screech ricochets off the inside of my skull and I find myself nodding. "I agree with her. I vote to leave now and live to see tomorrow."

Mar nods her head and then we all take off. Nat grabs my hand and pulls me along behind her until I get my pacing as we are running side by side. We keep throwing glances at each other as we run, a wicked smile plastered across my face even as my heart races.

Mar is keeping pace beside Rian while the remaining guards run up ahead of us. Usually that would be frowned upon but given the fact the horses are currently unattended, it is probably for the best. The last thing we need is for them to get spooked by the angry lion bird chasing after us and take off.

We make it back to the carriage and quickly climb inside. Nat slams the door shut behind us and jumps into the coach box. She wastes no time in getting the horses moving and soon we are racing down the road again.

"I don't understand," says Mar shaking her head, "what is a griffin doing out in the woods? They should be up in the mountains, hidden in a cave somewhere." Griffins are a part of the Air Realm, Eteri, which is why it is so unusual to see one so far from their home.

"Listen I don't really care where they are *supposed* to be, I just care that a very angry one is currently flying over us and doesn't seem too pleased we found it's hiding place." I dare a glance out the window.

The griffin is hot on our trail, flying close to the ground behind the carriage. I wished the damned thing would just shift back into its mortal form so we could have a civilized conversation, but apparently that would be too much to ask for. The griffin gives an angry squawk, clearly upset that we chose not to become today's lunchtime snack.

Mar pulls open the curtain at the back of the carriage, "Shit. It's getting closer."

Usually we don't have to worry too much about creatures like griffins or manticores, they prefer to stay hidden away in the mountains, far from the roads that lead between realms. Why this one decided to come down and party in the woods is beyond me.

I lean my head out the window and shout towards the creature, "Hey there. Sorry to disturb your home. We didn't realize someone was living in those trees. Our bad. Is there any way you could stop chasing us now?"

I lean back inside and Mar raises her eyebrows in question.

"What," I say with a shrug, "it's not like it could make things worse."

The wheels of the carriage are lifted from the ground and dropped back to earth as the roof is ripped off completely. Mar and I are tossed around, banging off of the benches as the griffin's large talons cut through the metal like it's a piece of paper. The griffin flies high into the sky before releasing the roof and sending it crashing towards us.

Mar and I share a split second look before we both jump over the side of the carriage and onto the road. I duck into a roll and feel small rocks and pebbles cut into my skin before I land in a crouch, Mar beside me. Looking around I see that Nat cut the horses free before jumping herself. One of the guards races after the horses while the rest circle us, waiting for orders.

I look up and find the griffin is soaring back the way we came, clearly pleased with itself. I shake my head and start to laugh. Rian hops down from his horse and approaches Mar, examining a small gash on her arm, most likely from the jump.

"Next time you want to scream at unknown creatures, please don't?" Nats asks with a half smile, her arm outstretched above me. I take her hand and let her pull me to my feet.

"Oh come one, that was the most exciting thing that has happened since we left the city."

Nat lets loose a warm laugh. "Yeah I suppose you've got that right. Still, I would rather not get the heir to the crown killed on my third week."

I look over my shoulder to where Mar is arguing with Rian. I give her one of our looks but she just rolls her eyes and shakes her head.

Rian throws his hands up and walks over to me. "Can you please tell your sister that she needs to allow me to treat her wound."

I throw my head back and laugh. "Yeah, good luck with that. First, I don't *tell* my sister to do anything, and you should give up trying. Second, she'll heal quick enough if she feeds, so what's the big deal?"

"We are at least a few hours from the nearest village and that is assuming you two can keep up on horseback. She should just let me take care of the wound so that we can get moving," he growls. His light blue eyes bore into mine, challenging me to argue with him.

"There. Taken care of," Mar says from behind us, holding her arm up. There is a bit of dried blood but the gash has completely vanished.

Rian stares at her dumbfounded as she walks straight past him.

I clap a hand on his shoulder, bringing his attention back to me. "Oh yeah. Did I forget to mention my sister's not half bad at healing magic? It's just another one of her many talents."

I turn and follow after Mar, leaving Rian and the rest of the guards to talk, argue, I'm not even sure at this point. We walk along the road until we find the mangled carriage and begin sifting through the wreckage.

Most of our bags were sent ahead of us so the only thing that was truly damaged was the food rations. Half of our traveling party are vampires so we don't need to worry that much about them. The other half consists of a cyclops, Nat who is a dragon, and myself, meaning we really only needed to worry about the three of us.

Mar and I gather up what supplies are salvageable and rejoin our travel party.

"We have a problem." Nat says, looking between my sister and I.

"Great, what happened now?" Mar asks, voice laced with surprising irritation.

"Before the carriage was destroyed I cut the horses free. We were able to catch them but when we did we realized that their saddles were damaged. There is no way you two will be able to ride them the rest of the way."

Mar frowns, "Why? We can just ride bareback, can't we?"

Rian walks over, laughing in Mar's face. "Bareback? You two? No offense princesses but I highly doubt you'll find the journey *comfortable* from here on out. Especially if you are riding on a horse with no saddle."

Mar's eyes narrow, "Is that so? Well, I believe my sister and I are fully capable of riding, saddle or not."

I whip to face her, "Yeah keep me out of this. I have no intention of riding a horse with no saddle. It's going to be uncomfortable enough as is."

"You can ride with me," Nat says with a smile.

I consider that for a moment. Nat's chest pressed against my back, our thighs brushing up against each other. Damn, I need to feed. Maybe if I'm lucky Nat will be equally excited by these new seating arrangements and I might be able to take the edge off. It's been over a week since I had a full meal and I refuse to *ask* a guard for assistance.

While my mother may be in the habit of buying me whomever she thinks will please me, I do my best to avoid partaking. There is something to be said about buying sex. It doesn't taste as sweet, literally. For a succubus, sex and pleasure is like the sweetest wine. The burn as you swallow their moans like a shot of pure adrenaline. My entire body heats at the thought of my mouth on Nat's. Drinking her in, her copper hair flowing down her defined back as her bright eyes stare into my own.

It's been a while since I've enjoyed the company of a female, an unfortunate truth. Men have their perks, don't get me wrong, but females, females know how to take care of each other. Most succubi take it wherever they get it, the nature of my kind. Ultimately it's the person, not the parts to me. So long as I feel an attraction and the desire is mutual, I am down for a good time with anyone. Male, female, neither, all of the above, makes no difference to me.

Nat raises her eyebrows at me and I realize I haven't responded.

"Works for me," I answer with a smirk. Feeling the slight flush burning my cheeks.

Mar is giving me her what the fuck look but I choose to ignore it. If she wants to ride by herself then go for it but no way I am suffering alongside her needlessly.

"Fine. Eve can ride with Nat and I'll ride by myself," Mar grumbles.

Rian cocks his head at my sister and smirks, "I bet you don't even last the rest of the day."

I shoot Rian a look, "It's a mistake to make bets with my sister. She rarely loses."

Mar smiles at that and I can't help but notice the glint in her eyes as she stares the guard down. I wonder if she is more excited by *him* or the challenge he promises.

"Come on Eve, let the man decide for himself. He seems confident enough," she says with a smirk.

"Oh I am confident. So confident that I'm willing to bet my favorite dagger on it," Rian says, unsheathing a dagger from his belt. It's gorgeous. The blade is black obsidian, the sun shines off the reflection of the smooth stone. The hilt is gold with a leather strap tied around the bolster.

I want it.

Mar's eyes shine with adoration as she takes in the weapon, "I win, I get that dagger. No going back."

"What about me?" he asks, "What do I get when I win?"

"*If* you win, you can have this potion," she says holding up a small glass jar.

"I'm supposed to give you my favorite dagger and you're going to give me some basic potion? Not gonna happen, princess," he says with a shake of his head.

"This is not just any potion. I made this myself. One sip of this, and even the worst wound will be stitched back together." Mar proudly holds the potion up between them.

"I take it that is how you fixed your arm so quickly?" he asks, eyes narrowed suspiciously.

"Of course. Why waste my magic healing a little cut when I have a potion that will do it for me."

Rian seems to consider the offer before extending his hand, "you've got a deal. You last longer than the night and you get my dagger. You give up any time before nightfall and I'm taking that potion of yours, *and* your pride."

Mar takes his hand, giving it a firm shake. "You're on. I wonder what I'll name the blade when I take it from you," she says with a smirk.

"No, absolutely not. If by some miracle you do win, you are not giving my blade a new name. You can take the name with the blade or take nothing."

Mar shrugs, "Fine, no new name. But it better not be something stupid."

Once the deal is settled we get to moving, gathering up the horses and what's left of the supplies, we each mount our horses. I take my seat in front of Nat as she wraps a gentle arm around my waist.

"Lean against me, we have a long way to ride and I want you to be as comfortable as possible," she says tugging me back.

She's a bit taller than me, her chin just above my head. I twist to look up at her and a shot of electricity shoots to my core. Her cheeks are a bit flushed and she keeps licking her lips.

I know that if I opened up and allowed myself to feed I would taste sweetness on my tongue. But I don't. It's not right to feed without the person's consent. And besides, if I let her get all worked up maybe I won't just be topped off at the end of the night, maybe I'll finally get rid of this aching hunger that has been gnawing at my insides for weeks.

I scoot my ass back and lean up a bit to whisper in her ear, "Believe me, with your chest pressed against my back, I'll be more than just comfortable."

I watch the blush spread across her cheeks as she swallows hard. I chuckle to myself and turn back around. This trip is finally starting to actually be some fun.

Chapter 7

Mar

My vagina is on fire. Scratch that, it's going to fall off. It's been almost three hours since we all climbed back on our horses and continued on our journey. Three *agonizing* hours for me.

I look slightly ahead where Eve is sitting comfortably against Nat. The two of them laugh in unison as Eve continues to whisper over her shoulder into her riding partner's ear.

How nice. For her.

"Feeling a bit uncomfortable?" Rian asks smugly from beside me.

It's been like this for over an hour now. Eve and Nat having the time of their lives, meanwhile Rian tries to goad me into giving up.

My eyes flick to the dagger hooked to his hip and I plaster a smile on my face. Looking at him with my eyebrows raised I shrug my shoulders casually, "Why would I be uncomfortable? I love riding."

My horse shifts beneath me and I have to stifle a groan. My thighs are aching, my back is burning, and I am pretty sure my feet fell off a while ago. I try to adjust to relieve the pressure between my thighs but that just makes it rub against the sore spots. I bite into the side of my cheek and continue staring straight ahead. Ignoring Rian as he continues to stare me down.

"Really? Is that so? Well, if you're so comfortable I guess there will be no reason for you to join me, will there?" Rian continues, rubbing a hand across his saddle tauntingly.

I shake my head, "Nope. No reason at all. I am perfectly fine riding by myself."

Rian nods his head slowly and begins to pull ahead on his horse. He rides beside my sister for a moment before continuing forward to the head of the group. Eve and Nat's horse slows a bit and then they are beside me.

"Come on Mar. Cut it out. This is just getting ridiculous," Eve says with a groan of frustration. Her cheeks carry a faint blush that I can only imagine has to do with her riding companion.

"No. I refuse to let an arrogant prick like him tell me what I can and cannot do." I shift again, wincing as I push into a particularly sore spot.

"He does that to everyone, princess. I wouldn't take it too personally," replies Nat with a sympathetic grin.

I stare into the back of Rian's head and hope that he can feel me watching him. Mentally setting him on fire and watching as his ashy blonde hair melts from his head.

The sun has nearly set and we are still a good distance away from the village. I hate to admit that Rian was right about anything, but unfortunately he was. I've slowed us down. It's not just uncomfortable to ride without the saddle, it's difficult to direct the horse. I'm not an experienced enough rider to comfortably give direction without the tools I have grown used to. My horse doesn't seem all that thrilled with our current predicament either. Constantly huffing or whipping its head back and forth dramatically.

Rian glances over his shoulder and sees me staring, a smirk spreading across his face. He holds a hand up to our travel party and we all come to a stop. He hops down from his horse and walks over to my sister and I.

"We're taking a short break. A few of the men need to relieve themselves. You should stretch your legs, if my map is correct we are at least another two hours from the village."

Nat hops down from their horse first then helps Eve, grabbing her by her waist and easing her down gently even though Eve is fully capable of getting off her horse herself. My sister bends over and touches her toes then stretches all the way back with her hands in the air.

I reach my own arms over my head, easing some of the pain in my shoulders before I move to dismount.

Rian appears before me, eyebrows raised, "Giving up so soon?"

"I thought you said we were taking a break?" I bite, eyes narrowed.

"Oh *we* are. But if you want to win our bet you won't be joining us," he says casually, walking away.

I open my mouth to call after him but decide against it, snapping my jaw shut. This is perfectly fine. Besides, if I got down now I might not be able to handle the pain of getting back up. I am tempted to take a sip of the healing potion I brewed but it was meant to be a gift for Rose. When I read her latest letter she told me how her rides through the woods often result in small cuts and bruises and she was worried about her mother telling her she shouldn't be riding.

It's a simple enough potion, a mix of herbs and a bit of elemental magic. What makes it truly special is a drop of phoenix blood. Difficult to come by if you don't know a willing phoenix, and almost impossible to brew correctly. Too much heat and the blood boils. Not enough heat and the herbs won't dissolve. A delicate balance that requires focus and attention to detail. Something that I learned from my mother.

I spent much of my early childhood learning how to brew potions by her side. She worked in the castle as a healer and was known for her tonics. It was how she met my father. He was injured during some kind of training exercise and she was the one who took care of him. Now, she has passed on a few of her gifts to me.

I've always excelled with my elemental magic. Fire is a difficult element to control, especially when emotions become involved. Yet for me, it came naturally. I could summon flame to my fingertips or warm my body from the inside. I used to centralize the heat in my face when I pretended to be sick. My mother never bought it. Father on the other hand would rush to the healer's wing and bring someone running into the room. They would always kick him out immediately and tell me to stop playing games.

Eve thought it was hilarious and made me do it often.

I stare at my thighs as they throb and consider the potion again. Shaking my head to myself, I try to lean back to take the pressure off my thighs. If I can just last till we get to the village I can use a salve that eases the ache. Only a few more hours. In the meantime, I will focus on coming up with as many scenarios of how to murder Rian as possible, the insufferable asshole.

~~~

I watch as the last embers of sunlight fade upon the horizon and smile to myself. The sun has set, and I am still riding. I take a moment to bask in my own joy and give Rian a smug smile.

His lips are set in a firm line and he refuses to acknowledge me.

Nat and Eve turn and give me hesitant smiles and I know from their looks that they can see my pain.

My body is practically screaming at me, demanding I stop riding at once. My muscles ache and I can feel every small bump as we walk over the uneven road, no longer capable of hiding the way my face contorts in pain or the small gasps that sneak past my lips. I'll feel better about my victory when we are in the village and I am off this damn horse. I squint my eyes ahead and hope to see some sign that we are near but there is nothing but black, even with my heightened eyesight.

Rian and another guard are a few feet ahead of us with their palms outstretched. One perk of fire magic, you never run out of light. The ground shifts as we begin to climb a small hill. I gasp as agony rips through my body. Eve turns to look at me with concern on her face, whispering to Nat and the two of them ride ahead.

After a few minutes of excruciating pain I catch up to the rest of our party, my body begging for reprieve as we crest the top of the hill. Then I see it. They all stare ahead where the village is lit up in the distance. The faint glow of lanterns nearly has me choking on a sob. We all start forward in a line and soon we are approaching the gates.

The villagers here are all tradesmen and women, they welcome travelers into their inns and sometimes their own homes in exchange for foreign goods. Then, after a few weeks they travel south along the border to the next village, and then the next, until they finally deliver their goods and start the process all over again in reverse. We've stopped here many times while traveling between realms.

Our small group makes our way to the stables and begins to unload. The guards remove bags from the horses and a few stablehands come out to meet us and tend to the horses. Everyone else has made it off their horse but me.

My sister and Rian walk over to me and look up expectantly. I try to swing my leg over the side but a sharp pain causes me to hiss. Rian's hands shoot out as if to catch me but I don't budge. I take a deep breath and grit my teeth, trying again. This time my body moves, albeit reluctantly. My leg slings over the side and I slide down till my feet touch the ground. I lean against the horse, struggling to put my full weight on my shaking legs.

Eve reaches out and places a light hand on my back. "How're you feeling?" she asks, voice laced with concern.

Rian steps towards me but I hold out a hand. Turning away from him, I keep my back pressed against the horse for support and let my head fall back. I close my eyes and take a few deep breaths before willing my body to move just a bit more. Looking into my sister's eyes I try to force myself to take a step forward but my legs won't hold. My knees buckle beneath me and my body goes falling towards the hard ground. Arms appear around me and I am lifted against Rian's hard chest. I open my mouth to protest but he casts me a silencing look. For once, I don't argue.

"Excuse me, we need a place to rest for the night. A few of our other party were sent ahead to prepare for our arrival," he says to a stable hand, his grip on me tightening ever so slightly.

The young boy nods and asks us to follow him. We walk behind him as he leads us through the village while I squirm in Rian's arms. He clamps down, immobilizing me, and staring straight ahead after the boy. I sigh but stop moving, trying instead to focus on anything but the pain in my legs aching, even as Rian carries me through the village.

The stable boy leads us to a small house at the very center of the village, the outside is covered in runes and wards preventing any violence within the walls. I snort which causes Rian to look down at me, a question in his eyes.

I shrug, "What? Don't you find it funny that they put us in the one house that is covered in runes?"

Rian cocks his head, considering my words, "No, not at all actually. I would imagine they were well aware of our impending arrival and prepared the house especially for us. I would like to think that your royal friends here did it out of an abundance of caution. Don't you?"

I bite my tongue to keep from responding. Rian has made it no secret that he does not trust any kingdom but our own. It's why he insisted on joining us this time. He is technically a part of our father's personal guard but when he learned we would be traveling such a far distance he demanded to be allowed to lead the party, and to choose the other guards.

In complete honesty, I was actually excited when I learned he would be joining us. I thought it might be a chance to get to know him a bit better, maybe even finish what we started in the training room. Turns out, Rian is actually just a douche with some sort of god complex. That much became evident before we even left the city. At first I thought it was an act put on for my father but oh was I wrong. Rian is an arrogant, egotistical asshole through and through.

"And what exactly has you smirking like that?" he asks, still looking down at me.

I bite my lip before I full on grin, "Oh wouldn't you like to know."

The door to the house is opened and we are gestured inside. We all stop inside the entryway waiting to be led to our respective rooms. An older woman steps into the room from what looks like the kitchen. "How many rooms will you be needing?" she asks sweetly.

Rian looks around our group before turning back to the woman, "three please. The females will all share one room, the rest of us will break off in pairs."

Eve shifts on her feet beside Nat who is trying to hide her laughter. Whatever they had *thought* was going to happen tonight was obviously off the table now that I would be joining them in a room. At least I *hope* it's off the table.

The woman nods and gestures for us to follow. She points out the first two rooms for the males and then a slightly larger third room for the females. She turns to leave us but Rian stops her.

"Excuse me, where is your bathing chamber?" he asks.

"That door there, at the end of the hall." she replies, pointing.

"Thank you."

I wiggle in Rian's arms to be set down but he refuses. I let out a huff of frustration. "Look, I'm fine now. Just put me down so I can crawl into bed."

"If you were fine you wouldn't need to crawl," he says plainly.

Nat and Eve watch with interest but don't move to interfere. I glare at them. Thanks for looking out *ladies*.

I give him my best scowl and narrow my eyes. "You and I both know that it was a figure of speech. Now, are you going to let me down or am I going to have to make you?"

Rian shrugs, "Suit yourself. It's not my fault if I laugh when you faceplant." He sets me down gently, his hands lingering for a moment before he releases me. Once he seems sure that I won't collapse, he turns to leave the room. "Nat, make sure you look at her legs, she's hurt and not hiding it nearly as well as she thinks," he says without looking back.

The door clicks shut behind him. I move to crawl into bed but I feel a light tap on my shoulder.

Nat stands behind me and gestures to my pants, "Are you going to take them off or am I going to have to do it?"

I roll my eyes, "You don't actually have to examine me. I'm fine. Just sore and tired from riding."

"Yeah bullshit. I saw your face while you were riding earlier, and then again when you tried to get off your horse. You're in pain, why won't you just let us help you?" Eve says with frustration.

I consider arguing but decide it's not worth the fight. I move to unbutton my pants and then start to pull them down. I'm half laying down on the bed which makes it difficult but I'm not sure I have enough strength in my legs to stand and balance. The pants get stuck over my thighs and I fail to hide my cry of pain. Hot tears threaten to spill from my eyes but I will them back.

"Oh my god Mar, how hurt are you?" Eve asks, a hand clasped firmly over her mouth. She winces as I continue to force the pants off.

I finally manage to wiggle out of them and throw them across the room. This is the last time I will travel anywhere wearing leather.

Nat and Eve both gasp as their eyes roam to my legs. The inside of my thighs are a marbled black and blue. Dark bruises cover my legs from the apex of my thighs to my ankles, some areas are a more brownish yellow and don't hurt as much. But the highest points? Those throb incessantly.

I allow my hand to gently touch one of the worst spots and cry out.

The door is thrown open and Rian stands in its place. He stares down at me in my half dressed state and takes in the damage I did to myself. Swallowing hard he slowly closes the door behind him and moves to stand in the corner. The four of us sit in silence, waiting for someone to say what I know they're all thinking.

"You're an idiot. Completely and utterly stupid," Eve says, stepping forward so she is right in front of me. "You allowed this to happen to yourself. Your own stubbornness put you here, and for what? For fucks sake you're bleeding!"

I look down and find that she isn't wrong, parts of my legs were chaffed so bad that the skin has torn and small welts of blood have sprung to the surface of my skin.

"I'm fine, Eve. Don't be so dramatic. Just go in there and grab my healing potion," I point to my bag next to Rian.

He is just standing there in the corner of the room, not moving and not saying anything. It's kind of creepy. His eyes are locked on my face but I can't help but feel exposed.

"Oh no, not gonna happen. I won't be an accomplice to you hurting yourself." Eve says viciously.

"Eve, that makes no sense. How is taking my healing potion hurting myself?" I say with a sigh.

"Because it's not about the potion! It's about you being so damn stubborn that you refuse to let anyone help you. One day it's going to get you killed. If I let you use that potion tonight you won't learn anything. You'll think it's alright to do shit like this and it isn't Mar! So no. Get it yourself if you must," Eve yells. She quickly turns on her heels and stalks out of the room, Nat following close behind.

Rian closes the door behind them, then turns to me, staring silently.

"Look if you're just going to stand there and stare at me I would prefer you leave. If you're here to help then fine, pass me the potion so I can get some sleep," I say, laying back.

I hear Rian move and then the sound of him rummaging through my bag. I crack one eye open and watch as he approaches. Standing above me he holds out the potion just out of my reach. Rolling my eyes I sit up and try to snatch it from his hands but he grabs my wrists, crouching down in front of me and putting us both at eye level with one another.

"Do you enjoy hurting yourself, princess?" he asks, his face close enough to mine that I can feel his hot breath. His grip on my wrist is firm, but not painful. I consider yanking my hand back but his eyes captivate me.

For a moment all I can do is stare into his furious gaze, watching as his light blue irises swirl with the storm brewing inside him. His jaw is set in a hard line, accentuating his plump lips and defined cheekbones. I kind of want to bite his lips.

Wait what?

Shaking that thought from my head, I realize he is waiting for me to reply. "No. Of course not."

He cocks his head and pulls me closer by my wrist, this time it hurts. "Is that so? Because the absolute wreckage that is your legs right now begs to differ." I pull against his grip and he eases it a bit but doesn't let go. Instead, he leans closer to me, our faces only inches apart. My tongue wets my lips involuntarily, his eyes track the movement.

He stares at my lips for a moment before his eyes flick to mine. Sighing he releases my wrist and stands, crossing the room to lean against the corner again.

I slump back and stare up at the ceiling.

"Why did you do it?" he asks out of nowhere.

"Do what?' I ask without moving.

"Make the bet."

"Why did *you*?" I throw back at him.

He doesn't respond immediately and I have to fight the urge to look at him. When he does reply his voice sounds much closer. "I thought you would give up. I thought it was a bet I was sure to win."

"And why would you think that?" I ask.

"Because, I wanted everyone else to be wrong."

I turn to look at him, "Wrong about what?"

He is suddenly much closer than before, sitting at the foot of my bed. "About you. Everyone told me you were this strong, stubborn headed female but all I could see was the fragile princess who needed protecting."

91

"I am anything but fragile," I retort. My blood heats as my magic begins to swirl beneath my skin. How dare he suggest that I am some weak creature? Someone who needs his *protection*.

"I know that now. And I'm honest enough to admit that I misjudged you."

I sit up a bit so I am resting on my forearms. "And how do you know that? Because I rode a horse bareback?" I scoff.

He shakes his head, "Because even when you could hardly stand you didn't ask for help. When you smiled at my taunts and threw them right back at me."

I smile a bit to myself.

"Do you know what else I learned?" he continues.

I nod my head no and he gives me a mean smile. "I learned that you're arrogant. Almost as much as I am. That you don't know when to say no or give in. I learned that you absolutely do need me, and your sister, and everyone else who has spent their entire life protecting you from yourself."

I grind my teeth and extend my hand, "Give me the potion and get out."

Rian smiles in my face, a kind of cruel smile that I have used many times myself. "No. Your sister is right. You need to learn to deal with the consequences of your actions. You drink this potion, you learn nothing. So I'll be holding onto it the rest of the journey," he says standing and pocketing the glass container.

"You can't do that. I won the bet. That potion doesn't belong to you and in fact, you owe me that dagger against your waist."

Rian looks down at the blade and shakes his head, "No one won that bet. You won't be getting anything from me."

"Liar," I say with a snarl, "You and I both know I won. Everyone else will back me. Besides, need I remind you who I am?" I don't love to throw the princess card in people's face but something about Rian has me wanting to use every advantage I can against him.

"No, princess, I am perfectly aware of who you are. I just don't think you've quite figured that out yet yourself," he says, turning to leave the room.

Before he pulls the door shut he tosses me a small metal tin. I unscrew the lid and open it to find a salve. I raise it to my nose and take a deep whiff, peppermint. My experience creating my own salves tells me it's a kind of numbing cream. Something that will ease pain but doesn't really do much to heal the actual wound.

"If you're so desperate to prove you're a fighter, start by learning to protect yourself first. You can't help anyone else until you've first helped yourself," he says, closing the door. I stare at the spot where he just stood in disbelief. That asshole stole my potion. The minute I can stand I am going to kick his ass and take my potion back, along with that dagger. I fall back with a huff of frustration and hold the salve tin against my chest.

My body is aching and demanding I pay attention to my wounds, but part of me is tempted to just close my eyes and let sleep claim me. I reach a hand down and touch my sensitive thigh, wincing at the contact. Applying the salve is going to hurt like crazy, but if I don't I'll feel even worse in the morning.

Sitting back up I scoop two fingers into the tin and grab a glob of the thick cream. The thick scent of peppermint invades the room as I tentatively touch the bruises. Hissing at the first contact I continue to smear the cream all over my inner thighs, focusing on the darkest blues and purples, even some black areas. I lay the cream on thick and fight back the tears that threaten to spill from my eyes.

It takes me what feels like hours before both legs are covered in the cream. Halfway through the first leg became numb which surprisingly made the other leg hurt worse. Almost like my attention had been split between the two but was now solely focused on the remaining wounds. After I finish I pull my tunic over my head, and toss it aside next to my pants. I manage to pull a thin blanket over me and curl up half on my side, a pillow tucked between my legs.

I close my eyes and hope that sleep claims me quickly. Preferably before my sister and Nat get back and keep me up half the night. Although I doubt any of us will be getting much sleep at all regardless. Between my pain, Eve's nightmares, and Nat technically being on guard duty, this room might as well just kiss sleep goodbye.

Still, somehow, sleep comes easily.

Chapter 8

Eve

"Princess! Wait up." Nat calls from beside me, jogging up to my side. She stops, not even a little out of breath.

I continue walking, feeling Nat's presence beside me even though she doesn't say anything as she follows me through the village. It's late and most of the villagers have gone home. The market stalls are finally closing up for the evening and soon the entire village will be dead quiet.

I love this village. Back when I used to visit Rose more often she would meet me here and we would travel together. Practically racing back to her family's home. There was a welcoming feeling in the Earth Realm, almost like it had a heart and lived. I tried to explain it to Mar once but she didn't seem to feel it.

Rose tried to tell me that earth magic was different, it was a give and take between the royal family and the magic itself. It didn't make sense to me. In Vulca, magic was everywhere. You could feel the energy hum in the streets, ready to be used. I love that about my home. I often feel drained, like my body uses up too much energy doing the most basic tasks. But no matter what I can call on my fire magic and it's there, waiting to be used. Even when it feels like that well inside me is ready to bottom out, there is always *something* left to grab on to. Some kernel of power deep within me.

I look around and realize we're all the way at the village edge. Looking over my shoulder I find Nat is there, silently standing guard while I deal with whatever it is that is going on inside me right now. I don't even really know why I am so upset. Mar is like this, stubborn to a fault at times. She never lets anyone help her, even when it is obvious to everyone around her that she needs it. It is, annoyingly, one of the things that we have in common.

Sighing, I plop down onto the damp grass, picking up a small twig and fiddling with it, weaving it between my fingers and over my knuckles like I would my dagger.

Dried leaves crunch as Nat moves closer. "Mind if I sit?" she asks.

I nod, not bothering to look up at her. She sits down close enough that I can feel her body heat and I can't help but smile a little as she bumps my shoulder with her own. "Is that a good smile or a smile I should be worried about?"

I chuckle, "I was just thinking about how warm you are, even so far from home."

"Ah, I see. Well I am a dragon and we are known for being exceptionally hot," she says playfully.

I look up at her and find a gentle smirk gracing her lips. "Is that so?"

Nat nods her head, her smiling disappearing and a look of nervousness slipping over her face.

I reach a hand out tentatively and brush my thumb across her delicate cheek. She is truly stunning. Her hair is pulled back away from her face, accentuating her high cheekbones. Pale blue eyes meet mine, pupils blown wide with the powerful pleasure I can taste seeping from her. I allow my thumb to skim over her full bottom lip and her breath hitches. The intoxicating taste of her lust overwhelms me. It's been a long time since I've taken control in these kinds of situations, usually opting to let someone else take charge.

Leaning forward I press my lips lightly against hers, testing her response. Her body shudders against me as her arm closest to me circles my waist, pulling me in further. I tilt my head so our lips brush again, a bit firmer this time. She makes this delicious noise that has me crawling into her lap. I straddle her, my arms going around her neck and tangling in her curls. I pull back lightly and she gasps.

Oh this is going to be fun. I love when they're responsive.

I lean forward, pressing my chest against her own. Her hands go to my waist and dig in. Deepening the kiss further, I wait for her to open for me. When she does, I let my tongue trace her lips before starting a sensual exploration of her mouth. We've moving slowly, *deeply*. My insides heat as her hands shift so that she is cupping my ass and I smile against her.

Maybe I won't have to take charge after all.

She nips lightly at my bottom lip and then suddenly I am under her. She's flipped us over like a pro, her leg coming up between my thighs and pressing firmly, drawing a gasp of my own. Things start to happen very quickly. Her clothes come off first, then my own, until we become nothing more than a tangled heap of limbs, our kisses never broken. Her tongue dances against my own, her taste so sweet, like the best wine. Her hands are everywhere, roaming across my bare skin, heat following their every path.

My skin is practically humming in approval. My shifted form is restless beneath my skin, demanding that I feed on this delectable pleasure. I try to shove it down, ignore the way it is making my skin prickle. The lust is thick in the air, making it difficult to ignore but I fight it anyways, focusing instead on Nat as she trails kisses down my neck.

Nat's lips press against my pounding pulse as she whispers in my ear. "I know what you need. You don't have to ask."

My whole body goes still. I didn't want it to turn into this. I mean, I did, but I didn't plan this. It's not like I intentionally lured her here so I could chow down on her pleasure. No matter how ravenous that little cuddle session atop our horse made me.

"What are you waiting for?" Nat asks, whispering in my ear again, her voice needier than before. Her hand slips between my thighs as she begins to rub small circles over my sensitive clit. A single digit dives between my folds, sliding easily through the wetness gathered there.

A moan escapes my lips as I pull her lips back to mine and give her a long, deep, kiss. With one last look into her eyes I can see how sure she is, how much she wants me to do this. I give in. My senses open up to hers and I feel the sweetest taste of her pleasure on my tongue as I begin to feed.

She lets out a noise that shoots right to my core. Our bodies move together as we both dive into this feeling. It's hard to really know what it feels like when a succubus feeds off you. We don't feel it the same way others do. I've been told it is a lot like every sense being dialed up to 1,000. Which I've got to say, sounds pretty damn good to me.

Suddenly, Nat sits up and I start to follow but she pushes me back down with a hand to my chest. I smirk but then I notice her eyes are trained on the forest not even 10 feet away. I taste bitterness as her emotions rapidly change.

Nat is off of me in no time, quickly picking up her weapons that were tossed beside our forgotten clothes. She stands fully naked and poised to strike at whatever is out there, lurking in the shadows.

Branches snap and a figure emerges from the woods.

I try to use my heightened eyesight but it's just too damn dark to see out here. I scramble to my feet and into a fighting stance. I don't bother searching for my discarded weapons, knowing that I can fight just as well hand-to-hand. Whoever thought it was a good idea to sneak up on us is in for a less than pleasant surprise. The figure steps forward and I summon fire to my hands, casting us all into a bright orange glow.

My eyes adjust and I see that the figure is in fact a man. Well, more of a boy really. The young stable boy is standing there, slack jawed as he takes in the two very naked females in front of him. Composing himself fairly quickly he bows his head and takes off back towards the village hastily.

I watch him run until he is too far, a laugh escapes me the moment he is out of view. Turning back to Nat I see she is far less amused with the turn of events than I was. "Hey, he's just a kid. Probably out messing around in the woods. I hear it's awfully romantic," I say, wiggling my eyebrows and stepping towards her.

Nat lowers her sword but takes a step back, away from me. Slowly she shakes her head as the putrid taste of regret coats my mouth.

I take another step forward but she holds up a hand between us. I quickly lock down my emotions, cutting off the connection between us, not realizing it was still open. She winces as the connection is severed and I instantly feel the cold that comes after a feeding wash over me. My body isn't humming anymore, no, it's like my veins have turned to ice.

"I'm- I'm sorry princess. I never should have allowed this to happen," she says, voice unsteady.

I move to the pile of clothes and toss Nat hers while I start pulling my own back on. "Of course, no worries. If you're not into females or if the succubus feeding thing was too much I totally understand," I say, unable to meet her stare as my cheeks burn.

When she doesn't say anything I turn back around to find her already fully dressed and standing at attention. "It's not like that. I prefer the company of a female but *this* was a mistake." I try to hide the hurt but it must show on my face because Nat takes a half step towards me before stopping herself. "This is my fault princess. I am your guard. I should have never- I am supposed to protect you," she says, stumbling over her words.

"Protect me versus what, fuck me?" I snap my mouth shut, biting my tongue and knowing that was a shitty thing to say. If she doesn't want to fuck me then that is absolutely her choice. It doesn't matter if she decided that before we got naked or after, even if the succubus side of me doesn't quite understand that.

Nat's pale cheeks are stained pink but she doesn't shy away. "Yes. If that boy had been an enemy you could have been hurt, or worse. I should have never allowed myself to get lost in my own emotions. It was unprofessional of me."

"I mean it's not like you pounced on me or something. I made the first move." I scoff.

"Still, as your guard I have a duty. Your safety should be my number one priority. Always. I can't guard you properly if I am... distracted," she says, avoiding my gaze.

I sigh. "Look, it's fine. I get it. No hard feelings, okay? Why don't we just walk back to the house and call it a night."

Nat opens her mouth to say something but decides against it. She nods and we start walking back, her slightly behind me this time. We walk in silence until we are outside the house. Before I can open the door Nat grabs my wrist. I look down at her hand and she quickly drops it, clearing her throat. "I-um...if you need..." she takes a deep breath and tries again, "If you need someone to service you I would be happy to find one of the other guards and establish a lookout."

Anger and embarrassment pricks my skin. I absolutely despise when people do this. My *mother* does this all the time. They think that just because I am a succubus, or because I do not have a preference when it comes to my partners, that I will fall into bed with just about anyone. It's part of the reason why relationships are so difficult, people think I will cheat or leave them for someone just because I'm running low on magic. As if that is all that matters, that emotion plays no part in it.

"Not necessary," I say, voice laced with unexpected venom, "wouldn't want them to get distracted, now would we?"

I walk inside and go straight to the bathing chamber. I know that Mar is probably in the room and if I go in there all pissed off I know she is going to want to talk about it.

Actually, now that I think about it, I'm pretty fucking pissed off at her right now too.

100

I take one look in the mirror and head back out, into the war zone.

I throw open the door, ready for a fight, but instead I find her curled up in bed. She's using her arms as a pillow while her actual pillow is tucked between her damaged thighs. Sighing I close the door gently and move to my own bed, yanking the pillow off and trying to slide it under her head without waking her.

She stirs but doesn't open her eyes. Damn, she must really be exhausted if that didn't wake her. Usually she will wake to the sound of a pin being dropped.

I stare down at my sister, wondering how it got to be like this. Sometimes I forget that I'm older, that I'm the one who's supposed to take care of her. Not that she ever lets me. I wish that there was a way I could take her pain from her. Not just now but every time she feels like this. Back when she lost her mom I would have done anything to be able to make her feel happy, even for just a moment. But that's not the way this works. I can take from others, steal their pleasure and happiness, but I can never give it in return, not in the way I wish.

I crawl into my bed and pull the covers over me, using my arms to support my head since I gave up my pillow, and try to fall asleep. A million thoughts race through my mind as I recall the events of the last 24 hours but eventually they start to fade away. I swallow hard as a sour taste invades my mouth.

Chapter 9

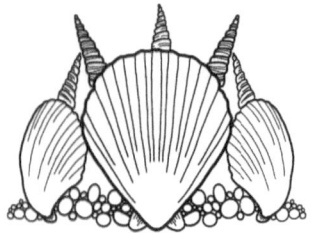

Cay

I pull my thick waves up into a bun and stare at my reflection, my round face flushed from training. Something woke me early in the morning and I had been unable to fall back asleep. Instead of tossing and turning, I opted to get in a bit of training before the guards arrived.

My muscles ache from overuse and forgetting to stretch, but otherwise I feel good. Strong and refreshed despite my lack of sleep. I had a breakthrough this morning and the lingering excitement has greatly improved my mood since last night. I bring my hands up and press the tips of my fingers into my cheeks, allowing my healing magic to flow. The angry red flush fades to a pink blush against my pale skin, my sea green eyes are practically glowing now.

Mermaids are natural healers, our abilities far surpassing any other species, even those of the other elements. They say I've shown promise from a very young age. My mother first noticed when I would heal my own small cuts and bruises without a second thought. She allowed me to meet with our healers regularly so they could teach me how to handle more complex injuries. I've even been called to assist with the guards who take it too far in training.

You didn't help Rose, the nagging voice in my head reminds me, sending a sharp pain to my chest. I brush the thought aside as I make my way through the halls towards the dining room and focus on what little facts I know from last night's conversation. Oliver was here for two reasons. He was going to help us meet with the manticore from Eteri, which is not uncommon given their realms relationship. The more concerning reason was the attacks he mentioned. I can assume based on my mother's reaction that it must have something to do with sirens.

A hard lump forms in my throat but I swallow past it. I cannot allow whatever happened in the past to darken my future. Sirens are a part of this kingdom whether I like it or not. I have a responsibility to them, same as any other species in this kingdom. I may be surrounded by mermaids in the city but on land there are hydra, nymphs, gorgons, and yes, sirens to consider.

There are days that I resent my upbringing. My father and mother have always been too protective, hiding things they think I'm not strong enough to handle. But not anymore, I won't be kept in the dark any longer. Steeling myself, I enter the dining hall and cross to my seat at the table. My father is absent, my mother engrossed in a conversation with Oliver, who apparently is sticking around for a while.

His eyes flick to me for a moment before continuing his conversation with my mother.

I had plenty of time last night and during my training to think about what to say. How to find a way into the conversation. I clear my throat and my mother looks up, smiling broadly.

"Minnow, how did you sleep? You look positively glowing," she says warmly. Her dark hair is styled away from her face into a thick braid down her back, highlighting her steel blue eyes and defined cheekbones.

I look to Oliver who regards me with interest. "Actually mother, there were some things on my mind that seemed to make sleeping quite difficult," I say, continuing to stare at Oliver.

His eyebrows raise but he remains silent. The ever present smirk gracing his full lips.

"Oh? What was bothering you?" my mother asks, a crease forming between her full brows. She shifts towards me, reaching out and placing her hands on the table atop mine.

"I want to know about the attacks Oliver mentioned." The words rush out of me in one continuous stream. My heart pounds in my chest as my hands grow clammy.

Oliver's smirk grows as he glances at my mother, waiting to see how she might respond.

"Oh, minnow, you don't need to concern yourself with something like that. We are handling everything. There is no reason to worry," my mother says, patting my hand lightly.

I turn to look at her, doing my best to control my expression. "I deserve to know, mother. I am the heir to this kingdom. If something, or someone, is attacking our people," I turn to look at Oliver, "or if our people are attacking our allies, I should know."

My mother gives a nervous laugh as eyes around the table fall on our conversation. I raise my brows, waiting for a response. I won't let her brush me off this time.

She quickly composes herself. "There is nothing to know. Oliver was mistaken. Simple as that." She reaches for her glass and takes a long sip of her wine. A bit early to be drinking yet no one says a word.

I shift my gaze to Oliver who is doing his best to hide his annoyance at my mother's insult. "Is that right, Oliver? Were you mistaken?" I ask plainly.

My mother opens her mouth but Oliver cuts her off. "I believe that the attacks were sirens seeking to cause chaos and unrest. Your parents seem to disagree. Which I find interesting given the clear evidence. The only creatures who could harm my people as they were, are sirens, that cannot go ignored."

I smile at my mother's shocked expression. It is clear that she never expected him to speak against her or my father so blatantly. Normally I would share her offense, but if what Oliver is saying is true then why were my parents trying to cover it up? They might make a habit of keeping me in the dark but that is not to say that they allow these kinds of things to go unchecked. Secrets aside, they are beloved rulers who care about their people above all else. They would never do anything to jeopardize our home.

A hush has fallen over the table but my mother recovers quickly. She stands and gestures towards the patio that overlooks the gardens. "Why don't we all move to the exterior and enjoy the view?"

The entire room stands and moves to follow her but I stay seated across from Rose's brother. Sometimes they are so alike but other times it is hard to imagine he is really related to her... or Terran. He looks nearly identical to his brother but he has a more wild side. Rose once said it was like Oliver was constantly trying to stir up trouble or turn things into a competition. I laughed back then, thinking about how competitive Rose is herself. Now, I am beginning to see what she truly meant.

Oliver doesn't stand either. Instead he remains seated at the table, staring at me as I take a swig of my mothers wine.

"I didn't think you had it in you," he says incredulously. He leans forward, setting his elbow on the table and resting his head in his hand. His gaze is calculating. It's clear he is looking for something but I have no idea what.

"Had *what* in me?" I ask.

Oliver smirks, "A backbone. That was the first time I have ever heard you actually speak up or go against what your parents say."

My eyebrows crease together. That wasn't *exactly* what happened. "Well, we learn something new everyday now don't we?" I say by way of response.

"True. Although given the fact I have known you your entire life I would imagine there isn't much you could do to surprise me."

I laugh, "That's the thing Oliver. You don't know anything about me. You may have watched me grow up but you never took the time to get to know me. Not really. You were too busy terrorizing us."

His hazel eyes widen, "Fair enough. But maybe it's time I start."

"Why would you do that?" I say, eyes narrowed suspiciously.

Oliver gives me another one of his signature smirks, "Well it seems my big brother certainly has taken an interest. Why shouldn't I?"

I choke on my wine, spitting half of it across the table and into Oliver's face.

"On second thought," he says, dabbing a napkin across his forehead, "maybe it's better I don't."

I finally stop coughing long enough to respond. "Why would you think that? Terran has no interest in me." I can feel the heat burning in my cheeks.

Oliver chuckles. "Is that so? Then why has he been sending you letters regularly for the past year?"

My heart is beating erratically but I don't let my face show any emotion. "Who's to say he has?"

Oliver stands and rounds the table, stopping beside me. "Are you truly going to deny it?"

I consider it for a moment. "Who's said I'm denying anything?"

Oliver leans forward, far too close for comfort. "So it's true? My brother has been sending you letters?"

I bite the inside of my cheek and look away.

Oliver's voice is hot against my ear, "What would the heir to the Earth Realm need from a princess like yourself? My imagination is running wild with the possibilities."

I push away from the table, forcing Oliver back, and turn to leave. I make it to the door before I feel his presence beside me. Of course he would follow me. I stop and stare at him. "What do you want, Oliver?" I ask bitterly.

Oliver's face is serious, more so than I have ever seen it before. "I want to know why my sister's best friend has refused to visit her for over a year now. I want to know why my older brother and future High Lord," he says disdainfully, "is constantly sending you messages yet *never* getting any response. I want to know why your people are attacking mine. Better yet I want to know why your parents are trying to cover it up. You see, I'm just *full* of questions."

I sigh and continue walking down the hallway, ignoring him as he walks by my side. After a while I decide it's not worth it if he's just going to follow me. "I have my reasons for staying away. Reasons that I am not about to discuss with you so don't bother asking again. I don't know what to tell you about Terran. He sends me letters, but I don't read them, I have no reason to." My mind goes to the letter in my desk. I don't know why I lie but it doesn't seem right to go around telling people what Terran has said to me in his letters. That's between him and I.

"I don't need to explain myself to you, Oliver, but since you're Rose's brother I'll say this. I love your sister, she is my best friend. The closest thing to a sister that I have. Nothing is going to change that. Our relationship is stronger than most and we don't need to visit each other to prove that," I say without looking at him.

"And what of your relationship with my brother?" he asks, his voice lower than before.

We turn down the hall that leads to my studio, the doors are slightly open which is odd.

"I don't *have* a relationship with your brother," I respond, squeezing my hands into fists. My fingernails dig into my palms dark enough to draw blood.

"Fine, keep your secrets," he says, grabbing my arm and stopping me in place. He uncurls my fist and heals my palms without mentioning it.

I stare between him and my palm.

Oliver looks around the hall and leans forward, once again invading my personal space. "If you won't tell me about my brother then what about the attacks? If you know anything, Cay, you have to tell me. These are my people being attacked. *My sister's people.*"

I shake my head, "I'm sorry, I don't know anything. Up until you mentioned them last night I didn't even know there had been attacks. And I don't know why my parents are acting so weird about it."

Oliver nods but doesn't say anything else.

"Oliver, what is it about these attacks? You-you aren't acting like yourself." Throughout my entire life, Oliver has been a constant presence. Usually unwanted but constant nonetheless. If there is anything that I have learned about Rose's brother, *brothers,* it's that they never do anything without a reason.

He drives his hand into the roots of his curls. "I can't say much, but these aren't normal attacks. It doesn't make any sense. The village is far enough inland that no sirens should be anywhere near there," he says with unusual candor. His jaw ticks as a mask of irritation slips over him.

"Then why are you so sure it was the sirens who did it?" I ask, a small shred of hope that maybe my parents weren't lying builds inside me.

Oliver's face turns haunted. "The victims, something was wrong with them. They didn't look right. Whatever it was, I wouldn't wish it on my worst enemy."

A shiver passes over me. "I don't know what to say. I'm sorry."

Oliver nods and we start walking again until we reach the door to my studio. "I'll be leaving this evening to head back to Sena," he says almost out of nowhere. He turns to leave, walking back the way we came from.

I think about Terran's letter again and bite my lip. I'd thought about it all night and even this morning. Taking a deep breath I call out to him, "Oliver!"

He stops, turning to look at me in surprise.

"Do you- do you think you have room for one more in your travel party?" I ask nervously.

Oliver smirks, "That depends. Does this person happen to be a princess?"

I roll my eyes, "And what if she is?"

Oliver raises his brows, flashing me a smug grin. "Well then I might be able to make some room. Meet me in the tunnel at sundown."

I laugh. "Do I need to remind you that we don't really have sunrise or sunset down here?"

"Good point. I'll find you," he says before turning to leave.

I stand at the door to my studio with my heart pounding. For the first time in over a year I will be leaving the city. We'll have to travel through the docks of Atran to make it out of the kingdom. Anxiety churns deep in my stomach and I almost call out to him to say forget it but he has already disappeared. Taking a deep breath I enter the studio and push the large doors shut behind me.

A pair of small arms circle my waist, nearly giving me a heart attack. Looking down I spot my little brother giving me a devilish grin.

"Finn, you scared me," I chide.

His boyish laugh echoes off the large room and back to me, making me smile.

"What are you doing in here?" I ask, reaching down to pull him off.

He releases my legs and wraps his arms around my neck instead, trying to get me into a choke hold.

"I snuck away from my guards and hid in here, waiting for the perfect moment to attack," he grunts, yanking me this way and that.

I reach back to pinch his side.

He yelps and releases me, stepping back and rubbing at his hip.

"And why were you waiting to attack me?" I ask with a sigh.

Finn just turned ten but sometimes he still acts far younger. Recently, he has taken to running off and scaring anyone who wanders into his path. It is quite annoying.

"Easy. Because I can," he says confidently.

I scoff. "Yeah, well be careful. Next time I might attack you back."

He laughs, "I can take you."

I turn to him with my eyebrows raised. Summoning water magic I send a stream shooting at him, knocking him off his feet. "Keep telling yourself that, little brother."

Finn climbs to his feet and looks down at himself. His clothes are soaked and his dark waves are stuck to his forehead, dripping water down his face. He gives me his angry face and stomps past me and out the door. He tries to send a blast of water back towards me but I deflect it easily.

I learned to stop babying him. He gets it enough from our parents and the court, he doesn't need it from me.

Finn was born too soon, his small body delicate and weak. He was sick a lot when he was younger and has only really grown into himself over the last couple years. He used to be sweet and loving. Now, he is more like a little terror. I love my brother but sometimes I wish I could grab him by the shoulders and tell him to grow up.

I walk over to the painting that's supposed to be for Rose and stare at it again. If I want to finish it in time I better get to work. Setting out paints and brushes I look at the canvas with newfound purpose. Oliver may have been right, something *has* gotten into me. I just hope it's something good.

Chapter 10

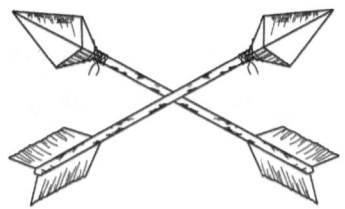

Oak

Crouching low to the ground, I move through the shadows, using my earth magic to soften the ground making my already light footsteps silent. My fae eyes cut through the darkness to follow the figures I have been stalking for the last two days.

Both males are gargoyles as I expected, though I was still in a bit of awe at the first time they shifted. They're huge, standing well over seven feet tall and made entirely of stone. Large wings protrude from between their shoulders and despite the solidness of the stone I know they're agile, strong yet swift. Gargoyles are reclusive in nature, rarely leaving their nests high in the trees and always living near the northern mountain, right on the border to Eteri. Which begs the question why they are walking through the forest more than 30 miles from the mountain's edge.

I hadn't expected to find them so soon but when I did, I didn't hesitate to follow. This mission is one I can't afford to fail. The fact that the high lady trusted me with a task so important only proves how much she has grown to trust and rely on me. Finally cementing my place in her court, in this *family*. I wish I could tell my cousin of all the things her mother keeps from her. How there are more and more villagers going missing. How new attacks are coming from both the north and the south. Even just to tell her to be careful.

But I can't, it's not my place. As her mother so often reminds me.

The gargoyles use their wings to shoot up into the tree where they have made a temporary nest. Groaning internally, I pull on the earth to create a ladder of vines that will bring me to my own makeshift home. The first time they shot into the trees I had remained on the ground not too far away, watching from a distance. I tried to use my fae hearing to listen to what they were saying, but the distance from the ground was too far. So up the tree I went.

I curl into the notch in the tree where I have been perched the last few days, watching and listening for anything odd or interesting. Not that there has been much to hear, they're practically silent all the time. I have only heard them speak a handful of times and never anything worthy of note. At first I welcomed the silence, a momentary reprieve from the chaos back at the castle, yet as the days continue to pass by I can't help but long for some sort of interaction.

I relax back against the tree, letting my mind wander a little. Rose's birthday is only a few days away now and if I want to make it there in time I'll have to leave before first light. I'll be returning empty handed, which is something I hate, but I swore to my cousin that I would be there for her. Even if that means shirking my duty. It's a choice that ends with me losing either way, even if it's not much of a choice at all. Not when I am unwilling to lose Rose.

She is one of the only people who seems to care that I even exist.

I'm only two years older than her but with how naive she can be you would think it was a much larger gap. Not that I can really blame *her*. Not when the high lady shields her from the real world.

Her mother keeps so many secrets, it would never be fair to expect Rose to know anything of real importance. I wish I could understand why it was necessary. The one time I asked, the high lady just smiled and told me that *some things are better kept a secret.*

I hate secrets.

My mother and father died for a secret that I will never know. I had hoped that by becoming my aunt's spy she might tell me the truth but that turned out to be a hopeless dream. Still, eventually someone will know something, someone will have answers. My brother and I *deserve* answers.

Rustling leaves in the gargoyles' tree gets my attention and I'm surprised to find that they have shed their stone form for once.

"We can't wait much longer. Eventually a decision must be made," says one of the gargoyles with a bite of annoyance.

"We don't move until he says so. There are laws that must be followed, Aldric," says the other with a hiss.

"I know the laws. I was there when they were written," Aldric retorts.

My eyebrows crease in confusion. This conversation just came out of nowhere. They have been sitting there in silence this whole time and then boom, straight into this tense discussion? I strain my ears to listen closer for any information on who 'he' might be.

"That may be true but the young king was not. You'd do well to remember his temper," says the second one. Aldric never responds and after a few minutes I hear soft snores coming from their direction.

So, whoever 'he' is, is a king.

An interesting thought really given the fact that there are only two kings in all of Estarynn.

All of the land in Estarynn is split between the mortal lands and the four ruling families, although there was technically once a fifth ruling family who have been gone for a millenia now. The Earth Realm, Sena, is ruled by the high lord and lady. Otherwise known as my aunt and late uncle. The Air Realm, Eteri, is ruled by the chief and chieftess. The two kingdoms, Water and Fire, are ruled by their respective kings and queens. Rayan is overseen by King Callan and Queen Mira, while Vulca is under the rule of King Basc and Queen Elani.

Searching through my memory of past interactions with the kings, nothing stands out as suspicious, not that I really was paying much attention at the time. King Callan, Cay's father, has never been one for ambition. King Basc on the other hand has raised two wild daughters; it might not be entirely too much of a stretch to imagine he would get himself involved in something less than favorable. Still, the most likely explanation is that whoever the gargoyles think their 'king' is, he is nothing more than a fraud. The question of their loyalty is one my aunt is sure to be interested in.

Looking through the branches and towards the ground at least 30 feet below me, my stomach flips and bile burns the back of my throat. I absolutely hate heights. Fae weren't meant to be in high places; the ground, the *earth*, is our friend. The fact that gargoyles are so comfortable in the air and soaring through the clouds is a mystery to me. Perhaps they were better suited for another realm, like Eteri, where they could soar above the treetops till their heart's content.

I could sleep for a few hours but with the daylight approaching quickly it won't really be worth it. Making my way back down my vine ladder I don't take a deep breath until my feet are back firmly touching the ground. Looking up towards the treetops I suppress a shudder. I could find somewhere else to rest but something is nagging at me that I should just leave now, get an early start back towards the castle. I dismantle the magic forming the ladder and let it collapse into just another pile of leaves as I accept that I will be returning home empty handed.

Somehow, even after living there for so long, I'm still not used to calling it my home. When my parents were alive we lived in the south, in a small village along the Rayan border. I loved it there. We weren't quite close enough to see the water but it was only a few hours away on horseback. My father was a royal guard and spent most of his days patrolling the border and ensuring that nothing was out of the ordinary. My mother owned a small store out of our home where she would help bind books and teach the little ones how to read.

Everything about our village was peaceful, calm. Nothing ever really happened there which is why I loved it so much. I didn't have any fancy parties to go to or foreign dignitaries to entertain. No, those times were reserved for when we visited my mother's sister.

My aunt and mother loved each other dearly but they had very different visions of the ideal life. While my mother was content to live in our home with my father, brother, and I, my aunt always seemed to want more. My mother liked to say she was just driven with ambition. Which worked out in her favor in the end. She is high lady after all.

Making my way through the woods in near pitch black is fairly easy with my eyesight. I can see every overturned log and hole in the ground with ease. Not to mention my magic allows me to sense even the smallest vibration of movement around me. I was never that good at magic until I moved to the castle. At home, my mother and father were my only teachers. In the castle, I had a private tutor for twenty different kinds of magic from healing to enchantments. Even for some of my *rarer* gifts. Now, I can command the element with ease.

Making my way through the woods silently, my mind wanders back to Rose. No matter how hard I try, I can't wrap my brain around the point of keeping so many secrets from her. Rose is no child, she will be 23 in a matter of days and soon enough she will fully settle into her immortality, or as close as we get to it. The worst of it all is that Rose *truly* believes that she knows everything. Her mother tells her just enough to stave off her questions and sate her curiosity.

A rush of static runs through my body as my magic alerts me to movement on my right. I stop dead in my tracks and press close against the nearest tree. In the distance I can see the faint glow of a fire and hear the rumbling of voices. It's not often that travelers stray so far from the main roads and designated paths. I silently make my way closer to the group.

There are horses tied off to the side along with a small group of tents lined up around the fire at what appears to be the center of their camp. I'm still far enough away that I can't see the people clearly but it looks like there are at least three or four of them. Creeping closer I note that two men are stationed outside of one of the tents, swords strapped to their belt and ready to be drawn at a moment's notice.

A female tends to the fire, stoking it with a stick and occasionally blowing on the fading embers. Voices are coming from inside the tent, confirming my suspicions. I look for any identifying features but neither of the men nor the woman gives anything away. The curtain to the entrance to the tent is suddenly pushed open and a tall man walks out, followed by a woman with long blonde hair.

"This is exactly why I am in charge, if you had just listened to me this would have never happened. The last thing we need is yet another delay caused by your sister's idiocy," says the man harshly.

The woman plants her hands on her hips, "Call my sister an idiot one more time and let's see what happens, shall we?"

My body freezes. I know that voice.

"Don't move and we won't have any problems," says a feminine voice from behind me. I try to look back but find the sharp point of a dagger pressing into the column of my throat. Glancing back towards the fire I find that sure enough, the female is missing.

Sighing, I raise my hands up in the air. "I mean you and your group no ill will."

The female laughs. "Forgive me if I don't take your word for it. Move," she says, giving me a gentle shove forward.

I walk into the clearing and the light of the fire. The angry man quickly turns to look at us, his gaze finding the female with her blade aimed at my jugular.

"Well, looks like someone has been taking their job seriously," the man says with a harsh smile.

The blonde steps around the man and meets my gaze.

"Oak? What are you doing out here?" asks Mar in confusion.

Shit.

Chapter 11

Mar

Oak, Rose's cousin, stands in the center of our small camp with a dagger pressed to her neck, which she seems totally unbothered by. Her hair is shorter than I remember, the ends are a vibrant shade of green. Her petite frame is swamped by an oversized tunic that hangs past her knees, the woven fabric thick, meant for riding long distances.

"Nat, you can remove the dagger. That's a member of the Sena royal family you've got beneath your blade," I say to Nat with a raise of my brows.

"Apologies, I didn't know," Nat says with a small dip of her head, sheathing her blade and leaving us to go back to tending to the fire. It's not cold enough yet to need the fire for warmth but the light is welcome in these dense woods. The wind carries through the leaves whispering in the darkness and sending chills skating over the back of my neck.

"Why doesn't she just use magic?" Oak asks suddenly. Her gaze locked on Nat as she bends over the fire and pokes it with a large branch to shift the wood.

Oak always did prefer to be more straightforward, never beating around the bush. The first time we met I thought she was just rude but in the years of knowing Oak I have come to appreciate that about her. Too many people waste time hiding how they truly feel when it would just be easier for everyone to get it out and deal with it.

"We're trying not to draw too much attention," I answer with a shrug.

Oak nods, her gaze roaming across the small makeshift camp. "Where's Eve?" she asks, somewhat hesitantly. Her body is tense as she continues to shift from one foot to the other, her hand running through her hair repeatedly.

I can't help but wonder what exactly Oak is doing so far away from the castle.

"Did I hear my name?" asks Eve, stepping out of the tent behind me.

Rian groans, rolling his eyes and joining Nat by the fire. Oak tracks the movement but doesn't say anything.

Eve peers around me, locking eyes with Oak. Both of them stare at each other for a long moment before Eve breaks the silence. "Oak. What are you doing here? I'm so confused. How did you find us?" she says breathily.

I look between the two of them, studying their faces. Oak and Eve have always had an interesting relationship. Rose told me the first time they met it was like they had known each other their entire lives. It kind of freaked her out. Oak is reserved, guarded even before her parents died. But with Eve it was like there were no walls, they just recognized each other inherently. They call to a part of one another than no one else does.

The silence is drawn out between them uncomfortably, I clear my throat, prompting Oak to acknowledge that Eve spoke in the first place. "Isn't it obvious? I'm here to escort you to the palace," Oak says with a tight smile.

Using my enhanced hearing, I listen out for the hint of a lie that can be heard in her voice and find her heart rate speeding up ever so slightly. I know she's lying, it's written all over her face, not that anyone else would notice. Her posture is tense, her heart racing, and her voice is pitched higher than usual. I glance at my sister out of the corner of my eye, waiting to see if she notices it herself.

Eve's face is still set in a mask of disbelief, her gray eyes wide and mouth hanging just slightly open. Between the look on her face and the fact that she hasn't even moved since she saw Oak, I know that my sister is deep inside her own mind right now.

"Oh? How did you find us? We're well off the designated road," I ask in return. Let's see if she lies again.

Oak shifts on her feet, "I used my magic. When I didn't sense anything on the main road I followed the vibrations into the woods."

"Seriously? That's so cool," Eve says in awe. She takes a step towards Oak but winces.

I reach my arm out and grab her shoulder. "You should be resting," I scold.

She tries to smile but it's more of a grimace.

"What happened? Are you hurt?" Oak says, scanning my sister from head to toe. Her hands reach out instinctively.

Rian forces a laugh from beside the fire, "What happened is that the princess can't follow basic directions and has almost gotten us all killed *twice* now."

Eve turns to him stiffly, "Are you really still mad about the griffin? That wasn't even really my fault. Besides, we're all alive." Eve throws her arms out, turning in a small circle and smirking at the guard.

Rian gives Eve a stare that would seriously concern me if she weren't the heir to the throne. A storm is brewing in his icy eyes, I can't help but get lost in the depths of blue that is so familiar and strange at the same time.

"For now. But who knows, maybe the third time really is the charm. Shall we take bets?" he says, locking eyes with each of us.

Oak flinches a bit when his gaze locks with her own, making his eyes narrow in suspicion.

Hm. Maybe I'm not the only one who can tell Oak is lying like her life depends on it.

"Ignore him," I say to Oak, waiting to see how she responds.

Rian gives me a look of mock betrayal and turns away to talk to Nat. The two guards start up an easy conversation and soon enough the others join in, gathering around the flame and passing around a small pouch of water.

"What's his problem? Isn't he a royal guard? He shouldn't talk to either of you that way," Oak says, nodding to Rian. Her dark green eyes are shooting daggers at the back of Rian's head and I swear his shoulders tense like he can feel her stare.

Eve snorts, "You would think so right? Rian has been a guard for a pretty long time now and he usually works directly with our father. He would never disrespect him, but us? That's another story. He's kind of a dick but don't hold it against him." My sister winks at Oak and casts a scathing look at Rian at the same time Nat turns to look our way.

The two lock eyes briefly before both turning away with a flush. Nat's one of embarrassment, meanwhile Eve looks closer to rage.

I let my eyes roam to Rian again, my mind drifting back to the morning in the training room. That version of Rian and this version feel very different. One playful and one stern. I just wish I knew what changed.

"I wouldn't put it past our father to put him up to it," Eve says with a shrug.

I turn back to the conversation, considering Eve's words. She's not wrong, there is a strong likelihood that our father gave some sort of order to keep us in line. Pointless as it might be.

"Put him up to what?" asks Oak, her shoulders stiffening.

"Well the way I look at it, our father knows us and how we can be sometimes. He would suspect that we, or I guess at least *I*, wouldn't make this journey easy on anyone. You see, I'm not exactly the best at long road trips," Eve says with a dramatic sigh, making me snort. She glares at me but continues, "Anyways, if I had to guess he probably told Rian to give it all right back to us. Call us out, yell at us, whatever it took to make sure that we behaved and didn't get anyone killed." She flashes a devilish smile.

It's not the worst theory I have heard and certainly isn't that far off from my own. Rian does seem like the traditional kind of guard, one who would be respectful and professional even when my sister does her very best to push his every button. I had been wondering what his sudden change of attitude was about. If our father gave him some sort of ultimatum that could potentially explain it.

"It's highly likely," I agree, "Don't get me wrong, it's certainly overkill but so far effective. Someone has to keep the *wild sisters* in check."

Eve laughs at the use of the nickname we have somehow earned here in Sena.

Oak rolls her eyes even as I spot a slight flush coming over her olive skin.

Setting aside my suspicions I nod to the tent behind us, "Come on, let's talk in private for a bit."

Eve practically hobbles back inside the tent as Oak follows us inside. It's a tight fit, cramped even with only two people but Oak is so small that it's not unbearable.

Once situated, Oak turns to Eve, "You never gave me a real answer. What happened?"

Eve groans as I laugh to myself. "Okay, so Rian wasn't completely off. I did sort of almost get us killed. We were riding along the main path but it was so dark, practically pitch black out there, and I could barely see anything so I sent just a small ball of fire out in front of me to light the way. Call it a tiny fireball. Well apparently the horses didn't appreciate the light and before I knew it they were all going wild trying to buck us off."

Oak laughs deeply, "I'm sorry what? That is so stupid. Besides, I thought people from Vulca had crazy good night vision or something like that."

"We do. All of us were doing just fine until Eve decided to go around throwing fireballs for no reason."

Eve gives me a bland look, "Listen, I didn't know that they would go crazy over a tiny bit of fire and I still don't believe you could see anything out there."

Oak waves a hand in front of her face, "It wasn't the fire they were upset about. It's all the creatures that your little light show must have woken up. It's no wonder they were trying to toss you off. I would too."

"Oh they didn't just try. The rest of us got the horses under control pretty easily but Eve over here only seemed to aggravate the poor thing further and it took off into the woods. We had to chase them down and by the time we had found her she was laying on top of a pile of leaves on the forest ground," I explain with a broad smile.

Oak breaks out into a fit of laughter, the noise filling up the small tent while Eve rubs at her ass. She healed the damn thing immediately but insists that the pain has *lingered*.

"Oh sure, go ahead, laugh. It was terrifying! I thought a tree branch was going to decapitate me and then next thing I knew I'm staring up into a dark abyss," Eve whines, shivering.

Oak narrows her eyes, still trying to get her laughter under control. "But I still don't get why you couldn't see in the dark?"

Eve rolls her eyes, "I would have if I could but for some reason lately I can't seem to get my damn eyes to work right. Any time I shift them I just end up seeing complete darkness."

"What?" I ask in alarm, "You never told me that."

She sighs deeply, "I didn't need to, it's really not that big of a deal."

"Of course it's a big deal, Eve. What if something is seriously wrong with you? Your mom is already-" I stop myself before saying too much while Oak pretends not to notice. I'm not sure who truly knows what is going on with the Queen but it's probably not the wisest decision to shout about it on foreign soil.

Eve's hand lands on my shoulder. "I get why you're concerned. But I promise, I'm okay. I probably just need to feed or something."

A smirk spreads across my face slowly, "Oh really? You didn't get enough the other night with Nat?" I ask, shimmying my chest at her suggestively.

Oak gasps loudly. "Hold on. What is she talking about? Eve, are you screwing one of your guards," Oak demands, sounding scandalized.

"Shhh! She could hear you!" Eve whisper shouts.

We both wait expectantly while Eve pokes her head outside the tent looking around. She settles back in with a sigh.

"Fine, I'll tell you everything but first you have to swear you won't laugh."

"Oh now this is going to be interesting," I say, giving Oak a broad smile.

She just shakes her head.

Chapter 12

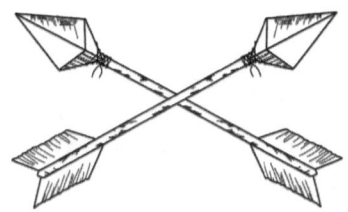

Oak

"This is why I shouldn't tell you anything. You swore that you wouldn't laugh," Eve grumbles.

"Okay, okay, we'll stop. I'm sorry." Mar continues to laugh.

We lock eyes from across the small tent, I try to swallow down the chuckle that is bubbling up in my throat but a small laugh escapes through my lips and we are both thrown into another fit of giggles. I clutch my stomach as Mar wipes at her eyes where tears are beginning to pool.

Eve starts smacking our shoulders, shouting at us, but after another shared look she is laughing along with us. Eventually our laughter dies off and we all share a knowing smile.

My stomach cramps from the laughter, a comfortable kind of pain that leaves my head feeling light and a buzz of happiness skating across my skin. It has never been easy for me to connect with other people. For so long I would separate myself from them, never letting myself really be a part of the conversation. Watching, observing, being a bystander in my own life. Yet somehow it has never been that way with Eve.

From the first time we met she forced me out of the safety of my comfort zone and thrust me into her own wild life, and in turn the life of her sister. Our first meeting is something I will never forget, I was maybe eight years old at the time. My mother had sent me to the castle to spend time with Rose over the summer. Rose had begged me to play some kind of game where she would count and I would hide. The only problem was Rose was barely six and lost interest in the game quickly. Running off to find some other game to play.

That's when Eve found me. I was sitting on the ground, knees curled to my chest, in a small alcove in a castle hallway. I looked up expecting to find Rose, but there was Eve, big gray eyes staring down at me. I didn't even know her and Mar were in the castle. I can still remember the way I anxiously asked where Rose was and the look of disgust on Eve's face as she told me Rose and Mar were playing in the library. A bitter taste was left on my mouth as I moved to get up but instead, Eve sat down beside me and started to huff about being left out.

She pulled a book out that was hidden behind her back and asked me to read it to her. I was so taken aback that I barely noticed it was my favorite story. We sat in that alcove talking for hours before Mar finally found us. Grumbling something about Eve running off, which of course she denies to this day. Ever since then, Eve has been my safe space. When she got hurt or upset I would be there to comfort her but more often than not it was her who found me, alone or crying somewhere no one would bother looking. Like our souls called out to one another at the smallest hint of trouble.

Now, looking at Eve's wide smile and bright eyes, I could hear that call loud and clear.

"I'm going to ask Rian how long we have before we need to leave," Mar says, sharing another knowing look with me. She spares a final glance at her sister before slipping out of the tent, pulling the opening shut behind her to give us some privacy.

Mar and I share a different connection. One that was forged in time spent together, running through the halls of the castle and chasing after her sister. Our souls might not call to each other as they do to Eve, yet the love I have for her is in no way less. Just different.

Turning to face Eve, I find her eyes distant, lost in some deep thought. Her gray eyes flick to mine as I lay down on my side. She mirrors me, watching each other in silence and letting the words go unspoken. After a few moments Eve rolls onto her back and closes her eyes.

Her pale skin is flushed pink, her thick eyelashes fanning her cheeks. She looks younger than usual, far too young to carry the worry that is evident from the tension in her body. I reach my hand out and take her own, threading our fingers together. Her body seems to relax a bit, a sigh leaking from her parted lips. I close my own eyes and let myself ease into the comfort of her presence.

We lay like this for a while, silent and just letting ourselves relax fully for once. No one else understands how our connection- just being in each other's presence- can heal our souls. It isn't about romance or sex, it isn't even really about love. It's knowing that this person understands you on the deepest level, that they would never judge you even when you judge yourself, and that no matter what, at the end… they are your person.

Rose asked me to explain it once before but I could barely put it to words. To anyone else, Eve and I were like opposites. Her, wild and constantly at the center of the party. Me, off in the shadows and on my own. Eve liked to be loud and to have attention on her, good or bad. I preferred to stay out of the spotlight, invisible and at peace. Eve called to others without even meaning to yet I pushed them away, letting myself remain alone. She is the only person who has ever really succeeded at getting me out of my shell. A fact that hurts people, people like Rose, and my brother.

Our friendship is something that I know makes them upset. Call it anger, jealousy, or maybe even just confusion. Either way, I've always noticed how other people look when Eve and I are in a room together. I see the way the high lady watches us, how she likes to ask questions that I'm not quite prepared to answer. So I pulled back. I stopped responding to Eve's letters entirely. I tried to create distance between us so that everyone would be happy and no one would get hurt. Better to be alone than to watch someone I love suffer because of me. Yet from the moment I stepped into this camp, I felt drawn to Eve's side, needing exactly what we are doing now, just *being* there for each other.

Eve doesn't question me. Doesn't demand answers for why I suddenly *disappeared* from her life. She doesn't need to ask, she just knows. From the beginning Eve has understood that at times I needed to just be with myself and my own mind. She's never pushed for an explanation. Even when my parents died and I ignored everyone. Eve was there, giving me comfort in her presence without demanding anything of me. No questions of 'how are you doing', 'do you need anything', just the comfort of someone sitting in a silent room with me while a million thoughts were running through my mind. Feeling my pain as if it were her own.

A ruffling of the tent flaps draws my attention. Sitting up I watch as Mar pokes her head in her eyes locked on her sister, concern written plainly across her face.

Eve must feel her gaze because she sits up quickly. Sparing me a glance before addressing her sister. "What's wrong?" she asks.

Mar shakes her head, "Nothing. But Rian said if we want to make it to the castle on time we need to get moving. We're still too far away to stay put for too long."

I nod, "She's right. It's not too much farther but it's far enough that we won't have time to stop again and traveling in the dark isn't a smart decision."

Eve sighs as she jumps to her feet, stretching out her muscles and twisting at the waist, filling the tent with the rapid *pop pop pop* of her back cracking.

Mar grimaces, "I wish you wouldn't do that while I was around. It's disgusting."

"What? This?" Eve says as she begins to crack every bit of her body, even her toes.

Mar practically runs from the tent, not even bothering to give us a second warning.

I stand beside Eve, looking up into her gentle face. Her bluish black hair is free, falling in gentle waves just past her breasts. Her gray eyes and dark hair are so at odds with her sister's bright appearance, if you didn't know they were sisters you wouldn't be able to tell just from looking at them. Mar takes after their father, all except his red hair. I wonder if the king was sad that neither of his children took his fiery locks.

I spare Eve another glance before following after Mar.

The guards are already packing up the few things they had set up and as soon as Eve follows me out they start on the tent. Looking around I see that they have plenty of horses but no carriage.

"By the way, why were you riding a horse and not inside a carriage like usual?" I ask Eve.

She groans, "It's a long story really. Nothing interesting I swear." The light dancing in her eyes promises that that is an absolute lie.

I look around to where Rian is watching us with distaste in his expression. I meet his stare with one of my own and watch as his lips curl back in a sneer, flashing one of his fangs. "It wouldn't have anything to do with the griffin you mentioned earlier, would it?" I ask with a smirk.

Rian's eyes narrow at me but he continues to adjust the horse's saddle.

"Do me a favor Oak and forget you ever heard about the griffin, actually just forget everything you heard tonight. Yeah, that would be perfect," Eve says with a self-satisfied smile plastered across her face.

I laugh. "Yeah, not going to happen. If I don't get it out of you before the end of this trip I'll just ask Mar and you know she'll tell me anyway."

Eve gasps, grabbing at her chest, "You wouldn't dare. My sister is loyal to me and would absolutely never betray me like that."

Raising my arm above me I call out, "Hey Mar, you up to tell me more about Eve and this griffin I keep hearing about?"

Mar looks at Eve's shocked expression and instantly catches on. "Of course Oak! Why don't you ride beside me and I'll tell you all about it."

~~~

It takes almost no time at all to get everything ready to go and then we are on our way. Rian begrudgingly gives me a horse to ride before mounting his own at the front of the group. I take my place beside Eve and Mar as we begin our journey. A few of the guards are on foot using their shifted forms to keep up with the group.

Mar tells me all about their encounter with a griffin, much to the horror of Eve, and we easily slide back into conversation. The pair tells me all about their most recent adventures, Mar talking about her brothers extensively. Envy builds in me as I think about my own relationship to my brother. I've allowed too much distance to grow between us since becoming my aunt's spy.

Our group moves in the darkness with ease and despite the presence I feel lurking close by, the journey passing quickly and without trouble, although every once in a while I catch Eve squinting towards the path in front of us. Luckily, daylight breaks through the dense woods and the terrain shifts as we get closer to the castle.

A few hours pass and the path opens up, the ground widening as it transitions into cobblestone and the castle comes into view. My back tenses at the realization that I will now have to explain how I ended up with Mar and Eve.

The high lady will likely have informed Terran of my whereabouts, but Rose, she'll have questions. I hate the idea of lying to her but for some reason her mother gave me direct instructions to never disclose my real work to my cousin. In the years of training and working for my aunt I've never found a reason why I should hide anything from Rose, yet I have. Countless times. All at the request of her own mother.

It never gets any easier to look her in the eye and make up elaborate stories and explanations. But this time is different. It's not just strangers or random citizens that could blow everything up in a moment's notice, these are our friends. Eve and Mar are practically family to Rose, inseparable since we've been children. The two of them rival my own bond with my cousin and if it came down to it I'm not sure that Eve would lie for me. Not to Rose.

As the castle walls get closer I know a decision must be made. I can't say anything too detailed or it will quickly unravel, simple half truths should work fine, they have to. If she asks how I found them I'll use the same lie I told Mar and Eve. The only difficult part will be how and why I left. It isn't exactly believable that I would leave the castle to meet up with the group without bringing a horse of my own. The castle is close enough to make out the carved details on the main door, intricate swirls and florals. The familiar crest of the royal family adorning the center, a large tree with wide branches and a myriad of flowers intermixed with the leaves.

"Are you okay?" Mar asks from beside me.

I take a deep breath before responding, "Of course. Why wouldn't I be?"

Mar slows her horse and I match her pace, watching as our group continues forward. Eve is practically at the front by now, eager to be done traveling. Though I notice her gaze occasionally drifting to a certain redheaded guard.

"Your heart is practically beating out of your chest Oak. You tell me," Mar says in a hushed, accusatory, tone.

I force a smile, "I'm just anxious for you all to be reunited. Rose has been so excited for your arrival and she will be so surprised when I deliver you to her."

Mar tilts her head, "Why would she be surprised? I thought you were sent to meet us."

I nod, "Yes, by the High Lady as a surprise for Rose. Call it a birthday gift."

Mar gives me a bland look. "Interesting." Mar instructs her horse to catch up to the rest of the group and I am left at the back, a distance away, as it should be.

Taking a deep breath I try to compose myself as our group approaches the main gates. Our arrival is announced throughout the castle as we all begin to dismount. I send a bit of earth magic to the high lady, informing her that I have also arrived. Only a handful of bags and supplies have been unloaded when Rose appears in the doorway.

"EVE! MAR!" she cries their names, gracefully running down the steps and sweeping the two girls into a tight embrace.

I watch from a distance. Their laughter and excited screams indiscernible. The guards hustle around me working with the palace staff to get things taken inside and to the proper rooms. Once that is sorted they are escorted to their own chambers, the horses taken to the stables. And then I am standing in the open, completely exposed.

Rose's gaze sweeps over me, she does a double take. "Oak? When did you get back?" she asks, confusion thick in her tone.

I clear my throat, "I just arrived. Surprise."

Rose looks to Mar who shrugs, Eve gives her one of her signature smiles.

"You arrived *with* them? How did you - I'm confused," she says, brows pinching together.

"Oak met us along the way, last night actually," says Eve.

My heartrate kicks up again, my pulse pounding in my throat. My gaze shifts to Mar and of course her gaze is firmly held on my neck. Her eyes move to my own and a sort of question lingers there.

I look back to Rose and smile. "After you and Terran told me they would be joining us I met with him and your mother to plan a surprise. I was going to meet their travel party and sneak the girls into the castle to surprise you but a few things happened and unfortunately I wasn't able to do it right. Sorry, Rose."

"What happened? Are you okay?" Rose asks, concerned.

Mar steps forward and stands beside me. She towers over me, my head barely reaching her shoulders. "Oak is fine, it's actually all Eve's fault. She decided to 'help' and you can imagine how that turned out," Mar says with a laugh.

Eve comes to her defense and launches into a full story about the horse and the fire. Rose laughs as she listens and is completely distracted. I move to sneak away but Mar grabs my arm.

"You're lying, and honestly I don't know or care why. But if you do anything to hurt my sister or anyone else I care about. I won't hesitate." Her voice is harsh but her eyes flash with the pain of her imagined betrayal.

I pull my arm free from her grip and stare up at her, "I don't know what you're talking about. I would never hurt Eve, and Rose is my cousin, my blood. Your empty threats mean nothing to me and beyond that, they're unnecessary." My blood heats as anger bubbles up inside me. I turn on my heel and stalk away but Mar follows me.

She grabs me by the shoulder, spinning me around. "Believe me when I say this, Oak, I never make empty threats. I don't care what your relationship is to them, or me. If you do anything to hurt them, physically or *emotionally*, I will make sure you receive the same treatment, only I won't be as kind." She raises her brows, waiting for me to challenge her further.

"Understood. Good thing you have nothing to worry about."

Mar turns and walks back to where Rose watches Eve perform some sort of elaborate reenactment, complete with fireballs for special effects.

Using this opportunity to slip away, I move through the corridors quickly until I am standing outside the high lady's private study. I knock on the door and it eases open. Poking my head inside I find that it is not the high lady sitting at her desk, it's Terran.

"Oh, hi," I say awkwardly, searching the room for any sign of his mother.

"Oak, welcome back. Please, come inside," he says with a smile. His chestnut curls have grown out a bit, falling into his face and giving him this boyish charm despite his advanced years.

I step into the room and pull the door shut behind me. He gestures to a small couch near the center of the room and I ease into it. He sits himself beside me and turns to face me.

"How was your trip?" he asks.

I look around the room before answering, "It was uneventful. Although I did learn a few things."

Teran's eyebrows raise, "Oh? What did you learn?"

I tell Terran about the gargoyles and what they said, his expression remaining at ease the entire time. His smile never falters. One of the reasons I admire my older cousin so much is his sheer capability to remain calm and collected. He never gets worked up, never stresses out. He is always the perfect picture of calm, cool, and collected. I wish I knew where he got it from. Perhaps his father.

Rose is easily offended, she takes things personally and will not hesitate to hold a grudge. Oliver is arrogant and sarcastic, he plays with people's emotions for fun and when he gets truly angry it's scary to watch. My younger brother, Reed, is a lot more like Terran. He is always relaxed, goes with the flow and never really asks questions. Admittedly he handled the move from the village to the castle with ease, unlike myself.

Terran claps a hand on my wrist, drawing my attention back to him. "Thank you for doing this. I know it must be difficult for you to lie to Rose. But this information is necessary, we need to know what is going on in our realm. I'll be sure to pass this along to my mother."

"What *is* going on in the realm?" I ask.

Terran sighs, "It is still unclear. We can only hope that Oliver comes back with more information, maybe even an answer to that very question."

Chapter 13

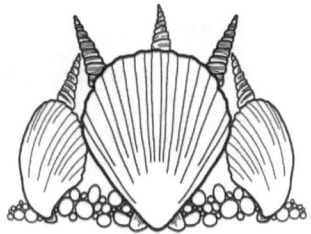

Cay

It takes me the better part of the afternoon to finish Rose's painting. Finally satisfied with the details, I set it to dry and clean up. Poking my head out the door, I spot one of the guards standing outside, keeping watch.

"Excuse me, can you please call ahead for assistance in packing? Have someone meet me in my rooms."

The guard gives me a quick bow and hurries off down the hall.

"Wait! On second thought," I call after him, "I'll take care of it myself." I have no idea how long I will actually be away since the decision to go has been so impulsive. I should take the time to choose things myself.

"Are you sure, princess? It's no trouble," he calls back, sounding unsure. His shoulders are still half turned in the direction he was headed, ready to move the moment I give the command.

I give him a broad smile, "Yes, I'll summon someone when I am ready. Thank you."

I start down the hall in the direction of my rooms, passing the guard with a smile. My knees crack with each step, my thighs rubbing together beneath my simple gown. I groan as I massage my aching shoulders, my body stiff between training and sitting on the floor all day to paint. The pathway splits and I pause for a moment. Rather than taking the one that leads back to my chambers, I turn to the left instead.

Walking through the halls I find myself in wonder at the beauty of my kingdom. The grand archways are lit by the soft glow of stained glass windows. Outside, the barrier pulses in a dome around us, my family's magic flowing through it like veins. I stop for a moment to marvel at the way the magic calls to me, like it recognizes the place in my soul where it lives and breathes. My eyes flutter shut for a moment as I revel in the feeling of being surrounded by magic. The water calling to me, an enchanted song that could rival any siren's.

Or mermaid's.

Letting out a soft sigh I enter the darkened hallway that leads to the chamber below the main castle. At the base of the winding stone staircase is a raging waterfall, one that will only allow a member of the royal family to pass. A spell to protect the sacred pools below. I step through, using my magic to part the water on either side of myself, emerging into an immense cavern. Small pools of water surround me on all sides as energy hums beneath my skin. I slip my shoes off before entering the chamber. Cool stone greets my feet and sends a chill through my body, goosebumps rising across the back of my neck.

Stepping up beside one of the pools, I dip a toe in. The warm liquid sends another burst of chills racing over my skin. I quickly strip off my dress, tossing it to the side and leaving myself bare as I sink into the water up to my hips and then shift. My thick thighs mold together becoming one, scales cover my skin in a mix of blues and greens. A large fin bursts from where my feet were and I sink into the water easily. My chest is bare from the waist up, my hair cascading down over my breasts and dipping into the water. Letting my body relax, I call on the healing magic in the water, small bubbles form around me and ease away my pain.

"Well, I'm not sure I've ever seen you look so relaxed," a deep voice calls from the entrance at my back.

I whip around, the bubbles fading and my chest completely exposed beneath my hair.

Oliver stands at the base of the stairs, his eyes heated, a smug smile plastered on his lips as his tongue sweeps across, wetting them.

"What are you doing here? This area is off limits for anyone outside the royal family. Leave," I shout, pointing up the stairs.

Oliver lifts his hands defensively, "Understood."

I wait for him to leave but instead he leans against the cavern wall, looking around and admiring the beautiful light radiating from the pools as the magic illuminates them from within.

"Hello? *Leave*. You can't be here, this is a *sacred* place," I admonish.

He cocks his head, letting his eyes roam over me from head to fin.

I wrap my arms around my waist and his brows crease before flicking back up to my eyes. A storm rages within me, threatening to burst free of my hands if he doesn't get out of here immediately.

"What's that look for?" he asks, brows raised. His eyes continue to roam over my shifted form slowly.

For a moment I consider shifting back but my clothes are too far and I would rather him *not* see my entire naked body. I move my arms to block his view a bit further. "What are you doing here, Oliver? It can't possibly be time to leave yet," I protest.

He leans back against the wall lazily, looking down at me through his familiar hazel eyes. Only it's not *his* eyes that are familiar.

An entirely new ache builds in my chest.

"I wanted to check on my favorite princess and make sure she wasn't having any second thoughts," he says with a shrug.

"First, I am not your favorite princess. Nor do I want to be. Second, of course I'm not having second thoughts. Why would you even suggest that?" I bite.

Oliver moves to step towards me but when my gaze turns deadly he chuckles and stays where he is. "Oh you see that's where you're wrong. You *are* my favorite, and admit it, that makes you a little bit excited," he says with a wink.

I have to fight back a gag as my stomach rolls, hot bile threatening to make an appearance. Oliver can be absolutely nauseating at times. His smugness is an artform that he perfected from an early age. Growing up he would tease all of us incessantly, especially me. Taking extra care to knock me down and hurt my feelings at every chance he got. Terran was the one who always came to my rescue.

When I don't respond he sighs and rolls his eyes. "Fine. I'll wait for you at the top. Make it quick."

Before I can respond, he is making his way back up the stairs and out of view. I contemplate ignoring him but don't trust that he won't come back down here to drag me out. I quickly shift back and step out of the pool, use my magic to dry off, and quickly pull my clothes back on before walking back up the stairs.

Oliver stands waiting at the top as he said he would, his arms crossed over his broad chest and eyes closed. I stare at him for a moment, taking in the strong line of his jaw, so like his brother.

His curls are a bit looser, and longer, but still the same chestnut brown as his siblings'. His ears have the familiar point to them marking him as fae. His dark bronze skin is dusted with freckles covering his cheeks and the bridge of his nose. His smile shifts, revealing a hint of a dimple in one cheek, though it's gone before I am ever sure it was really there.

"Stop staring," he says without opening his eyes.

I jump back a step as heat burns beneath my cheeks. Turning on my heels, I quickly make my way to my room, Oliver following close behind. I push open my door and he tries to follow me in but I spin, planting a hand in the center of his chest and blocking him from going any further. "Wait here," I growl.

His eyes widen at my tone and he gives me another teasing smile. One with no dimple.

I quickly race to the dressing room and stare at a closet full of clothes still with no idea what to pack. Frustrated, I throw myself down on my bed. What was the weather like right now? Here in the city the temperature stays around a crisp 40 degrees year round, which can make it difficult to keep track of the seasons if you aren't visiting land frequently.

Which I *clearly* have not.

I try to think back to Rose's past birthday events; it was always held indoors but she had mentioned in a letter that she hoped to enjoy the courtyard this year. I stare up at the ceiling and wonder if this was a mistake. I can only assume that Eve and Mar will also be in attendance which means I'll have to answer to them as well.

Oliver knocks on the doorframe, reminding me that he is still here.

I roll out of bed with a groan and walk over to him. "What now?"

He raises his brows at me, "Watch it. I'm here to help. If you let me in I can help you pick what to wear. I do have excellent taste." He runs a hand over his fitted tunic, his biceps flexing subtly.

A laugh tumbles from my lips. "Yeah, not going to happen. You stay right here. No further." Crossing my arms over my chest I stare up at him, wishing I was taller so I didn't have to crane my neck.

Oliver leans forward, invading my personal space and tucking a strand of damp hair behind my ear. "Is that so?"

I take a step back to gain some breathing room but he takes this as an invitation, pushing past me and ignoring my shouts of protest.

"So, this is the, what does your mother call you? Little minnow? This is the little minnow's bedroom," he says with a smirk.

Grinding my teeth I step in front of him, halting his advance. "I think that is far enough. There is no reason for you to be in here. You checked on me. I didn't change my mind. Now go, you can return when it is time to leave."

Oliver's gaze roams across every corner of my room and snags on my empty trunk. "You have no idea what to pack. You do realize we are leaving within the hour, right?" He easily maneuvers around me to stand at the entrance to my wardrobe.

"I was working on it. Besides, I could focus on packing if I didn't have to worry about *someone* barging into my chambers," I say, exasperated.

Oliver's hand snakes out, reaching into the closet and pulling out a silk nightgown that is practically sheer in some places. "And what do we have here? Princess Cay, I am shocked," he says mockingly. His eyes darken as they roam between the gown and my body, lingering on my chest before trailing further down. When his gaze reaches my thighs beneath my gown he seems to sigh to himself.

I snatch the grown out of his hands and throw it onto the bed. "Get out. Now."

Oliver laughs and moves to a chair in the corner of the room, making himself comfortable. "No thank you, I'm perfectly comfortable right where I am."

I fight the urge to grind my teeth again and decide if he insists on being here he might as well make himself useful. "Fine. If you're going to stay, you're going to help."

This peaks Oliver's curiosity although he doesn't say anything.

"What is the weather like in Sena right now?" I ask.

Oliver snorts, "Has it really been so long that you don't remember?" he asks.

"Are you going to answer the question or should I call for guards and have you removed from *my* bed chamber."

"The weather is changing already. Summer is fading and autumn has made its appearance. Warmth lingers in the days but in the evening the sun fades and a chill permeates the air," he says with a shrug of his shoulders.

Finally, something helpful. Nodding to him, I look through my closet and begin pulling out some dresses. Once I have a few picked out I move onto sleepwear. I pack a single pair of silk sleep shorts and an accompanying camisole. I throw in a few nightgowns and then sheepishly grab the one off the bed.

"Planning for a bit of nighttime fun are we, Cay? And who might that fun be with?" Oliver asks devilishly.

Blushing, I ignore him and continue packing.

Why was I packing that gown? I never wear it at home so why would I wear it anywhere else? Pushing the thought aside I continue packing. I search through my more formal gowns until I find one perfect for the ball. Finally I choose a few necklaces and jewels that I might wear to the party and move on, satisfied with my choices.

"You know, this is really quite boring. You could at least talk to me while you're at it," Oliver says, running a hand through his soft curls. How they never turn frizzy is beyond me. Knowing him he probably has a magical cream or spell cast so that they always look perfectly styled. It's utterly infuriating. Nothing ever bothers him, nothing can crack his cold exterior.

I ignore Oliver and move to another part of my closet where I keep my undergarments. I grab a few items and quickly move to shove them into the trunk but Oliver snatches a corset out of my hands.

He holds it out between us and inspects it with keen interest. "I've got to say, Cay. I'm a bit disappointed. Here I thought you were going to at least try a few things on for me."

I snatch the item back and shove the lot into the trunk, slamming it closed and doing the latch all while my cheeks burn a deep shade of red. "Are you done mocking me, Oliver? Because I have had quite enough."

Oliver licks his lip, eyes alight with mischief, "Oh, princess, I'm just getting started. Actually, you might want to be nice to me, seeing as we have at least a day's ride back to my home. Plenty of time for us to get to know each other better."

I blanch and he laughs. I smooth my hands down my sides and he tracks the movement with his eyes. Looking back to me his face is devoid of all emotion.

"Time to go," he says, turning and walking straight towards the door.

"Wait, we're leaving right now?" I ask, suddenly anxious.

"Yes. I'll send one of my men to fetch your trunk," he says looking over his shoulder, "You should get changed. As magnificent as that dress looks on you, it will be uncomfortable for traveling. Get moving."

My skin crawls and my stomach rolls again. I turn back to my closet and pull out my favorite travel set. A pair of linen pants and a pale pink tunic to go over it, I grab a matching coat that cinches at my waist and draws attention to my curves nicely. I change quickly and soon Oliver's men are knocking on the door to retrieve my things.

Anxiety bubbles up inside me as I watch them carry it out and follow them down the halls. I had barely had time to speak with my mother and inform her I would be leaving, now I am walking out the door. She was excited for me but also nervous. She insisted I take an entire entourage of guards but I managed to convince her to just bring two. After all, Oliver had his own royal guards with him and it wasn't like I was totally defenseless anymore.

Not that she knows that.

A thought shoots through my mind like lightning and I quickly break away from my escorts, shouting that I forgot something. I rush over to the training room and quickly grab my trident. I trigger the collapsible feature which shrinks the large weapon into a single tube the length of my forearm. I hook it to the belt of my coat and take off after the guards.

Oliver looks up as I approach, his eyes immediately going to my belt. "Took you long enough. What's that?" he says gesturing to the tube.

I smile innocently. "Just something a girl needs to survive. Nothing you would know anything about I'm sure."

He eyes me suspiciously but doesn't say anything else. Instead, he moves through our group, barking orders and telling them where to put everything. Once everything has been settled he instructs me to climb into the carriage. I sit down and begin to get comfortable when he follows in after me, sitting directly across the small space.

"What are you doing?" I ask, eyebrows raised.

He scoffs, "What does it look like I'm doing? This is going to be a long trip and I would prefer to ride comfortably."

"Why does that mean we must share a carriage? Certainly you are capable of riding on your own."

Oliver smirks and looks out the window as we begin to move, "Too late now. Besides, if I didn't know better I would think you didn't want to spend time with me."

I shift in my seat, trying to avoid looking out the window as we start moving through the tunnel towards the surface. "Well, for once you would actually be right." I begin to wring my hands together in my lap. As we make it closer to the surface I choose to stare at a spot beside Oliver's head, willing myself to block everything else out.

He turns to look at me and his expression shifts. Suddenly he leans across the cabin and pulls the shades down on the windows. Without saying anything he settles back in his seat. We sit in silence as we make our way through the tunnels. One of the guards tells us to prepare ourselves as we begin to shift from under the water to the land.

My hands are balled into fists, my sharp nails digging into the soft flesh and drawing blood. My heart is racing, the beat pounding hard enough that it might just burst through my chest. When the terror starts to overwhelm my senses I squeeze my eyes shut. Magic washes over us as we cross the final barrier and the full weight of everything settles on my chest. Something touches my hand and I flinch, my eyes shooting open.

Oliver's hand is placed gently over mine, his eyes locked on my face, expression unreadable. He pulls on my fingers until my fist relaxes. We both stare at my palms, covered in small crescent indents and dots of blood poking through the skin. I start to heal myself but before I can even pull on the hum of magic underneath my skin they have already vanished. Looking up, Oliver is back in his seat, staring out the window and ignoring me again.

He used his magic to heal my palms, again. My mind chooses to focus on that fact rather than the noises of the busy docks as we make our way through the village.

Why did he heal me? I was fully capable of healing myself. I stare at him as he continues to ignore me, fascinated by whatever we pass outside this carriage. My stomach churns at the idea of what he would say later. How he would hold it against me. He could tell Rose, tell Terran. Show them just how weak I really am. I take a few steadying breaths and try to calm my racing thoughts. There's nothing I can do about it now. What's done is done. Besides, it was just a few small marks.

A guard calls out to inform us that we have cleared the first village and my body relaxes. Tension eases from every muscle but a lingering ache remains. The farther away from the city the weaker my magic grows but it's always there, a hum beneath my skin, begging to be used.

I've barely been away from the city and I already feel the effects on my power, I can only imagine what it is like for Oliver. Or any of my friends for that matter. The city isn't like other realms or kingdoms. When you're under the sea you are basically entirely cut off from your magic. Unless you are a water elemental of course. The wards that protect the city make it difficult to call on earth or air, and nearly impossible for fire users. One of the reasons that Eve and Mar so rarely visited. Not that I blame them after what happened with Rose, even if they don't know that.

I settle back into the seat, opening the shade again and seeing land for the first time in over a year. The scenery has changed, colorful leaves show just how close to true autumn we really are. The coastal look of my kingdom begins to fade and is replaced with more trees and greenery the farther we ride. The piers of Atran become nothing but a speck in the distance. Then we cross the border into Sena and the dense forest surrounds us. The smell of wet moss and florals are thick in the air. Even inside the carriage it is palpable.

Looking across the carriage, Oliver's eyes are closed. His head leans against the window pane and his mouth is parted ever so slightly. Looking at him like this I begin to wonder if he is really as bad as he seems or if it is all just an act. The tension in his body has relaxed a bit and he almost looks peaceful, at ease. For once no smirk, just a soft smile as his chest rises and falls steadily.

<div align="center">~~~</div>

Oliver sleeps for all of two hours before waking up and demanding that I entertain him. At first it was almost reasonable. He asks me about my kingdom's stories, our great rulers, even how the magic that protects the city works. I answer his questions, sometimes in full and sometimes with half truths.

Even if he was Rose's brother, I need to be careful what I say to him.

After a while he gets bored of history and his questions change. I am forced to endure his disgusting questions about my *experience*, for too long before he decides to become a storyteller instead. He shares tales of his many exploits in the bedroom, much to my horror.

Finally my patience breaks and I call a guard. "If I have to spend one more minute listening to this obnoxious, smug, *crude*, excuse of a male, I am going to blast the smirk off his face myself." Thankfully whatever look was on my face was enough to convince the guard to take a break.

We stop in a clearing about halfway to our destination. I quickly disembark from the carriage and place myself far away from Oliver. He seems to get the hint and chooses to talk with the guards rather than follow me. I sneak off into a denser part of the woods and take the time to relieve myself. It is important that I stay hydrated while away from my home but that does mean some needs come more frequently than others.

As I'm walking back to the group I sense something off to the side. My magic hums in response and I follow it. I allow my magic to guide me further into the woods and to a small cave, the closer I get the more my magic hums. Just as I am about to take a step inside the cave, someone grabs me. I whirl around quickly, my arm forming a perfect left hook. Only the face that my hand is racing towards is Oliver's.

He catches my fist before it can make contact with his face. "What do you think you're doing?"

I look back over my shoulder at the cave, ignoring how his arm is wrapped around me. "There's something in that cave that my magic recognizes. It's going crazy trying to get me to go to it."

Turning back to Oliver I pull my arm free and wiggle out of his grip. With space between us I get a clear look at his face.

His arrogant smirk is back and his eyebrows are raised, "So, your magic started going haywire and you decide to just follow it? Into some random cave where anything could be inside?"

Rolling my eyes and pushing past him I start walking back towards the carriage. "Forget it, you wouldn't understand."

Oliver follows behind me, grabbing me by my arm again and pulling me to a stop. "Try me," he says in challenge. His eyes boring into mine with a seriousness I am unused to from him.

I try to pull my arm free but he just squeezes harder. "Release my arm. *Now*, Oliver."

His smirk deepens, "And what if I don't want to?"

Rage boils my blood and I am seconds away from finding out the answer to that question myself. "Release me, or I'll make you release me."

This seems to spark something inside Oliver because he pulls me closer, grabbing my other wrist and forcing me to look up at him. "I'd like to see you try."

My already thin patience snaps and I launch myself at him. We engage in a sort of fighting dance, me attacking, him evading. I throw punches and kicks and try to summon every bit of my miniscule training that I have. He dodges everything I have and never once tries to give it back to me, infuriating me even more. "Fight back!" I scream.

Oliver laughs, "Oh, princess, it wouldn't be much of a fight if I did. You forget, I've got years of training over you and I actually *use* mine. Unlike you. Remind me, what was it you did when you let my sister be attacked by *your* creatures? Oh wait, that's right, I remember. Nothing."

I freeze for a moment as what he says settles in my mind.

"That's right, Cay, I know what happened. In fact, I know a lot of things. Fuck, I even know what my savior older brother did afterwards."

The mention of Terran breaks whatever bit of restraint I had left in me and I take Oliver to the ground. I straddle him, throwing punches straight at his smug face but before I can land a hit he grabs my wrists and flips us so I am pinned beneath him. He gathers both my wrists into one hand, holding them above my head. He uses his legs to pin my own down and his body weight settles over me, leaving me completely immobilized beneath him."If my hands weren't trapped right now I would wrap them around your neck and squeeze until the light faded from your eyes," I say, voice dripping with venom.

"Hmm, interesting offer, princess. But if anything is going to be wrapped around my neck I would prefer it to be your magnificent thighs," he says with a smirk.

My entire body burns red with embarrassment and rage. A scream rips past my lips as I send a jet stream of water straight for his face, shooting him off of me. He lands ten feet away, drenched from head to toe. Scrambling to my feet, I walk back towards the carriage, not bothering to spare him another glance.

Chapter 14

Rose

Walking through the castle corridors I listen to Mar talk about her little brothers with my hand in hers, my other arm looped through Eve's. There is a sort of easiness to moments like these. Growing up in the castle I loved my home, but it always felt sort of empty. Of course there were hundreds of staff and people constantly visiting the palace, but no one ever really stuck around.

Even my brothers were never really around. Terran was, and still is, constantly off handling some political matters or tending to the lands. Oliver only ever seemed to want to tease me and beat me in games, and once he fully matured he stopped hanging around entirely. Running off chasing after Terran and trying to *prove* himself to our mother. Of what he was trying to prove I will never understand.

No, it was always the girls who made this place come alive. We would run through the halls wreaking havoc and terrorizing anyone who came into our path. Eve and Mar were around the most; they spent a large majority of their summers here. Cay was always difficult to meet up with because her parents kept her under close supervision. If we *were* able to spend time together, it was usually on their terms, and in their kingdom. Oak spent the majority of her childhood in the southern village with her parents. It wasn't until they passed that she spent any extended time here. Same with her brother, Reed.

As wrong as it sounds I was excited when Oak and Reed came to live with us. Reed was still so young, he didn't really understand why he lived in the castle now, just that he got to run around and play wherever he wanted. There are days where my heart aches for Oak, for how she used to be before she convinced herself that it was easier to shut people out. She denies it but I know that's what she does. She pushes everyone away and pretends that she is still here. It's more painful to have her just out of reach than actually gone.

There are moments when I think she is really here, when her snark will come back and her personality slips through the cracks. Only, it never sticks around for long. And then there are the secrets. She thinks I don't notice but I do. Whatever she was really doing out in those woods, it had nothing to do with Eve and Mar.

Eve has this sort of blissful smile on her face, a happiness that can't be shaken. I've laughed more since she arrived than I have in the past six months. Mar gives my hand a squeeze and I look into her eyes. She's the only one I don't have to *literally* look down at, our height evenly matched. She flashes me a cheeky smile and a wink, making me laugh. We walk like this for a while before Eve finally begs for food.

"Listen, nothing against the grand tour and all that but we've been here a million times and honestly all I can think about is the delicious sweets I know you have hidden in that kitchen of yours," she says, practically salivating. Her gray eyes are wide and bursting with an energy I only wish I could bottle.

Shaking my head I pull her after me to the kitchen. The large room is full of staff preparing for the party. Pastries are being baked, imported goods flown in, I even see a large carafe filled with a dark burgundy liquid. Mar's attention is captured by it and it takes no genius to guess what is in the glass.

"Come on, let's go into the dining hall and have someone bring out a whole platter of treats," I whisper to them both.

They share a grin and nod their heads, following after me. We enter the dining hall and find that it's not entirely empty. Terran is seated at the head of the table, a collection of books and a map laid out in front of him.

There is a deep crease between his brows as he flips through the pages of a thick tome, looking between it and the map. He's wearing an emerald tunic that stands out against his deep olive skin, his curls are kept short so that they don't fall into his face. He looks up at us as we enter and gives us a wide, toothy grin.

"Well, hello there, ladies. Pleasure seeing you all. Eve, Mar, you both look lovely as always," he says, standing and walking towards us.

Eve rushes forward and gives him a bear hug which he returns. Mar is next and this time he lifts her feet off the ground a little.

"I won't be able to do that for much longer I'm afraid. You're getting too tall," he says to Mar, bumping her hip with his own.

She laughs and steadies herself with his arm. "I've been the same height since I was 16 Ter. You're just in denial that you're getting old," Mar teases, jabbing a finger into his ribs.

Terran grabs at his heart and contorts his face in mock pain. "You wound my ego, Mar. I may be getting older but I'm not old yet."

Eve chuckles and claps him on the shoulder, "Keep telling yourself that, grandpa."

The four of us make our way over to the table and take our seats. Terran gestures to a server and he nods without even hearing the request.

This makes Eve's round eyes grow even bigger. "Wow, you didn't even say anything to them," she says in amazement.

"I didn't need to. I'm in the presence of two princesses and my darling little sister. What else could you three possibly want other than sugary sweets?" Terran asks with a smile. His hazel eyes flick to mine for a moment, his gaze brimming with love that my heart has so desperately been missing.

"Good point," says Mar, "but could they also bring me a glass of that O-positive I smelled earlier. It's been a while since I've fed and I wouldn't want to get all hangry when I've just arrived."

"Of course," Terran nods and another server quickly leaves the room.

We sit there talking and eating for hours before Terran excuses himself from the table. Eve is rubbing her stomach and staring up at the ceiling in a daze. Mar just shakes her head at her sister and gives me a look that promises fun; and maybe a bit of mischief.

I narrow my eyes at her and she raises her brows a few times. Oh I have been waiting too long for this. The two of us circle the table until we stand on either side of Eve. She doesn't even see it coming when we grab her by the arms, dragging her from her chair.

"Wait, no, not right now, please," Eve begs, "I've just eaten my weight in cake and I can't even think about walking let alone anything else."

Mar and I ignore Eve's pleas and pull her into the courtyard off the dining room. It's not as big as the one where the party will be held but it's still large enough to serve its purpose.

"Here are the rules, same as always. No hiding outside the castle grounds, no using magic to conceal yourself, and the first one found has to sneak into the library and steal one of the locked tomes from my father's private library," I say, dramatizing my voice. It's the same game we've played since we were children, the only difference being the difficulty in finding a hiding place the others won't already know. It may seem childish but it's moments like these that remind us not to take things too seriously, we have plenty of time for that later, much later.

Eve is practically bouncing on her feet, waiting for the game to begin despite her earlier protests. Mar looks half ready to make a run for it but her eyes tell me otherwise, the pupils blown and ready for a bit of a hunt. The competitive nature of all of us rising to the surface in an instant.

Eve moves to stand at the very center of the courtyard, turning so her back is facing Mar and I before calling out, "You have three minutes! One! Two!"

I don't wait to hear her count to three. I take off running, turning down a hallway as Mar zooms past me. "Hey! No fair, no vamp speed!" I call after her.

I race through the hallways until I find the small sitting room by the main entrance that is unoccupied. I walk over to one of the lounges and lay out comfortably.

Eve has never really been good at this game. Usually giving up after ten minutes or so after getting frustrated at never finding anyone. Still, it was fun enough and got the heart racing a bit. I look around the room, unsurprised to find it filled with bookcases and scrolls. A small pile of them sit on a desk by a large window. I cross the room and begin sorting through them.

Most are maps, old drawings of the entirety of Estarynn only very outdated. These maps show not only Eteri to the north, Rayan to the south, and Vulca to the east, it also shows a small patch of land beneath Vulca. Cansu. I sit at the desk and inspect the map closer. Cansu is a blip of a kingdom on the map, dwarfed by even the mortal lands.

Although, what is really odd are the mortal lands themselves. On current maps there were clear lines drawn along the edges of each realm and kingdom, leaving the mortal lands at the very center. However, on this map, their borders extend further into our lands and even into Vulca. I pull out other maps that are dated around the same time and they are all drawn the same. I flip over one of the largest books on the table and it includes a history of the mortal lands.

Nothing out of the ordinary. It explains the story of the Goddess Vana, how she gave life to all creatures and then left us to live in peace, protecting us all when we need protection. Closing the book with a sigh, I look out the window and am surprised to find an entire travel party making their way up the cobblestone path. The royal flag of Sena is proudly flown on top of the carriage which means one thing, Oliver is home.

Kicking back the chair I quickly leave the room and stalk down the pathway. He has some nerve ditching me like that; making me think I had won our race. Not to mention the fact that he was traveling so close to Cay and he didn't even bother to let me know. Oh no, he is going to have to answer this time.

I am fed up with everyone keeping secrets around here and refusing to tell me anything. I may not be a man but neither is my mother and she is the high lady. I have just as much right as either of my brothers to know what is going on around *our* kingdom. I won't be cut out of the conversation.

I stalk up to the carriage and wait for him to open the door. Only, when it opens, it's not Oliver I am staring at. No, instead of hazel eyes these are a beautiful seagreen. Where I expected chestnut curls, long dark waves frame a delicate face. Cay steps out of the carriage and stands in front of me, a hesitant smile on her face.

"Hi," she says, voice small and tentative.

I say nothing as I rush forward and envelop her in a fierce hug. It takes a moment but her arms sweep around me, squeezing me tightly. Hot tears threaten to spill down my cheeks but I hold them back. As much as I want to, I can't let them free. I can't let Cay see me cry, as it would only hurt her more.

Oliver steps out behind her and clears his throat. Untangling from our hug, Cay casts him a look filled with contempt. Turning my own gaze on my brother the sudden need to deliver a kick to his groin nearly takes over. Still, I fight the urge, focusing instead on his delivery of Cay. A million questions run through my mind but only one thing truly matters.

Turning, I ignore my brother entirely and focus on my friend. I say the one thing that I have wanted to say for the past year and a half. "I love you, I missed you, it wasn't your fault. I don't blame you," I say, my voice coming out shakier than I would have liked.

Cay gives a sharp inhale and then tears are flowing down her cheeks. I reach forward and wipe them away. She grabs my hand and squeezes it tightly. "I love you too. I missed you so much, I am *so sorry*."

I pull her back into a hug and we both begin to cry harder. Our bodies shaking with the force of our tears.

Chapter 15

Mar

Using my vamp speed I zip through the bustling halls, dodging staff as they move about preparing for the party. Once I am sure I am far enough away from my sister, I stop, looking around for a place to hide. My body is yanked into a room from behind, the door slamming shut in my face. I struggle against the arms locked around my waist. I move to throw my head back and start on a series of attacks but a voice whispers in my ear.

"If you hit me, I hit back," Rian's deep voice growls.

My body relaxes a fraction but I don't move. "If you'd let go of me I wouldn't need to hit you."

Rian releases me and I spin to face him. He's leaning against the wall casually, his expression unreadable. His eyes search my own, lingering for a moment before looking back towards the door. "I thought you were being chased," he says simply. His sinewy body is tense, his thick arms crossed over his broad chest.

I laugh. "I sort of was," I say, making his eyebrows raise. "We're playing a game, Eve is the one in charge of looking. Rose and I are trying to hide," I explain with a shrug.

Rian steps forward but I stand my ground. He continues his pursuit until we are practically standing chest to chest. He's a head taller than me so standing so close I have to look up at him. It pisses me off.

"Tell me more about this game of yours. Does it involve fighting?" he asks, staring deep into my eyes.

"Not necessarily. Whoever is the first to be found has to do something. Usually something that is likely to get them in quite a bit of trouble," I say staring back, refusing to break eye contact.

He tilts his head, curiosity lighting his pale blue eyes, "Oh? In trouble with who? Is this something I should be worried about?"

"Why would you need to be worried?" I ask with a raise of my brows.

He gives me a bored look, "I'm your head guard, it is my responsibility to protect you."

I allow my gaze to run over him quickly. He's wearing a simple tunic, dark burgundy with gold embellishments that mark him as a member of the royal guard. It's sleeveless, showing off his toned biceps. My gaze returns to his face and I find his eyes heated.

"It's not your job to protect me. You're only here because Eve is. She's the important one," I say with a smile.

He takes a step forward forcing me to move back or else our bodies will become flush with one another. He does it again and this time my back hits the wall behind me. He places his hands against the wall on either side of my head, effectively caging me in.

"Why would you think that?" he says, staring me down.

I tilt my head back to meet his gaze, "It's the truth. Eve is the heir. She's the one who should be protected. Not me."

Rian leans forward but I refuse to back up any further. "Is that what you believe? That you're not important?"

The sound of Eve's voice in the hallway outside the door echoes into the room. My eyes shoot towards the door. Rian's hand moves to my mouth, pressing firmly as his entire body pushes into mine, pinning me between him and the wall.

A gasp slips free as my eyes widen and I start to tell him off but he shushes me.

"Shh. Quiet, unless you want the precious heir to hear you," he says with a smirk.

I bite my bottom lip, holding back what I was going to say. Eve's voice is fading as she continues walking past the room. When I can't hear her anymore I pull his hand off of my mouth. "If you ever try that shit again you'll regret it," I say, my heart racing.

Rian moves so his forearm is pressed into the wall above me and he leans forward, right in my breathing space. His cedarwood scent invades my senses. "Is that a threat?"

My heart is racing, my entire body heated with rage and a bit of something else. His chest is pressed against mine, his leg pushed between my own, parting them. He is close enough that I can feel his hot breath on my cheek and practically taste the blood pumping in his veins. My mouth is poised perfectly over his neck, I lick my lips.

His eyes track the movement and his gaze darkens, "Whatever you're thinking about, little one, you better get that look off your face."

I stare up at him through my lashes and try to understand his expression. Part of him looks like he is in pain, the other part looks hungry. I tilt my head a little, exposing my neck to where his mouth hovers only mere inches away.

He closes his eyes and takes a deep breath in, pushing his hard chest into mine. He trails his nose up the column of my neck. I raise my hand and place it on his chest; to stop him or pull him closer I'm not sure. His eyes shoot open with the contact and his pupils are completely dilated. Rian stares down at me, very clearly fighting with his own self control.

I move my hand up his chest and a shiver rolls through him as I tangle my fingers in the hair at the nape of his neck. He tries to pull away, shifting slightly, and I feel something hard digging into my hip. My eyes widen in realization as I drag my hand down and let it stoke over the spot where his pulse is pounding, almost as erratic as my own.

"Don't," he says harshly. Adjusting his hips so that his hard length isn't pressed against me.

I continue tracing my finger up and down along his vein.

When I get to the sensitive spot beneath his ear he hisses out a breath. "I'm not joking, princess. Knock it off," he says, groaning. He grabs my arms tightly, pushing me back further into the wall.

Smiling at his reactions I lean forward and place my lips right above his neck. He moves so quickly, grabbing me by the shoulders and holding me arm's length away from him.

"Enough," he says sternly.

I smirk at him, "What? Not in the mood to play?"

He laughs huskily, "Not with you."

"I thought you liked playing with me. At least you seemed to in the training room that morning," I say trying to lean forward and close some of the distance he made between us.

Rian holds me back, pressing me firmly into the wall. "I'm not playing games, little one. I'm your guard, I am here to do one thing, my job."

I scoff. "What is it with you guards and your duty?" I say, thinking about Eve and Nat. Seriously this whole duty thing seems to be getting in the way of everyone's fun.

His face morphs to one of confusion, "What's that supposed to mean?"

I roll my eyes, "Nothing. Back to us."

Rian let's go, taking a few steps away from me. "Absolutely not. This conversation is over," he says. He drives a frustrated hand through his hair.

Pushing off the wall I get all up in his personal space, just like he did mine. "Actually, this conversation is just starting. So why don't you sit your ass down and we can talk for real." I trace my hands up his stomach, feeling the defined lines of his abs beneath the tunic.

He moves around me, effectively removing my hands, and starts towards the door.

I appear in front of him, blocking his path. "You don't get to just walk away whenever you don't feel like doing something." Irritation is beginning to cloud whatever pleasant feelings he was bringing up inside of me.

It only takes a moment but he moves me across the room and sits me in a chair. "I'm leaving. You stay," he demands, walking away.

"You don't get to tell me what to do. No one does," I say, following him.

He turns quickly, grabbing me by the chin and tilting my head. My pulse increases and my body ignites, fire racing beneath my skin. I try to focus on his words and not his actions but all I can see is his pulse, his blood, pounding in his neck and practically begging me to let it out.

His fingers squeeze against my jaw and my eyes find his. His stare promises something that I would very much like to find out, but instead of saying anything he releases me. He stands there, staring down at me, not touching me but not leaving either.

"I know you want this. I can read it all over your face. I can hear it in the way your heart is racing, same as mine. Why not just give in already and give us both what we want?" The words come out breathlessly. Magic swirls in the pit of my stomach, warm and intoxicating. It begs to be set free any time Rian is around, which makes me wonder, what is it about him?

Rian laughs, reaching out to grab my ponytail and giving it a slight tug. My body pulls taut at the action and I swallow my gasp. "You don't even know what you're asking, little one. So stop." His fangs peek out from between his parted lips.

Before I can respond he shoots out the door. Shit. I race after him but as soon as I leave the room Eve appears in front of me.

"HA!" she cries, "I finally found you!"

I look around trying to figure out which way he went but Eve snaps her fingers in front of my face.

"Um hello? Mar. Are you in there?" she asks, clearly annoyed.

I sigh, "Sorry, Eve. Just distracted."

Eve smiles, her eyes narrowing. "Would your distraction have anything to do with the highly attractive vampire guard I just saw running down the hall?"

I give her my best look of innocence, "I have no idea what you're talking about."

"Mhmm, and that's why your cheeks are flushed and your breath is coming out all wonky." She smacks her lips together, tapping a finger against her temple. "Oh, what's that I taste, lust?" she draws the word out, her pupils already expanding from the bit of magic she steals from me.

I cut my sister a look and give her a mock laugh.

"Hey, no judgment here. You know I wanted a taste of guard myself. No shame in admitting it," she says with a shrug.

I roll my eyes. "There's nothing going on. Let's just go find Rose and finish the stupid game."

Eve throws her hands up, "You two are the ones who dragged me, literally as I recall, into this game. If you didn't want to play we didn't have to." We start walking down the hallways side by side.

"I didn't mean it like that. I'm just- I don't even know, maybe I am hangry after all," I say with a sigh.

Eve gives me a smirk. "Oh I'm sure you're hungry. Just not for blood," she says, wiggling her brows at me.

I roll my eyes and walk with my sister through the grand halls. Sena is so different from Vulca. Besides the fact that it isn't inside a dormant volcano, there's this sort of formality that we never enforce back home. Each staff member we pass gives us a nod or a curtsy, some even a full bow. It's not that I particularly mind them doing it, it's just weird. We're treated more like *royalty* here than we are back home.

We continue through the halls in silence, walking the familiar paths that we have learned from years of summers spent visiting. We pass by the library and I spare a peek inside, wondering if Rose had chosen to hide here. When we don't find her we keep looking.

Eve gets bored of the silence and she starts talking about all the places she has already searched, trying to narrow down the potential hiding spots. "I've looked pretty much everywhere I could think. The only place left would be the main entrance I think."

I nod and follow her lead as we walk back towards the grand doors that we arrived through. Again, so at odds with our home back in Vulca. Our *palace* is one tall building that looks almost identical to the rest of the city. The only difference is the large banners that fly beneath each window and the guards that wait by the entrance in secret.

Personally I prefer the subtlety, not caring much for all the politics that comes with a palace like this. Still, the city Tepis in Rayan is far more formal than even Sena. I've never been invited to Eteri, few outsiders ever have, so I can't speak to their court. I like to imagine that their realm is one big cloud that everyone lives on, floating high above the mountains and looking down on all of us; much like their attitude suggests.

I always thought it would be cool to fly but I don't know about the whole being thousands of feet above the ground thing. Seems like a really easy way to go *splat*. I still have another two years before I settle into my immortality and I would really prefer to not die before then.

We turn down the hall that leads to the main entrance and notice a group of horses outside the window. Their handlers appear to be taking them to the stables.

"Hm, I wonder who is here," Eve says, pointing them out to me.

"No idea. Probably more party guests," I say with a shrug.

Chapter 16

Rose

There are things that people need in their life to survive. Food, water, shelter. But there are also things that people need for their soul. Feeling Cay's arms wrapped around me, squeezing me in a hug that was long overdue, I know that I need my friends. They are a part of me as much as my family, as much as the magic that courses through my veins.

I give Cay another squeeze and we release each other. My smile is so wide that my cheeks ache and I'm sure I look like a crazy person. Cay's face is red and blotchy from crying, her eyes swollen ever so slightly and her round nose is running. I laugh a little and she frowns.

"What? What is it?" she asks.

I shake my head, "Nothing. I'm just happy to see you."

"She's laughing because your face is all red and you have snot dripping from your nose," Oliver says from a few feet away.

Cay frantically wipes at her nose and casts healing magic on her face. Within a second she's glowing, her skin flawless and her eyes shining brightly like she just woke up from the best sleep.

I fix my obnoxious brother with a stare. "Was that really necessary?"

Oliver smirks, "Apparently so, seeing as you were content to lie to the poor girl. I mean truly, some friend you are. What if *someone* were to see?" He shares a knowing look with Cay that catches my attention.

Cay's face flushes but she says nothing. Part of me wonder's what he is talking about but given the fact that it's Oliver it can't be anything important.

I march up to my brother and stop directly in front of him. "If I find out you upset or hurt Cay in any way, you're going to regret it."

My brother raises his brows and nods towards Cay, "She's the one who attacked me. I didn't do anything to the little princess other than give her a free ride and protection."

I turn to Cay, mouth agape and eyebrows raised. "Please tell me he is telling the truth for once. Did you seriously attack him?"

Cay smiles broadly and flashes my brother a sinister grin before turning back to me. "Absolutely. He had it coming."

"I don't doubt that for a second." A laugh bursts free, as the image of Cay knocking my brother down a peg flashes in my mind.

Oliver walks between the two of us, stopping in front of Cay. "What's the matter, princess? Can't take a little joke? Or is it that you don't want my sister to know about your little secret?"

Cay's hand shoots out so fast I can barely see where it's headed until it's there. Oliver catches her wrist just before her fist makes contact with his smug face.

He tilts his head at her, "Hasn't anyone ever told you that hitting isn't nice?"

Cay jerks and Oliver jumps back, narrowly avoiding a knee to the gut.

"Neither is kicking," he says with a snarl. He looks between the two of us, rolls his eyes, and walks away, heading inside the castle.

Just as he turns the corner two figures step around him. Eve and Mar stop dead in their tracks when they see Cay standing beside me. Eve is the first to recover, she comes bounding down the stairs and practically throws herself on Cay, nearly knocking her over.

"I can't believe you're here!" she screams into Cay's ear, making her jerk away.

Mar is not far behind her sister. "Me next. I need one of those," she says as Cay untangles herself from Eve's arms.

The two share a long hug and then I'm being pulled in too. The four of us share an epic group hug filled with laughter and lots of teasing of one another. When we finally pull apart everyone is smiling more than I have seen in far too long. A familiar feeling warms my chest as I look between my closest friends. The last time we were all together was two years ago. Looking at the three of them side by side, I am already choking back tears again. The only person missing is Oak.

"Nope, none of that. No crying," Mar says, taking my hand in hers.

We all stare at each other for a moment until all we can do is scream into the sky. We let our voices carry through my land and echo back to us. The sound is a symphony to my ears as each voice mingles together. Once we've calmed down a bit from the excitement we all turn to face Cay. She hasn't even come inside yet.

"Come on, let's get you settled and we can all catch up," I say, nodding towards the castle.

~~~

It doesn't take long to get Cay settled into her rooms and then we are off. We sneak through the castle and out of a hidden door that leads to what used to be my father's private gardens. No one comes here except for us.

We first found the gardens while playing a game one of the summers that Eve and Mar came to visit. At first we had no idea what it was. It seemed like a scary cave that was dark and definitely not a place for little girls to hang out. Of course that meant we just had to explore.

To our surprise the cave opened up to a small garden, moss covered the stone walls that surrounded it. The flowers were overgrown and weeds had taken root. Thankfully Oak and I were able to use earth magic to restore it and we were left with a beautiful place just for us. We've claimed the gardens as our own ever since.

Once inside the gardens we all take our usual spots. Eve flops down onto the ground on her back, an arm thrown over her eyes. Mar takes a seat on the swing hanging from the large tree in the center of the gardens, she swings her long legs back and forth lazily. Cay props herself in a wicker chair as I lay out on a stone bench. My fingers trace over my father's name carved into the stone sending small tingles up my arm, like some kind of magic lingers here.

Hours pass as we all catch up with one another. We talk about everything from the latest books we've read to the most recent chaos in our families.

"I don't know what to do. Finn has no interest in learning anything about our kingdom and he insists on trying to *overthrow* me," Cay says with a groan.

Surprisingly, Eve offers her own advice, "He's still a kid. You can't expect him to grow up so quickly. We have to let kids enjoy themselves while they can, before they get sucked into all the boring meetings and parties."

Mar scoffs, "You're one to talk, Eve. You've been skipping out on meetings for months now and making me cover for you."

Eve smiles at her sister, "And I love you for it."

Mar rolls her eyes, swinging her legs harder beneath her, getting higher on the swing. The breeze blows her pale blonde hair back over her shoulders, the strands catch in the sunlight and appear more golden.

"You could have it worse. Just look at my older brothers," I say with a grimace. Flashes of Oliver's smirk fills my head.

Eve and Mar laugh.

Cay sits up straighter. "Terran's not that bad.'' Her cheeks are slightly flush, just the palest shade of pink dusting the tops of her cheekbones and the tips of her ears.

Cay and I decided to tell the others what happened in Rayan. We thought they deserved to know the truth about what was going on between the two of us. They were upset at first; at the situation and the way we handled it. Truthfully they seemed more upset at the sirens than anyone else, including Cay. Eve strung together some delightfully colorful language to describe the creatures. When we finished our story I asked Cay about the time my brother spent in her kingdom but she quickly changed the subject. We let it go then, now we won't.

We're all staring at Cay, waiting for an explanation but she doesn't seem to get the hint.

"And why do you say that Cay?" I ask, raising my brows.

She tries to hide the deepening blush but the color is so bright against her pale skin that it's nearly impossible not to notice.

Eve gasps, sitting up fully. "Wait, wait, wait! Cay, do you have a *thing* for Rose's big brother?"

"What? Of course not!" Cay says, her face now a vibrant beet red.

Mar jumps off the swing and lands beside Eve who flinches. She crosses the small garden and stands directly in front of Cay, staring down at her face and into her eyes. Pale blue meeting seagreen eyes. At first I think Cay isn't going to crack but her expression falters and she throws her head back.

An excited noise slips from Eve's lips and Mar gives me a triumphant smile. I turn to face one of my best friends. "Cay, are you and my brother... " I can't finish the sentence. Terran is the closest thing to a father to me since our actual father passed. Something about the idea of Terran and Cay together just feels... off. Though I would never try and stop them if they truly cared for one another.

Her gaze whips towards me and she begins shaking her head vigorously. "No! I promise, Rose, it's nothing like that. I just admire him. He's an heir like me and he seems to have it all figured out. When he was in Rayan he helped me come to terms with everything. That's it, I swear," she says vehemently, her ocean eyes pooling with emotion.

I nod, trying to ignore the pang of hurt that goes through me. There has always been this unspoken divide between Cay and Eve, and Mar and

I. Two heirs and two spares. It's not that they have ever treated us any different or thought less of us for our positions, it's just the way it feels.

Not getting invited to a ball or party. Never being included in the decision making. Constantly fighting to know what is going on in our own realms. Cay and Eve never have to worry about those things, at least not in the same way Mar and I do. Oak can feel even more distant at times, she will never know the crushing weight that being in line for the throne holds, no matter how far down that line we are.

Turning to Eve I change the subject. "Eve, you have to tell me what's been going on between you and Sebastian," I say with a wiggle of my brows.

Mar bursts out into laughter and Eve sighs.

"What? What did I say?"

Eve shakes her head, giving her sister a scathing glare. "Quite literally, nothing. Seb was just a bit of fun. Nothing worth keeping around for long," she says with a shrug.

Her sister's expression tells me that she agrees, not that I would have expected anything less. Eve has always had a way with others. Her succubus nature calls to people and she has more *experience* than anyone else I know. She was barely 13 or 14 the first time if I remember correctly. Cay and I's jaws were left slack when she told us all about it. In *excruciating* detail.

"I hope it's not rude to ask, Eve, but how do you feed when you're not..." Cay fades off, her pale face flushing once more.

Eve chuckles and smiles at Cay, "When I'm not in a relationship? It's not really something that I have to worry about and my body doesn't really care either way, relationship or not. It's about the connection with the person and yeah of course the attraction, but ultimately it's just what happens in the moment."

Cay nods in understanding but my curiosity is piqued. "That makes sense but I have a follow up question. How exactly did you feed while traveling here? I didn't notice any *help* traveling with you?" I try to choose my words carefully, knowing how uncomfortable Eve has always been with the *arrangements* her mother makes.

Paying people to make themselves available to her daughter at all times. Eve once told me that it feels like a violation, going as far as to describe how it tastes different. I was a little grossed out but interested all the same. Mar and Eve's powers require feeding; unlike Cay and I, we can replenish our magic just by being around our element. It's these slight differences in our species that have led to me spending hours with my head buried in a book, studying everything I can about the species who call Estarynn home.

"Oh this is a great question. Eve, why don't you tell them about Nat. I do love this story," Mar says devilishly. She plops down into the grass beside her sister, crossing her long legs and resting her elbows against her knees, she places her chin in the palm of her hands.

"Nope, not going to happen. We've been through this once, I'm not doing it again," Eve says firmly.

Cay and I share a look before we launch into a full-scale show of begging and pleading. Eventually we get her to cave and she tells us about her unfortunate encounter with her guard. The conversation stays light-hearted at first but quickly shifts when she lets slip how long it's been since she fed.

"Eve, you should really feed. It's not good to wait so long. I fed multiple times on the way here *and* since arriving," Mar says, voice laced with concern.

Eve shakes her head, waving her sister off. "I'll be fine. Succubi can go a lot longer than vampires can between feeding. Just another reason we're the superior species I guess," she says mockingly.

Mar seems ready to argue but Eve changes the subject again, effectively diverting attention away from herself.

We stay in the garden for hours, sharing stories and telling each other every small detail about our lives. It doesn't matter that we talk often, that our letters to one another are always long and thorough, we talk as though no time has passed and simply enjoy one another's presence. In the passing moments I feel my soul begin to piece back together, unaware of when it first started to feel so broken.

Chapter 17

Eve

We spend most of the day in the garden. Oak joins us late in the evening and we all decide to go back to Rose's chambers. We've all been given our own but we prefer to be together. Everyone else fell asleep hours ago while I've been awake, pacing the room. I walk towards Rose's vanity and spot a beautiful collection of jewels and hair ornaments.

A small box catches my eye and I open it. Inside is a rose quartz ring with a dainty gold band. I wonder if this is part of Rose's ensemble for the party. Rose always looks put together, perfectly styled and behaved no matter the occasion. I've always admired her ability to do that, just as I admire her ability to charm a room. She has always excelled in political matters whereas I have run from them at every opportunity. It's not as though I don't love my kingdom, I just don't find any particular interest in learning about rules and policies.

Sighing I close the box, jumping from the loud snap of the lid shutting. Mar stirs from across the room but doesn't wake. Looking around at my friends, I feel my heart warm. Rose is in bed with Cay, the two curled on their sides facing each other, in exactly the same position as when they fell asleep. Mar is curled into a ball on the couch, looking so small despite her towering height. Oak lays on the floor, a pile of cushions beneath her and taking up as much room as possible despite her petite frame. I snort at the two polar opposites before me.

I slowly cross the room and slip out the door, pulling it gently shut behind me. I wander through the familiar halls of the castle until I find myself in a place that calls to me, no matter where I am. The palace training room is surprisingly small. A few rows of dummies lined up along the far wall and a selection of weapons hung beside them. It is similar to the training room back home only ours is large enough to host the training practices for the entire royal guard, whereas this is a private space. Intimate.

I remember the first time I stepped foot in this room. I thought it was perfect. It forced people to get close to each other. You can't rely on long range weapons here, only hand to hand combat or, my preference, small blades. I shrug off my robe and am left in a thin camisole and silk shorts. Not exactly the ideal training attire but it will work.

Power hums beneath my skin, an incessant buzz demanding to be used. My magic always seems to stir with my emotions, sometimes impossible to ignore. Magic builds up over time, growing stronger and replenishing until the person's threshold is reached. Then, it demands to be used, released back into the universe. The stronger the person the more magic they hold, and in turn, the more often they need to use it.

The first punch leaves my hand stinging, my knuckles a bright angry red from a bad hit. Shaking out my hand, I go through my usual combinations. Right hook, palm heel strike, middle punch, kick. I spin on my left leg, bringing my right around for a vicious roundhouse kick that threatens to tip the dummy over. I run through these a few times, warming my body up, and then I start to let my magic slip free.

It's not exactly a physical strength that determines one's magic though. It's a combination of that, genetics, and most of all, their will. Because magic has a mind of its own, it can be dangerous, especially if the one using it is unfocused or untrained. Or worse, if they allow their emotions to control them. Some magic is easier to use than others, like the elements. Most people find this magic the easiest to control because they are born with it. The element is as much a part of us as our soul, our mind. Being surrounded by it in our realms is what keeps us strong, though depending on the person they can keep that power no matter how distant from their land.

I bend over, grabbing a small pair of daggers. The moment the blades are in my hand I feel my senses heighten and adrenaline kicks in. It's the middle of the night and all my friends are sleeping soundly, but I can't quiet the fire in my body, demanding to be used. I cut the blades through the air, slicing and stabbing at something that isn't even there as I work my muscles to the point of exhaustion. I call on my fire, sending bursts of flames out of my fists and sometimes wrapped around the blades. My skin is burning from the inside and I know it's not going to be enough.

The element that we can control is determined by our species. The species that control earth consists of; fauns, centaurs, gargoyles, wolf shifters, and fae. Meanwhile water is controlled by; gorgons, nymphs, hydra, sirens, and mermaids. Air is reserved for; harpies, sylphs which are otherwise known as wind spirits, pegasi, manticores, and griffins; like the one that attacked us on the way here. Cyclops, dragons, phoenix, vampires, and succubi are all able to wield fire magic. Out of all the elements, fire is the most difficult to command. The most volatile.

Magic has a strong control over our bodies. It forms a direct line to our emotions and even our actions. Tonight, my fire is threatening to burn through my skin and set the entire room ablaze. A sort of anxious energy has settled in my chest ever since leaving Vulca. At first I thought it was being so far from the home and a constant source of fire, but now I'm not so sure.

The elements are the foundation for all magic and how we replenish it when it gets depleted. Our bodies were born with the magic in our veins, if we use too much too quickly we can become weak and sick, possibly even die. Now I realize that it's not just the absence of my element making me feel so off. Just being around the element isn't enough for magic to truly replenish itself. Each species needs something different, mine just so happens to need positive emotions; passion, love, happiness, *sex*. Though I loathe to admit it, Mar was probably right.

Ignoring the unsettling feeling building in my chest I push harder, calling only the fire that rests just beneath my skin. Elemental magic isn't the only kind we can use. Spellcasting, incantations, curses, and even healing are all within the realm of possibilities. Growing up I received private lessons for each, practicing day and night and learning the intricacies of each kind. I excelled at spells and curses, yet struggled with healing. For some reason I have never been able to release my power enough to actually heal more than a few small cuts and bruises, even my own. There were times that I wished I had that sort of power, that I could just fix whatever it was that was broken or wrong, never needing to rely on someone else for their help. Maybe if I could heal I could fix whatever is wrong inside me.

Breathing heavily and drenched in sweat, I stand, staring at the single mirror in the room. My reflection looks unfamiliar. I'm paler than usual, my eyes wider and cheeks more drawn, my waist is more narrow and the outline of my ribs is visible through my camisole as it clings to me. Sighing deeply, I turn away from myself and start to clean up. Hints of daylight are peeking through the windows and I need to bathe, badly.

As I start to place the blades in their respective places my vision goes fuzzy. A buzzing starts up in my head and then I feel it. The cold numbness ricochets through my bones and into my brain. Before I even have a chance to brace myself I am falling. My vision goes completely black, my senses dulled.

A creaking sound is distant in my ears and I try to force my eyes open. I feel something warm grab me and panic shoots through my veins. I need to pull myself together, dammit. I am screaming at my muscles, demanding they listen but they refuse. I lay there on the floor, utterly helpless. I try to calm my racing heart, steady my breathing, but it feels like each breath is taken through a straw. My body is shaking violently and I can hear the faint sound of yelling.

But then it's over. My senses return, my heart rate slows, and it feels like every ounce of energy in my body has been completely drained. When the blackness fades and my vision returns, I am surprised to find that my body is not shaking, it's being shaken.

Reed, Oak's younger brother, stares down at me with terror in his bright green eyes. He is calling my name frantically and shaking me by the shoulders. His unruly curls stick up at every angle.

I try to move my arm, it takes an extreme amount of effort but I manage to place my hand over his and halt his unintentional assault. "Geez, Reed, what're you trying to do, shake my brains loose?" I groan.

He curses and pulls me into a sitting position gently, "Evie! Thank Vana, I was so worried. I was walking back to my rooms when I heard a crash from in here. When I opened the door and saw you, I thought you were *dead*."

Laughing I push him off me and pull my knees to my chest. "Sorry to scare you. I'm fine."

Reed doesn't seem all that convinced, his face contorting in worry. "What happened?"

I move to stand and he helps me up. "It's embarrassing, really. I couldn't sleep so I decided to train for a bit and I must have exhausted myself. It's nothing to worry about."

Reed looks towards the door hesitantly, "Should I go find someone? My sister or maybe yours would be better?" His eyes continue to dart between my face and the door.

If Reed tells either one of them what happened I am going to be facing a full on interrogation. Not to mention they'll probably hover around me constantly until they are satisfied I'm not going to have any more spontaneous naps.

I smile at Reed. He's grown a lot since the last time I was here. He is Oak's male opposite, nearly identical if not for their height. Where Oak is short enough to pass as a kid on most occasions, Reed is taller than Mar. He might even be as tall as Terran by now. His wavy locks have grown out, curling more than I remember and giving him this sort of boyish charm. Though a boy he is no longer.

"Don't bother. I'm going to take a quick bath and then head back to bed. No use in waking them up now, it's still early," I say, picking up my robe and wrapping it around myself, trying to hide the way my body shivers. A layer of sweat coats my skin and makes the slight breeze nearly unbearable.

It always happens this way. I feel it a moment before it happens and then I am on the floor. It fades quickly, but the side effects linger for hours, sometimes days. One of the signs I have come to recognize was exactly what I tried to ignore for days. My magic was getting out of control, demanding to be used and when I didn't, it found ways to release itself.

Like what happened with the horse. The first time it happened Mar was away visiting her brothers and I was lucky. Since then, not so much. She found me one day and I had to brush it off as forgetting to eat breakfast. She scolded me for not taking care of myself and then let me be. Somehow I doubt she will be so unquestioning a second time around.

"I really think I should get someone. I could find a healer if you need. Or I could help take you there if that is easier. I'm studying to be an apothecary now, I might even be able to whip up a potion for you myself," Reed says somewhat stubbornly.

Turning to leave I try to keep my steps even, to not show any sign that I might collapse a second time. Something that is starting to feel more and more likely with each moment. Stopping by the door I cast Reed a look over my shoulder, he is standing by the spot where he found me, staring down at the ground like he still expects to see me there. I feel a pang of guilt in my chest. I wish I could let him help me, to tell someone what is wrong, but that's not what comes out.

"Thanks for your help, Reed. You should really head back to bed. Oh and, do me a favor?" I say. He nods and I continue, "Don't tell anyone else about this okay? Wouldn't want to worry them over nothing."

Reed gives me a hesitant nod and I leave.

Walking back down the hallway towards my chambers I am forced to use the wall as a crutch. My magic has been thoroughly depleted, its absence leaving my body cold and feeling hollow. It takes me longer than I would have liked to make it into my temporary room. As soon as I am inside I move to a small trunk, reaching inside and rummaging around. I pull out a small vial filled with a dark swirling liquid.

I down it in one swig, sitting on the floor. I lay back and prop my ankles up on the trunk pushing blood back towards my head and heart. My eyes drift shut for a brief moment and I think I might get lucky and actually sleep for a while.

It doesn't take long for the beginning of the nightmare to find me in the darkness; refusing to grant me even a moment of peace. I fight to keep my eyes open as I stare up at the ceiling. When exhaustion finally claims me, I fall back into the familiar scene with the same familiar screams.

Chapter 18

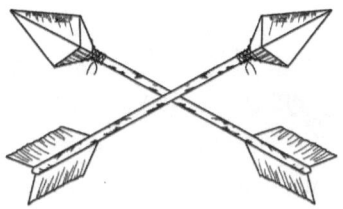

Oak

I wake up on the floor of Rose's chambers. I'm sprawled across my pile of cushions like a starfish. Sleep lingers in my bones as I stretch my arms and legs, flexing my muscles to wake them up. Sitting up, I survey the room. Everyone else is still asleep, except Eve, who is already gone. Yawning, I stand and leave the room silently.

Once in the hall I start towards my rooms down the hall. They're smaller than most, simple and free of clutter. When I first moved into the castle I thought it would only be temporary, that eventually I would be able to take Reed and myself back to our *true* home. Now, that seems like more of a fantasy.

Entering my room I quickly walk to the bathing chamber, strip off my clothes, and sink into the deep tub. The water is warm, comforting my aching muscles as I move the soap over my body and then apply a shampoo to my short hair. Once clean, I quickly change and move back into the main room. There is a large bed, desk, vanity, and a wardrobe. Pulling open the wood doors I grab out a simple pants and tunic combination before making short work of brushing my hair back and using a simple spell to hold it in place.

Satisfied with my appearance, I head towards the high lady's chambers. I never got the opportunity to check in with her about the gargoyles and I know I shouldn't delay any longer. By now, Terran will have filled his mother in, but I can only assume she would want to get the full story from me directly.

Even if she hasn't summoned me since my return. Words are easily twisted, even when unintentional. I have found that going straight to the source is usually the best way to get the closest thing to the truth.

Moving through the halls I pass dozens of staff as they rush to set up for the evening's festivities. In a matter of a few hours the castle will be full of guests and music. The courtyard looks like something out of a dream and if it is anything like the usual balls, there is sure to be lots of delicious food. Dishes of rice and the perfectly cooked meats, bright vegetables and fragrant spices already fill the air. My stomach grumbles at the mere thought. I close my eyes for a moment, picturing the desserts that will come after the dinner, and run straight into someone.

My eyes fly open as an apology tumbles from my lips. Looking up I find my little brother, Reed, smiling down at me. "Oh, it's you."

Reed's smile slips, "You don't have to say it like that."

I grimace, "Sorry, I didn't mean it in a bad way. I just wasn't expecting you."

There is something disconcerting about one's younger brother being more than a foot taller than them. His hair is disheveled and looking up at him now he looks so much like our father that I can hardly breathe. I move to step around him but he steps into my path.

I raise my eyes to his, a question in my stare. "Are you going to move? I have to see the high lady."

Reed runs a hand through his wavy hair, tousling it further and looking anywhere but at me. He steps to the side with a sigh and starts to walk away.

Turning on my heels I call after him. "Wait a minute. What's going on? Why won't you look at me?" I ask, narrowing my gaze. My brother wears his heart on his sleeves and his every thought in his expression.

He stops but doesn't turn, keeping his back to me. "Nothing. I'm just heading to my rooms." His voice is steady, deep like our father's was even at a mere 18 years.

I cross my arms and stare into the back of his head. "Spill it. What do you know?"

Reed sighs, turning to face me and throwing his hands up in the air, "Nothing, okay? Why does everything always have to turn into an inquisition?"

I hold my ground, raising my brows as I wait for his real answer. If there is anything I know about my brother, it's that he is a horrible liar, and even worse at keeping secrets. We stare at each other for a few moments before he curses.

"Fine. I ran into Eve, that's all," he says with a shrug. Running that same hand through his hair, a nervous habit most of our family shares.

My arms drop to my side, my expression turning to one of confusion, "Eve? What's she got to do with you?"

Reed shrugs again, "Nothing. I just ran into her, that's all." Reed continues to look anywhere other than my eyes. Staring above my head or out a window.

"No, what aren't you saying?" I ask.

When Reed doesn't answer I ask again. He refuses to answer me so I do what I always do when I want answers. I pull on my magic and ask again, this time my words come out thick. This particular bit of magic is rare, very few people can accomplish it correctly. But not me, my persuasion comes out flawless, undeniable.

Reed tries to fight off the magic but gives in reluctantly. "Fine, Eve passed out on the floor of the training room. I had to work really hard to wake her up. She wasn't responding to her name or when I shook her."

My mouth drops open and I step forward, pushing my magic into him again, "Do you know why she passed out?"

Reed sighs, "She said she was working out and must have exhausted herself. But she didn't look good, she was pale and super thin, I was really worried about her."

I release my magic and turn to face the hallway where he came from. Eve had seemed fine last night. She was joking around with us, drinking, having a good time like always. There has got to be more to the story here.

"You know I hate it when you do that," Reed says angrily from behind me.

I mutter an apology but he doesn't let it go.

"You know you can't just go around forcing other people to say and do whatever you want, Oak. It's wrong!" he shouts.

I turn back to him.

His fists are clenched at his sides and his face is a mix of emotions. I take in his tense posture and the way his jaw seems to flex as he grinds his teeth. It is rare to see Reed so angry. In this moment he looks much older than he is. A slice of pain cuts through my chest as I imagine our father again. His hulking form dominated any room he entered, his mere presence taking command of each and every space. Reed is so much like him and he will never really know it.

Sighing I step forward, placing a soft hand on his arm. "You're right. But if something is wrong with Eve I need to know about it. She is the heir to the Vulca throne, we cannot allow anything to happen to her or we risk dire consequences."

Reed raises his eyebrows at me, "Do you really think if something happened that her father would come after us?"

I nod, "He's a king, Reed. If something happens to his heir while on foreign soil, he would *have* to do something about it."

Reed seems to think about it for a second before nodding.

"Thank you for telling me."

He scoffs, "You didn't give me much of a choice."

I flinch a bit at his words and the truth behind them. I hate using my power on the people I love, even when necessary. But I start to wonder, was this even one of those times? An uncomfortable feeling creeps into my gut and I push away the thought, looking at my brother.

"I'm going to find Eve and check on her."

"I thought you were going to see Aunt Ayana?" he asks.

Shit, I was going to do that.

I consider my options for a moment. Go straight to the high lady and check in with Eve later, or go straight to my friend now. If Eve is sick or injured or in any way needs my help then that means she is my top priority, and it has nothing to do with her title.

Making up my mind I smile at Reed, "It can wait. I'll go to Eve first."

He nods to me and after a moment of awkwardness he turns to leave.

I watch him walk down the hall but I can't get the pit in my stomach to go away so I call out to him. "Reed!"

He turns back to face me, "What?"

I give him a sheepish smile, "I'm sorry I used my magic on you."

He rubs the back of his neck, "You know you didn't have to right? I would have told you what was going on. I was just trying to figure out how."

I nod, watching as he walks away again. This time I let him go.

~~~

It takes me longer than expected to find Eve but when I do she is in the dining hall. I look her over from the entrance to the room. She seems perfectly fine. Her ashy black hair is pulled into a slick ponytail, her face seems bright beneath it, not even a dark circle to be seen. She locks eyes with me and smiles as she eats her breakfast. Her plate consists of fresh fruit, a small portion of plain rice, and a single piece of toast with honey. Nothing out of the ordinary.

"Good morning," I say sitting down across from her. She immediately pushes her plate towards me.

"Here, please finish this for me. I am so stuffed I can't even think about taking another bite."

I stare down at her practically full plate, "Is something wrong with the food?"

She shakes her head vehemently, "No, of course not. I'm just full, that's all."

I push her plate to the side and try to catch her eyes as they roam, "Eve, is everything, alright?"

Eve looks back at me with a bemused smile "Why wouldn't it be? I'm here with the people I love most in the world." She bumps her shoulder against mine lovingly.

I take a deep breath knowing she isn't going to like what I say next, "I ran into Reed. He told me what happened."

Her smile doesn't falter, she barely shows any reaction at all.

Okay, something is seriously wrong.

She laughs, rolling her eyes, "Of course he did. I told him it was nothing to worry about but he seemed pretty shaken up by it."

I reach my hand across the table, taking hers in mine. "Eve, if something is going on, you can tell me. You know that right?"

Eve laces her fingers with my own, giving me a bright smile. "Of course, Oak. But nothing is wrong. I promise. Reed was overreacting, really."

I search her expression for any sign of something wrong but only find mild amusement. Sighing, I let go of her hand, sitting back against my chair and picking at her fruit. "I'm sorry, I'm just on edge. A lot has been going on lately."

Eve's eyes widen at that and she leans forward, resting her elbows on the table, "Oh? Well don't be shy, tell me what's been happening."

I give her a half smile, knowing I can never really tell her the truth. She may be my best friend but this is something I can't tell anyone, not even her. I wave my hand in front of my face. "Just normal court drama, you know how it is. The party has everyone going crazy, I swear."

This set's Eve off on a long tangent about the gown she will be wearing. A million questions about my own spilling from her lips faster than I thought possible. I listen to her intently, answering questions when I can, and enjoy the ease of being with my friend. My soul feels lighter already.

Part of me knows that she is downplaying whatever is going on with her, but the other part of me knows that pushing her never got me anywhere. A dark thought pushing me to use persuasion crosses my mind but I shove it back. Reed had a point about using that magic and I know Eve will tell me when she is ready.

My heart constricts, knowing I can never return the favor.

The rest of the girls stroll into the dining room looking like they just rolled out of bed. Eve teases them for it and an easy banter starts up immediately. I watch as the four of them go back and forth. My gaze catches with Mar's as she gives me a look that promises our earlier conversation isn't over.

Chapter 19

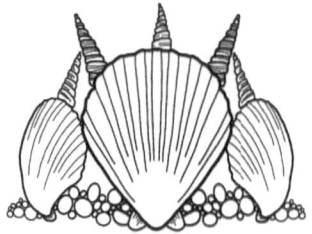

Cay

It's been almost a full day since I arrived in Sena and somehow I have managed to avoid Terran the entire time. At first I wasn't really *trying* to avoid him. I was just more focused on catching up with my friends and making up for lost time. But somewhere along the line something shifted, I started to walk through the halls more cautiously. Being careful to listen around corners before turning. Not that I seemed to need to do any of that. In the 24 hours since my getting here I have yet to hear or see a single sign of the Sena heir.

The other girls are all getting ready in Rose's room. An entire team came in to try and do our hair and makeup but Rose sent them away, opting to do it herself so we all decided to help. I headed back to my room not long ago to retrieve a few items from my things. Our dresses were already brought to her rooms but I left my family jewels safe in their box under the bed.

As I am about to turn down the hall that leads back to Rose's room I send a wave of my magic out, waiting to see if I sense anything. It's something I started doing at home some months ago and can't seem to stop. I start to turn but then I feel it; the brush of magic against mine, hesitant yet firm. Familiar. I suck in a sharp breath as static shoots across my skin, making goosebumps rise.

This magic is powerful, wild even. This is the kind of magic that demands to be used rather than the other way around. Before I can decide what to do, the person who controls such magic steps around the bend and I am staring up into hazel eyes beneath a head of chestnut curls. My heart rate kicks up for a moment but then a knowing smirk crosses his face. A rush of anger races through my blood.

"You know for someone who has been avoiding my brother all day you seem awfully disappointed I am not him," Oliver says. He towers over me, his large frame dominating as he invades my personal space.

I fight the urge to grind my teeth and try to step around him.

"Woah, where do you think you're going? We're having a conversation here, don't be rude."

My eyes lock with his, "We're not having anything. Unless you would like a rematch of what happened in the forest?" I hold my hand out between us, summoning a small whirlpool into the palm of my hand.

"Careful how you speak to me, *minnow*," he says with a growl, using my mother's nickname for me.

I step forward, going chest to chest with him. The heat from his body presses into me. "I could say the same to you. After all, only one of us here is an heir, and it's not you." It's a low blow, one that makes me regret the words almost immediately. My position is not one to lord over others. Shame rises in me but the apology is stuck in my throat.

Oliver clicks his tongue and pushes past me. I turn the corner and quickly make my way into Rose's rooms. All of the girls welcome me back as they continue getting ready.

"Rose, would you still love me if I killed your brother?" I ask, falling down onto her opulent bed.

She snorts, "I'm assuming you're talking about Oliver, in which case go right ahead."

"Hey at least you all have a brother, I've only got Mar," Eve says with a dramatic sigh.

Mar slaps her arm and Eve holds her hands up in submission. Watching them I am reminded of how it used to be with Finn, before he started growing up and decided he had to compete against me. Even when our parents made it perfectly clear that that was *not* how we were to behave.

"Trust me, Eve, you aren't missing out on much." I say with a sad smile.

Mar sits beside me on the bed, knocking her shoulder into mine, "What's up with Finn? Last I saw him he was hanging onto your every word and was practically a shadow following you through the halls. I know you mentioned he was acting up but it seems bigger than just that."

"I don't even know where to begin. All of a sudden he is mouthing off and terrorizing the entire court. Not to mention he has finally reached an age where he can truly start to learn about our kingdom and the politics of being a prince but he wants nothing to do with it," I say with a groan.

Eve mumbles from her spot on the couch something that sounds an awful lot like 'join the club'.

Mar shakes her head and grabs my hand, "He's still young. He has plenty of time to learn all about the crappy parts of being royal. Let him enjoy the good parts for now. Believe me, as a second in line myself, there will be more than enough opportunities for him to learn his place in this world."

Another bout of shame at what I said swirls in my stomach making my skin prickle, but Mar continues, drawing me back into the moment.

"Besides, little brothers are just like that. One day they love you and think you're the coolest person in the whole world and the next they're your mortal enemy. A few weeks ago, Hagan set my bed on fire because I wouldn't teach him some advanced spell."

I laugh a little as Oak decides to chime in.

"Oh if you think that's bad, wait till they are teenagers. When Reed was 15 he thought it would be a good idea to try and *ride* on the back of a centaur."

A gasp echoes from all of us except Rose who nods in confirmation.

Species are divided into those who shift partially- dimidiums - and those who shift fully, plenus. Depending on the creature it can be seen as extremely rude to ride them, dimidiums almost never allow it. Centaurs are an incredibly proud dimidium species, they prefer to spend most of their lives shifted, rather than 'deny their true form'. The fact that Reed was still alive after trying it must mean that the centaur in question was *very* forgiving, if not indebted to the crown, or I suppose now the other way around.

Once the shock of Reed's actions passes we all fall into an easy conversation. We get ready together, scattered across Rose's large room. Oak is currently applying a black kohl to the rim of her eyes. Mar uses her magic to heat a brush as she drags it through, making her platinum blonde hair perfectly straight. Eve is casting a spell on her dark hair so that it falls in subtle waves around her face.

I work my hair into an intricate braid, pulling pieces away from my face and letting others hang down. I start adding my pearl pins strategically and then slip on my family ring. It's a simple thing, a gold band that waves towards the center, holding a small pearl. An heirloom passed down to me by my mother and all the way back to our oldest ancestor. I wear it as often as I can but truthfully I fear losing it. The ring looks dainty on my finger, matching my pins perfectly and pulling the whole look together. My eyelids have a light dusting of pink powder and a thick layer of black coating my lashes, making the color of my irises stand out.

I look around the room as we all add our finishing touches.

Mar is wearing a blood-red, satin gown with a deep neckline. Two slits extend all the way up to her hip, creating a single panel in the middle. One wrong move and everything will be on display, yet somehow Mar moves in it with ease. Her blue eyes are framed with gold and a darker shade of brown. Powder shimmers on her cheekbones making her sharp features stand out even more. Her lips are coated in a shade of red that matches her dress perfectly.

Eve on the other hand has a much subtler look. Her face looks natural, her features only accented by a light dusting of blush and a subtle shade of brown to the lids. Her lips are covered in a thick gloss and something makes her skin glow all over. She wears a simple, floor length black gown that is nearly entirely sheer. The neckline plunges to the waist where it is cinched, accentuating her curves and showing off the generous swell of her breasts. A single slit reaches her hips, showing off her leg and a dagger strapped to her thigh. We all shake our head at her as she carefully adjusts the strap holding the dagger in place. Leave it to Eve to wear a weapon as an accessory.

Oak is across the room running her hand through her short hair again. Instead of a gown, she wears a deep emerald green top made of the smoothest velvet. The sleeves are long and buttons go up the front, stopping at the sloping neckline. She has paired it with a pair of black high waisted trousers sporting three matching buttons. They hug her legs and make them appear longer, despite her petite height. Her face is completely bare aside from the thick lining of black around her hooded eyes, making the green of them stand out. Her freckles are on full display, splattered across her nose and cheeks. She continues to run her hands through her short hair, twirling pieces around her finger and trying to style it exactly how she likes.

I'm wearing a sleeveless ball gown made of an intricately designed brocade that gives the fabric a glorious texture. The dress is powder blue, the simple bodice stops at the waist where it billows out into beautiful folds, a knee length slit hidden on one side. It accentuates my waist without losing any of my curves. It also draws attention to my neck where a thin gold chain holds another pearl. The necklace was a gift from Rose back when we were teenagers; I thought it was only fitting to wear it tonight.

I glance around the room looking for Rose to show herself but she is nowhere to be found. "Girls, has anyone seen Rose? Where did she run off to?"

Eve and Mar look around the room, giving me a shrug.

"Did Rose not tell you? She will be escorted in by Terran so she had to leave early to get into position. We're all expected to be escorted by partners as well," Oak says, continuing to mess with her hair.

Eve raises her hand, "Am I the only one who has no idea what you're talking about."

Oak turns to look at us and her mouth hangs slightly open, "Oh no. Please tell me you have all arranged escorts for the evening?" she asks desperately.

The three of us shake our heads in unison and Oak groans.

"Okay, not to worry. I figured something like this might happen. Leave it to me, you all go on ahead and I'll meet you by the entrance with your partners," she says, hurrying from the room.

Mar rolls her eyes and follows her out the door, Eve in tow. The two of them walk elegantly despite their towering heels. My own feet are in thin flats, and I am grateful for it as we bound through the silent halls as a trio. Most of the guests will have already arrived and are waiting for Rose to make her grand entrance. I trip over my own feet for a moment as realization sets in.

I may have been avoiding Terran well enough so far, but tonight he will be there and there is no way I can escape him now. We cut through the kitchens to save time and I snatch a glass of bubbling wine off a tray, downing it in one sip.

Eve is leading the way ahead of us but Mar walks close to my side. She watches as I snatch another glass on the way out and raises her brows.

"Sorry, it's been quite some time since I've been away from the city, let alone to a ball," I say, blushing. My entire body feels like it is about to burst into flames, an uncommon occurrence for a mermaid. I summon a bit of my magic to the surface and let it cool my skin from the inside out.

Mar smiles at me and takes the glass from my hand, taking a sip before handing it back with an odd expression. "You're going to do fine. First, you look gorgeous. And second, all you have to do is be your usual, *regal* self."

Mar's right, I just have to be myself. I give her a broad smile and down the last of the wine as we make our way to the main entrance. I can do this, it will be as easy as swimming downstream.

Chapter 20

Eve

As we approach the entrance, Oak turns to face us. She gives us all a hesitant smile and steps to the side. Behind her are Reed, Rian, and Oliver. Reed is giving us all a look of awe while Rian is looking anywhere *but* at my sister. Oliver on the other hand is staring straight at Cay. His gaze locked onto her like the rest of us didn't even exist. His mouth is drawn in a hard line and his eyes burn with some emotion I can't quite place. Though I certainly taste *something* of interest.

I glance at Cay out of the corner of my eye and her face is red, flushed either from the wine or something else. We stop in front of the males and turn to Oak for further instructions.

"Okay, Rian, you'll escort Mar. Oliver you're with Eve. Reed you have Cay, got it?" Oak says hurriedly.

We form a line, Mar and Rian at the front. I take my spot as second but Reed steps up beside me, not Oliver. I give him a questioning look but he just shrugs. I don't have to look behind me to know that Oliver has taken Reed's place beside Cay. The two are whispering something back and forth but before I can question them about it, the large doors leading to the courtyard open.

Mar's name is announced and she steps forward, her arm laced delicately with Rian's. He is wearing dark leather pants and a red tunic that matches Mar's dress so perfectly it makes me wonder if they had planned it. All of the eyes are on them as they enter. Mar looks beautiful but there is something about her standing next to Rian that makes them mesmerizing. His ashy blonde hair has been styled perfectly, accentuating his defined cheekbones. He gazes down at my sister as he leads her in and I can't help but try and get a taste of whatever might be rolling off of him as well.

Before I can, my name is called next and I step forward. Reed takes my hand in his and holds it out before us, leading me down the path. I finally get a good look at the rooms as we make our way down the entrance.

The tables lining the exterior of the room are covered in beautiful moss and candles, casting a warm glow around the entire space. There are flowers everywhere, shades of white and pink amongst the hanging vines. Orbs hang from the ceiling, filled with some kind of magic that is making them glow. Energy hums as earth magic flows through the land and the many citizens of Sena. A large wisteria tree commands the space, drawing the eyes to the high lady perched beneath it. We stop in the center of the room, bowing slightly to Rose's mom before stepping off to the side.

Cay is called next, Oliver by her side. He is wearing brown linen pants with a dark green tunic, the color makes his hazel eyes stand out nicely. His loose curls have been pushed back away from his face leaving his many freckles on full display. Where his skin is bronzed, Cay's is porcelain.

Her dark hair makes it look even paler in the low light. She looks stunning, her pearls the perfect accent to her pale blue gown. Standing next to Oliver she looks unsure, her posture is stiff and her shoulders are drawn up. She glides across the floor elegantly yet she looks hesitant. They stop in the center of the room, bowing slightly just as we had done before them.

Oliver takes a second step forward, giving his mother another deep bow, his hand placed over his chest in a show of respect.

She smiles at him knowingly as she stands. Oliver and Cay fall into line beside my sister and I as the high lady addresses the room.

"My dear friends, family, thank you all for being here this evening. My daughter must be blessed by Vana herself to have so many people who care for her. I myself am incredibly proud of the beautiful young female she has become. So, without further ado, please allow me to introduce the guest of honor, my daughter, Princess Rose," she says, gesturing broadly to the grand entrance where we had all just come.

For a moment I wonder where she was hiding so we didn't see her, but the moment she steps out the thought vanishes from my mind.

Her chestnut curls have been expertly styled on top of her head, a few strands hanging down to frame her face. She wears a sage green, tulle gown, pulled together at the waist with a delicate white floral belt. The dress is complete with matching white petals, perfectly scattered over the bust and down the side, held up with thin straps. There is an underlayer of white tulle that peeks through as she glides towards us. Her wide, downturned eyes are lined with brown that makes her own freckles stand out. I am so mesmerized by how beautiful she looks that for a moment I don't even notice her escort.

Terran walks beside his sister, leading her through the path and giving polite nods to his people as he passes them. He is dressed similarly to Oliver only where his tunic was simple, Terran's is full of intricate detail. It is made of a brocade similar to Cay's, the color softer, more complimentary to Rose. His pants are form-fitting, hugging his thighs in a way that shows off the muscles beneath. His tight curls are cropped close to his head and show off defined cheekbones and a square jaw. Terran's skin is darker than the rest of his family, a deeper olive similar to his cousins. Everything about him exudes confidence and control.

They both stop before their mother and like those before them, give her a deep bow. As soon as they rise, her mother claps her hands above her head and music springs to life all around us. With that, the party begins. Everyone moves at once, rushing to Rose's side and gushing over her. Terran disappears into the crowd.

"Oh my, Rose, you look stunning," Cay says with wide eyes.

Mar gives her an appreciative once over, "Wow, you look hot."

I pull Rose into a tight hug and whisper in her ear, "You look like a goddess. Truly." I press a quick kiss on her cheek.

Rose laughs and pulls back, giving us all a brilliant smile. "You all are too much. Thank you. I am so happy you are all here." Her gaze lands on each of us, the swell of emotion evident in her eyes.

The ground beneath our feet starts to shift and then suddenly we are standing on a large marble dance floor. People begin making their way towards us as the music changes to a softer, slower song.

Reed steps forward and extends a hand to me, "Your highness, would you care to dance?"

I smile up at him and nod my head. As soon as I do he grabs my hand and pulls me against his chest. I stare up at him as he twirls us around the room, laughing and smiling. The music shifts and Reed effortlessly changes with it. My arms are wrapped around his neck as we sway together.

Reed is handsome, yet different from the other Sena men. Where Oliver and Terran are all muscles and chiseled jaws, Reed is more delicate. His features are softer, still clinging on to the last bits of boyishness. I've watched him grow up over the years and in my eyes he will always be the kid who used to chase after us. I study his face but his eyes are looking over my shoulder. He licks his lips and a slight flush comes over his bronzed cheeks. I turn to look at the spot where his eyes are locked and find an extremely handsome wolf shifter standing across the room.

The shifter has curly black hair, tan skin, and a killer smile. I can tell he is a wolf from the crescent moon inked on his shoulder. The two boys stare at each other, locked into an intense conversation happening with nothing more than their eyes. The mystery male smirks and I feel Reed's hands tighten around my waist. My gaze shifts back to him and he seems utterly entranced by this boy.

Something delicious swirls on the tip of my tongue and I am forced to slam my mental walls up, blocking myself from feeding. "So, who is he?" I say, clearing my throat.

Reed looks down at me, eyes a bit unfocused for a moment.

I raise my brows at him and he swallows hard.

"What?" he asks, a bit breathless.

I chuckle, "I asked who the boy that you won't stop staring at is."

Reed looks away from me but I gently force his eyes back.

"What's the matter? You can tell me," I say with a smile. I give his shoulders a reassuring squeeze.

Reed shakes his head as he continues to lead us through the dance, never missing a beat. "That's Mateo. An alpha who's pack roams just outside the castle grounds. I've run into him a few times while out riding or when I make deliveries for the apothecary. We've never spoken."

I look back over my shoulder and Mateo is talking to a few faun girls, his gaze still locked on Reed. "Maybe you should. He is giving you some very intense eye contact right now."

The music shifts again and Reed dips me low, pulling me back up so I am flush against his chest. He lifts me off my feet by my waist and spins me around effortlessly. When my feet touch the ground again I stumble but he is there to steady me. Who knew Reed was such a great dancer?

"I can't. He's an alpha," Reed says darkly.

I cough out a laugh, "Reed, you do remember that you are royalty, right? By all true definitions of the word, you're an *alpha* yourself."

He fixes me with a pointed stare, "Barely. My father was a soldier. My mother may have been the high lady's sister, but my aunt married into her power. I have no royal blood to speak of."

I roll my eyes, "That doesn't matter. You know as well as I do that magic is what decides who rules. If it were up to blood then the high lady would have never been allowed to remain in charge after her husband died."

Reed lets out a deep sigh, "Sure but blood is what carries your magic, what makes you powerful. It's something you are either born with or not. So yeah magic might be what puts people in control but the power comes from the blood itself."

"You're not wrong, most families keep their power since the strength of magic is passed down through the blood line, but you only helped prove my point. The high lady, your *aunt*, is powerful enough to rule, and last time I checked her blood ran through your veins."

Reed pulls us off to the side of the dance floor and we both struggle for a moment to catch our breath. He smiles down at me and looks back towards where we last saw Mateo. He leans over and places a soft kiss on my cheek, "Thank you, Evie. I guess I'm going to go talk to him. Wish me luck."

I smile at his nickname for me and return the kiss, "You don't need it but good luck anyways."

Reed leaves me on the side of the dance floor as I struggle to regulate my breathing. My lungs refuse to fill and my vision is a bit spotty. I walk towards a long table and lean against it. Once my vision has cleared I start to look around the room. At first I'm not really sure who or what I am looking for, but then I see her.

Standing by the entrance is Nat, her fiery red hair is pulled back into two thick braids that hang past her waist. She's turned away from me, showing off her open back gown. It is black satin and clings to her curves, her ass looks absolutely amazing. I sink down into my chair and grab a glass of the sparkling wine, downing it in one go, then I go back for another. If there is one thing that the earth realm knows how to do, it's wine.

I haven't spoken to Nat since we arrived, feeling too awkward to seek her out. I stare at her back from across the room, thinking of all the things I should say to her. *I'm sorry* for one. I acted completely out of hand back in the village, and none of it was her fault. She was only doing her job. For a second she stiffens up, almost like she could feel me watching her, but then Rian walks by quickly and she follows after him.

I watch as she leaves. Sighing, I down another glass of wine, but this time it seems to leave a bitter taste in my mouth.

Chapter 21

Mar

Reed escorts Eve onto the dance floor and I am left alone with Cay. Her fingers wrap around the ends of her braid, twirling them anxiously.

"Are you okay?" I ask her, raising my brows.

She gives me a quick smile, and snatches another glass of wine from a passing waiter. "Never better," she says, downing the whole thing. I've lost track of how many glasses she has had and the smallest bit of unease stirs inside me.

I open my mouth to press her further but Rian steps in between us, extending a hand to me. "Care to dance?" he asks politely.

I narrow my eyes at him but take his hand nonetheless, letting him guide me towards the dance floor. He pulls my body flush against his as we begin swaying to the music. I spy my sister and Reed laughing and twirling on the other side of the dance floor. A smile spreads across my lips and I let myself get lost in the music.

Rian isn't the best dance partner I've ever had but he's still far better than some of the others around us. A poor girl to my left keeps yelping as her partner tramples on her feet. The music swells and I am lifted off my feet and set back down gently.

A laugh escapes me and Rian leans forward to whisper in my ear, "You have no idea what that sound can do to a male."

I tilt my head, observing him. His look is serious yet his lips are turned up slightly in the corners, the smallest hint of a smile which is rare on his usually scornful face.

I lean forward, letting my lips brush his cheek, whispering back, "Enlighten me."

Rian swallows thickly, another crack in his harsh demeanor. The music slows and he pulls me forward again, fitting my chest to his. I can feel his racing heartbeat and the warmth of his skin through the thick fabric of his tunic. My ears catch on the sound of blood rushing through his veins and I feel a prick as my canines elongate.

"Careful there, wouldn't want to go all bloodthirsty in the middle of the dance floor now would we," Rian says with a chuckle. His hand glides up my back, tracing the path of my spine beneath my silk gown.

I watch him for a moment, considering my response. Rian has had a stick up his ass since we left Vulca. Yet in the odd moments like this one I feel like there might be something more to it. I just need to push the right buttons to get it out of him. Wrapping my arm around his neck, I lean forward, running my tongue up the side of his neck slowly. "I don't know. Does it count if we don't get caught?"

He freezes, missing a few of the dance steps and nearly getting us run over by another couple. Still, he recovers quickly, easily catching up to the music.

Okay, maybe he is a better dancer than I thought.

I laugh, "What's the matter? Worried about what others might think?"

Rian's hand slides back down, tightening on my waist, "No, but *you* should."

I cock my head, "When have I ever been known to give a damn about what other people think of me?"

199

Rian smirks, "You seem to care an awful lot about what *I* think of you."

"And what exactly led you to believe that?"

"Don't play coy. It doesn't suit you." He lifts me again and as soon as my feet are on the ground, I counter.

"Believe me, being coy isn't really my thing. Although if that's what you're into I'm sure I could find someone for you."

Rian yanks me forward and skates his teeth across my neck, making my pulse spike. "I've never been into the whole shy and innocent thing myself. I prefer someone who isn't afraid to take what they want."

I smirk, "Is that so? Well then Rian, tell me, what is it you think that I want?"

Rian's face goes hard, "It's not my place to know what you want."

"What is that supposed to mean?"

Rian dips me low then pulls me up quickly, making the room spin. "It means that I am your *guard*. My only responsibility is to protect you and your sister. *That* is what I am concerned about."

I snort. "Sure. Though, in case you haven't noticed, my sister is perfectly safe dancing around this very room and I am quite literally in your arms," I say glancing down at where our bodies are pressed against each other.

"That's not what I meant."

"By all means, explain it to me." I flash him a sinister smile and lean into his chest.

"Is that an order?" he asks, his voice huskier than usual.

"Does it need to be?" I answer.

"Fine. Mar," he says, my name sounding like a sin on his lips, "you want me to explain it to you?"

I nod, staring at his blue eyes that burn with an intensity I have never seen in them before.

"Let me make it perfectly clear. I am here for the sole purpose of protecting you, as is my duty. I never asked to be here, in fact I asked the opposite. Yet here I am, bound to do everything in my power to keep you safe, even when all I want to do is shut that mouth of yours up. To wrap my hand around your wrists, so that you can't move while I suck and lick that pretty throat of yours until you beg me to give you what it is you want."

I swallow hard. We stopped moving, standing at the center of the dance floor while couples spin and twirl all around us.

"You want to know what you truly want?" he asks, "you want to let go of all that control you cling on to so desperately and let someone else make the decisions for once. You want to feel teeth dig into that sensitive spot beneath your ear and suck down all that extra magic that you have no clue what to do with. You want to let go, relinquish the power for once. And for some fucking reason you seem to want me to be the one to take it."

My entire body burns from his words. One of his hands is digging into my hip, the other wrapped tightly around the back of my neck, holding me completely still. I breathe deeply, letting my lungs expand fully yet my words still come out breathless, "Then do it. If you're so sure that's what I want then what's stopping you?"

Rian's grip on my neck tightens and he tilts my head to the side. He places his lips right beneath my ear, in the exact spot he somehow knew existed. A shiver skates down my back. He breathes one word to me, "No." His hands drop away from my body and he takes a step back. My body feels cold from the loss of contact.

"No?"

Rian smirks, "No. You see, princess, you can't just get everything that you want all the time."

I stare dumbfounded at him as he turns to walk away. Shooting forward I grab his arm and turn him back to face me. Before he has a second to even think I wrap my arm around his neck and pull his face to mine. Our lips meet firmly against each other. For a second I think he is going to pull me closer but instead he pushes me away with a growl.

"We're done here," he says, turning to leave again.

"What's your problem?" I call after him.

Some of the couples have stopped dancing and are openly staring at us now. Fuck it, let them watch. I place my hands on my hips and raise my brows, waiting for an answer.

Rian glances around us at our new audience and walks back over to me, getting up in my face. "My problem is that you are my princess. So unless you are in some sort of danger at this precise moment. Drop it."

This time when he turns to walk away I let him. I stand there awkwardly at the center of the dance floor for a few moments before I regain my composure. Cutting through the crowds I make my way to the table where they are keeping the blood.

I grab a large glass and down it in one go. My head buzzes from the hit of magic but it quickly clears. Looking around the room I spot Rose chatting with a few members of her court I have yet to meet. Eve is by a table, staring very obviously at Nat, although she seems oblivious to the many stares she is getting herself. Cay is still standing on the edge of the dance floor, another glass of wine in her hands.

You know what, that's the right idea. Screw Rian and his mind games. Whatever crawled up his ass and made it's home there can stay for all I care. Moving over to the alcohol table I pick up a large glass of wine and take a sip. The bitter taste hits my mouth immediately and I have to fight the urge to spit it out. What the?

Sena wine is known for being sweet and delicious, whatever this was it was certainly not that. I leave the wine and grab a glass of something else. Without thinking too much about what it is I down it in one go. There is a lingering taste of magic that makes my whole body feel alive. Before I really know what I'm doing I am crossing the dance floor and joining in again, letting the many bodies move me to the rhythm.

I feel hands all over my body, running up and down my back, over the curve of my hip and even brushing across my ass occasionally. The music has changed to a more rhythmic tone that's perfect for grinding against someone. I let my body move naturally, my hands roaming over my body and into my loose hair.

Suddenly hands are grabbing me and I am pulled out of the crowd of people. Opening my eyes, not having realized they had closed, I stare into Rian's stern face.

"What the fuck was that?" he demands.

I glance back over my shoulder at the large group of bodies moving as one.

"It's called dancing. Haven't you heard of it?" I ask sarcastically.

Rian lends forward, invading my personal space yet again, "*That* was not dancing. That was barely a step removed from fucking some random male in front of half these people."

I snort, "If you consider that borderline fucking then I feel sorry for whatever poor girl ends up in your bed."

Rian grabs me, pulling me against his chest, "Keep that mouth of yours shut before I show you exactly what fucking me looks like."

Fire courses through my body and I fight to push it back. I struggle with my instincts for a moment before I give in. "Don't make promises you won't keep."

Rian tucks a strand of hair behind my ear before whispering into it, "It's not a matter of won't, sweetheart. If I had my choice I'd bend you over one of these chairs and fuck you right here while everyone watched."

I feel my body tense, my thighs pressing together involuntarily. Rian lets a single digit trace a line down my arm and back up. The sensation makes chills rise over my overly sensitive skin. "What's stopping you?" I ask breathlessly.

Rian shakes his head with a sigh, "More than I would care to admit. So please, do me a favor and keep the *dancing* to a minimum."

"That sounds like a challenge to me," I say with a smirk.

Rian laughs fully at that, "Trust me. It's the opposite. Now, go have fun with your friends or your sister or something, anything other than this."

I consider defying him for a moment but then I think of something even better. I nod my head and make my way back across the room to the bar, grabbing two more of the mystery drinks and dowing them in one go. I turn back to face Rian and shift, letting him see my canines extend as my senses heighten, listening for the reaction I want from him.

"Vana help me," Rian groans.

Chapter 22

Cay

The party is in full swing around me, music is playing, people are dancing, but I stand to the side. My head is fuzzy, too much wine has made my thoughts a little less coherent. My skin is hot, my face flush. Part of me knows that I should drink some water, maybe sit down for a bit, and definitely eat something. The other part of me, the part that is winning, knows that the moment my mind is clear I'll feel even worse.

When Terran walked in it was like all the air had evaporated from the room. His eyes landed on me immediately, almost like he already knew exactly where I was. My throat was already parched but when his hazel eyes met my own it felt like I had swallowed a jar of sand. I tried gulping down more wine but it only made me feel unsteady.

Luckily, Terran had been pulled away, leaving me to people-watch on my own from the side of the dance floor. Rian and Mar had looked ready to rip each other's clothes off; or heads, it really could have gone either way. I lost sight of the others a while ago but I can still hear Rose's bubbly laugh from somewhere across the dance floor.

I want to be out there, dancing with them and enjoying the party, but every time I move I feel a rush of dizziness. The crowd on the dance floor splits into two lines, gracefully going through the moves like they have all done it hundreds of times before. Knowing how Rose's kingdom loves to throw parties it wouldn't surprise me.

Watching the dancers twirl makes my head spin. I feel off balance even just standing here. I start to fall to the side but a hand steadies me.

"Cay, are you feeling alright?" asks a familiar voice from above me.

My head clears in an instant and my eyes snap to his face.

Deep bronze skin, perfectly styled chestnut curls, and warm hazel eyes that are so familiar it makes my heart ache. Terran is staring down at me, concern etched across his beautiful face. A million thoughts race through my head at once. From the last conversation we had, to the night before *it* happened, all of it rushes to me like a wave. My skin pricks with a nervousness that only he brings.

Clearing my throat I take a step back, out of the reach of his hand. "Yes, fine, just feeling a bit dizzy from watching all the dancers," I say with a smile.

Terran raises his brows at me, a subtle smile gracing his lips. "Is that so? Well, then I guess a dance is out of the question, isn't it?" His posture is preternaturally stiff, his shoulders tight with tension.

I fight back a grin at his suggestion. It wouldn't be the first time Terran had escorted me to the dance floor, although the last time was quite different. I flush at the reminder and his eyes widen slightly, almost like he knows exactly where my mind went.

He takes a step forward, grabbing my hand, "On second thought, I must insist. Dance with me." His hand dwarfs mine, the thick calluses scraping across my sensitive skin.

I nod silently, letting him guide me to the dance floor. Our hands fit together like they were made for it, perfectly positioned as we glide across the floor. I'm lost in him as he leads me through the movements. His eyes are locked on mine, searching for something in their depths. I stare back at the familiar greens and browns, a singular fleck of gold holding me captive. Terran's eyes are warm, comforting. I would spend hours just staring at those eyes.

Terran chuckles and I realize that he said something and here I am staring at him, like a complete fool. It never used to be like this, I could speak to him with ease, the words just flowed naturally. Now, I can hardly look at him without feeling like I might implode.

He's staring down at me, waiting for an answer.

I force a laugh, "Apologies, I was just a bit distracted."

Terran chuckles, "I could see that. What's on your mind?"

I try to look anywhere but at his face, a difficult feat when dancing. Someone bumps into me from behind and I am pushed forward, into Terran's arms. He steadies me, his large arm wraps around my waist gently as he turns us so he is in my place instead.

"Cay, if this is about what happened..." he trails off.

My face burns, "I- no. It's not"

Terran nods, looking over my head. He sighs deeply and leans his head forward, our foreheads almost pressed together. The scent of pine and rosemary invades my senses. The smell is so inherently Terran that for a moment I can do nothing but breathe it in.

"I feel like it is. You've been avoiding me since you arrived and you can hardly look me in the eyes." His voice is low, his words meant for my ears alone.

I bite the inside of my cheek, "I haven't been avoiding you."

He laughs, "No? Well, my mistake. I shouldn't assume such things."

I look up at him and he is giving me an expectant look. "Fine, maybe I was. But, not for the reasons you think," I say with a sigh.

"Oh? And what reason would that be then?" he asks.

I feel my cheeks flush and look away. His hand leaves my waist and cradles my cheek, turning my head to look at him. The rough calluses of his fingertips trace the lines of my face.

"I can't tell you how sorry I am for what I did," he says gently.

I blanch, "What? Sorry? Why would *you* be sorry?"

He lets out a deep sigh, pulling us off the dance floor and to the side. "You know why. Do I really need to say it?"

I fight to find the words, staring at him dumbfounded.

"Fine, Cay, I'm sorry because what I did was inexcusable. I can't blame you for avoiding me. For hating me." His face is contorted into one of barely restrained anguish.

"Terran…" I start but he cuts me off.

"No, please, just let me apologize. I should have never taken advantage of you like that. It was wrong and I understand if that changes things between us. I just want you to know that I am deeply sorry." He studies my face, watching as I process his words, my mouth hanging slightly open.

Out of all of the things I thought Terran might say to me, that was never one of them. At least not seriously. He continues before I can regain my composure.

"You had been drinking, you were upset. It was wrong of me to do what I did," he says, squeezing his eyes shut tightly.

I take a deep breath, letting it out slowly. "Terran, you didn't take advantage of me. I knew exactly what I was doing. I- I practically forced myself on *you*. I should be the one apologizing."

Terran's eyes snap to me, a war of emotions written on his face. "Don't. You and I both know you weren't at fault here. I hadn't had a sip to drink. You were…"

"I wasn't drunk, Terran. I knew what I wanted. What I *still* want."

His eyes shut as his body shudders, "Please, don't say things like that."

"Why?" I ask, my voice comes out huskier than I expect it to be.

He stares down at me with a hunger in his eyes, "Because if you tell me that I might do something bad again. I might do something that can't be undone." Terran's grip on me tightens.

My entire body heats with his words, my stomach tightens as my skin becomes sensitive even to the air. "What's stopping you?" I ask breathlessly. I know it's wrong. I shouldn't push like this. But when his arms are around me, our faces mere inches apart, I can't help but give in to the part of me that craves him. His mind. His laugh. His *touch*.

Terran curses under his breath.

I reach up and place my hand on his cheek as he stares down at me, his gaze searing. "Listen to me, you did nothing wrong. Nothing I didn't want." *Still want.*

His hand covers my own, pulling it away from his face. He lets it hang between us, not letting go. "Please don't try to make me feel like I'm not the bad guy here. I knew you were drunk. I crossed a line."

"What line? Because the only line I see is the one you are drawing yourself," I say.

He squeezes my hand, "I won't argue with you about this. What I did was wrong. I just wanted to apologize for my behavior."

I yank my hand from his, throwing them both up in the air, "Are you listening to me? I'm telling you that there is nothing to apologize for." The bitter haze of frustration invades my mind, clouding all the good emotions Terran brings out in me.

"Would you say the same if someone forced themselves on Eve, or on my sister?" he demands.

"That's entirely different."

"How? How is it any different?" His voice is hushed but his words are laced with pure frustration. *Yeah well the feeling is mutual.*

"Because you didn't force yourself! I-" I stop myself. My mouth slams shut so hard my teeth ache. My heart is racing.

We stand there in silence for a moment.

"I don't want to argue with you. I just want to try and make things right between us before-" he's cut off by one of his advisors calling him away. Some urgent matter that needs his immediate attention. He hesitates for a moment. His eyes roaming over every inch of me before a deep sigh escapes his full lips.

I watch as he walks away. He pauses for a moment longer, looking over his shoulder but then he is gone, lost in the sea of people.

My body relaxes as the adrenaline fades. Looking around the room I expect to see people staring our way but no one is looking. I am utterly invisible. I quickly make my way to the bar and grab another glass of wine, gulping it down. The moment it's empty I grab another, then another. I reach for one more but someone snatches it out of my hand.

Oliver downs the glass in one gulp and gives me a smirk. "Thanks for that. I was feeling rather parched."

My teeth grind together as I reach for a replacement. He snatches this one too, holding it above me and outside my reach.

"I think you've had enough," he says with a grin.

My head is fuzzy again, my body uneven on the ground. The entire room is spinning around me like I am still on the dance floor.

"Please do not throw up on me. I have this thing about vomit," Oliver says, staring down at me as my eyes glaze. His face is fuzzy. Well, all of him is fuzzy actually. Just a big blob. A laugh escapes my lips. "What's so funny?" he asks, his voice sounding far away.

I blink slowly. Oliver grabs my face in his hands and stares at me. "How much have you had to drink tonight?"

A giggle escapes me. Then another. Then another until it turns into full on laughter. I try to fight it but every time I stop another laugh bubbles up and I can't resist. My insides feel so warm. I am pulled away from the bar and to the corner of the room. A warmth spreads against my forehead and I realize it's Oliver's hand. "What- what- you…"

"Quiet. You should think twice before drinking so much that you can't even speak right," he says irritated.

"I can shpeak. I jus don wanna speak with you." I point a finger at him as I sway on my feet, my brain and mouth feeling full of cotton.

Oliver rolls his eyes, which I can now see clearly. Healing magic is washing over me but the fuzziness is still there, just less.

"Why?" I ask.

"Why what?" Oliver replies.

"Why are you he-helping me?" I say with a hiccup.

Oliver drops his hand, "Good question. Why am I helping you?"

I feel my legs start to give out and Oliver curses. He helps guide me to the ground, leaning me against the wall.

"Okay seriously, how much did you drink? That wine wasn't even strong," he asks with a groan of irritation.

I laugh but it comes out choked. My throat feels tight, like I am holding back tears but I don't feel them. I probably could cry, if I wanted to. But why would I want to cry? Oh right, Terran and his dumb honor. Hot liquid splashes against my cheeks.

"Are you crying?" Oliver asks, disgusted.

I shoot daggers at him with my glossy eyes. "No. Just leave me alone."

He laughs, squatting down in front of me, "Bot a chance. So, what did my perfect brother do to make you drink yourself stupid. Because you are, you know? Stupid that is. I mean, you would have to be to cry in front of me."

I don't bother responding. Instead, I focus on trying to clear my head. Oliver's healing helped but there is a sort of cloud around my mind. A fog so thick I don't know how to find my way out. My vision at least has cleared a bit. "What do you want, Oliver? Just leave me alone. Go find Mar or Eve, literally anyone else to terrorize," I say, fighting the hiccups.

"Easy. I want to know what is going on between you and my brother. Tell me that and I'll leave you alone."

I snort, "Not gonna happen. You might as well leave and enjoy the party."

His jaw tics and he looks over his shoulder. When he looks back his eyes shine with a wickedness I have never seen before. He grabs my hand, yanking me to my feet awkwardly, my dress getting caught beneath me.

"What are you doing, Oliver, just leave me alone," I say, the room around me spinning as the haze closes in again.

He smirks. "Not gonna happen." he says, mocking me, "let's go. You and I are going to dance."

I glance at the dance floor and people are spinning around, it makes me want to throw up immediately. I shake my head no but Oliver is already pulling me towards the dance floor. Once we're there he pulls my body against his and starts twirling us around. At first I just want to puke, then, the fuzziness turns into something else and I find myself actually having fun.

My body is burning up from the wine and the dancing, my skin almost as hot as Eve's and hers is practically on fire. I try to call on my water magic to cool myself but I can't seem to find it within me.

Oliver spins me around and my mind forgets all about getting cool, instead focusing on not throwing up again. Oliver pulls me close to him, our faces inches apart, "Now, how about you tell me what happened with my brother."

Chapter 23

Rose

My mind is in a million different places. I am swept away from the moment I enter the room. I am passed from person to person as they wish me a happy birthday, compliment my dress or the party, and ask me a hundred questions.

Thankfully, Oak pulls me away and towards the dance floor. We join in the crowd, twirling around the room and letting the music move through us. Music is a huge part of my realm, almost as much as earth itself. Where there is music, my people will dance.

My friends are scattered throughout the party mixed in among the blur of other guests as I spin until I can't see anymore. A sort of desperate ache to be by their side rises in me but being the guest of honor means entertaining all of the foreign dignitaries and addressing the larger court. This small reprieve on the dance floor is the only escape I have.

Oak eventually leaves me and her brother takes her place. He lifts me off the ground, spinning the both of us before setting me down on unsteady feet.

My cheeks ache from the constant smile plastered across my face. I needed this, I hadn't realized how much my heart had been aching. I had grown so used to the pain that I stopped realizing just how bad it hurt. I let myself become numb to the things that hurt me and the ways that I hurt myself. That is until now, until I felt what joy is supposed to feel like again. What it was like to do more than just go through the motions.

Music fills the entire room, magic courses through me like a drug. Everyone is laughing and drinking, there is just no room for pain, not anymore. I look around the room trying to find my friends again.

Mar is across the room at the bar talking with someone I don't recognize. Her dark skin is flawless against a soft yellow gown. The fabric wraps around the back of her neck and drapes beautifully down the front. As she turns to get another drink, I find the back completely open revealing a myriad of intricate swirls and designs inked onto her dark skin. The two of them lean against the bar casually, watching as the other party guests dance wildly. Whoever she is, she has found a friend in Mar tonight.

I take a break from the dance floor as I continue to let my gaze roam, searching, and find Cay dancing with Oliver which is very odd. I consider going over to rescue her but she throws her head back, loud laughter bursting from her mouth. The joy on her face is infectious, yet I am still surprised to see my brother crack a genuine smile for once, a deep dimple indenting his cheek. His eyes are bright and filled with a light that I haven't seen from him in years. Oak has vanished as per usual but it's Eve I am surprised not to find. I walk the edge of the room, peeking through gaps in the crowds trying to spot her.

A small group moves towards the bar and I see her. Eve is slumped in a chair way off in the corner of the room, swirling around a half empty glass of wine. I cross the room easily, people part for me as I approach.

"Get up," I say, looking down at Eve.

She glances up at me and gives me a pathetic smile. Hey gray eyes looking unusually dull.

214

"Oh no, not on my birthday. Today is a day for joy, for happiness, no *whatever* this is, allowed," I say, grabbing her hands and yanking her to her feet.

Eve groans, "I'm sorry. Really. I just- I'm not feeling in the partying mood at all."

My mouth drops open, "Clearly something is seriously wrong with you if that is true. The Eve I know would never turn down a chance to party."

She smiles at me, a sort of broken half smile. I look down at the table where she set her wine.

"I'm surprised there is anything left in that glass."

She shrugs, "Too bitter for my taste."

Bitter? Our wine is known to be exceptionally sweet. I call over a waiter and grab two glasses off his tray. I take a sip of the first glass then the second, the taste of fresh-berries greets my lips.

I extend a glass to Eve, "Here, this one isn't bitter. Drink up and let's go dance."

Eve takes the glass from me, downing it in one go. The moment her glass is empty she smiles at me, a real smile. Taking my hand she leads the way back towards the dance floor. The music has changed again, moving away from a slow waltz to something more upbeat, like Eve listens to back in Vulca.

Raising my brows at her I nod my head to the musicians, "You wouldn't happen to know anything about this change in tune would you?"

Eve flashes me a bright smile and shrugs her shoulders innocently.

We quickly make our way to the center of the dance floor. Moving with the rhythmic music, swaying our hips and letting our hands roam over our bodies. Eve's curves are obvious in her dark gown, mine are somewhat hidden beneath all the layers of tulle. Yet when I look around the room I find many eyes locked on my movements, how my hands skim over my thighs and waist. I can only imagine what my mother is thinking right now. But it's my birthday so she will most certainly wait to reprimand me.

I let the music fill me, leading me through a dance that I didn't realize I knew. Eve is lost in the music too. Her eyes are closed and she spins around, her hands tangled in her hair. She opens her eyes and extends her hand to me, taking it and spinning us in a wide circle. People around us jump to get out of the way. We keep spinning until we stumble, a bit dizzy. I quickly right myself but Eve struggles. She tries to stand upright but doesn't quite make it. Stepping forward I steady her. "Are you okay?"

She's holding her eyes tightly closed, her breath is coming out erratic. "Yes," she gasps, "I'm fine, just need a second. Must be the wine."

I have seen Eve drink more than I thought possible and then proceed to do cartwheels down the hall, all while singing at the top of her lungs. She never missed a beat.

"Are you sure? Should I get Mar?"

Eve waves her hand in front of her face, "Yeah, promise. Just one too many spins."

I look around the room but everyone else seems to have gone back to what they were doing. Mar is still by the bar, the mystery woman no longer beside her. I try to catch her eye but she is in the process of shooting daggers at Rian from halfway across the room. I hope to never be on the receiving end of that stare.

A hand wraps around my own and I turn to find Eve, upright and smiling. "Come on, the night is still young and you, birthday girl, have lots to do," she says mischievously.

I let her pull me away from the dance floor and towards a cluster of advisors. One second her hand is tugging me forward and the next it is tugging me down. Eve collapses in front of me, folding in on herself quicker than I can react. I try to catch her as she falls but she slips right through my arms.

Only Oak is there. My cousin wraps her arms around Eve's waist and tugs her up a moment before she can hit the ground.

I help grab Eve and pull her to the side, setting her down in a chair.

Mar appears beside us in an instant. "What happened?" she demands.

I shake my head, unsure what to say.

"She collapsed. I was watching them dance when I noticed Eve struggling," Oak answers.

I stare at my cousin, "Why were you watching us dance?"

"Because, this isn't the first time Eve has collapsed since she arrived. I was just keeping an eye on her to make sure nothing happened. Clearly I was right to do so."

Mar whirls on Oak, "What do you mean this wasn't the first time? Eve hasn't mentioned anything to me."

"Me either," I add.

"She didn't say anything to me either, technically. Reed says he found her passed out in the training room. She told me it was nothing, that he was overreacting. I let it go back then but I knew she was lying. She's barely touched her food since she got here and I'm pretty sure she hasn't *fed* either," Oak says as she tries to coax Eve to open her eyes.

"You noticed all that?" I ask, a bit surprised.

"Of course," Oak says it like it's obvious.

"So, you didn't think to inform me that my sister has been passing out around the castle?" Mar challenges.

"It wasn't my place to. Eve is grown, if she wanted you to know, you would have."

Mar's expression turns deadly, "What the fuck is that supposed to mean?"

Oak sighs, looking up at Mar, "All I meant is that Eve is fully capable of taking care of herself and that clearly she didn't want *any* of us to know."

"Clearly she can't, not when she has collapsed on multiple occasions and not just here," Mar whispers angrily.

"Wait, what? This has happened before?" I ask, confused. This entire conversation gives me whiplash. Fear for Eve gets muddled with the frustration of more secrets from my cousin.

Mar lets out a long breath, "Yes. I found her passed out back home a few months ago. She gave me some excuse and I didn't really think anything of it. I had no idea it was still happening."

Eve groans, her head rolling as she starts to wake.

"Listen, whatever this is. We need to be supportive, so can the two of you please stop arguing for two seconds so that we can help Eve?" I ask pointedly. Eve groans and my head snaps to her, watching her intently.

Oak and Mar stare each other down for a moment before nodding. We all circle around Eve as her eyes blink open and refocus.

"Hey, what happened?" she asks groggily.

"You passed out," Oak answers.

"Again," Mar emphasizes.

I roll my eyes at the two of them. "Eve, what's going on? What aren't you telling us?"

Eve sighs, "Nothing, okay. It's not a big deal."

Mar laughs mirthlessly, "Yeah, not going to cut it this time. We deserve the truth."

Eve narrows her eyes at her sister. "Fine, you want to know the truth. The truth is I haven't fed in too long, my magic is almost entirely depleted, and it's making me have these little episodes. Happy?"

Mar throws her hands up, "Are you serious right now? Really? Out of all the things?"

I place my hand on her shoulder, silencing her. "Eve, you really shouldn't do that. It's not healthy. You could seriously hurt yourself." Letting your magic get too low can be seriously dangerous, even deadly if it gets bad enough.

"If you need us to find someone to feed off of, we can make that happen," Oak offers, already looking around the room like someone will simply materialize and strip down at a moment's notice. Though given Eve's succubus nature, that might hold some validity.

Eve cuts her a glare, "No. I refuse to feed off of someone unwilling just because I'm running a little low on magic at the moment." Her face is set with determination.

Mar rolls her eyes, "We've been over this a hundred times. They *are* willing. Just as willing as the people who donate blood for vampires. You know this, why are you being so stubborn?"

Eve shakes her head, "They aren't, not really. Agreeing to let me suck out their happiness, their joy, their passion, all to make enough money to live? That's not right. I won't do it."

I grab Eve's hand, squeezing it, "Eve these people, they volunteer to do these things. We all know that you need this just as much as Mar needs blood. It's nothing to be ashamed of."

"I'm not ashamed. I'm a succubus, it's my nature to crave these things. To seek out the positive emotions and let them feed my magic. I have no problem doing so with willing participants. But no, I won't do it just because someone is getting paid to, it's not really their choice at that point."

This isn't the first time we have heard this argument from Eve but still, I never thought she would let things get to this point out of pure stubbornness or some skewed sense of right and wrong.

"Fine," Oak says, stepping in front of Eve, "then feed off of me. Take my emotions. I'm as willing as it can get."

"Absolutely not," Eve says in complete disgust.

"I'm going to try to not be offended by that reaction just now," Oak says quietly.

"I'm sorry, but there is just no way that I am going to feed off of you, Oak, off of any of you," Eve says, fixing us all with a determined look. She sighs, "Look, I can't take away the happiness from any of you, not knowing what you could feel in the aftermath."

I glance around the room, trying to find Cay so that she can hopefully talk some sense into her but she has vanished from view. Something about that makes the anxiety bubble up inside of me but I can't focus on that now.

Eve pushes up from her chair and starts to walk forward but she stumbles again. She takes another step but immediately collapses again. This time Mar and Oak both catch her, gently placing her back in her chair.

"Let's just take her back to her room, start a fire and hopefully that will get her magic juiced up some. Then maybe she can stay conscious long enough for us to convince her to feed for real," Oak suggests.

Mar nods, looking around the room, eyebrows creased. The two of them move to grab Eve and haul her to her feet. Oak is almost a full foot shorter than Mar which makes it a bit awkward but they manage to get a solid grip on Eve.

"I'm going to try and find Cay and we'll meet you in her room." I say continuing to look around the room.

"No, it's your birthday, you should stay and enjoy yourself. Let us take care of Eve," Oak says.

Mar nods her head in agreement, still looking around the room, searching for something or someone.

"There is no way I'm just going to go back to the party and pretend like one of my best friends isn't currently in need of a major intervention," I say. Just the idea of abandoning my girls for some party has nausea stirring inside me. When something happens to one of us, we're *all* going to be there for each other. I won't let any of them suffer alone, not again.

The two share a look. Oak seems to give in first, letting out a low curse. "Fine, but don't make it too obvious. Your mother will kill all of us if she realizes you are ditching your own party."

I nod and watch as the two of them carry Eve from the room. Now, looking around at the dense crowd, I begin my search for Cay.

Chapter 24

Mar

I want to kill my sister.

Eve has always been reckless, especially when we were younger. She would dare me to do things she knew would get us in trouble, egging me on and testing the limits of our father. I never questioned it, or her. She was my big sister, I trusted that she knew what she was doing, what she was getting the two of us into.

Now, it has become abundantly clear that she has absolutely no fucking clue what she is doing. I carry most of her weight as Oak helps guide us through the halls and back towards Eve's rooms. She's still passed out, although occasionally she'll mumble something under her breath and we pause to listen. It's not exactly words but it seems like she is trying.

We turn down the last hall that leads to her room and Nat nearly runs into us.

"Oh sorry, I didn't see- is that Eve? What's wrong with her?" she asks startled, her voice thick with concern.

Oak looks at me, waiting to see what I will say.

Good, she's learning.

When it comes to my sister I will never back down. Especially not when her safety is on the line.

"It seems my darling older sister has been refusing to feed for Vana knows how long," I say, shifting more of Eve's weight to my back.

Nat looks between us, her mouth left slightly agape. To her credit, she regains composure quickly. Snapping her mouth shut and pulling herself together, stepping into her role as a guard in a moment. "I am here to help however I can, princess, just tell me what to do," Nat says. Her eyes are firmly locked on the limp noodle that is my sister.

Oak snorts and gives me a grin as I fight with the urge to roll my eyes.

"You can start by dropping the whole princess thing. Mar will be just fine. Besides, it seems you've already taken to calling your future Queen by her name, why would I be any different," I say, letting the insinuation hang in the air. Eve might hate me for it later but what kind of sister would I be if I didn't tease her crush just a little.

Nat blushes but otherwise shows no response, waiting for my orders, I realize.

"Fine, can you help me carry her? Oak is a bit too short to really be of much help," I offer.

"Excuse me, who was it that caught her when she fell? Oh right, me. Plus, I could easily carry her myself if you would just let me," Oak argues, tugging more of Eve's weight her way.

"Eve is *my* sister. If anyone is going to take care of her it should be me."

Oak scoffs, "No one here is saying otherwise. I'm just saying that if you would stop being so unbelievably stubborn for five minutes, maybe Eve would actually ask for your help."

I tug Eve back towards me, "So, we're back to this are we? Why is it that things are always my fault with you, Oak? For once can you take some damn responsibility for your actions." It's not unusual for Oak and I to butt heads, our personalities just different enough to instigate things. But for some reason this trip feels different, like Oak has already pushed me away and this time she might never let me back in.

"Oh no, don't go trying to make this about me. These are your issues, not mine. I have no problem owning up to my actions." Oak's green eyes flash with a hint of her magic, the power stirring just beneath the surface.

I roll my eyes, "Give me a break. If that were true then why did you lie about meeting up with us. Why are you keeping secrets from literally everyone, huh? Explain that then. You're supposed to be our friend." I can't help the hurt that creeps into my voice.

"Um…" Nat says between us.

"Stay out of this," Oak barks.

"Don't tell my guard what to do," I bite.

"Righhht, so now you're a princess again. You know, since it's convenient for you." Oak scoffs.

Eve is stirring between us, her mumbles becoming louder, but still as incoherent.

"Excuse me?" I say.

Oak rolls her eyes, "Give me a break, Mar. I've known you almost my entire life and you have never once cared to act like the princess that you are. No, instead, you use Eve as an excuse to play heir whenever it pleases you. But you and I both know that when that time comes, Eve is going to be the one sitting on the throne, not you."

It takes me a minute to process Oak's words. To take in their meaning and really break it down. She thinks I want Eve's throne. That I would be so cruel as to steal it from my own sister. "Is that what you think I've been doing?" I ask with barely restrained fury.

"It's not about what I think. It's about what I know," Oak says dryly.

My eyes flick to Nat who is solely focused on Eve's limp body between us.

"And how exactly do you *know* this?" I ask pointedly.

Oak stares into my eyes, "I think you already know the answer to that question."

"Enough," Nat yells, "Eve is currently unconscious and clearly needs our help. So either get over yourselves and take care of her or let me."

Oak and I stare each other down.

"For Vana's sake," Nat says, stepping forward and scooping Eve up into her arms with ease, "leave. I've got this."

We both hesitate and Nat sighs. "Look, I've got her, okay? Now go work out whatever it is that's got the two of you looking like you're ready to murder one another. Aren't you supposed to be friends?"

With that, Nat turns back down the hall with Eve, disappearing into her room. Oak and I stand in the hallway for a moment before I turn to leave. I'm trying to keep my steps even but my blood is pounding with a rage that is demanding to be set free. Small flames lick at my fingertips from magic slipping past my control. I can hear a constant screaming in my head and my hands keep clenching involuntarily, making the flames stronger.

"Mar..." Oak starts.

I hold up a hand, silencing her. I keep walking until we are close enough to hear the roar of the party and then pull her to the side into an alcove. "Look, I don't know what it is that Eve told you but I'm not trying to take her crown," I say quickly, the words tumbling from my lips.

Oak sighs, running a hand through her dyed green hair. "I know that. I didn't mean what I said, I was just... angry. And for the record, Eve knows that too. All she mentioned was that you've been going to some meetings in her place or something like that."

I snort, "Yeah, because *Eve* keeps ditching said meetings and begging me to cover for her."

Oak's expression is one of clarity and maybe a bit of frustration. "Well. Yeah that um, that sounds like Eve alright."

The two of us sit there in silence for a few moments before I feel the anger ease from my body slowly.

"Look, I didn't mean the things that I said. I'm just frustrated with so many things and I'm on edge. I feel like I'm constantly at war with someone or something," Oak says on an exhale.

I nod, "I know what you mean. I love my sister, don't get me wrong, and I actually enjoy attending these meetings. But I also know that every time I let it happen I am enabling her to do it again. I'm telling her that it's okay, and if she is serious about one day ruling she needs to start stepping up. A lot has been going on and I'm not sure she even knows the beginnings of it."

"Yeah, same here. There are so many things that I wish I could say but *can't*. I hate keeping secrets but these aren't things that you just tell someone out of nowhere," Oak says despondently, her eyes haunted.

I look at how much regret and despair is written all over her face. Oak rarely shows so much emotion, especially with me. "Why can't you say something? Share that burden with someone?" Maybe if she told me what is going on I could help, or at the very least understand her better. Lately it feels like I don't even really know Oak.

She sighs, "It's not that easy. Rose, she's too innocent for some of the things going on out there, it would be too much for her."

I smile, thinking about Rose and her light smile, her hazel eyes bright and shining. Her soul is still so pure, untainted by the horrors that wait just outside these castle walls.

"That could be true. Or," I say drawing out the word, "you could think of her as the grown up woman she is. Rose is strong. Stronger than any of us have even begun to realize. Don't you owe it to her, as her family and her friend, to tell her the truth? Regardless of if it might hurt."

Oak smiles slightly, "Yeah I guess you're right. Maybe it's time that I start telling her the truth about the crazy shit going on out there." A shudder rolls through her and I can't begin to imagine what is running through her head.

"Ditto," I echo, "There's been attacks all across the border back home. Villagers who live on the outskirts of the kingdom, outside of the protection of the volcano. My father has been sending more and more troops out to help but they can't figure out who's responsible." It's a risk, talking so openly about court business, one that I really shouldn't be taking but in the end I know I can trust Oak with this as much as I can trust her with my life.

"Seriously? That's insane. What kind of attacks are they?" Oak seems shocked, but not as shocked as I expected.

"I'm not sure exactly. My father didn't want me to see, he said they were too disturbing." I answer with a shudder.

The two of us let the silence stretch on for a moment. I start to ask what is happening in Sena but a crash outside the alcove interrupts me. Oak springs into action and I follow her back into the hall.

"What the…" I watch Oliver drag a giggling Cay down the hallway.

"Oliver, what in Vana's name did you do to her?" Oak demands in a whispered scream.

"Why is it that you assume *I* am responsible for this?" Oliver spits back.

Oak raises her brows and Oliver looks to me for help but quickly finds I am waiting for the same answer.

"I didn't do anything to her. She did it to herself," he says angrily.

Oak crosses her arms over her chest, clearly not buying it. Looking at my friend as she half rolls around on the floor, her fingers playing with the end of her braid, I am starting to think I know what is going on.

"Is she drunk?" I ask, shock evident in my voice.

Oliver gives me a mock smile, "Geniuses, truly. Yes, she is drunk! Look at her. The damn girl practically drank all of the wine at the party. Would have kept drinking if I hadn't stepped in."

Oak narrows her eyes, "Why? What made you step in."

Oliver rolls his eyes. "The why doesn't matter. But you," he says looking at me, "should take her back to her rooms before she does anything *else* exceedingly stupid."

Oak looks between us, "Why just her?"

Oliver looks at his cousin grimly, "Because, You and I are needed in the high lady's chambers. Immediately."

Chapter 25

Rose

I do another lap around the room, searching for Cay among the crowds of people. The last I saw her she had been on the dance floor with Oliver, but knowing her she would have already found a way to escape my brother. I spot Terran on the far side of the room talking to a few of our advisors. I begin weaving through people as I walk towards him, the closer I get the more clear it becomes that they aren't talking, Terran is *yelling*. Terran never yells.

He is always the perfect picture of composure yet in this moment he looks ready to rip someone's head off. As I approach, I catch the end of what he is saying.

"I don't care what you have to do, just get someone there, immediately," he shouts.

I step beside him, placing my hand on his shoulder. His head whips to mine angrily but the moment our eyes meet he softens.

"Rose, I hope you are enjoying your birthday," he says with a forced smile.

"Terran what's going on?" I look between him and the advisors.

They shuffle away, not too far but enough to give us privacy.

"Nothing, just something that needs to be taken care of, that's all."

My eyes roam over him. His hair is a mess, his curls frizzy from running his hands over them. He has shadows under his eyes that weren't there when we first entered the party. I'm not sure I have ever seen him look quite like this. Utterly disheveled. "I know there's more to it. Just tell me," I say adamantly.

"Have you seen Cay lately?" he asks suddenly.

Taken aback, I don't respond at first. His eyes roam across the room, looking straight past me as if I don't even exist.

"Um, no, I was actually coming to find you to ask you the same thing."

His eyes shoot back to mine, "what do you mean?"

I consider telling him about Eve. He could probably help, he would know what to do about this sort of situation. He always knows what to do. But Eve would be so angry with me, and Oak would probably yell at me later too for worrying him. Besides, Cay is the priority right now.

"Nothing, I'm just looking for her, that's all," I say with a shrug, trying to remain casual.

An advisor steps forward, "My lord, you are needed in the high lady's chambers, she has been waiting for you. I must insist that we depart at once."

Terran runs his hand over his hair again, disrupting the curls further. He sighs deeply, "Fine, let's go. Rose, do me a favor and go find Cay."

"Why do you want me to look for Cay? Tell me what's going on," I demand.

The advisors are growing irritated, clearly not happy about my holding my brother here any longer. "Sir, we really must leave." Their eyes flick between the two of us anxiously.

"Just give me a damn second to talk to my sister," he bites.

My eyes widen at his uncharacteristic outburst. They all take a step back in unison. Terran moves us a step further away from them and leans forward.

"There's nothing you need to worry about, just enjoy your party. Dance, drink, have fun with your friends. You deserve it," he says, smiling sadly.

I narrow my eyes at him, "Why are you lying to me? What's going on that is so bad you won't tell me?"

Terran just shakes his head.

"I knew it. Tell me, right now." I hold my ground, refusing to be kept in the dark yet again.

"We must go, *now*," the advisor says again, his voice much firmer. This time, Terran nods and starts to follow after them. So I do the same.

The advisors hesitate for a moment so my brother turns to me. "What are you doing, Rose? It's your birthday, you should stay at your party. You're the guest of honor after all."

"If you think I'm just going to ignore whatever the hell is going on and go dance around the ballroom then you must not know me at all." I raise my brows at him.

He stares at me for a moment before seeming to give up, he nods his head and I follow after him.

My mother's chambers are on the opposite end of the castle than the ballroom, a security feature my father had insisted upon after they were mated. The entire walk there my heart is racing, I can hear it pounding in my ears. No one speaks as we walk through the corridors. Halfway there, guards join us and form a tight circle around us, causing my heart rate to spike.

The grand doors to my mother's chambers come into view, surrounded by guards. They are lined up along the walls, down the hall and it seems like there are even more inside. A lump forms in my throat that is impossible to swallow down. The last time I saw this many guards was outside my parent's room right after my father died. My mother locked herself away for weeks, silently grieving and leaving my brothers and I to deal with the repercussions of losing our leader. Then, she emerged stronger than ever, like it never even happened.

"Terran…" I say hesitantly.

He looks down at me from my side and takes my hand in his, giving it a tight squeeze before releasing it.

A pair of guards move to open the door as we approach, my brother follows the advisors inside and I slip in behind him. The moment we enter the room we are thrown into chaos. Guards and advisors are shouting at one another. Dozens of people are in the room crowding around tables and chairs with countless maps and scrolls laid out upon them.

My brother crosses the room straight to where our mother is staring down at a table. She is still wearing her gown from the party but her hair is a mess, much like my brother's. I follow Terran and find that Oak and Oliver are both already there.

Oak is staring at a group of guards as they all talk over one another. Her face is devoid of all emotion, her eyes almost glossed over as she is lost deep in thought. Oliver's face is a mask of barely restrained anger. I feel waves of power emanate from him as I approach. I draw up short as I feel the strength of his magic, meanwhile he barely acknowledges my presence.

Terran goes straight to our mother, taking her hand and whispering something in her ear, she nods and he lets out a deep breath. His eyes flick back to me for a moment before they resume their whispering, far too low even for my enhanced hearing to pick up.

"Can someone tell me what in Vana's name is going on?" I ask no one in particular.

Silence is my response. Oak doesn't even look at me and Oliver just stares, his silence speaking volumes about the gravity of the situation. I'm a moment away from asking again when my mother finally answers.

"Rose, darling, there has been an attack," she says grimly. She refuses to look at me, her eyes glued to some document placed in front of her.

I look between my family, waiting for an explanation. "What do you mean there has been an attack? An attack on who? Where?"

Oliver stands and stares at me, "The city."

"*What* city?" I demand. My heart is in my throat, icy fear washing over me.

"Atran," Oliver confirms.

With that one word a thousand thoughts run through my mind.

Rayan is under attack; Cay's *home* is under attack. I can barely acknowledge them as they pass through my head, one after another after another. I try to pick the most important but they come so quickly that I can barely discern one from the next. "The Queen and King?" I ask, voice shaky.

Oliver sits back down so I turn to my mother, she shakes her head.

"We aren't sure. The reports we have received are difficult to understand. We aren't even sure who it is that is attacking. Hundreds of people are fleeing the city as we speak. Everything is complete and utter chaos, " Terran answers from behind me.

I turn to face him, "How can that be? How do we *not* know? Surely someone has eyes on their *King and Queen*."

Terran takes a step forward grabbing my hand. "It takes time. There are a lot of things we won't know for a while. Our men on the borders were able to get word sent to us as soon as they became aware but they have a job to do."

I pull my hand from his, "What do you mean?"

"He means that our men have been ordered to stay where they are," Oliver bites from his chair.

"What? Our men should be out there, helping them. Whose orders are they following?" My voice rises with indignation and alarm.

"Mine," my mother answers from her desk. She's sitting now, a glass of something in her hands, steam billows over the rim as she gently raises it to her lips.

I stare at her in shock while Oliver snorts a derisive laugh.

"The high lady had to make a difficult decision to do what is best for everyone," Terran offers. His jaw is locked, his teeth pressing together tightly as he forces himself to remain composed.

I shake my head turning to look at him, "How can that be *best* for anyone? We have to help them. We should be helping them. What about all those people?"

"The castle walls are strong, they will hold. Besides, our reports have shown no progress into Tepis itself. Rayan has a strong army. I have trained with them myself. Our focus should be elsewhere," Terran says, looking away from me and at the ceiling.

I turn back to my mother. "Rayan are our allies, for what reason would we possibly abandon them in their time of need?"

"Rayan isn't the only city being attacked. We have heard reports that something is also happening in Eteri, possibly as far as Vulca. We must anticipate that something is coming for our home as well," my mother replies simply, like it makes perfect sense. She waves her hands and a guard appears with a small vial of something that she downs in one long swig.

"So we ignore the real threat to protect against something that *might* or *might not* happen? What about Eteri? Vulca? Are we really just going to sit here and do nothing while my friends' homes are being destroyed?" I ask, trying to hold back the anger in my voice.

"No, we wait. And only when we are sure it is safe to do so will we consider sending assistance elsewhere. If we were to send our troops away and then find ourselves facing a similar attack, we would be defenseless, it's too risky," she says, like it's the most obvious thing in the world. As if I'm acting silly or childish for not understanding her decision to abandon these people.

I look around the room at all the people talking, planning. But none of them are doing anything. Not taking any real action at all. I think about Eve, she is already so weak. Mar has so much on her plate taking care of everyone else. Cay's family could be in serious danger. I look at my own but they're all avoiding my gaze. I step in front of Terran, forcing him to look me in the eyes. "And you're okay with this? Do you agree with this decision?" I challenge him.

"I agree with the decision of our high lady to protect our people. It is our duty to ensure they are safe, first and foremost," he answers, looking me straight in the eyes.

I stare my brother down, "Does Cay know?"

It's Oliver that answers, "She is in no state to handle this right now."

I whirl on him, "What did you do?"

Oak snorts.

Oliver throws his hands up, "Why is it that I am constantly being accused of things for which I am completely innocent. If you must know, your friend decided to drink herself stupid this evening and is now most likely curled up in bed next to a bucket. That or she is off throwing herself at whoever happens to be walking by," he adds the last part under his breath.

Note to self, talk to Cay about drinking habits. Although I am curious as to what he meant by that last comment.

"It is also not our place to inform her of this," Terran adds with a sigh.

I blanch, "*Not our place?* Do you all hear yourselves right now? Cay is the *heir* to the Rayan throne; if her kingdom is under attack she is the *first* person who should know."

Oliver murmurs something that sounds an awful lot like agreement.

"What's our next move?" Oak says, the first thing I have heard from her since I arrived. She's standing now, looking only at my mother. At this moment I want nothing more than to grab her by the shoulders and shake her till she sees reason.

"For now we wait. Rose, you should head back to the party, let us worry about all this," my mother says with a casual smile.

"Fuck that," I say turning to leave. If they won't tell Cay then I will. There is no way I am keeping something like this from her. Even if she wasn't the heir, she is still my best friend. I reach for the door but it is yanked open.

A guard rushes in, out of breath.

Terran pushes past me immediately, going straight to him.

"News from the border..." he says out of breath, "the castle walls have fallen, the tunnels breached."

The world stops moving.

"They have entered the city, Tepis is under attack."

Chapter 26

Cay

Darkness envelops me like a long-awaited hug. My body feels hot, yet cold at the same time, there is a faint buzzing in my head. A feminine voice is talking to me, light and airy, almost like the words are whispered on a gust of wind. I can't make out what the voice is saying but it is oddly comforting. Hearing it makes my body relax, like it knows I am safe. I let that voice seep into my flesh and bones, filling the cracks and smoothing the rough edges. Seeking out every imperfection and invading the space, filling it with a song that I can hear almost as clearly as the voice itself.

My eyes are shut but the faintest hint of light can be seen through my closed lids. My body is oddly numb, like every sensation has been dulled. Something gently shakes me but I try to resist it, focusing instead on the lyrical voice, on the song in my bones. This voice is important, more important than everything else. The world could fall apart but so long as this voice was here in my mind I would welcome it. Some part of me knows if I open my eyes she will be gone and I can't bear that thought. I wish I could stay here, in this darkness with the voice, just listening to the words until I can make sense of them. The voice continues speaking in that singsong way, the same familiar yet impossible tune over and over again.

Hands grab me, touching all over my face, pressing against my forehead and against my heated cheeks. They feel more real now; like whatever is dampening my senses is fading and touch is beginning to surface. The most sensitive brush of skin against me sends painful pins and needles shooting in its wake. A chill runs over my body, followed by a scorching heat that has my throat drying up. I try to swallow but my throat feels like it has forgotten what it feels like to drink water, like swallowing sand.

Frustrated, I dive deeper into the darkness, into the voice's waiting embrace. Then, I hear it and it makes sense. It's one word, but more than that it's a name. A name both familiar and foreign. The shape of it rolls around in my mouth before dripping off the tip of my tongue. The sound of the name penetrates the haze in my mind and sends sharp pain shooting throughout my body, making me gasp.

I sit upright involuntarily, my eyes fly open and search my surroundings. I am in a dimly lit room, lying on a plush bed covered in blankets and still dressed in my gown. Everything is fuzzy, like my thoughts have been placed inside a jar and shaken around. A giggle bubbles up in my throat before I can stop it. I look at my tingling hands, running them over my bare arms. My skin is oversensitive, my own touch tickling to the point that I can't fight back the burst of laughter that escapes me.

A blond girl appears in a doorway, she rushes over to me the moment I make a sound. She crouches down beside me on the bed, looking me over from head to toe. "Hey, how're you feeling?" she asks, placing her palm on my forehead.

I lean into her hand. "I feel wonderful," I say with a hiccup.

The girl chuckles, pushing me back gently so that I am leaning against the pillows and not her hand. "Yeah? I'm glad. You had me worried there for a second. You passed out as soon as you hit the bed and then started to shiver like crazy. Your whole body felt like ice."

No, that doesn't make sense. I look down at myself and throw the blankets off. Standing up and pacing, "I'm hot. Burning, my skin is burning."

"Cay? Are you sure you're alright?" the girl asks. She's familiar, her voice and worried expression pricks at something in my memory.

"Who are you?" I say tilting my head.

"Geez, Oliver wasn't kidding, how much did you drink? I'm Mar, remember?" Mar says, raising her hands out in front of her slowly, as if not to startle me.

I look at her hands and then my own. My skin feels too hot, itchy beneath the heavy gown. Looking around the room I spot the doorway Mar came out of. I rush over to it, pushing the door open as wide as it will go. Inside is a glorious white tub, filled to the brim with frothy water.

Running forward I grip the edge of the tub and hoist myself inside. I hear a curse from somewhere behind me as I let my head slip under the water. Bubbles start to form around my legs and then they are gone. My legs fuse together into one, large, beautiful tail covered in turquoise scales. The same shade as my eyes.

Hands grip beneath my arms and pull my head above the water.

I squirt out a little stream of water from my mouth before descending into another fit of giggles.

"Cay, do you think that now is really the best time for a bath?" Mar asks, her arms dripping wet and the front of her gown soaked, the fabric clinging to her.

I giggle some more, sinking down until my nose is just barely above the water. Shifting around I free my tail from where it is stuck beneath me and let the end flop over the rim. My dress covers most of my scales, frustrating me. I yank at the fabric, trying to pull it off. It's heavy, the water saturating the fabric and weighing it down.

"See, this is why we don't take baths fully clothed," Mar says with a sigh, stepping forward to help pull at the heavy fabric. It takes a great deal of wiggling but she is able to yank the fabric up and over my head, plopping it in a sopping heap next to the tub.

The water soothes my scorching skin, as the ache eases I begin to hum the same tune the voice had whispered to me. Not that any of it makes any sense, only that name. I stop humming, sitting up a bit in the tub.

"What?" Mar asks, confused.

"I forget," I answer, wistfully.

"Forget what? The entire evening? Because honestly that wouldn't exactly surprise me given the fact you are currently sitting in a bathtub full tail and tits out," Mar says sitting with her back against the tub.

"The name. She told me the name but I forgot it already. Why can't I remember?"

Mar looks over her shoulder at me, "Remember a name? I mean it's not that uncommon really. Eve forgets everyone's name within 30 seconds of meeting them."

I sink back down into the tub, water sloshes over the side and soaks Mar further if her curses are any indication. "I heard a voice. It was trying to tell me something, only I couldn't understand it. Just the name."

"I wouldn't read too much into it. I have some crazy dreams myself even without drinking an insane amount of wine. Which reminds me, what exactly possessed you to drink so much? Was the wine really that good?" Mar asks in disbelief.

I shake my head, "The wine was bitter. Not good."

"If the wine didn't taste good then why did you keep drinking it?" she presses.

The water is helping clear some of the fog in my brain, the haze that was making everything so difficult to understand. But with this understanding comes the rush of embarrassment that I was so desperately trying to avoid. A groan escapes me as I cover my face with my palms.

Mar looks at me, sighing and moving so she is sitting behind my head. She starts the process of undoing my hair, meticulously finding and removing the pearl pins I had placed earlier. We sit there in silence as she lets the braid loose and then picks up a comb, starting at the ends and working her way to the top. I let the feeling of her hands in my hair ease the anxiety bubbling up in my stomach.

I take a deep breath, letting it out slowly, "I kissed Terran."

Mar's hands still in my hair, I pause for her response but she doesn't say anything so I continue.

"It was a year ago. He came to check on me after everything happened with the sirens. I didn't want him to but he insisted. At first he would just sit outside my door, talking to me about anything and everything. Eventually I felt bad so I opened the door. But he didn't come inside, he just sat in the doorway, leaning up against the frame," I say, the image surfacing in my mind like I'm still there, curled up on my bed and watching him watch me. Our eyes locked together as we shared things with each other that we've never shared before.

"He told me about his own struggles. How he feels unsure of himself every day. But this was Terran, Mar. Terran who's always had it together. Who always knows what to do or say. Yet he looked at me and shared his deepest concerns, his fears. He didn't have to do that. I even told him so to his face," I say ardently.

"Truthfully, I was actually quite annoyed when he first arrived. I wanted nothing to do with the *healing* he was trying to show me was possible. But over time, listening to the things he told me but never told anyone else, I realized that Terran is so much stronger than any of us have ever thought. Or at least I had," I say with a smile.

Terran's gentle smile and chestnut curls flash into my mind. The way his hazel eyes light up when he talks about his family or his people. The way he laughs, deep and free, unafraid of what others might think. The way his calloused hands felt against my skin. My cheeks heat.

"It sounds like you really... admire him." Mar says from behind me, pulling my thoughts back to the conversation.

I laugh, "Yeah, I really do. But it's more than that. There was one night that changed things." I pause, taking a deep breath before I finally speak

239

aloud what happened over a year ago. "I was supposed to be attending a court banquet and Terran was also there as a guest. They happen so often, I hadn't even stopped to consider what it might be about. As soon as I walked in I knew exactly the reason. Standing across the room was my father, he was talking to the leader of the sirens, and standing next to them was the same siren who nearly killed Rose." Bile burns the back of my throat.

I hear Mar's intake of breath and take a second to steady my own racing heart. The feelings of complete and utter betrayal, the way my entire body locked up in that one split second. "It was like I was back there, helpless and unable to do anything, even breathe. Then he was there. Terran appeared before me and helped talk me back to reality. He never left my side, never left me alone. The more the night went on the more I drank. I didn't even realize what I was doing at first. Terran realized just how drunk I was and offered to take me back to my room."

"I don't know if I should be excited or scared of where this is going," Mar says from behind me.

I let my head fall back against the rim of the tub so I am looking up at her. "He walked me back to my room, and then turned to leave but I pulled him inside. I pushed him on the bed and..."

"Oh my Vana, Cay! I had no idea you were so *assertive*," Mar says, wiggling her brows.

I groan.

"Don't stop there, keep going, what did he do? I need details." Mar says, giving my shoulders a light shake.

For a brief moment I am reminded of the fact that I am naked from the waist up and in a bathtub, though it's nothing Mar hasn't seen before. Moving past it I continue the story.

"So I pushed him onto the bed and then I... climbed into his lap," I bury my face in my hands, "full on straddled him. At first he held me away from him, really tried to put some distance between us but I was determined."

Mar smirks at me knowingly and I roll my eyes.

240

"He tried to stop it from happening. But I was persistent. I kissed him. *Really* kissed him. And Vana did it feel *right*. It was unlike any other kiss I have had before. Only, he wasn't kissing me back. At least not at first. So I obviously panicked and pulled away but then he grabbed me by the back of my neck and back to him...."

"And? Did he kiss you back?" Mar presses when I pause.

"Yeah, he did. His lips were so soft, so at odds with the way his hands felt against my skin. It felt so good, Mar, and I sort of took that and ran with it. I got a little more adventurous with my hands..." I say with a sigh, squeezing my eyes shut against the rising embarrassment.

"Cay, what exactly did you do?"

"I don't know what came over me really but I just.... grabbed *it*. At first I thought he might even like it. But then he grabbed my wrist and pulled my hand away. I swear, Mar, I have never wished to die more than I did at that moment."

"I'm sure it wasn't that bad," Mar offers. Though the way her face is contorted tells me otherwise.

"Oh it gets worse. After that he pushed me away completely, just stood up and left. Walked right out of the room. To make matters worse, the next morning at breakfast he apologized to *me*. Like I wasn't the one practically forcing myself on him."

"Yeah, that's not great," Mar agrees, shaking her head.

"I have been completely avoiding him ever since that night. Only that was obviously much easier when I wasn't staying in his castle." I throw my hands over my face, forcing the world out and silently wishing the world would open up and swallow me whole.

Mar laughs, "I can see how that would be true."

I groan. "Mar what am I going to do? He's Rose's *brother*. Not to mention the heir to Sena. There is just no way this will ever work, but I *really* like him."

Mar moves my hands from over my face so I am looking at her again. "Hey, it will all work out. If you are both serious about this then we will find a way to make it work. But before we do anything else you should probably put some clothes on. Not that I don't love seeing you like this but the water has got to be freezing."

I splash my tail a bit, shaking my head, "Actually no. Mermaid bodies are designed to handle extremely cold water since that's where we spend the majority of our time. This feels great to me."

"Fair enough," Mar says, standing and grabbing me a towel from off a stool.

I let my magic move through my body, shifting back to my mortal form with ease. Once my tail becomes legs again, I stand, letting the water drip off my body for a moment before wrapping myself in the fluffy towel. Stepping out of the tub I follow Mar back into the main room.

Looking around I realize that I'm already in *my own* room so I walk over to my trunk and pull out a silk nightgown. The same nightgown Oliver had teased me about. My cheeks burn with the reminder as I drop the towel and pull the gown over my head.

Meanwhile Mar warms the bed with her fire magic.

"You don't have to do all that," I say with a laugh.

"I like taking care of people, so hush," she replies, continuing to move her hands over the bed until seemingly satisfied.

I crawl under the covers. "Are you going to sleep here tonight?" I ask.

Mar shakes her head, "I'm going to hang out for a bit then check on Eve before going to bed."

"What's wrong with Eve?" I say sitting up.

"I'll tell you about it tomorrow, for now just get some sleep. I'm not sure what you were up to earlier but I have a sneaking suspicion that you won't be feeling so great tomorrow."

I narrow my eyes, "What does that mean?"

Mar laughs, "You'll have to ask Oliver about that."

My mouth drops open as a thousand horrible thoughts race through my mind. Vana help me.

Chapter 27

Cay's breathing steadies as she falls asleep. As soon as I see her body relax I slip into the hall, leaning against the door frame for a moment before sliding down to the floor. My forehead falls against my bent knees as I squeeze my eyes shut. There is a slight burning in my throat, letting me know that I didn't get enough blood today. A little warning bell telling me that something is wrong and I need to take care of it.

I snort. If only Eve listened to her own warning bells, then we wouldn't be in as big of a mess as we are. Rose is probably walking around her party alone and trying to not show how upset she truly is. Knowing her she probably won't even say anything, she'll just check in on everyone else and pretend that everything is fine. But it's not fine.

Never, in all my years of knowing her, have I seen Cay like this. She was like an entirely different person. I want to be excited that she is finally letting go a little and actually enjoying herself. But a heavy ball of dread has found a place in my chest. Something about the way the high lady snuck off so early. She spent months planning this, yet she disappeared just as the party had barely begun. Something is going on and I want to know what.

Between Eve and Oak I'm really getting tired of everyone around me lying and keeping secrets. Cay's words float through my mind; she has feelings for Rose's brother. While there is nothing particularly wrong with that it certainly doesn't help the situation at hand. It feels like everyone around me is making decisions and doing things without considering how it will affect others.

I can feel the rage building inside my chest. It burns hot and threatens to spill over at anyone who crosses my path. My head falls back against the door, as I let out a deep exhale. If I don't do something to channel this rage I'm going to go off on someone who doesn't deserve it, probably say something I'll regret later.

Cay is asleep and hasn't really done anything deserving of my anger, although I do think we need to have a conversation about what she told me. Oak is probably back at the party, hopefully attempting to get Rose to actually enjoy her birthday. Eve is probably passed out still, or with any luck, feeding, as much as I do *not* want to think about that.

The training rooms are always an option but it's not my body that wants to release the tension, it's my mind. No amount of kicking or punching is going to ease the storm inside my head. I sit upright. There is still one other person who has done a fantastic job of pissing me off lately; Rian. Standing up before I can give it a second thought, I start walking towards the party, the last place I saw the damn prick. Not only was he acting like a complete ass earlier, his face just pisses me off. Screaming at it might lessen that a bit.

Marching through the halls I notice that there are a lot more guards now, one stationed every few hundred feet. I speed up as I walk past them. As soon as I enter the party the air changes. People are huddled up together and whispering, the dance floor is empty although the musicians are still playing hesitantly. I look around the room but it's a sea of unfamiliar faces.

I grab the arm of a passing guard and ask him what's going on but he just pulls away, hurrying off into the hall. My heart is racing, my blood pounding in my ears. What the fuck is going on? I push through the crowd

244

of people towards the center of the room, calling out for Rose and Oak. Strong hands grab me from behind and I whirl around. This is not the time for some pervert to try something. A split second before my fist meets his face, Rian dodges.

"That wasn't very nice of you," he says pulling me closer to him as the crowd around us

starts closing in.

My breathing becomes uneven, aware of just how little space there is between and around us. I try to focus on Rian and what's going on, but bodies press against me on all sides, the air feels thin as I try and gulp it down. Panic consumes me as I realize I can't take a deep breath, it feels stuck in my chest like it can't quite reach my starving lungs.

"Just breathe, Mar, in and out. I'm going to get us out of here so grab on to me okay?" Rian whispers against my ear, his hand makes soothing circles on my bare arms.

I nod my head and grab on to his waist from behind as he pushes through the crowd. At first we hardly move, I keep my head pointed straight ahead staring at Rian's back. The hushed whispers are becoming louder, more frantic as people start to realize how little space there really is. I don't know why everyone ended up huddled together like this but I do know I want out. The farther away from the center we go the easier it is to breathe.

Once we're out in the open I take a deep breath in, letting the air fully expand my lungs before letting it out slowly. I look back at the crowd behind me and realize that the reason why people are pushed together so tightly is that the guards are bringing more and more people into the room, herding them into one giant cluster of bodies.

"What's happening?" I ask Rian as I feel the remaining panic slowly fading.

Rian spins me to look at him and I focus again on the feel of his hand on my arm. His calloused fingers smoothing circles over the sensitive skin, such a tender gesture. He saved me. He saw how upset I was and he got me out of there. "Where the hell have you been? And where is your sister?" he yells. Oh yeah, *asshole*.

"Excuse me? What gives you the right to speak to me like that? Actually you just reminded me why I am even here in the first place I have something to say to you ass-"

"Enough, you can yell at me all you want later. Where is your sister?" he demands, staring into my eyes with a determination I have never seen from him.

"She's back in her room with Nat, she isn't feeling well. Why?" I ask, looking back over my shoulder again. More people continue to spill into the room. I spy Reed on the far end of the room being practically dragged away by a guard as his eyes search frantically through the crowd.

Rian grabs my wrist and pulls me after him, "We're leaving. Immediately."

I pull on my arm but he refuses to release me. "I'm not going anywhere with you so let go."

He yanks harder, causing me to stumble. "I don't have time for this. *We* don't have time for this. We're going to get your sister and we are leaving."

I narrow my eyes on him, "Leaving to go where?"

"Home. Back to Vulca. We'll have Nat fly us there, it will be faster."

"What? Why would we be going back to Vulca? Tell me what's going on. Now," my voice leaves no room for argument yet it seems he hardly hears me.

We make it to the doorway and one of the Sena guards tries to stop us. They say something about it being *safer* here but Rian just pushes past him, ignoring his shouts as we practically run away.

"Rian. Tell me what's going on," I demand again, yanking against his grip hard enough that he lets go this time. I plant my feet firmly in the middle of the hallway, refusing to move.

He turns to face me, his jaw ticking with irritation. "Fine. There have been reports of attacks and it is no longer safe for us to stay here. Now, you can either come with me to retrieve your sister or I'll throw you over my shoulder and carry you there anyways."

My mind empties. This night just keeps throwing things at me and at this point I'm not sure I can handle anything else. "What do you mean by attacks? Here?" I ask, my voice surprisingly steady.

His expression turns hard, "Rayan."

I stare at him in disbelief. Attacks in Rayan. "Tell me everything you know."

"Fine, but we're going to get your sister," he compromises, turning to walk away.

I nod and start to follow him.

"Reports started coming in a few hours ago. It wasn't much at first, just some vague talks of unrest. Then it got worse. The last I heard they had breached the city." His steps are hurried as we practically race through the halls.

I stop dead in my tracks. "Wait. We're going to Cay first. She needs to know what's happening."

Rian continues walking away. "No. She's not my priority, you and your sister are."

"If Rayan is under attack then Cay should be the *only* priority. It's her kingdom, she's the heir." If the enemy has reached Tepis then Cay's entire family is in danger.

Rian stops, turning to face me, "Yes, but not *my* heir."

That rage that had diminished is quickly making its way back into my body. "Neither am I," I challenge.

Rian lets out a long sigh, "That's different."

I snort. "It's not. Which is exactly why I am going to help my friend, whether you come with me or not." I turn on my heels and start walking back towards Cay's rooms. I have no idea how I'm going to wake her up and tell her her home is under attack, but she deserves to know. She needs to know, even if she isn't ready to hear it. Though I'm not convinced anyone would ever truly be ready for something like that.

Rian curses and catches up to me, "We don't have time for this. We need to get out of here before things get even worse."

I glare at him. "It's bad already, taking a few extra moments to check on Cay isn't going to change things that much."

He walks beside me. "You don't know the full extent of things. It's not just Rayan. Yes, they have it the worst but there are reports coming in about attacks from all over."

I hesitate for a moment but continue walking, "Vulca?"

He nods, "Something is moving at our southern border. No reports from the northwest. If we leave now we should be able to make it there without any issues."

"The south? There's nothing in the south that makes no sense."

Rian says nothing, his lips pressed into a line.

I stare at him out of the corner of my eyes, "What do you know?"

He doesn't respond. I sigh, shaking my head and letting it go for now. The only thing that matters at this moment is making sure my friends are okay.

We turn down the hallway to Cay's room and Rian grabs my arm. "What are you going to say to her? We don't have time to deal with an emotional breakdown."

I look down the hall to her door, behind it she is sleeping soundly. "I don't know. But it's not going to get any better waiting around till I do," I say, walking up to the door and pushing it open.

Rian follows in behind me, stopping at the door and giving us some privacy.

I cross the room and put my hand on Cay's arm and immediately yank it back with a hiss. Her skin is freezing cold, so cold it hurts to touch. I call out to Rian but he is already beside us, his hands roaming across every inch of Cay's still form.

He starts shaking her but she doesn't stir. Doesn't show any sign of response. He presses his palm to her face. "Her skin is like ice," he says with a curse.

"This doesn't make sense. She's a mermaid, mermaids don't get cold. She told me so herself." I shake my head in denial.

"That's not exactly true, they can handle extreme colds when they're shifted but when in their mortal form they are more susceptible. Still, the room is comfortable," He says, pulling back the blankets and looking her over from head to toe.

"What's wrong with her? I was *just* talking to her, she was completely fine," I say, watching his inspection.

He grabs her hand and takes a close look at her fingertips, the tips are a pale purple. "What exactly happened before you left her?"

"She was drunk so I put her in bed. She woke up and said she felt really hot so she got in the bath. We talked, she seemed fine- sober even-then she went back to sleep. Did I- was there something I missed?" My mind runs over every minute that I spent with her in this room, searching for any sign or warning that I should have noticed before.

Rian shakes his head, "No. The water likely saved her."

Cay's body jerks and then she is vomiting. Her body trembles, from aftershocks or cold, it's unclear which. She's shaking so violently that Rian has to pin her to the bed to stop her from hurting herself.

"Rian, what do we do?" I ask, terrified.

Cay stops trembling and Rian looks at me, "I don't know. I don't know what's wrong with her. She needs help. *Now.*"

Chapter 28

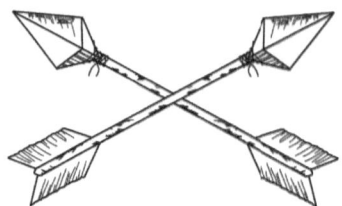

All it takes is one look from Oliver and I know he is thinking the same thing I am. There is absolutely no way that we are just going to sit here and do nothing. The last time I did nothing, people died, I won't let that happen, not again.

Rose bursts out of the room and we both follow after her. Once we get some distance from the high lady's chambers, Oliver pulls us both into an alcove.

"I'm going." he says plainly.

Rose stares at him in shock but I nod my head.

"Me too," I agree.

Oliver gives me a nod and turns back to his sister, "Stay here. Let us take care of this."

Rose shakes her head, "What? There's two of you. How do you expect to *take care of this*?"

Oliver smirks, "You have such little faith in me." He puffs his chest up, letting the smallest bit of his magic free so that we can feel the power resting just beneath the surface of his skin waiting to be used.

"There's no way the two of you can handle this alone. You're going to get yourselves killed," she says. A mixture of fear and anger flash across her face, the fear seeming to win out momentarily.

"Oak can take care of herself, and I'm too stubborn to die," Oliver says with a shrug. His words do nothing to encourage me that we actually *can* be of any king of assistance.

"Oliver…" Rose starts.

I cut her off, "Arrogance and idiocy aside, he's right. We've got this. Besides, we won't be alone." The lie rolls off my tongue easily, though I know it's only a half lie. A part of me regrets the words instantly. Oliver cuts me a glare but I continue, "The entire Rayan army will be fighting whoever is attacking them. By the time we get there they might not even need us."

Rose gives me a look that says she is unconvinced but Oliver pulls her to the side, speaking directly into her ear. Her expression turns shocked at whatever Oliver says but it seems to convince her. She nods, turning to me. "Take care of each other. I mean it."

I laugh, "Of course. We'll be okay. Now, go check on the others. Cay wasn't looking so good last I saw her and she'll probably need more help than us."

Rose nods, looking between us, "Whatever this is, stay safe. Don't die. I can't lose either of you."

My breath hitches and the urge to pull her into a hug takes over as a lump forms in my throat. My parents' faces flash in my mind followed by Rose's father. Oliver turns to me and we both take off towards the stables. Once outside, we have to sneak around the guards to where the horses are kept. The moment the high lady catches wind of what we're trying to do she'll send people after us to bring us back. Each of us takes a horse but it's going to be far more difficult sneaking them out than us getting in.

"I've got it," Oliver whispers. He kneels down, pressing one hand against the dirt and sending a pulse of magic into the earth. Two grunts echo from outside and then he stands, leading the way outside and past the two guards, now tangled in a web of vines. We lead our horses out and wait until we are far enough into the woods to mount and take off. It's still pitch black outside as we ride through the forest side by side.

Oliver stares straight ahead, pushing his horse to gallop harder, faster. He's hardly said a word since we left Rose. We ride in silence, feeling the weight of our actions and the uncertainty of what we are heading into hanging like a sword over our heads. There is very limited information on what is really happening in Rayan but if the reports are to be believed it won't be good.

For hours we ride at an unrelenting pace, the cold wind biting against our face. The temperature is dropping despite the fact we are traveling south. A fact that does not bode well for the long journey ahead of us. If we ride non-stop we might be able to make it there in about two days, the horses will never last that long without rest. Besides that, it's already the middle of the night and neither of us have slept.

I look at my cousin but he shows no sign of fatigue. His face is a mask of determination as we race ahead. My back is aching, and my legs are numb either from the cold or from riding so long. "Oliver, we need to take a break," I call out to him.

He ignores me so I gallop up beside him.

"The horses need rest, we've been riding for hours. They can't keep this up." I fight back a groan as I imagine laying down for even a moment.

Oliver shakes his head, "If you need to stop then stop. I'm good."

I sigh, "No, you're not. You need rest."

He glares at me from the corner of his eyes, "Don't tell me what I need."

"Look, I get it. I want to help just as much as you do. But we're no good to anyone if we're exhausted."

"Like I said, I'm good," he responds firmly.

"*Stop*," I say, my voice thick.

Oliver forces his horse to stop. He turns to me with a look of pure rage on his face, "*Never*, I mean *never*, use your magic on me again. Understand?"

I give him a small nod, a dark feeling swirling in my stomach.

He jumps down off his horse and I follow suit, leading both our horses after him as he walks off.

"You needed to stop. I made sure you did. You can thank me later," I say with a shrug, feigning indifference.

He whirls on me, "I can promise you that I will never be thanking you for anything. If you weren't my cousin you might already be dead from a stunt like that."

I snort, "Go ahead, do whatever you want."

Oliver steps towards me, "Watch yourself, Oak. My patience is already running thin." He turns on his heels and walks us forward into a small clearing.

I shift into my fae form, letting my heightened senses guide me as I tie the horse's reins to a tree and watch as he moves around, holding his hands out in front of him. His magic seeps into the air as he begins casting a protection spell around us, masking our presence from anyone on the outside. When he finishes with that he closes his eyes, starting on a new incantation.

"What's that one for?" I ask, stepping closer to him.

"I'm releasing the energy from the earth, unless you'd rather freeze to death."

I watch as his magic calls to the earth and waves of heat begin washing up from beneath my feet.

"That's incredible. Where did you learn to do that?" I ask, amazed.

"I didn't. I designed it myself."

I stare at him in shock, "You created this spell on your own?"

He ignores me, continuing to chant. He spits on the ground and opens his eyes, the spell complete. "Yes. Now, if you don't mind, I'm going to sleep. Seeing as I wasn't given much of a choice in the matter," he says, laying on the ground and folding his arms behind his head.

"If you're looking for an apology you won't get one." I won't regret forcing him to take a break, not when I *know* that he needs one, that we both do.

"No, but a little gratitude would be nice," he says with a smirk.

I stare at him, "And what exactly do I have to be grateful for?"

Oliver raises his brows at me. "You and I both know that my mother is only using you as a spy because Terran suggested it."

Rolling my eyes I plop down beside him, staring up at the night sky. "Are you still upset about that?"

He laughs mirthlessly, "Upset? I'm not upset about anything other than you acting so high and mighty all the time."

I roll over so I face him, "Is that so?"

He turns to face me, "Yeah, it is. So do everyone around you a favor and get over yourself already. You want to be special but surprise, everyone else can see just how desperate you are for attention."

I smile at him broadly, "While we're on this subject how about you explain to me what your deal is with Cay, hmm? What's got you so interested in her all of a sudden?"

Oliver barks a laugh. "Believe me, I have no interest in her. My brother however, now that's a different story," he says with a shrug.

"Terran? What does he have to do with anything?" Tendrils of dread sneak up my spine. If Terran and Cay have something going on he might have told her all the lies I've been keeping. It doesn't seem likely but who knows, people do crazy things when they're in love.

"You tell me. Why did he spend weeks in Rayan, *without* Rose? Why was he sending Cay letters every day? Why has he been meeting with my mother for months and sending me on scouting missions to the south?" he says suggestively.

I shake my head. "I don't know. But whatever his reasoning is, why do you care?"

He shrugs. "Call it curiosity."

I narrow my eyes at him. "Yeah, I don't believe that one bit. There's got to be more to it. Something's got you acting like an even bigger asshole than usual."

"Maybe I'm just not a nice person," his voice is teasing.

I fight a grin. "Yeah, that's absolutely possible."

"Ouch, you didn't have to agree so quickly," he says, clutching his hand over his heart in mock pain.

I snort, "Don't make it so easy to believe it then."

We sit in silence for a while, staring up at the sky. Oliver's spell keeps us warm, releasing the energy from the earth beneath us. It's genius, honestly. Our entire family has always been good at incantations but something like this, it would change so much about the way we live.

"We'll rest until daylight, that should give us a few hours. Then we're riding until we get there. No more stopping," Oliver directs from beside me.

"Agreed. Oliver?"

"What?" he says, clearly irritated again.

"How bad do you think it's going to be?" I ask, doing everything I can to mask the fear in my voice that has been creeping in since we left.

"I don't know. But expect the worst." He rolls over, giving his back to me.

I stare at him for a while before I feel my body pulling me under into a deep sleep.

Chapter 29

Eve

I wake up with my head resting on something soft and warm. I squeeze my eyes shut, nuzzling against it. I inhale deeply as I press my face into the softest pillow. Someone clears their throat and I'm surprised by how close the sound is and how I could *feel* the vibration of the noise in that person's chest. When I open my eyes the last thing I expect is to be in someone's arms. More specifically, Nat's arms. Yet here I am.

We stare at each other as realization comes crashing in on me. My hand is placed lightly against her chest but my face is buried against her full breasts. I breathe in deeply again, her scent of spiced rum invading my senses.

Horror seizes me as I take in her delicate flush, the way her pupils are bigger than usual. I start to struggle to put space between us but her grip on me tightens. She's laying in my bed but I am curled up in her lap.

Vana help me.

Her bright eyes are locked onto mine, almost in a trance. I try to escape again but she doesn't let go. "Stop moving. You were so comfortable, just go back to sleep," she says, looking away from me at last. A light blush paints her cheeks.

I struggle to form words, my mouth opening and closing multiple times. What the fuck is happening? The last thing I can remember clearly is talking with Rose, everything else is a bit hazy. "Um, Nat, what's going on?" I look around the room, my brow furrowed. Nothing seems out of place except for the dragon guard beneath me.

"I found Oakley and your sister carrying you back to your room, they said you collapsed." She raises her brows at me accusingly.

Shit. That's not good. Oak is probably pissed at me but Mar might *actually* kill me. Maybe if I feign passing out again they will be a little easier on me. Though that plan does have equal potential to backfire the more I think about it. Looking around the room, I expect to see them standing by, waiting to rip into me.

"It's just us if that's what you're looking for." Her voice is smooth even as her heart is beating erratically in her chest.

I look at Nat again, surprised to find her face still flushed. Reaching out I tuck a strand of copper hair out of her face. Her skin is hot, like all dragons. Her lashes flutter shut for a moment as my fingers skim over her cheek. Her chest rises on a deep inhale and I pull my hand back, fighting the urge to reach out for a taste of her emotions.

"I don't mean to sound rude, but, why exactly am I in your arms?" I ask, raising my brows. Something stirs deep in the pit of my stomach but I continue to ignore it.

"I offered to watch over you while you recovered. Your sister didn't seem pleased, neither did Oakley, but I managed to convince them," she says with a sheepish smile. Her hand is trailing against my hip bone absently, the same small circles over and over.

I smile a bit to myself. "I would imagine the two of them were more interested in fighting each other than you."

"Actually yes. Did something happen between them? Why do they hate each other so much?"

I laugh openly this time. "Oh, they love each other. As much as I love either of them. They have always been like this though, butting heads on just about everything. I think to everyone else it must look like you said, that they hate each other. But in reality, it's just about how they do things. Mar isn't afraid to speak her mind and tell you exactly what she thinks of you. Oak would rather keep those thoughts and feelings to herself. It has led to some rather interesting arguments. Though I'm not privy to whatever it is that has them so riled up this time."

"It sounds like it, they seemed ready to tear each other's heads off," she chuckles.

"Nat?"

"Yes?" she hums.

"Can I move now?" I ask sheepishly.

Nat's face turns blood red as she nods.

"Can you move your arms?" One arm is tucked under my leg and grabbing onto my thigh, the other is wrapped around my waist, still drawing circles against my hip. As soon as I speak she releases her grip on me and I start to shift. I scoot over so I am sitting beside Nat instead of on top of her. For a while we sit there in silence, wondering who will be the first to speak.

There is an unusual awkwardness that I am not quite used to. Before the *incident* in the village, we were talking so easily, like we had known each other our entire lives. Now, it just feels like there is a weight pressing down on my chest. The feeling is more than uncomfortable, it's unbearable. I turn to her at the same time she turns to me. We both open our mouths to speak but stop when we see the other.

"Sorry, you go first," she says with a nod of her head.

"No, you go."

More silence follows us but then she speaks. "Why didn't you tell me? Back at the village, if I had known…" she trails off.

It takes me a moment to understand what she means but then it clicks. Oak and Mar must have told her why I passed out. Part of me wants to be angry at them but the other part knows that they only want to help. I take a deep breath, letting it out slowly, controlled. "I didn't tell you because it's not something you need to worry about."

Nat gives me a pointed stare, "I'm your guard. Of course it's my problem."

I sigh. "See, that's exactly why it can't be your problem. I don't want anyone to feel forced into taking care of me. Especially when it comes to *this*. I am fully capable of taking care of myself."

"If that was the truth then why did you pass out? Why did you let it get to this point?" she challenges.

"It's not as simple as that. There are other things going on than just feeding. That's just one part of it," I sigh.

"And can you control the other part? Is that something that you are capable of doing?" Her words are cautious, like she is testing the water to see how I might respond.

My mind goes back to the vials of unopened tonic sitting in the bottom of my luggage. I nod my head, answering her question.

Nat turns, facing me fully, "So you can control both things yet you don't? You let it go this far?"

"It's not as though I want it to. I just- it's more complicated than that," I groan.

"So explain it to me," she practically begs.

"I can't." We sit there in silence as I stare down at my hands, fiddling with the lace of my gown. There are things I wish I could say, to explain. Not just to her but to everyone. My sister. My friends. Even my father. But some things are better left unsaid, just like my mother wants.

Nat shifts and for a second I think she is leaving but as I look up I see her shift closer, not away. Her body moves so quickly that I almost miss it but then she is there, hovering above me, legs straddling my hips. She reaches forward and grasps my face in her rough hands, calloused from her training.

"What are you-"

"Let me take care of you," she begs, cutting me off, "let me ease your burden. Please."

I start to shake my head and tell her no but she leans forward, closing the distance between us. Her lips capture mine instantly. I nearly moan at the feeling of the soft skin pressed firmly against my own. She tilts her head to the side, her long hair falling forward and brushing the tops of my chest. One of her hands moves from my face to the back of my neck, right at the base of my hair, her fingers tangling with the dark tresses.

Thoughts of protesting vanish from my mind, replaced only by the sole focus of her lips moving against my own. I lean forward slightly, my hand moving to cup her elbow, her waist, everywhere that I can. Her skin is velvety smooth and oh so warm. She presses her chest against my own and I stop fighting. I return her kiss fiercely, moving with her.

Her tongue skims over my bottom lip and I open for her, deepening the kiss. Her tongue sweeps inside my mouth and she makes a soft whimpering sound and that breaks whatever restraint I have held on to. Somewhere in the pits of my stomach I feel my magic reserves buzzing, waiting to be filled. I ignore them, focusing instead on the stunning creature currently seated in my lap.

Her hand moves further into my hair as my own drops to her hip, tugging her closer. The movement has her grinding down against me and she makes that sound again, the noise causing my magic to thrum insistently. I groan in the back of my throat, deepening the kiss further and fighting the pull of hunger that is threatening to take control. My nails dig into her waist, drawing a gasp from her lips.

Nat's free hand skims up my leg to where the slit in my dress is, stopping in the middle of my thigh. She pulls back, staring down at me with wide, lust filled eyes, "Is there a fucking dagger strapped to your leg right now?"

Shit, I forgot about that. "Yes?" I say hesitantly.

She leans forward, capturing my mouth in a quick yet scorching kiss. "That's so fucking hot," she says against my lips.

I smile and she takes the opportunity to deepen the kiss once more, her tongue battling my own. Our kisses become sloppier, more frantic as our hands roam over each other. I have one hand squeezing her hip, the other hooked around the back of her knee.

Nat leans back slightly, pressing her forehead against my own. "Please. Let me help you."

"Nat, I don't know."

She kisses me again, this time long and slow, burning. "I want this. I want *you*. Helping your hunger is just an added benefit."

The reminder of hunger sends the buzzing racing through my entire body until it is a hum I can't ignore. I can feel my magic screaming to be refilled, desperate to pull from her what she is so willingly offering. But is she willing? The question is stuck in my mind as Nat leans back. Her arms move to her waist and before I can really comprehend what she is doing her dress is already halfway over her head. All it takes is a single moment and that dress is in a pool on the floor next to the bed. She is wearing no undergarments, her entire body hovers over me completely bare.

Fuck.

An ache builds in me as I take all of her in. Her hair is cascading down her back and over her shoulders. Her skin is flushed, full breasts heavy with need, aching to be kissed. I let my gaze roam down her body, finding small scars and marks across her stomach. Her strong legs are still seated on either side of my hips, she sits up higher, lifting her center away from me. Nat reaches for my hand and guides it between her thighs. She's practically dripping. "Do you believe me now?" she says a bit breathlessly.

I swallow thickly, letting my hand slide through the wetness that has gathered there. Her hips jerk a little as I pass over that bundle of nerves that begs for my full attention. I look up at her head tilted back, staring up at the ceiling. Her eyes close as a single digit presses against her opening. I let the finger slip inside, feeling the warmth and wetness waiting for me. Her breath hitches and her internal muscles spasm, clamping down on me. I add a second finger and her hips jerk again, begging for movement. But I wait, two of my fingers still inside of her.

"Please," she whimpers.

The hunger is building inside of me and I know that if I continue to fight it, passing out will be the least of my concerns. Here, perched above me, is a beautiful female who wants to give me the very thing that will help me. Why shouldn't I take it? Fuck that voice inside me that says otherwise.

"Okay," I say.

She drops her head, staring down at me, fire burning behind her irises, "Okay?"

"Yes. But if- if I do this. It's about you, your pleasure. Not mine."

She opens her mouth to argue and I withdraw my fingers out a bit. Her hand snatches my wrist before I can pull my hand away, she eases down, impaling herself on my fingers.

"Yes. Whatever, just… please," she moans.

I smile at her, leaning forward to kiss her delicate lips. She opens for me the moment we make contact and I nip at her bottom lip. As soon as I have captured her mouth I start to move. My fingers slowly gliding in and out, curling and spreading inside her warmth. I move my thumb to her throbbing clit and press down. Her entire body jerks and I smile against her.

"More," she demands of me, a hand grabbing my shoulder, the other her chest. She pinches one of her pink nipples between the pad of her finger and thumb. The sight makes my stomach tighten.

I continue curling my fingers, pushing my thumb down harder as she rides my hand. My magic starts to pull from Nat as her pleasure builds. I feel the hum coursing through my body. The sweet, heady, taste of her pleasure fills me, my energy already becoming stronger. I open my senses to her and let my succubus magic release. I'm not sure how it works really but when I open my senses like this, whatever emotion I am feeding off of becomes heightened. If someone is happy they become downright blissful. If someone is feeling pleasure…

"Oh fuck…" Nat moans, her head falling back as she continues to writhe on my hand.

I wrap my free hand around the hair at the base of her neck tugging back slightly. Her breathy moan is music to my ears. My entire body heats at the feel of her thighs clamping down on either side of my own. Her body starts to tremble as I continue to work her opening and clit. My magic is humming happily, heightening her pleasure and feeding me at the same time. My energy is close to being completely replenished already, a testament to just how much Nat is enjoying herself.

Smiling, I pull Nat's mouth back to mine and give her a slow, lingering kiss, nothing like the frantic ones we shared before. Her body begins to shake harder as she tightens around me. I quicken my pace, pressing down firmly against her bundle of nerves and curling my fingers at the same time. I press a third finger into her and her inner walls coil tightly around my hand, as she releases a breathy moan and slumps forward, hitting the crest of her pleasure.

Her thighs tremble as small whimpers slip past her lips. Her arms grip me on either side, fingernails biting into my skin. I kiss her through it, my fingers continuing to pump into her as she comes down from her release. I let my magic pull on every bit of her pleasure until I feel completely replenished. My head is a bit dizzy from all of the magic. It's been too long since I recharged and the feeling is unfamiliar.

Nat eases off of my hand. Scooting backwards and lowering herself down onto her stomach and pushing my dress up until it bunches around my waist. She lightly pushes against the inside of my thighs and I spread them for her involuntarily. My body moving of its own accord.

"What are you doing?" I ask, eyebrows raised.

"Did you get enough?" she asks, smiling up at me.

I narrow my eyes at her, my pulse already quickening. "Yes…" I say hesitantly.

She wets her lips before leaning down further and placing a soft kiss on my chest, then another on the flat expanse of my stomach. She continues her path down until she reaches the waistband of my undergarment. I suck in a breath and try to remain focused. A difficult feat given that while one hunger may have been sated, another is being rather insistent at this moment. I try to control my breath as I exhale but it comes out shaky. Nat's hands roam up and down the sides of my thighs, leaving goosebumps in their wake. The chilled air and her touch make my nipples harden.

Nat removes my dagger, setting it down gently on the nightstand. She pushes aside the fabric of my panties, exposing my heated center to the cool air and making it impossible to hide the wetness pooled between my thighs. My chest tightens as Nat leaves a trail of kisses from my thigh to my clit, eliciting a gasp from me the moment her mouth closes over it. She looks up at me through her lashes, and places a hot, wet kiss there again.

My hips buck off the bed. "What're you doing?" I ask again, my voice barely a whisper.

Nat smiles, "Well, seeing as your magic is now fully replenished, there is no need for this to only be about me."

I feel her mouth move against me, drinking in my wetness. My body flashes hot and cold as her tongue works me, lapping at my dripping cunt. I move my hands into her hair, lightly holding her against my center as she devours me. I pull a little on her hair and she groans against me, the rumble of it sending a shock of sensations through my body.

She looks up at me again, licking her glistening lips. "You taste so fucking good. This is a sweetness I would never grow sick of." Nat lets her tongue move through my folds, licking and sucking up every bit of me as I squirm beneath her.

My body is trembling already. My magic still affects all of my senses, making things that much more sensitive. I try to clamp down on it, let the magic relax back into me but I can't. If anything, it feels like it's getting stronger, like every one of my senses has been dialed up to 100.

My entire body bows as Nat inserts a single digit, a moan bursting from my lips. Her mouth continues to move over my clit, licking and sucking, pushing me to my breaking point. My brain is going absolutely haywire at the mix of emotions racing through me all at once. I try to focus on what Nat is doing but it's overwhelming, the sensations of everything crashing into me like a tidal wave. Without warning my release rips through my body, tearing a scream from my throat.

Nat guides me through it, as I had her. Her fingers working me, her mouth glistening wet. The trembling in my body begins to calm. Nat crawls up beside me, laying down on her back and starting up at the ceiling. A shiver moves over her naked body so I pull the blanket up and over her.

My skin is still too hot to even think about joining her. We lay like that, our breathing slowly returning to normal. I roll over onto my side as Nat does the same. We stare into each other's eyes in silence, wide grins set on both of our faces. "Well…" she says with a shake of her head.

I lean forward, placing a soft kiss on the tip of her nose.

"That was- I have never experienced anything like that before," she admits, still a bit breathless.

I laugh, "I take it you've never been with a succubi before?"

She shakes her head again.

"Well," I say echoing her, "our magic does more than just take positive emotions from people. It can also heighten them. Heighten everything really. It's not particularly intentional but rather something that just sort of happens."

"I- I don't think I even have words."

I kiss her forehead, her eyes shutting briefly at the light contact. "I'm not even sure most people realize that is what's happening. Don't get me wrong, most succubi are truly superb in bed, but even if they weren't they could just increase their partner's pleasure and they would never really know the difference."

"Do you do that?"

I clutch a hand over my heart, "Ouch. That hurt. Do you really think so little of my skill?"

Nat's eyes widen. "No! I mean, absolutely not. Your *skills* cannot be questioned," she says, a light flush covering her entire face. Even the tips of her ears turn that adorable light pink shade.

I kiss the top of her ear, eliciting a light laugh from her.

"What was that for?" she asks.

I shrug, "Nothing. Just wanted to."

For what feels like hours we lay there, staring into each other's eyes and talking about anything and everything. I asked about her family; because her parents were both royal guards she was practically raised by her older brother. She joined the royal guard as soon as she possibly could, following in her parents and brother's footsteps. He's also a guard, but he isn't stationed in the city, he guards the border to the south. They don't get to see each other often but they try to make time when they can. Their relationship reminds me so much of Mar and her brothers. How she stepped up when her mom passed away.

After a while we get to know each other even further. Learning every inch of each other's bodies and memorizing the sounds we make as we fall apart at the other's hands. By the time we slump back against the mattress, my magic is so full I feel like I could run to Vulca and back faster than Mar. Our bodies are so sated that we can do nothing but curl against each other breathing heavily.

We fall asleep with our hands intertwined and foreheads pressed together. And for the first time in what feels like years, I get some real sleep. My mind shuts down, my body relaxes, and when my eyes drift shut there is no tunnel. No screams or blood. Just blissful darkness.

Eventually, that darkness turns into a dream. A dream full of mist and shadows. Whispers blow on the wind and the air feels stale. Dream me tries to push through the growing mist, looking for a sign of anything other than this barrenness. In this place my body feels cold and oddly like I had been dipped in a bath full of ice water. I try to call on my fire magic to warm me.

Before this version of me has a chance to do so, a knock sounds on the door. Not a dream door, the real door. Nat stirs beside me but I drape my arm over her waist, pinning her to the bed. "Leave it, they'll go away soon enough."

The knock sounds again, this time harder.

I squeeze my eyes shut, trying to bring myself back to the fog, to the blissful darkness that promises me the most rest I have gotten in a long time.

When the knock sounds a third time I groan. I slip off the side of the bed, pulling the blanket up to fully cover Nat's sleeping form. Crossing the room to the door, I'm suddenly aware that I am entirely naked and quickly reach for my gown where it was tossed onto the floor. I slip it on and yank the door open angrily, ready to tear into whoever interrupted us.

Only that anger immediately vanishes as I take in the state of the person on the other side of the door. Rose is standing there, hair disheveled and face blotchy like she has been crying. I grab Rose's arm and pull her into the chamber, closing the door behind her.

"What happened?"

Chapter 30

Rose

The moment I am inside of Eve's room my emotions begin to bubble up inside of me. I take a few deep breaths, trying to calm my racing heart. I ran here the moment Oliver and Oak left. I have no idea where Cay and Mar are but I knew that Eve should be here. "Eve, oh Vana, it's- it's bad. I don't even know where to start."

She shakes her head, "It's fine, just tell me everything. What's going on? Are you alright?"

A lump forms in my throat, the words getting stuck there too. I shake my head fighting the tears burning in my eyes and threatening to spill over. Now is not the time for this. I take one, long, deep breath and let it out slowly. My body relaxes and my thoughts become clearer.

The words rush out of me in a single string of thoughts. "Rayan is under attack, the city walls have been breached, I can't find Cay and Mar, the borders aren't secure, people are panicking, and my brother and cousin just took off against my mother's orders."

Eve just stares at me for a moment, her mouth hanging slightly open. Motion catches my attention behind her and my gaze shifts to her bed.

Nat sits up, rubbing at her eyes. "What's going on?" she asks sleepily. The blanket covering her slips, exposing her bare chest as shock washes over me.

Eve steps in front of me, blocking my view as my eyes widen. I raise my brows at her in question but she ignores me. "Wait. That was a lot, let me make sure I heard you correctly. Rayan is under attack?" she asks slowly.

I nod, "Yes, and the city walls have been breached."

"You have no idea where Cay and my sister are?" she continues.

"Yes, Oak mentioned something about Cay being drunk so I was going to check her chambers next after yours."

"Okay, and Oak? She left with Oliver or Terran?"

"Oliver."

"Did anyone else go with them?"

I bite my lip, shaking my head.

Eve lets out a slow breath before looking back to Nat. "Get dressed, we need to go. I'm sure Rian is already looking for us both."

Nat nods, wrapping the blanket around her as she moves around the room gathering up clothes.

Eve nods towards the door and I step back outside, she follows and pulls it shut behind us.

"Um, did what I think just happened, happen?" I ask.

"Now is really not the time to be discussing that, is it?" Eve groans.

"I think it's as good a time as any." I place my hands on my hips, allowing this new development to momentarily distract me from everything else imploding around us.

"Seriously? Does Cay even know what's happening right now? *She* is our priority. Not my love life," she adds in a hushed tone. Her words are a harsh reminder of reality but her tone is nothing but teasing.

"Not yet, and yes I agree but I still think we can take a moment to acknowledge what is happening inside that room at this very moment." I nod my head towards the door.

She rolls her eyes as the door opens again, Nat emerging fully clothed and ready to move. She passes Eve a dagger and shifts her fingers into fierce talons.

"Alright, let's go find Cay right away. If we're lucky maybe we'll find Mar there with her," I say hopefully.

The three of us move as a small unit. Nat walks slightly ahead of us, her dragon claws at the ready just in case we encounter any surprises. Knots form in my stomach the closer we get to Cay's rooms. Finding her is one thing, knowing what to say, that's something else entirely.

My heart races as we turn down the hall. Vana help me. I don't think I can do this. Fear seizes my body and I freeze, Eve and Nat continue marching forward without me. A cry for help cuts through the silent hall and for a split second all thoughts empty from my mind. I know that voice, that's Mar's voice.

The three of us take off running down the remainder of the hall. Nat pushes inside the room first, followed by Eve. I walk in at the moment Nat makes it to the side of Cay's bed. Mar is standing to the side, hand collapsed over her mouth in horror. Eve immediately moves to her sister's side, begging for an explanation.

Rian answers from beside Cay, "We found her like this. She is completely unresponsive, her body is weak and ice cold."

"That's impossible, mermaids don't get cold," Eve says with a shake of her head.

"Yeah well apparently this one does so either help or get out," Rian shouts.

Mar takes a step forward, always ready to defend her sister but Eve blocks her with an arm. "Listen here, asshole, that girl is as much a sister to me as Mar is so I'm going to ask all the questions I fucking want. Understand? Or do I need to remind you who *I* am," Eve says, her voice strong and confident, never wavering. In that moment, it is impossible to forget she is the heir to the Vulca throne.

I stare at my friend in wonder. Pride swells within me at the strength that Eve shows, even in the face of chaos. The sisters face each other, whispering quick and low while Mar explains the situation at hand.

I move to Cay's other side, watching as Nat moves her hands over her body. "What's wrong with her?" I ask softly. I grab Cay's hand and find that they aren't lying, her body is like ice, her skin has this odd sort of purplish-gray hue to it.

"I don't know, I've never seen anything like this before," Rian says from behind Nat, frustration clear in his voice.

"She's been poisoned," Nat says looking up at me from across the bed.

"What do you mean poisoned?" I ask.

"I've never seen one quite like this before but my mother is somewhat of a village healer. She's not the best but I used to help her in her shop sometimes, just simple stuff, grinding herbs and things like that."

"Do you know how to help her?" The question comes from Mar.

"I'm not sure. Poisons are very finicky, each one requiring a very specific antidote or spell. I'm not the best healer myself, are any of you?" Nat looks between all of us.

Mar and Eve shake their heads. Rian does the same.

Nat looks at me but my heart breaks as I tell her the truth. "The best healer out of all of us is Cay. She is always the one to take care of us when we get hurt or do something reckless. She taught me a few things but nothing like what you're suggesting. I could call for one of the staff but with everything going on the entire castle is in complete chaos, I have no way of knowing when they might get here."

Nat nods, placing her hands on Cay's arm gently. "Well, if we don't know what the poison is then it's not safe to give her anything. Our best bet is to burn it out of her system."

"Burn it out? Won't that hurt her?" Eve asks fearfully.

271

"Not if we do it slowly, moving from her heart and working our way out, it should be enough." Nat's gaze rakes across Cay, observing every minute detail and thoroughly checking for any sign of what might be going on.

"To do that the person heating her will need a lot of control, if a mermaid gets too hot…" Rian trails off.

I watch as Rian and Nat's gazes shift to the sisters.

"I-I can't, I don't trust myself," Mar says with a shake of her head.

Eve stares back at four sets of eyes, her expression showing nothing but complete confidence. "I'll do it. I'm good to go, just tell me what to do and I'll do it."

Mar shakes her head, "You barely have any magic in you there is no way you are going to be able to do this."

Nat's entire face turns blood red but Eve just gives her sister a look. "I promise, I'm good to go. All topped off."

Mar's eyes shift to Nat for a fraction of a second and I swear I hear Rian snort.

Nat clears her throat, drawing attention back to the issue at hand. "If you're going to do this you need to do it now. I don't know why her body is so cold but if I had to guess it's probably the poison trying to stifle her magic."

Eve steps forward, taking her place beside Cay's frozen body. She takes a deep breath and sets her hands down on the center of her chest.

"Okay, Eve, now think about drawing warmth into her body. Of building that heat steadily. Nice and easy. Just don't think about fire, fire is too hot, it will burn her from the inside out," Nat adds and my mouth drops open.

"I really wish you hadn't said that because now all I can think about is that mental image," Eve groans.

"Don't, ignore it. Let that image pass and focus. All you need to do is warm her chest, then her stomach, move over her legs and then her arms. Be very careful with her head, you don't want to melt her brain."

"Seriously Nat, I'm going to need you to shut up because you are not helping with the whole mental images thing," Eve bites as she guides her hands over Cay's body.

Nat chuckles, "So bossy. Still, you need to listen. Cay's body won't be able to handle the heat for too long, Rian was right about that much. We need to warm her slowly, let her adjust and then cool her body back down. Nothing too extreme or too fast, we don't want to send her into further shock."

Eve nods her head, following Nat's commands with a level of focus I have never seen from her before. Slowly she hovers her hands over Cay's face. We all hold a collective breath until we see Cay's chest expand and then fall steadily. We release our breath with her.

"Good, now let the warmth recede, not too much and not too fast. Just guide her body back to a slightly hotter than usual temperature," Nat says, her voice calm and even.

After another few minutes Eve removes her hand and we watch as Cay's chest begins to rise and fall a little more evenly. Nat checks her temperature and nods. "She's good. We just need to move her into a room temperature bath now. The water should help activate her magic and force whatever is left of the poison out of her body."

Rian steps forward and scoops Cay up into her arms. Mar leads him from the room and into the bathing chamber. I hear a light splash and my body begins to relax. Rian appears in the doorway and props himself up against the frame.

"How is she?" Eve asks him, her voice a bit more timid than before.

"She seems okay, your sister is in there with her if you want to join." Rian runs a hand through his hair, his fingers slightly damp and slicking the ashy locks back.

Eve nods, standing on somewhat shaky legs. I hope she didn't just deplete her magic too much again. Although, based on what I saw in the room earlier, it seems that might not be an issue any longer.

I follow after my friends and sit down beside Eve on the side of the tub. Mar plays with Cay's hair as it hangs over the rim, soothing a hand over her forehead gently. For a while we all just sit there in silence, waiting. My entire body is sore from how tense the past few hours have been. My muscles aching from being held so tight. I roll my shoulders and stretch my arms above my head. When I look down I find Cay's skin has returned to a normal color, no longer sporting the grayish tint. My gaze roams to Cay's face and I see her eyelashes flutter. She opens her eyes briefly and I gasp.

"Look! Her eyes opened," I exclaim, relief washing over me.

Mar and Eve both look down at Cay with hope. Her eyes flutter open and closed again, this time staying shut. We all let out a grateful sob. Rian and Nat appear in the doorway.

Eve turns to them, "She opened her eyes. That's a good sign right?"

Nat smiles, nodding her head. "Yeah, that's a good sign. We should move her to the infirmary, let the real healers look her over."

Nodding, we all stand and watch as Rian lifts Cay from the water, getting himself completely drenched in the process. He walks through the room and Nat follows.

I turn to Eve and pull her into a tight embrace. "Thank you. For saving her." I whisper into her ear.

She squeezes me back tighter. "Of course. I would do it for any of you." she whispers back.

Mar joins in and the three of us clutch onto each other's back desperately. My heart cracks a bit knowing that this embrace could have been for an entirely different reason.

Chapter 31

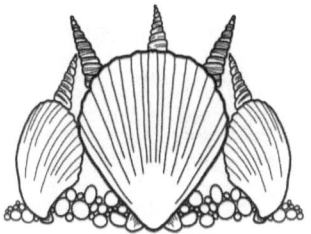

Cay

My entire body aches. I feel it first in my arms, then my legs. The muscles tighten and throb with any bit of movement. Even my eyelids feel heavy as I try to force them open to look around and get some answers as to what exactly is happening. They flutter open and a flash of bright light breaks through the darkness, I squint against it, my eyes struggling to adjust.

The first thing I see is the tall ceiling, ancient stone covered with a layer of vines. I turn my head and find a small table, on it is a single glass of water. My throat burns suddenly. Like the mere thought of water reminded my body of something that my mind can't recall. I reach out a hand hesitantly but it's too far out of my reach. I'm lying in a comfortable bed, propped up slightly by a pile of pillows. Using the leverage they already give me I push myself so I am fully sitting up.

Movement draws my eyes to the foot of the bed. Eve has a chair pulled up beside the bed, her chest sprawled across the mattress as her dark hair spills out around her sleeping face. I allow my eyes to roam across the large room. Rows of beds are lined up one by one, each with a small table beside them. Most are empty, but Mar has claimed one nearby as she curls in on herself. Rose is standing by a window staring out as raindrops cascade down the glass, her mind appears far away locked in thought.

I reach for the water again but groan as my muscles protest the movement.

Rose's gaze snaps to mine and her mouth drops open. She stares at me for a moment before rushing to my side. "Eve! Mar! Wake up, Cay's awake," she says, her voice cracking on my name.

The sisters wake up faster than I have ever seen them capable of before; Eve instantly comes to my side. She takes my hand as her sister stands at the foot of the bed. I turn to Rose as she hands me the water, her eyes are glossy with tears threatening to spill over at any moment. My mind is a mess of jumbled thoughts and memories, most making little to no sense and feeling a lot more like a dream.

"What happened?" I ask, my throat hoarse.

My friends exchange a loaded look. Eve squeezes my hand. "Cay, there is no easy way to say this but you were poisoned. It's been three days since Rose's birthday," Eve answers hesitantly.

Rose turns away from me, staring out the window once again. Mar doesn't come any closer than the foot of the bed. The three of them seem on edge, like they're scared. Which I guess given the fact I just found out I was poisoned, is a valid thing to feel. "What kind of poison?" I ask Eve. They don't seem surprised by my question, more frustrated than anything.

She shakes her head, "We don't know. The healers have never seen anything like it. It attacked your *magic*." Her words are choked off on a broken sort of sob. She squeezes her eyes shut, a singular tear sliding over her pale cheek. "You would fight it for so long but then your magic would be near empty and it got bad again. We didn't- we weren't sure you would..." her words drift off, the weight of them washing over me like a crashing wave.

I stare at her, taking it all in. If my body was fighting through some sort of poison, would that be why it aches so much? Can you get sore from that kind of internal battle? I run a mental check, reaching out for my magic and finding it there, depleted but still accessible. An undeniable emptiness settles in my stomach, begging to be filled with magic in a way I have never experienced before.

"You woke up for a little while one day, but then you started screaming. You were in *so much pain.* It was the scariest thing I have ever seen in my life," Eve whispers, swallowing hard. When she opens her eyes again the gray swirls for a moment before settling. The sight of it sends a chill racing down my spine.

"Well that would explain why my throat hurts so much," I say with a smile.

Eve launches herself at me, wrapping her arms around my shoulders and pulling me into a fierce hug.

"Eve, be careful, she's still recovering," Mar reprimands. She takes a hesitant step towards us, ready to intervene if her sister pushes things too far.

"Yeah, well I needed this so I'm sure she does too," Eve retorts, wrapping her arms tighter in emphasis.

I try to lift my arms to return her hug but they barely make it to her waist before the pain becomes too much. I let them close there, squeezing her back as hard as I can manage, it isn't much. She pulls back and looks at Rose, concern written plainly across her face. Mar is avoiding eye contact with me entirely.

"Okay, what else? What am I missing?" Though the pounding of my heart in my ears might be a sign that I am not ready for that answer. I'm met with three stares, none of them encouraging.

Eve looks like she is about ready to burst with whatever she is holding in. Rose is about on the verge of tears. And Mar's expression is unreadable, which is almost worse.

"Someone just spit it out already. What can be worse than getting poisoned?" I ask, jokingly, a mirthless laugh dying on my lips when my friends flinch.

Rose steps closer to me, sitting down on the edge of the bed. Before she speaks a word I know that it *is* worse. Her eyes are filled with regret and a sorrow I have only seen in her once before, when her father died. Fear steals my breath, my body grows numb in an instant.

"Is someone dead?" I ask, my voice surprisingly even.

Rose recoils from the question. "No," she cringes, "well, we aren't sure. There is- you've missed a lot, Cay. I'm not even sure where to really begin. But please know that I am *so sorry.* For everything. For the poison and- just, I'm so sorry, Cay." I can see the regret written plainly across her face, echoing what I saw in the mirror for the last year.

I wait for her to continue but she doesn't so I turn to Eve, begging her silently to just tell me what happened before the panic threatens to consume me.

"What was the last thing you remember?" she asks.

I try to sift through the fog in my brain, the last clear memory I have being my conversation with Terran. My cheeks heat and Mar nods her head knowingly. That does not make me feel overly confident in what is to come next.

"You were drinking wine at the party, we believe that's how you ended up poisoned. Oliver thought you were just drunk so he handed you off to Mar and Oak for safe keeping," Eve explains.

"Oliver? Why was I with him." I search my memories but Oliver is not among them. Only the warmth behind Terran's eyes as we danced together. The heat of his palm pressed against my back. The familiar curve of his lips as he smiled down at me. My cheeks heat as I pull myself from the memory.

"Not sure, I was… incapacitated myself actually," she says with a blush.

I try to dig deeper into my mind for answers but everything after my conversation with Terran is covered in a misty darkness that I can't see through. A thick fog that writhes and grows the deeper I search for answers. Frustrated, I give up looking. "Alright, what else? Please just tell me," I beg.

Eve looks to her sister and Mar huffs. "There was an attack," Mar says plainly. Always one to skip the theatrics and get right to the point. This time, her bluntness is welcomed, even if it causes my entire body to go hot then cold.

Nausea builds in my stomach and bile burns the back of my throat but I force the words out. "Okay, go on, please." I take deep, even breaths to try and calm the rising panic in my chest.

"Reports started coming in from all over Estarynn about different attacks. It was pure chaos, no one knew what was happening until we realized that most of the attacks were just a distraction. Something to pull the attention away from the real attack. Rayan."

My heart skips a beat. The steady thump of my heart silent for a split second, the world seeming to freeze around me. An echo of a voice in the back of my mind calls to me but I ignore it, focusing instead on what Mar said. I need to say something, ask more questions, step up and get this all well under control. But I can't. It's like all logical thoughts have emptied from my mind and one word has replaced them all. Rayan.

My home, my people, my *family*. The beautiful city beneath the water, the way the waves on the surface create ripples of light below. The laughing of people filling the halls. My brother. My parents. My soul in every way that matters most.

The heart of my magic itself. Every realm and kingdom has a city or royal estate of some kind, none quite like my own. Tepis is the very heart of all my people, not just me. The life that is breathed into them and runs through their veins comes from the magic the city produces.

If Rayan falls, so will my people.

I clear my throat, suppressing the rising sob. "Is- did the city fall?" Every millisecond that passes while I wait for the answer has my magic growing uncontrolled, even in its depleted state. Mar and Eve focus on one person so I do the same, praying to the Goddess that she has the answers. "Rose? Please, do you know *anything*?"

Rose turns to me and the tears have finally escaped, they run down her cheeks in a steady stream. Her hazel eyes meet my seagreen. "There are no words to explain or excuse the failure that I...." she cuts herself off. Her breaths come out in short pants.

"Rose, you have to pull it together. This isn't about us. Cay deserves to know," Mar says, her expression firm. I can feel ripples of power rolling off of her, small tendrils of her control slipping through her fingertips.

Rose nods, wiping her tears from her face, "I know. I'm sorry. Cay, three days ago the attackers breached the walls of the city, Tepis. As far as I know the barrier has remained intact but.. we have not heard any news since the initial attack and truthfully, my advisors fear the worst."

The nausea overwhelms me and I desperately search for something to throw up in. Eve quickly hands me a bucket that appears out of nowhere. I empty the limited contents of my stomach and then continue to dry heave. My stomach muscles clench and retch forcefully, painfully, until a sheen of sweat coats my forehead. Once I finally get myself under control enough to stop heaving I collapse back into the bed, my entire body shaking.

"Breathe, Cay. You have to breathe," Rose demands. She places a hand against my cheek and sends a bit of healing magic into me.

I gulp down air but it gets stuck in my chest. I feel like my insides are being wrung like a wet towel, my chest cracking open with the pain that my brain can't even begin to process.

"Don't let this break you. Cay, you are stronger than this. You are not alone. It hurts, I know that, but you have to fight it. For your people. For yourself," Mar commands, her eyes searching mine for a strength that I'm not sure I have anymore.

I've never been the strong one, I've just learned how to hide it well. I never learned how to push past the pain, I just shoved it so deep inside myself that I could pretend it wasn't there. For a while at least. But now, this pain is so strong, so potent, it can't be ignored. It screams through every fiber of my being, demanding to be heard. To be felt. If I could just breathe through this… but I can't. Every breath is like swallowing razor blades. Magic bubbles up inside of me and I have to force it back down before it becomes too much to handle.

Eve shakes her head. "No, you're not okay. Don't try and pretend you are. Feel it. But don't let it consume you. What do you want us to do next?"

The question catches me so off guard that for a moment I forget the cracks, the sharp pain in my chest, and I laugh. At first it is just a singular burst but quickly it dissolves into a sort of hysterical chuckle.

"I don't think she is in the best state of mind to be making important decisions at the moment," Rose counters.

"No, this is the perfect time to make these decisions. So tell us, what do you want to do now, Cay?" Eve says, determined.

There is only one thing I want to do. I want to stop this pain. But there is only one way to do that. "I want to go home," I say, between gasping laughs, the sound broken and out of place in the somber room.

Eve nods, "Okay, so that's what we'll do."

All of the laughter dies in an instant, replaced with a sort of calm that should scare me. "Really?"

"Let's do it. The only way to get the answers you need is to see for yourself, so, let's go," she says with a casual shrug.

Mar and Rose exchange worried glances but I pay them no mind.

The only thing that matters is that I am going *home*.

Chapter 32

Mar

I watch as Cay turns to Rose hesitantly. For a moment she seems alive again, present in this moment, but then reality hits her and she grows silent. Her face still has an odd grayish tinge to it. Her eyes are ringed with dark circles and glistening with unshed tears. Every move she makes is cautious, like she is in pain and not just the emotional kind. Cay's breathing is shallow and every inhale comes with a slight flinch. Whatever the poison was, it did a number on her.

The night that she woke up the first time we had all been so relieved. But before any of us could even consider telling her what had happened she started screaming. At first we thought maybe she was just frightened, having some sort of nightmare. Then we realized she was screaming in agony. The kind of pain that tears a person apart from the inside. And we had no idea how to stop it. For hours we listened to her destroy her vocal cords until her screams became silent and she collapsed back into a deep sleep.

None of us slept after that. I stayed up watching her writhe in her sleep, battling an unseen enemy and feeling every bit as helpless as when I found her in the room. The mere thought of how cold her skin felt, how rigid, it makes me want to grab that bucket Eve had earlier. Every second of that moment is burned into my mind, replaying on a constant loop.

The same way it had when I saw my mother lying on her bed covered in her own blood. My newborn brothers' crying in the other room, desperate for a mother that never got to hold them. Their father was sobbing over my mother's lifeless body, demanding Vana bring her back. I grabbed her arm, ready to beg for her life beside him, but the moment her skin touched mine I knew she was gone. Even as young as I was, I felt the life drain from her body. Leaving a shell of who she was behind, cold and rigid. Just like Cay was.

It's been difficult to reconcile the image of Cay as she was with the way she is now. A part of me is scared to believe she is here, alive and talking about rushing to the middle of what could very well be an all out war. Yet I wouldn't for a moment consider denying her. Not when I saw how instant her cracks began to spread. How she was a second away from crumbling. Cay needs this, and since there is no way we are letting her do it alone, of course we are all in. No matter the cost.

Rose echoes her confirmation and we immediately get to planning.

"Alright, when do we leave?" Eve asks, terrifying excitement evident in her voice. Energy crackles in the air around her, charged by her magic.

"Now. I want to leave right now," Cay says adamantly. She struggles to swing her legs over the side of the bed.

"You need more time to rest, to heal. It wouldn't be safe to travel in your current condition," Rose says. She gently pushes Cay back, trying to stop her from standing too quickly.

I nod my agreement.

"I'll heal twice as fast if I am back in my kingdom, especially once I am under the water. My magic will replenish faster than I can deplete it," Cay counters. She is buzzing with an anxious energy, one that will eventually crash and leave her vulnerable.

"Sure, but there's no way you'll be able to travel for days through the woods and not at least feel the effects." Sure there are other ways we can get there, namely a certain dragon who Eve seems to have wrapped around her finger, but I'm not about to go offering that option up, not when it will only encourage her further. I am willing to do whatever it takes to help Cay but putting her at risk is something that I don't feel comfortable with.

Cay smiles wistfully, "that's why we won't be traveling by horseback."

We all share a confused grin but Cay just says she'll explain later.

"Okay, now that transportation is apparently taken care of. What kind of backup are we bringing? Don't get me wrong, I think the four of us are pretty badass as is but it wouldn't hurt to have some help," Eve says, in a rare display of forethought.

"What about Oak? She'll come won't she?" Cay asks.

Eve and I look at Rose, who sighs. "Oak and my brother left the night of the party. We haven't heard anything from them," Rose says, calmly. Between her cousin and brother leaving, and Cay being sick, Rose has barely held herself together. Each day that passes has pushed her closer to her breaking point.

Cay's eyes widen, "Which brother?"

"Oliver," Rose groans.

A strange look crosses over Cay's face. My mind flashes with the image of Cay in the bath telling me about another one of Rose's brothers. I wonder if maybe that wasn't entirely the full story. If so, good for her.

"And Terran?" Cay asks, regaining her fragile composure.

"He had to stay here. My mother was anxious about possible attacks on our realm. Technically she didn't even approve the other two to go, but when have they ever listened?"

Cay nods to herself.

"What about Rian?" Rose asks, looking between my sister and I.

Eve makes a look of disgust. "Do we really *want* him to help? He's been getting on my nerves a lot the past few days and I seriously doubt sir 'it's not safe, we need to return home immediately' will be thrilled about the idea of us running *towards* the danger."

I snort, "You're just mad because Rian doesn't do everything you want like a certain dragon does."

Eve grins devilishly, but before she can respond, Cay cuts her off. "Wait, did I miss something else? Did something happen between you and Nat?"

Rose smiles to herself and I roll my eyes. Eve sits up proudly and launches into a very detailed story that I do my best to try and block out. I don't care how close we are, there are some things I really do not need, nor want to hear. Especially given the specifics that my sister so delightfully shares.

"I don't mean to interrupt but I'm pretty sure we have a time sensitive situation on our hands," I say, mostly to my sister although Cay gives me a sheepish smile.

"Okay, what else do we need?" Rose asks.

"We'll need weapons," I answer. If we're about to rush into a fight I want to be prepared and magic isn't always reliable. Especially being so cut off from our sources. There are things people can do to prevent magic, but a physical weapon? That you can always trust.

"I can take care of that," Eve offers with an only slightly concerning smirk.

"Anything else?" Rose asks.

I shake my head along with Cay.

"Let's do this then," Eve says, jumping up. She bounds from one foot to another, clearly energized by the prospect of a fight.

I roll my eyes at my sister as my heart begins to pound. Eve and I have been training since we were young. Rose only recently, and Cay even more so than her. There are a thousand reasons why this is a bad idea. Yet the way my sister looks to all of us makes me feel like nothing can touch us. Sometimes it's easy to forget she's the oldest. Especially when she so often lets other people take charge. But when she steps into these moments and *leads*? It makes me excited for the day she will be my queen.

Looking between Cay and Rose I realize just how much is really riding on this, and fear spikes in me again. The sound of Cay's screams echo through my mind, the faint sound of babies in the distance. I push away the memories, focusing instead on what needs to be done. I can't let anything go wrong. We need to do everything in our power to protect each other. *Everything.* "You need to top off your magic," I say to Rose.

She nods, "What about you?"

"I'll take care of it," I say with a smile.

Cay looks exhausted, only heightening my concern for her and whatever idea she has to get us there faster.

"Cay, you should stay here and rest until we're ready," Rose suggests.

Cay shakes her head, "I've been laying in this bed for three days. So aside from maybe a bath and something to eat, I'm done resting. I just want to leave as soon as possible."

"At least let a healer look you over," I push.

Cay nods reluctantly. Rose leans forward and pulls her into a hug. My heart aches. "I'll have some food sent over and send someone to check on you," Rose promises.

"Alright but I'll take mine without poison this time," Cay says with a forced laugh.

Rose blanches and I can't help but cringe.

"Too soon?" Cay asks.

Rose just shakes her head as she leaves. I linger for a moment before turning to leave.

"Mar?" Cay says hesitantly.

I look over my shoulder, "Yeah?"

"Did something else happen?"

"What do you mean?" Fear shoots through my veins.

"You just seem… off." Cay leans towards me, reaching out a hand.

I smile, taking a subtle step back. "No, nothing else happened. I'm just tired. I'm really happy you're okay. I love you." I don't wait for her response before leaving the room. It takes a few steps before I am aware of where I am going. I let my body lead me to the room that I know will have just the person that I am looking for. Entering the training room I look around for a sign of ashy blonde hair and an overinflated ego.

"Looking for me?" Rian asks from the corner of the room where he is putting dummies back in their place.

"Actually, yes," I say, smiling to myself at the timing.

His eyes narrow, "I don't trust that smile."

I roll my eyes, "Scared?"

He snickers, "Of you? Never."

I use my vamp speed to shoot over to him and strike at his throat. He easily dodges my bite but when he looks down he finds a small blade barely pressing against his gut. "Maybe you should be," I say with a smirk. We step apart and I slip the blade back into my boot. "I need a favor," I say looking over my shoulder and checking the doorway.

"No," he says immediately.

"You don't even know what it is yet," I counter, annoyed.

"I don't need to. Between you and your sister, any favor has got to be bad." He's not exactly wrong. Though something about his assumption rubs me the wrong way, after all, Eve *is* his future queen.

"Hear me out. You're going to want to help me when you hear this. Only rule is that you have to listen to everything I say before freaking out. Deal?" I confirm.

He glares at me for a moment before sighing deeply and running a hand through his hair. "You're going to do whatever this is with or without me, at least with me I can keep an eye on you both."

"Good luck with that." I scoff.

"You know that doesn't exactly make me feel confident with the current situation."

"Are you in or out?" I ask impatiently.

Rian takes a moment to study my face before extending his hand to me, "Please don't make me regret this."

The moment his hand is in mine my smile changes, "No promises."

Chapter 33

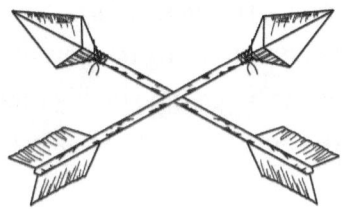

Oak

It has taken us three days to travel from the center of Sena to the border. Throughout the journey I spent an abundance of time imagining what we might find once we got there. Never did I picture what lies before us. For a moment I forgot what it meant to travel this path, what we would have to go through. But as we ride through the village, I cannot ignore the nausea rising up inside of me.

There are no people, no animals, no life at all. Worse than that, there are no bodies. It appears as though the villagers have simply disappeared. Like they just walked away, leaving everything behind. A thick fog makes it difficult to navigate the path, in some areas, so dense that I can't even see my hand in front of my face.

Darkness surrounds us, the moon high in the sky as Oliver rides ahead of me, silent as ever. His entire body is tense, either from the long journey or the disturbing silence around us. We would have been here sooner had it not been for my insistence on resting every few hours. Something that Oliver is sure to harbor resentment over.

A chill moves down my spine and I have to steady myself on my horse. I've spent years spying for my aunt. The things I have seen and heard often plague me with nightmares. But none as unsettling as this. The utter emptiness around us makes every sound and breath feel like a growing target on our backs.

My magic is itchy beneath my skin, a sign of how uncomfortable I truly am. The urge to speed through the village as fast as we can is strong. I keep my gaze fixed on Oliver's back, refusing to allow my eyes to wander down the familiar roads. I spent so much time in this village as a child, our own being close enough to the border that it was easy to check in and visit my parents' friends.

An ache throbs in my chest but I ignore it. Focusing instead on moving forward. We're getting closer to the docks outside the city. Tepis makes up the majority of Rayan's territory and with it being located at the bottom of the ocean, their actual *land* is limited. Atran, the small city connected to the docks presses up against our borders and makes it all too easy to get inside, going both directions. I recall playing with Reed along the border, hopping from one land to the next calling out, "I'm in Rayan," "I'm in Sena," he would always laugh as he watched.

The fog grows thicker the deeper we move through the village and we've barely entered Rayan's lands. Dread is steadily building inside me, like a warning sign to turn back now. I reach for the bow slung across my back, reminding myself that it is there and calming my racing heart.

Oliver has no visible weapon, opting instead to rely on his magic. His spellwork is exceptional, something that I never realized until now. The way he commands the element to bend to his will is on a level unseen before. His sheer power alone likely rivals that of his brother and mother.

Even more surprising is how quickly he is able to replenish his magic. Every time I am sure he must be near empty he pushes on, almost like he has a secret magic reservoir that no one else has. Asshole. Watching him extend his palm out in front of him he continues to make the ground even, softening the steps of our horses. Such a simple spell yet crucial in moments like these. Many warriors might be too hubristic to resort to such spells but not him. It appears that while Oliver is the epitome of arrogance in all other situations, he is rather humble as a fighter. Trusting the basics to work in his favor.

Suddenly, Oliver's hand closes into a fist, signaling me to stop. My horse stops beside him, huffing loudly. "What is it?" I whisper, letting my eyes search the area around us.

"You don't feel it?" he asks.

"No, what do you sense?"

"Magic. A lot of magic. The air itself is thick with it." He searches the darkness for something, a sign or source of the power.

I move my hands through the air around me, dispelling the fog for a moment then watching as it quickly reforms. "Do you think it's the fog?"

Oliver does exactly as I did, waving his hand through the mist and letting the tendrils pass between his fingers. "Possibly. It's hard to tell. This magic is unlike anything I have ever felt before. It feels ancient."

A hard blast hits me in the chest and I am thrown backwards off my horse, who immediately takes off running. I roll around on the hard ground trying to regain my breath but it feels like my lungs have collapsed.

Oliver is off his horse and beside me in an instant. "Get up. We're not alone. Get up now," he says, extending a hand out to me.

"I'm fine, thanks for asking," I wheeze out, grabbing his hand and letting him pull me to my feet.

"I don't have time to coddle you. I can sense at least five people surrounding us so get ready or get out of my way." The earth rumbles beneath our feet as Oliver prepares for an attack.

I bull my bow off my back and quickly notch an arrow. Not the best for a close up fight but it will have to do, my whips are strapped onto my horse. Which is now gone. I could use magic but when you have no idea who you're up against it's better to err on the side of caution.

Another blast shoots through the mist but this time I dodge it, releasing the arrow in the direction it came from. A twig snaps behind me and I whirl around in time to see a blade come cresting towards me. I duck, dropping low to the ground and popping up again, back to back with my cousin.

"Any idea who they are?" I ask, staring into the thick mist. A bright blast of power cuts through the air beside my head.

"No clue but I've seen blasts like those before." Oliver summons a wall of stone around us as a combination of attacks break through the darkness.

I turn to him, taking the moment of reprieve to look my cousin over from head to toe. "Oh? Care to elaborate?"

Magic cracks off the other side of the wall until a small hole appears, the rock crumbling and leaving space for a blast aimed directly at Oliver's chest. He moves his hands faster than my eyes can track, the wall reforms perfectly, thickening into an impenetrable defense. "When Cay decided I needed a shower," he says bitterly. His jaw is set as he fights to maintain the barrier between us and our attackers.

A laugh bubbles up in my throat but I suppress it. Now is not the time. Later, though, I will absolutely be laughing and high-fiving that girl.

"Screw this," Oliver grunts, dropping the wall and sending out a series of rapid-fire blasts of his magic. Large spears of rock slice through the air.

I notch and fire arrows one after another, not even pausing to breathe. For a moment we seem to have them at our mercy until the attacks start to come quicker and we are dodging blasts every few seconds. Jets of water careen towards us until they harden into deadly icicles. I continue to fire arrows but with the fog so thick I can't even tell if I'm hitting anything or just wasting time and energy. "This isn't working," I groan.

Oliver blasts away another icicle. "You think?"

Slinging my bow across my back again I drop to the ground. My fingers spread in the dirt, sending waves of vibrations through the ground until I sense the person closest to me. Crawling through the mist I pop up behind the attacker, slipping a small blade free and pushing it against their stomach, right between their ribs. I let the blade dig in a little bit, not enough to draw blood but leave no room for escape. "Knock it off or your friend here will find out how hard it is to breathe with only one lung," I yell into the fog.

In an instant the mist recedes, revealing four others surrounding Oliver as he fights to regain his breath.

"Thank you," I say with a smile.

"You gonna remove that blade now or what?" says the man in my grip.

I push the point in just a bit, "Nah, I think I'll wait to hear why exactly you are all attacking us."

"Fine, we'll tell you as soon as you tell us why you are here," a man says from beside Oliver.

"Not gonna happen," Oliver answers with a cruel smile.

"Well then I guess we are at an impasse, aren't we," says the man beneath my blade. He's awfully relaxed for a hostage.

I examine the man next to Oliver. He's tall, broad shoulders and a sword gripped tightly in one hand. He's wearing a plate of metal over his chest and leather pants. I squint across the darkness to examine the crest on the plate. A familiar trident insignia is pressed into the thin metal.

"Wait, are you all Rayan guards?" I ask.

"And if we are?" says a feminine voice from behind me. Something sharp and cold presses against my jugular.

"Well shit," I say, releasing the man in my grip and holding my hands up.

Oliver's annoyed expression tells me enough about my getting caught.

"Now would probably be a good time to mention that we are here to help. Call us, backup?" I shrug.

The female laughs beside my ear, "Sure, two lone fighters on horses with no supplies and a single weapon between them. Really helpful."

"Technically I have my blade too which counts as a second weapon," I counter.

"Barely. Now, tell us why you're really here," she demands.

Oliver steps forward, staring over my shoulder at my captor, "Ny name is Oliver. I am the second heir to the Sena throne and emissary of my realm.

I am a friend to Queen Mira and King Callan. My *cousin* over there is telling the truth. We have come to help with your situation."

The female steps back, releasing her hold on me. "Lies. Why would the Earth realm send not one but two members of the *royal* family? Especially when they have sent no reinforcements," the words are bitter, giving us little room to argue.

"I guess we're just that disposable," Oliver offers with a grin. Something about the way he says it makes me think he might actually believe that.

"Lucky us," I say under my breath.

The guards all exchange a look then turn to the female. I look over my shoulder and examine her. She is tall, with carved muscles and dark brown hair that brushes the tops of her shoulders. Her determined eyes are a vibrant green, similar to my own. She looks to be in the latter half of her third decade which means she's likely closer to 400.

"I'm Lieutenant Regan Auger, of Rayan," she says, lifting her chin up proudly.

"Tell us, Lieutenant, what is the status of your kingdom?" Oliver asks calmly, his voice taking on a more regal tone.

Her chin drops slightly. She takes a deep breath before answering, "The city walls have been breached. All of the citizens living on the docks have fled. The tunnels leading to the city have been completely destroyed. Our squad was helping evacuate Tepis when the blasts started, we barely made it out before they collapsed. I am not sure of what is happening on the inside."

Oliver nods his head like this all sounds perfectly normal and not like the craziest shit we've ever heard. I didn't even know it was possible for the tunnels *to* collapse, I thought they had some kind of magic that prevented it.

"Wait. You said the citizens on the docks fled. Where did they go?" I ask.

"The enemy came from the East, the citizens scattered. When people started to evacuate Tepis they became more frantic. There was a mass exodus to the west, likely fleeing into your own realm," she explains sullenly.

"We didn't see a single refugee on our way here. If they crossed into Sena territory, they would have likely stopped in this village first. They also should have immediately reported themselves to the high lady upon entering the realm," Oliver announces. A crease forms between his eyes as he seems to get lost in thought.

"That news is disappointing. We had hoped that by coming to the village we might get a reprieve from the fog, maybe be able to rest for a while before resuming our attempts to get back into the city," Lieutenant Auger shares with a sigh.

"Speaking of, what's the deal with this fog anyways? Is this your magic?" I ask looking at the fog that surrounds us yet doesn't invade our circle.

"The fog came first, making it nearly impossible to tell where the attacks were coming from. It took us a while to realize that, even though we couldn't dispel the fog, we could manipulate it so we could move and fight easier," she answers. Her hands move through the fog fluidly, controlling the wisps and bending them to her will.

If the fog came from the East and made it all the way here, it must extend the entire width of the kingdom, possibly further. It would make traveling through it impossibly slow, not to mention we still don't know what's going on inside the city.

"Do you know anything about the enemy?" Oliver asks suddenly.

She shakes her head, "Only that they came from the East and used magic that I have never seen before in all my years."

Oliver nods, pacing the small circle quietly.

I stand in silence, unsure what to say or do. When we left Sena we had no idea what to expect but part of me still believed there would be some kind of fight. A battle to defend the city. We came here to help but how can we expect to do anything when so much is still unknown? I look at my cousin but his expression is distant, lost in thought. "What can we do to help, Lieutenant? Are there more guards out there?" I ask.

"Please, call me Regan. Most of the guards were rushing towards the city, many were caught in the tunnels as they collapsed. We lost a few of our own," Regan shares.

"I'm sorry to hear that," I offer, placing a light hand on her shoulder.

"It's an honor to die protecting our people. I only wish we had been able to do more. Maybe if we had made it back through the tunnels we could help from the inside but as it stands, there is not much else we can do," she says sorrowfully.

"We can," Oliver says suddenly.

All gazes turn to him, shock written plainly across many faces. "The tunnels were destroyed, it would be nearly impossible without far greater magic than we possess," Regan dismisses with a shake of her head.

"Wait, everyone in the city is trapped?" I realize.

"Until someone with a great amount of power is able to reform the tunnels, I fear so, yes. They were originally constructed by our first king," Regan says proudly.

"Good thing I'm here then," Oliver smirks.

I stare at him, mouth agape and fighting back my twitching hand as it yearns to smack that arrogant grin off his face. This is not the time.

"That's impossible, you would need immense power. And besides, I believe I am right to assume that you do not carry the ability to wield water," says Regan.

"I might not be able to use water magic but I have more power than you think. I can create a dome using my earth magic and walk us to the city, like our own personal air bubble," Oliver says with a shrug.

My entire chest tightens at the image formed in my mind. Something about a concrete dome and the bottom of the ocean just doesn't sit well with me.

"Even if you were capable of such, it would take hours to reach the city from here and the oxygen would run out far before we made it there," Regan counters again, picking at flaws in this undeveloped plan.

"Well then I guess we better get moving. You have until we make it to the shore to figure out that whole oxygen problem," Oliver says, turning on his heel walking towards the direction our horses ran off to.

"Is he always like this?" the big guard asks.

I sigh, "Worse, if you can believe it."

Chapter 34

Mar

"So, I know I said I was cool with this plan but are we sure this is the best way to get there?" Rose asks hesitantly, fiddling with the straps on her leather pants holding her throwing daggers. She's wearing a matching leather vest with extra pockets to 'hold fun things' as she excitedly told me this morning.

She, Cay, and I all stand in our hidden garden, away from prying eyes. It's still early, the warm glow of the rising sun peeking through cracks in the stone walls. I struggled to find something to wear, and had to opt for the riding pants and tunic I wore on the way here. Had I known I was going to be running off into a battle I would have packed something a bit more practical.

"The best? No. The fastest. Absolutely," Cay answers, continuing to work on some sort of spell. She seemed even less prepared in the realm of fashion. Her long, cotton dress sweeps the floor as she walks around the garden. Her long sleeves billow around her arm as she extends it out beside her, pouring sand in a large circle around us then moving to fiddle with a bowl of water at the center.

I watch her ministrations in a mix of awe and confusion. I've never seen such a spell before. In Vulca, we mostly focus on elemental magic and honing our shifted forms. I learned some basic healing magic like simple tonics and potions from my mother but aside from that I have a rather limited knowledge.

"What can I do to help?" Rose asks, looking around the garden and fiddling with her braid now. Nervous energy is practically rolling off her.

"Just make sure that everything we want to go with us is inside the circle. I can handle the rest," Cay says, continuing her work. Sweat drips down the side of her face as she continues to use what limited power she has remaining after fighting for her life. Her steps are slow, her breathing labored, yet she never relents. Her determination to get home propels her forward and gives her strength, even where others might fail. Thankfully her power should restore much quicker once we arrive in Rayan.

Rose starts gathering up our supplies and quickly places them within the circle. We decided it was best to pack lightly, necessities only. For me that included a few tonics and potions in case anyone ended up hurt. I scoff at myself; big help they were when Cay was poisoned. The image of her laying in bed flashes again through my mind. My skin instantly pales as I try to shake the unwanted memory.

Taking a few deep breaths, I banish the picture from my mind, focusing instead on the clear sky above me. The birds are chirping in the trees, a slight breeze rustling the highest branches. If I ignore the two girls preparing for war in front of me, I can almost enjoy this moment. It's not often we get to spend time in the sun back home. My heart pangs with hurt, it's already been almost two weeks since I left home but so much has already changed. I can't help but wonder about my brothers, if they are safe and if someone is taking care of them.

They may have their father but he has to work and he can't always be with them to make sure they don't get themselves into trouble. Keegan is still too young to really take care of the twins. Flint and Hagan cause enough problems *with* supervision, and I try not to think about what they get up to without it. Unease builds in my stomach but I know that this is the right decision. Maybe not the smart decision, but certainly what is *right*.

"There, it's all set for whenever Eve gets here," Cay says, turning to look over her careful work as she pulls her thick hair into a bun on the top of her head

"I'm here!" Eve calls from the entrance. Her arms are full of various weapons for each of us. She opted for her own riding attire with the addition of her daggers strapped to her thigh.

I rush forward, taking a collection of blades from her before she slices off her arm. We begin handing out weapons. Cay gets some kind of cylindrical tube that she takes from me carefully, the shape of it reminds me of my own staff. Rose refuses the sword Eve hands her and opts for additional daggers and small throwing knives. I look back towards the entrance, my grip tightening on my staff as I hook it to the belt strapped around my waist. "Are you sure you weren't followed?" I ask, worry building in my chest.

"Positive. I would know if someone were following me," my sister says proudly, hiding blades in various places on her body. She slips a miniscule blade between her full breasts and I can't help but shade my head at the absurdity.

"Remind me to add stealth to your next training session," says a deep voice from the entrance.

I turn in time to see a flash of fire before Rian removes his concealment spell.

Oh thank Vana. For once the man actually listened.

Rian looks around the garden, locking eyes with me for a moment, understanding flaring in his gaze. He turns to my sister and gives her a firm look. "Let's go. Whatever idiotic plan you have worked up is done. We're going back home." He steps forward, reaching out to grab Eve by her arm and drag her out of here if need be.

Eve's mouth drops open then shifts into a grin, "I'm sorry did you just try to order me around?" She takes a step back, putting distance between them without appearing like she is retreating.

Rian's jaw clicks with tension.

"The last time I checked, *I* was *your* queen. So, how about you try that again?" Eve says smugly. It's rare that she chooses to use the queen card but in this case, I am not surprised in the least.

Rose and Cay both look nervous for wherever this conversation is headed. My own heart races with the hope that Rian will follow through on our deal.

He scrubs a hand over his chin, drawing my attention to a bit of stubble I hadn't noticed before. The hair is surprisingly dark, a stark contrast to the mess of blonde atop his head. "Fine. But the moment that anything goes wrong, we leave. And for the record, you aren't my queen *yet*."

"Not to state the obvious but it's not exactly like we'll be able to just *walk out* once we're there," Eve counters.

"Perfect, so you're running into a potential warzone with no backup, no real training, and no escape route. Tell me again how this is a good idea?" Rian sneers.

It's Cay that responds, stepping forward and commanding the attention to herself. "You're right. This isn't a good idea. But it's the only one I've got, so unless you can tell me a better way to save my kingdom, I suggest you keep those comments to yourself."

Rian opens his mouth to respond but Eve holds up a hand, silencing him. To my surprise, it actually works. Rian begrudgingly snaps his mouth shut, crossing his arms over his chest and shrugging as if to tell Cay she is good to continue.

"Okay, everything should be good to go. Is everyone ready?" Cay asks our small group.

"Wait for me," yells Nat, bursting through the entrance, her coppery curls bouncing in a ponytail.

I turn to my sister with a smirk but she shrugs, a slight smile on her lips. Rian looks to the poor guard with a look of complete and utter betrayal. Clearly, he hadn't expected to see the dragon here.

"Alright, now that we're all here," Cay says, pausing to see if there are any more interruptions, "the spell itself is pretty simple. I can use my magic to open a kind of doorway that will let us cross through and appear just outside the city. Because of the wards we won't be able to open one directly in the castle but this will get us pretty close."

"Have you used it before?" Rian asks gravely.

Cay shakes her head. "No. But my father taught it to me in case there was ever an emergency. Or maybe for something like this…" her voice fades off and a despondent look creeps over her.

I take a step forward, reaching out my hand to hold hers but pulling it back just before it touches her bare skin. I stare down at my arm, frustration building inside me.

This is idiotic.

It's just skin.

I've held Cay's hand a hundred times before. I start to reach out again but she turns away, gesturing to the circle.

"Everything inside the circle will be able to travel with us, anything left on the outside is disconnected, left behind. It's extremely important that we all stay close to each other and don't let go of each other's hand." She locks eyes with each of us, confirming we understand.

"We have to hold hands?" I ask before I can stop myself.

"No, but the connection is weaker if we don't. I'm using my water magic to activate the spell, since none of you carry that magic it can get a little tricky. Better hold hands to be safe," she says with a gentle smile.

I hesitate for a moment and this seems to give Cay the wrong idea. Her expression shifts to one of sympathy. Rage boils in my blood at my own actions, my hesitation. We're about to face an unknown enemy and I can't even hold my best friend's hand.

"Listen, I know you all want to help. And I appreciate it, truly. But this will probably be very dangerous. I understand if you don't want to take on that kind of risk. I won't be upset if you decide to stay behind," she says, the truth of her words weighing heavily on my heart.

Eve steps forward, taking Cay's hand, Rose follows without a moment of hesitation. They turn to me expectantly. I give them a wide smile and nod. Cay's face lights with relief as a lump forms in my throat. Here she is, ready to rush into a battle, only having just recovered from being *poisoned*, all to save her kingdom, and I can't even hold her hand while she does it. My body begins to shake with rage.

A warm hand presses against my lower back firmly. "So angry already? It's only morning, I'm sure there is plenty more I could do to deserve your rage," Rian says with a wink.

Taken aback, I forget my rage, focusing instead on the warmth of his hand, how it fits perfectly in the small of my back. My chest tightens for an entirely different reason and if his smirk is any indication, he noticed. I roll my eyes, "If I didn't know better I would think that you were excited about that."

Rian chuckles deeply, leaning in to whisper in my ear, "We both know the answer to that. I think I prefer you all fired up."

Someone clears their throat and we both turn to face the group. All eyes are on the two of us. My face heats and Rian laughs. I quickly shove my elbow into his gut and he lets out a rough breath of air. "Sorry, you were saying?" I ask sheepishly.

Cay smiles knowingly and continues to walk us through the spell, "Once I activate the spell we should be able to see the city. All we have to do is step through and we'll be right outside the tunnels."

"Question," Nat says hesitantly, "can't I just fly you all there? I've carried more people before and I'm not exactly loving this whole portal idea. I would feel a lot more comfortable flying."

Rian nods his head in agreement.

"That would be a good idea except right now we have the element of surprise on our side. They won't be able to see us coming until we're right there in the thick of things. If we choose to fly in, we would lose that," Cay answers kindly. We spent hours trying to come up with alternative plans but this was the best one that we could think of. Despite my reluctance.

"What about a concealment spell like the one Rian just used? I could cast it over all of us, problem solved right?" Eve asks.

Rian and Cay both shake their heads. "There are charms surrounding the border to the entire kingdom, the moment we crossed into Rayan lands the spell would fall away," Rian explains.

"He's right. The best chance we have at sneaking in is this. Any other way and we risk being seen before we're ready. This is the safest way to go," Cay emphasizes.

Rian looks like he is ready to argue that particular point but chooses to keep his mouth shut. We all look around our small group and step forward to form a circle. Rose takes the spot on my right, Rian to my left. Nat takes the spot on his other side, joining hands with Eve who takes Cay's hand. Cay and Rose close the circle and then it begins.

The hum of energy fills the circle and then the water in the bowl rises, creating a sort of archway. For a moment, it's empty, I can stare straight through it at my sister. She gives me a wiggle of her brows and flashes a look at Nat. I laugh inwardly, poor Nat has no idea what she is in for.

The archway begins to ripple, the water cascading down and forming a sort of waterfall. Then, it's there. At first the image is fuzzy, just a brief shot of the beautiful sea and the docks along the shore. A thick layer of fog makes things difficult to see clearly but then the image sharpens and we can see the grand entrances to the tunnels.

Only..

They're not standing proud and tall like they always have. No. The tunnels have collapsed inwardly on themselves. The ghost of the magic used to preserve them left haunting the place where they once stood. Pulverized bits of stone float on the surface of the water.

I hear Cay's cry of pain as she gets the first glimpse at her kingdom, at its destruction. The sound is a mix between a scream and a sob. The ground beneath us begins to tremble. The image becomes jumbled, showing us broken fragments of the city in rapid succession. It flashes a sliver of an image, some sort of mural, the stone is cracked and stained. The water explodes around us, dragging us into its depths as the images begin moving faster and faster, to the point where I can hardly discern one from the other.

A vortex of water surrounds us as we clutch onto each other's hands. Magic is pulling against us, trying to force us apart. I look around the circle as we all struggle to hold on. Cay's face is contorted, distraught, tears streaming down her face openly. It's her, well, her magic. Her emotions are out of control. Whatever Cay's feeling, whatever she is *seeing*, it's affecting the spell.

Magic grabs onto me firmly and yanks against the hold I have on my friends' hands. I watch in horror as Eve's hand is ripped from Nat's. Rian's hand tightens around mine, I stare down at it, willing the magic to release us. I feel his grip slip and lock eyes with him as he is pulled away from me and, along with Nat, goes tumbling through the vortex. A scream gets lodged in my throat.

Eve is clutching onto Cay, refusing to let go. Rose looks between me and Cay, fighting to grab us both. I feel her hand loosen and fear races through my blood. My heart pounds. Then her hand tightens around my own.

"I've got you! I'm not letting go!" Rose screams through the thunderous water as it crashes in waves around us.

We're being pulled along, caught in its rip as it decides whether to spit us out or gently set us in the place of Cay's choosing. Another wave comes barreling towards us, right at *Cay*. My sister screams. A split second before it is about to take the two of them out, Rose loses her hold on Cay's hand and we are torn away; completely at the mercy of a magic that we cannot control.

Chapter 35

Eve

The vortex spits us out onto a cold marble floor. My body aches from the impact. I roll onto my back and stare up at the cracked ceiling as I run my hands over myself, checking for any potential injuries and finding nothing of concern. Thank Vana for small miracles. Sitting up I look around the room and spot Cay, bent over on all fours.

I rush to her side as she dry heaves, grabbing her shoulders to steady her. Her skin is sweaty as she calms herself enough to sit up and take a deep breath. Her face is blotchy and red, her eyes swollen from crying. Her body continues to twitch violently.

"Are you okay?" I ask, my voice barely a whisper.

Cay shakes her head, "I don't know." I watch her as she tries to steady her breathing, taking deep breaths in and then letting them out slowly. She squeezes her eyes tight for a moment before taking in our surroundings. A gasp slips through her lips as she realizes where we are.

I wasn't sure at first but the way her eyes water tells me my suspicions were correct.

We're inside Tepis. More than that, we're in Cay's art room.

She takes a moment to survey the damage. Paintings have been thrown around, destroyed. Her supplies are strewn across the tables like someone had been rummaging through everything. I follow her eyes as they take in each broken and missing piece, then I watch as they land on the ceiling. It's missing huge pieces of the mural of Cay's parents, lying scattered across the room in piles of stone and dust. A large chunk with her mother's face, her gentle smile, is at the top of a heap, broken off from her father's.

A rumbling starts beneath our feet as the entire room begins to shake. I turn to Cay, her entire body is shaking too. Wait, no, *she* is making the room shake. Her pupils dilate and energy swells inside the room. It's like what happened with the spell before everything went crazy. I shoot forward and wrap my arms around her, pulling her into a tight embrace.

My magic hums violently beneath my skin as I try to calm her down. "It's going to be okay. We'll figure this out. Cay, I'm here, I've got you." The room continues to shake so I squeeze her harder. "I know this is a lot to take in. But you're not alone, okay? I'm right here with you. We're in this together, we just need to figure out what we're going to do next. But we can't do that if your magic is all over the place. I need you to take a few more deep breaths, can you do that?" I ask, my voice coming out shakier than I would have liked. Something stirs inside me, dark and consuming. The image of my forgotten tonic floods my mind, the dark vial sitting at the bottom of a trunk where it has remained for the last three days.

Pushing aside everything else, I focus on calming Cay down, speaking soothing words in hushed voices and doing my best to keep her magic under control. It takes a minute but I feel her nod her head. I wait until the room stops shaking to let go, keeping my arms on her shoulders for an extra moment.

She stares up at the ceiling, her eyes devoid of any emotion while the rest of her looks on the brink of something. The fissure of energy coursing through the room fades, the static taste of magic burns my tongue. "I never gave Rose her birthday gift," she whispers.

"What?" Her words catch me off guard, out of place in this moment of chaos."Her gift. I was going to give it to her after the party. It's a painting of her forest. I think she would have liked it." A singular tear trails down her cheek, splashing against her collarbone.

I stare at the ceiling with her. The cracks continue to grow even as we sit here watching. With every passing moment the entire city is that much closer to complete collapse, literally. "Well then, let's figure this out so we can all go back and watch you give it to her then," I say with a forced smile.

Cay gives me a slight nod.

"Cay, do you know what happened to the spell? Where are the others?" I hesitate to ask, afraid of what the question might do to her fragile control.

"I don't know. Something went wrong," she says defeated.

I brush my unbound hair away from my face.

"Here," Cay says, bending down to grab a ribbon off the floor and offering it to me.

"Thank you." I take it and quickly twist my hair into a braid, using the ribbon to secure it so it's out of the way. "Alright, we need a plan. First thing we should do is find some of your guards. They've got to be hiding around here somewhere."

"If they're not all dead," Cay offers plainly.

"Yes, as long as they're not dead. But I'm feeling rather optimistic at the moment so let's just assume that they're not. Deal?" It might just be wishful thinking but a part of me refuses to believe that the city could crumble so easily.

We push open the doors and turn down the hallway only to find ourselves face to face with five cloaked figures, shadows and mist spilling from beneath their thick black cloaks. Their faces are hidden behind a black mask and with gloves covering their hands, no skin is visible whatsoever. The hall is dense with magic, a heavy power that has my own writhing inside of me, desperate to escape.

"Shit." I quickly unsheath the dagger at my thigh, "get behind me Cay."

The shadowy figures move in unison, walking towards us slowly as mist seeps out from their gloved fingertips. It billows towards us, a cloud drifting along the marble floors.

"What the..." I start as one breaks free of the group, shooting towards me like a whizzing arrow. I dodge the fist aimed for my face at the last second, ducking and popping up on the other side. I counter with a wicked roundhouse kick that catches the attacker in the side. They don't miss a beat before they come at me again. Hands grab me from behind and I deliver another kick to their back, turning around just in time to block another punch.

The two figures decide to come at me at the same time, taking turns throwing punches and kicks while mist continues to pour from beneath their gloved hands. Something about it makes my skin crawl and my senses heighten. My heart is racing as we fight back and forth, no one landing any real hits. The mist creeps up my legs, and the utter repulsion that shoots through me has me throwing caution to the wind.

"Screw this," I say, sweeping my arm out and letting my blade slice right through the center of one of them. They burst into a cloud of mist, leaving behind nothing but a cloud of smoke that quickly dissipates.

"What the absolute fuck, did you see that, Cay?" I yell at her while my remaining attacker tries to get a hold of my blade.

"Sorry, I'm a little busy over here," Cay grunts.

I spare a glance over my shoulder to see her fighting off two of her own figures. "Wait, weren't there fi-" I am cut off as my body goes flying into the wall. I slide down, hitting the ground on my ass, all the air knocked out of me. Two cloaked figures stalk towards me, hands outstretched.

The mist washes over the floor in a thick fog, racing towards me. I don't have time to stand so I hold up my hands drawing magic and heat into my palms and then I let loose pure fire. My flames shoot out in a solid stream, blazing a fierce red and quickly devouring the mist in its path. The figures continue pouring more mist out but my fire reaches their feet. I push more energy into the magic and it consumes the two figures from the ground up.

They make no sound as they are enveloped by my flames, leaving nothing behind.

I watch until my flames flicker out and my magic settles deep in my gut. Happy to be used yet already hungry for more power. Pushing to my feet, I turn to face Cay as one of her attackers bursts into his own cloud.

The remaining attacker is caught off guard as Cay shoves a pointed trident straight into its chest and turns it into nothing but a cloud of mist just as the others had. Cay pulls the weapon back, whispering something to it, the entire thing collapses into a small tube that she tucks into a pocket of her dress.

"Um where did that come from?" I ask, my voice laced with shock.

She pulls the tube free from her pocket, turning it over in her hand, "My father had-"

"No, not the weapon. Although I would also love to hear more about that later. Where did you learn to fight like that? *When* did you learn?"

"I started learning a while ago from the Guards..." she clears her throat, "Terran also taught me a few things while he was here."

I raise my brows at her but she just shrugs.

"It's not a big deal. I just wanted to learn how to defend myself."

"Well clearly you succeeded. Seriously, Cay, that was some badass stuff back there." I walk forward and pull her into a hug.

She squeezes me back, "Yeah, but what about those things? Were they even people?" She shudders.

I shake my head. "No idea. But that whole mist thing? Vana... I've never seen or felt anything like that. At least not..." I cut myself off.

"Not what?" Cay presses.

"Nothing. It's just something about it. It was familiar, that's all." I swallow the lump in my throat.

"Do you know where you might know it from?" Cay asks.

I tighten the ribbon around my hair and inspect my blade, not a single drop of blood. "No. But maybe it will come back to me." Looking around the too empty hall as the creeps settle in my chest. The lack of bodies should be comforting but it just leaves this fear lodged in my chest.

A loud noise comes from down the hall and Cay quickly pulls me into an alcove. "We can't stay out in the open like this," she says in a hushed tone.

"True, but how else are we going to find the guards?" I try to peek around the corner but another noise has me pressing against the wall.

She shakes her head, "I don't think it's worth it. Clearly we can take care of ourselves. Let's just go straight to finding my parents." Her voice is firm, her eyes set with determination.

I stare at her for a moment, unsure how to respond. On the one hand she's right, we're pretty badass without the guards and they would probably just slow us down. But, going to the center of the fight with just the two of us, that's a different story. "What about finding the others? We got dropped inside the city. Maybe they did too?"

"It's possible, but the city is huge. There's no guarantee that we would be able to find them. Our best bet is to find my parents," Cay pushes adamantly.

"There's no guarantee that we can find your parents either," I counter.

Cay grabs my arm, "Please, Eve. I need to find them. I need to know that they're okay."

I sigh, "I'm trying to be the voice of reason here."

Cay laughs, "You? The voice of reason? Never. Where's the Eve that dared all of us jump off the pier when we were only, what, six years old?"

"You promised you would never use that against me," I say, holding a finger up. She gives me a grin that doesn't quite reach her eyes. We sit in silence for a minute before I shake my head. "This is a terrible idea. Even I know this. But, I would be lying if I said I'm not a little bit excited."

Cay flinches.

"Sorry, I didn't mean it like that," I say genuinely.

"It's fine. Let's just find my parents so we can fix this. Maybe we can figure out what the deal is with those mist things along the way," she nods back towards the hall.

I agree and then we are off.

We slip out of the alcove silently and then Cay leads me to a small door around the corner. She pushes it open and it opens into a small tunnel. "These caves are for the servants to get around easier. It leads throughout the entire city. I used to play around in them when I was little and I think I still know how to get to the throne room from here."

"The throne room?" I ask.

Cay nods, "I can't explain it but it's like my magic is calling me there."

"No, I get that. It's the same with me and my mom. I can always sort of tell where she is at. Like my magic seeks her out or something." Even now, half a world away, I can feel the same familiar thread of her power drawing me back to her.

"Only your mom?" Cay asks, leading us through the dark caves. The walls are tight, with very little light to guide us.

"Yeah, not sure why but I never feel a strong pull towards my dad," I say as Cay stumbles in front of me. "Here let me." I step up beside her and create a small ball of flame in my palm.

We walk the rest of the way in silence, just the crackle of my flames echoing off the cave walls and the occasional scruff of our shoes on stone. The deeper we go the more I begin to question whether this was a good idea.

Chapter 36

Rose

Air rushes out of me in a scream as my entire body smacks against something hard. I fight to drag air into my burning lungs as I blink away black dots in my vision. I roll onto my side in time to see Mar drop beside me, a crack echoes around us as her head makes contact with the solid floor. Crawling to her, I find her eyes closed and her breathing shallow. My heart races as I try to shake her awake. She doesn't even blink, causing panic to build inside me. How hard did she hit her head?

I reach for her with shaking hands and place my palms gently on either side of her head, feeling a wet warmth along the back of her skull as I call on my healing magic. It stirs inside me and travels to my hands, the warmth seeping through my fingertips into Mar's head. I focus every ounce of energy I have into the small bit of healing magic I learned after Cay was poisoned. I continue to push my magic until Mar's eyes peek open.

She stares up at me as her hand reaches up, hesitant to touch her head. She winces but otherwise seems to be doing better.

Breathing a sigh of relief, my hands fall limp at my side. "Thank Vana, you're awake."

"How long was I out?" she croaks, her voice barely a whisper.

"Not long." I watch her face intently, watching for any sign of lingering pain or injury.

"Vana my head hurts. Did you use healing magic?" she asks through a groan.

"Yeah, but I'm not sure how much it helped so you should be careful," I sit up, and a deep ache makes its way across my entire body in protest. Whatever happened, it hurt.

"Got it," Mar slowly pushes up beside me. It seems to take her an equal amount of effort as it did me, though her eyes are squeezed shut as she does it.

"Any idea what happened?" I ask. One second everything was fine and then next I felt like my insides were being ripped apart. Voices seemed to be screaming from every direction and I couldn't tell up from down.

She shakes her head and grimaces immediately, "No. But it probably has something to do with Cay's magic. We never should have let her do this. This was a terrible idea."

My head whips to her, "Obviously! Why didn't you say anything before we let her summon some sort of portal or whatever that was." Cay was determined to make it home and everyone else seemed just as eager to help her, which is the only reason why I didn't argue against this idiotic plan.

"What was I supposed to do, Rose? Tell her that it was an awful idea and that we *shouldn't* save her kingdom? Her family?" Mar says, throwing her hands up.

I bite the inside of my cheek before spitting out, "No, but maybe if you had said something we could have waited, come up with a *better* plan."

"As much as I hate to admit it, Rose, there was no better plan. We were running out of time. Still are actually. So, do you know where we are or should we continue to sit here and argue about the past?" Mar pulls her long legs up so that they're bent. She rests her forehead against her knees and takes long, deep breaths.

Letting my frustration go, I look around the room. It's small, full of boxes and what looks like bottles of wine. "I don't know, maybe some kind of storage room?" I push to my feet and start to open a box.

Mar stands up beside me, albeit slower, and starts to take a dive back towards the floor.

I grab her by the shoulder, steadying her on her feet. "Are you alright?"

"Yeah just dizzy, my vision went a little wonky there for a second," she says, shaking her head and almost immediately wincing with the movement."Stop doing that. You hit your head pretty hard and you keep flinching when you do that." The temptation to use more magic rises inside me but I know that I'll need to reserve my power for whatever is out there.

Mar goes to nod but stops herself, "Right."

We start opening boxes quietly. The first one I open is filled to the brim with some kind of herbs and spices, the scent of them wafting up and filling the air around us. A peek into Mar's box finds it filled with seaweed. "Food?" I mutter confused.

Mar continues opening boxes before turning to the door, a quizzical look crossing her face. Without warning she pushes open the door to our small room and I push back against a wall. Mar stalks through the door without pause and I stare after her helplessly. After a moment her head pokes back into the room. "Come on, it's just the two of us."

I take a step towards her hesitantly. "Where are we?"

She gives me a wicked grin. "We're in the kitchen."

I follow her out and admire the large space, long countertops with piles of bowls and pans, discarded knives left out, early signs of rust already forming on their blades. Everything in the space is left abandoned. "It's like everyone just got up and left," I breathe.

Mar walks around the room, taking in all the details and letting her finger glide over the smooth countertops. "My guess is that whenever the attack happened, everyone scattered. It looks like they just stopped whatever they were doing and ran."

"That isn't exactly comforting," I say nervously. I let my hand run over the throwing daggers attached to my thigh, reminding myself that they are there and we aren't completely helpless.

"Agreed. Come on, we should keep moving," Mar says walking confidently towards the door.

I scramble forward, grabbing her arm. "Wait! We can't just go out there blindly. What if there are enemies?"

Mar raises a brow at me, "Enemies?"

"Yes. Seeing as we have no idea who or what attacked this kingdom, I'm pretty sure enemies are *exactly* what to call them," I exclaim, throwing my hands up.

She considers it for a moment, "fair enough. Still, we can't just hide out here. We need to find my sister and Cay, then we need to figure out what's going on. We can't do that from inside the kitchen."

I sort through my brain for a better plan. What would Terran do? What would my mother do? Hell, what would Oliver do. I'm that desperate. Oak must be here by now, maybe if we find her we can get a better understanding of the situation.

"Rose, we don't have time. Let's go," she says, already starting to push the door open.

I throw my hands up, "Fine. But for the record I think this is a terrible plan."

"Well this is the only plan we've got." Mar moves to open the door but I grab her arm again.

"Hold on. Let's just go over this one more time. What's the plan?" I'm stalling and we both know it, even so, a little extra preparation never hurt anyone.

Mar sighs deeply, "Find the others, save the kingdom. Simple enough right?"

"Vana help us. Okay, it's not going to get much better than that. Let's just hope we find Oak and Oliver along the way and maybe we can get some answers." I move to open the door but this time Mar stops me.

"Rose, there's something you need to know. About Oak."

"What?" I ask, taken aback. Fear burns through my chest in an instant.

"Oak has been lying to you. That story she told you about coming to meet us? It was a lie. We found her sneaking around our camp in the woods." Her lips are pressed together into a thin line.

I stare at her for a moment while her words process. I had already suspected that Oak wasn't in those woods to meet them but confirming it is entirely different. If Oak wasn't meeting them then why was she in the woods in the first place? "I don't understand. Why was she sneaking around your camp?"

Mar shakes her head, "I don't know. But if I were you, I would want to know." She squeezes my shoulder.

I nod my head slowly, "Yeah, thanks. I will deal with it later I guess." Nothing new I suppose, just another secret and lie to add to my family's growing collection. At this point I'm pretty sure I'm the only one *not* keeping secrets. Though my cousin Reed seems more inclined to honesty so that might not be the case afterall.

"Alright, let's just go." Shoving thoughts of family and lies aside I push the door open and step out into the hall with Mar by my side.

We walk through the empty corridors as quietly as possible, staying close to the wall and using our heightened hearing to listen for any sign of friend or foe. The walls are cracked and dust falls freely from the stone archways over our heads. I shield my eyes as we walk under them.

An eerie silence surrounds us, our breathing and footsteps the only sound to be heard. I start to turn another corner when Mar grabs me from behind. She places a finger over her lips and points to her ears. I nod and focus on listening closely, letting the noise inside my head fall away. The muffled sound of voices drifts into my ears. Their words are too difficult to understand but they are slowly becoming clearer. Clarity floods my brain at the same moment Mar realizes.

We look up and down the hallway frantically, trying to find a spot to hide. The voices are becoming clearer because they are getting closer, and we're sitting here completely exposed. I grab Mar by the wrist but just as I am about to attempt a concealment spell a hand closes over my mouth from behind. A scream builds in my throat as both of us are yanked backwards *into* the wall.

My vision goes completely black for a moment as I thrash against the hands holding me. The hands vanish and I whip around ready to release the throwing daggers already in my grip. Only, it's not enemies that grabbed us. It's servants. Standing in what appears to be a cave of some sort are two young girls, maybe a few years younger than us. Their hair is the same shade of onyx and braided over one shoulder. They wear matching simple dresses, torn at the hem like they ripped them to be shorter.

I open my mouth but they frantically shake their heads. Mar and I both nod as they look at each other cautiously. The girl on the left stares directly into my eyes, she steps forward and extends her hand, sparing a glance at her companion who does the same. I share a similar look with Mar who just shrugs and reaches out her hand. Sending a silent prayer to the goddess I take the other one's hand and hope that this isn't a trap.

They pull us along behind them as they quickly maneuver through the tunnels. I try to memorize the specific turns we take but quickly lose track as they all look the same. They stop outside of a door, looking back at us one last time before knocking three times fast, then once slowly. The door is pulled open from the other side and we are ushered into a small room full of people.

There are servants everywhere, moving boxes around the room and folding up piles of blankets. I watch in awe as the scene unfolds before me. What looks like nearly a hundred people all huddled up together in this small room, silently working together. A few look our way but most just continue working.

Mar looks at me then turns back to the girls. She mouths 'can we talk?' silently. They nod their heads but do not answer audibly. "Where are we?" she whispers.

One of them holds up a hand while the other one rushes off.

"Thank you, for saving us back there," I offer quietly. The remaining girl nods and then rushes off after the other. We stare after them when an older woman appears, maybe around Terran's age, possibly older.

"Hello girls. You are welcome to speak to me but please, keep the volume to a minimum," her voice is warm, welcoming, even at a whisper.

We nod and Mar repeats her question, "Where are we?"

The woman smiles at us sadly, "My name is Alma. You are currently in the king and queen's servants chamber. Or at least what remains of it."

I look around the room at all the people, "Are all of these servants?"

She smiles fondly, "Yes. We all serve the king and queen. The princess and prince too."

I tuck that information away, glad to know that these are friends to Cay which hopefully means that friendship will extend to us as well.

"What happened here?" Mar asks.

"They came at night. We couldn't see them at first, the fog was so thick. It was everywhere, even in the castle. It all happened so quickly that we didn't have time to do anything except hide. We heard the others trying to escape and then nothing, complete silence."

"Who are they?" I ask, shivering as a chill skates down my spine.

"I'm not sure. They don't talk, don't eat or drink, they don't even sleep. The only sounds we could hear from the other side of the walls were the soldiers fighting. And even that only lasted for a short while." Mar and I exchange a look. That's not a good sign. None of this is a good sign. We need to find the others. Panic swells inside me and I try to take calming breaths before it overwhelms me.

"Rose!" a small voice cries from across the room.

A wave of shushing noises fills the room before I see him as he comes racing across the room, his small body weaving through the crowd until he launches himself into my arms. I wrap my arms around Cay's little brother, and thank the goddess that he is alright.

"Finn, I'm so glad you're alright," I whisper into his ear.

His arms wrap around my neck and squeeze me tightly, I feel hot tears drip onto my shoulder and I pull back to look at him. He has a small bruise on his cheek but otherwise he looks unharmed. I reach my hand out and heal the bruise with a smile. "Where's Cay?" he asks me, sniffling.

Mar steps forward and crouches down so she is eye level with him. "Hey, I don't know if you remember me, it's been a while and you're so much bigger than when I saw you last."

Finn gives her a shy smile and broken laugh, "Of course I remember you. You made me that potion that made my stomach stop hurting after I ate too many sweets." A faint blush stains his cheeks. Looks like someone made an impression.

Mar smiles at him, her eyes brimming with tears. "Yeah that's right. Look at that, I guess you do remember me afterall."

"Where's my sister?" Finn asks again, his voice more even than before.

I squeeze his shoulder reassuringly. "She's here to save everyone of course. Right now, she is off fighting the bad guys so you and I can see who can swim the fastest."

He laughs, "I'm a merman, of course I would win."

Mar raises her brow at him. "I don't know. I'm a pretty good swimmer." She's so good with him. I can see in her eyes that he reminds her of her brothers.

"You'll see, I'll beat you no matter what. Cay and Rose can be the judge that way it's fair," he says proudly.

Mar stands up straight, ruffling his dark curls. The ground beneath us begins to tremble and shake. People are knocked to the ground and silent panic spreads across the room. Finn grabs onto my leg. Nearly a minute goes by before the shaking stops.

"It's getting worse," Alma says, brushing dust off her shoulder.

"What was that?" I ask, looking at the growing cracks on the ceiling.

"Not sure, but whatever it is it's been getting worse. The entire city seems to be crumbling around us and we need to continue preparations." Alma turns away, handing out hushed demands as servants rush by.

"Preparations for what?" May asks, bringing her attention back to us momentarily.

"We are going to leave the city. It's no longer safe for us to stay here," Alma says, looking around as the others continue working.

I stare down at Finn as an unsettling feeling builds in my gut. "I understand. You should go, quickly." Right now Finn is the only member of the royal family that we *know* is safe, we can't afford to risk that, no matter what.

"You girls should come with us." Alma says, giving us both a pointed look.

I turn to Mar and her face says exactly what I'm thinking. "Thank you for the offer, but we have more to do here. We can't leave yet." I smile.

"I want to stay with Rose," Finn says, clinging onto my leg tightly.

I bend down and wrap my arms around him again. "I wish you could. But it's not safe. You need to go with Alma and the others." My heart breaks at the idea of abandoning him with strangers.

"No!" Finn yells, calling attention to our small group. Worried glances are thrown our way.

Mar squats down beside us. "We need to go help your sister but we have a really important job for you. See all these people?" Finn nods his head. "These people are counting on you to lead them. To keep them safe. Do you think you can do that?"

Finn looks around the room and then turns back to us, "I want to help Cay too."

I smile at him. "This *is* helping her. You keep everyone here safe so Cay can focus on what she needs to do."

He bites his lip and then nods, tears slipping free. He's still so small, too small to be dealing with all of this. I can tell Mar is thinking it too, her eyes are glossy though she holds the tears at bay.

The ground begins to shake again and Alma looks around, "We need to get moving. You two should at least follow us so you can see the way out."

Mar and I nod and follow her, Finn holding our hands in between us. Within a minute the entire group has their things gathered and follows after Alma down another tunnel I hadn't noticed. We move quickly, the shaking growing louder and more frequent beneath our feet. Just as we exit the caves into a small courtyard the tunnel begins to collapse behind us, the last of our group rushes out at the last second.

Alma appears before us, "Time to go little prince."

Finn looks up at me and I give him an encouraging smile. Alma reaches out her hand and Finn takes it, giving me one last longing look before turning to look up at Alma.

"We're at the heart of the city so it's easier to go up. You'll need water magic to get through the barrier though. All you need to do is go straight up then make it to the surface," Alma says, pointing directly above us. Her words are casual but something about the look on her face tells me that it's not as easy as she makes it sound.

"Here," I say, slipping a ring off my finger, "take this. It's got my royal seal. You should all go to Sena, use this and tell them that I sent you. They'll take care of you. Make sure Finn is safe."

Alma takes the ring and looks between Mar and I, "You two stay safe and please, protect the princess."

Mar smiles at her, "We will. Now leave before you miss your chance."

Alma nods and returns to the center of the group, everyone crowding in around her so they're huddled up tightly. Their hands raise into the air and a water funnel forms around them, shooting them into the air and bursting through the dome barrier surrounding the city, quickly fading from view as they pass through.

"Come on, I'm sure that drew some attention and I don't want to be around when someone comes to investigate," Mar says, looking around nervously.

"Alright follow me, I think I know where we are. The throne room is on the opposite side of the city but if I know Cay then that's where she is headed."

Chapter 37

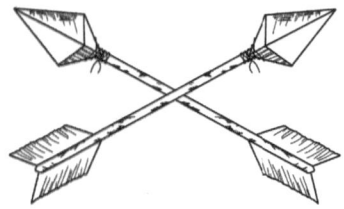

Oak

The sand beneath our feet is the only sign that we have reached the shore, the fog so thick we can only see a few feet ahead of our small group. Regan takes point, followed by Oliver and I with the rest of the guards circling us.

My connection to my magic shifts as the ground does, not exactly cutting me off but changing the feeling of it, putting a damper on the strength of my power. At the heart of Sena, my magic thumps incessantly through my veins, demanding to be used, but here, it's more like a soft call. Whispering to me and urging me to use it, not as demanding. I reach out to it and let a small succulent bloom in the palm of my hand, calming my nerves. Focusing on the small plant I mutter a transformation spell and it turns to sand, slipping through my fingers.

A fissure of energy rolls over my skin and shoots down my spine as thunder cracks over our heads, deafening in the otherwise silent darkness. A flash of light follows as we all look towards the sky. Clouds swirl and shift creating a kind of funnel of energy. My magic hums beneath my skin in warning as a dark figure appears at the center and starts to rapidly descend.

"Shit." I throw my hands above my head creating a small shield of stone. Glancing around me I find the others in similar positions. Oliver however, just stands there, staring up with squinted eyes. I call out to him but he ignores me.

"Is that-" the dark figure crashes into him, knocking him down and cutting off whatever he was about to say.

I shoot forward, pulling the body off of him and checking to make sure my cousin is alright. Oliver groans and curses but otherwise seems unharmed.

Regan steps to our side, her sword aimed at the figure who fell from the sky.

I whirl on them, my magic burning at my fingertips even here. Using vines to bind the figure's hands and legs to the ground, I get all up in their personal space. A flash of red light flares appears between us and I jump back.

Fire dances in the palm of a hand, lighting up a familiar face. Ashy blonde hair peeks through the darkness as Rian's face becomes clearer. The vines disappear as he pushes to a sitting position, coughing and shaking sand out of his hair. Before I can ask him what is going on another figure falls beside him. Rian doesn't even flinch.

Nat releases a fierce growl as she shoves her copper hair out of her face. "I am *never* doing that again. From now on, it's flying or riding."

"Likewise. I don't know how I let them convince me to agree to it in the first place," Rian echos.

"Who the hell are you two?" Regan demands, sword still poised to strike at a moment's notice.

Rian and Nat stare up at the guard and then look at me expectantly. What the fuck am I supposed to say to that? *Oh no worries Regan, these are two guards from Vulca who were visiting Sena but now have fallen from the sky.* Totally normal, makes absolute sense.

"They're with us," Oliver explains easily. He lightly touches his hand to his face and casts healing magic against his cheek where a shadow of a bruise is already forming.

"Is that supposed to make me feel better?" Regan challenges.

Oliver moves past us and continues walking towards the water. Regan stares after him, shaking her head, then sheaths her blade and offers a hand to Nat instead. Nat takes her hand and jumps to her feet, flicking her hair over her shoulder.

"What are you two doing here?" I ask, concern building with each passing moment.

Nat looks to Rian who just rolls his eyes and throws his arms up, walking off after Oliver.

"It was Eve's idea. After the Rayan princess was poisoned and the attacks got worse we came along to help but something went wrong with the spell and we ended up here," her words come out rushed, one continuous stream.

"Wait what? I don't understand, this was Eve's idea?" I shake my head in confusion. Of all the stupid ideas that girl has come up with...

Oliver appears between us in an instant, grabbing Nat by her shoulders and yanking her towards him. "What do you mean Cay was poisoned?" he demands.

"Ow, that hurts, asshole," Nat says, breaking free of his grasp.

"I'm sorry, did you mention our princess?" one of the guards asks.

Regan steps forward, concern clearly written across her face.

Nat nods, "Yes. We're still not sure how it happened or what exactly it was but, it was bad. She spent days with the healers and even then, we weren't sure she would pull through."

"Is she..." I hesitate to finish that question.

Nat's eyes widen as she waves her hands in front of her, "No, no, sorry. She's fine. Cay's fine. I mean she was fine the last time I saw her. But then again the spell did go a little crazy so maybe she's not? I think, physically, she is probably okay, maybe, I think."

Oliver shoves Nat away but Rian is there, pushing him back and getting up in his face. "Do that again and see what happens. Please. I've been itching for a fight." Rian bares his fangs at my cousin, pressing his chest up against his.

Oliver's head tilts dangerously, "Excuse you? I'd watch your tone when you talk to me."

Rian laughs in his face, "I don't care who you are. And while we're on the subject, I don't like you either." Which is interesting considering I'm not sure when they have ever even interacted with one another.

Oliver steps forward, looking down just enough to show he is bigger than Rian, "Great. Join the club. I don't need or want you to *like* me. But you will respect me." His magic pulses through the air, clamping down on everyone else in a show of dominance.

"Alright, that's enough of that," Nat says, pushing against Rian's chest so he is forced to take a step back. The two males stare at each other for a moment longer before Rian turns and drags Nat away, whispering to her hurriedly.

I step up beside my cousin and punch him straight in his arm. He doesn't even flinch, instead he continues looking down at me with his brows raised. I punch him in his arm, "What the hell was that about? We don't have time for this."

"He started it," Oliver grumbles.

My eyes widen. "Seriously? That's your excuse? Are you a child?"

Oliver's jaw ticks.

"Oh what, nothing to say to that?" I snort.

Regan steps up beside us, "Alright, enough of whatever this is. We've wasted enough time. Are we going or not?" She turns her fierce eyes on the two of us, a demand burning in their green depths. We follow after her as she calls her guards back to formation.

As we continue our mission I sneak up beside Nat. "Hey. What was the spell you were talking about before?"

"I don't know honestly. The princess, Cay, said it was something her father taught her. Some kind of portal?" she says with a shrug. Nat fills her place in our group naturally, her and Rian both blending in seamlessly, not even questioning what the plan is.

"Did she explain how it works? Maybe one of the guards can use the spell to get us inside." Or at the least it might be a valid exit strategy should this all go south.

"I know it had something to do with water magic but beyond that I'm not really sure. One second we were in the garden and the next I was falling through a whirlpool and landing here. I'm sorry I can't be of more help." Nat gives me a sad smile, smoothing out her hair where it got messed up.

I return her smile. "No, it's a huge help. I'm happy you're here." I look ahead to where Rian is keeping pace beside my cousin. "I'm happy you're both here." Even if it complicates things. More people mean more opportunities for someone to get hurt, for someone not to make it out.

"I hope you don't mind my asking but what's the deal with that one?" she says, nodding towards Oliver's back. He straightens for a moment, letting me know that he is very much listening in on our conversation.

A devilish grin spreads across my face, "Oh don't mind him. He's just jealous because Cay actually likes Rian, and you, pretty much everyone else except him. You see, he's got this little problem with ego and any time he isn't the center of attention he acts out so people will just *have* to look at him."

Nat listens to me with her mouth agape, clearly not the answer she was expecting. I shake my head at her and point to him with my eyes. Understanding flashes behind her eyes and she smiles a little. Her gaze shifts to Rian's back and her eyes narrow. "Yeah well, Rian's not much better. Pretty sure he's got a thing for Eve's sister but he's too much of a coward to do anything about it."

A laugh escapes me before I can stop it. "Good luck with that one. Mar is not one to mess around with. If he truly does want anything with her, he'll have to work for it." My mind vaguely drifts to our arguments over the past few days and I can only hope that we can move past it given the situation. If we leave things as they are not, I won't be able to bear it. We walk side by side for a while, Nat chewing on the inside of her cheek and clearly fighting back saying something.

"You okay? I mean other than the whole walking into battle thing?" I ask, nudging her with my shoulder. My head barely reaches her shoulders so it ends up driving into her side awkwardly.

She looks down at me while worrying her lip between her teeth. "Can I ask you something," she pauses for a moment, "about Eve?"

My steps falter but I quickly recover. "Um, sure, why not."

"Do you think- is this a terrible idea?" she whispers.

A small smile tugs at my lips. "You and Eve? No. I actually think it might be good for her." The way that Eve lit up talking about Nat, even despite how terribly things went before, it's a kind of happiness that I haven't seen from her in a long time.

"Why do you say that?" Nat asks nervously.

"Well, Eve has a habit of... well let's just say she doesn't have the best track record when it comes to picking who she shares her bed with." That sleaze Sebastion was nowhere close to the worst person Eve has told us about.

Nat lets out a strangled laugh. "Yeah, I could see that. Eve is literally a succubus..." her voice grows higher as her eyes widen with panic, "and a princess. Oh god, *she's my princess*, what was I even thinking? Of course this is an awful idea. I am so stupid. If my-"

"Whoa, whoa, calm down," I soothe, pulling on Nat's elbow so she stops beside me, "there is a lot you still need to learn about Eve and if you truly care about her I'm sure you'll take the time to do so. Just know that when it comes to who she is, status, title, none of that matters to her. It's all about who you are as a person. So don't get so in your head. Just, give it time."

"You must know her really well. Did you two ever..." Nat trails off.

I let out a harsh laugh, "No. Never. Eve and I- I like to think we are platonic soulmates. Drawn together in ways that only the other's soul can recognize but never like that. Never romantically. I just understand her better than most." Eve is the other piece of my soul, something that I can't live without.

Nat nods, seeming to accept my answer. "She really cares about you too. She wouldn't stop talking about you and her other friends on the way to Sena. It was driving Rian and the other guards crazy."

"And you?" I ask.

"I thought it was sweet." Nat's lips widen into a genuine smile, her full cheeks pushing up into her eyes and making little creases appear in the corners.

Regan calls to us from ahead, waving us over. Nat and I lightly jog till we're at her side and standing at the edge of the water. The waves are completely gone, the water unnaturally still. "We're here. We should hurry, something doesn't feel right," Regan demands, looking around anxiously.

Oliver walks a few steps into the water and bends down on one knee, digging his hand into the wet sand. I feel it the moment his powers connect with the land. The pulse of energy rolling through me and calling to my own magic like a current of power. The ground vibrates for a moment before a dome made entirely out of stone bursts from the ground and encases our entire group.

Nat grabs onto my arm tightly, her nails biting into the skin. I look up at her with my brows raised and she leans down to whisper in my ear, "Is now a bad time to mention I really hate being under water?"

I grab her hand and stare into her eyes, letting my voice thicken. "*You won't be afraid anymore.*"

Nat's eyes flutter open and shut before they glaze over, the persuasion taking root in her mind. "What was that?"

"Just a little spell I know. Don't worry, it will help you. Now let's go," I say, releasing Nat's hand with a smile. See, I can use this power for good things too.

"Alright, here's the deal. We're going to walk under the water, straight towards the city. I'll use my magic to keep the dome air tight so that no water gets in. We can't risk coming up for air so no talking, it'll waste oxygen. Whenever we inevitably run out of oxygen, I will open a small crack in the dome to let in some water." Oliver explains.

"That's where I come in," Regan continues, "I'll isolate the oxygen inside the water using my magic and add it to our air supply so that way we never have to go back to the surface."

"How long do you think it will take before we're in the city?" I ask. Anxiety rises in me as I picture how thin the air will be.

"It shouldn't take more than an hour. The real problem is going to be getting inside the protective barrier that circles the city," Regan answers. Her gaze roams over our small group, nodding to each of her own guards expectantly.

"We'll figure it out along the way, clearly we'll have plenty of time. Now, can we go?" Oliver requests.

Nodding my head I see the others doing the same. Even Rian, standing close to Oliver's side. His face is a mask of distrust and maybe a hint of contempt. Still, he doesn't say anything, letting Oliver take the lead and do what needs to be done.

As we take the first steps into the water I am surprised to find the compacted sand easy to walk on. The guards use their magic to control the water as we move forward. Regan is casting some sort of location spell to guide us as Oliver puts all his efforts into keeping the dome locked tight.

Thoughts race through my mind as we make our way to the city. Nat and Rian seem a world away as they walk side by side, hands resting on the hilt of their swords, ready for anything. There are so many things that could be happening inside that city right now. For all we know there could be no survivors, no one left to save. All of this could be one big trap. Although that is highly unlikely seeing they would have no possible chance at knowing what we were up to. No, more than anything, I hope that wherever Eve and the others ended up they are okay.

Chapter 38

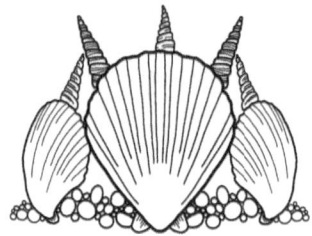

Cay

The caves are a lot more complex than I remember them being as a child. Maybe it's because I haven't been in them in a while but it feels like an eternity goes by as we get closer and closer to the throne room, my parents' magical signatures drawing me towards them.

Eve walks beside me, lighting the way with a small fire in the palm of her hand. Her gray eyes reflect the light and I swear they swirl for a second. "What?" she asks, startling me.

"Hm?"

"You're staring at me. Is something wrong with my face?" Her lips pull up into a slight smile, her brows raised.

I laugh nervously, "No. I just never really noticed your eyes before."

"Oh? In what way?" She glances at me for a moment, her brows furrowing before continuing to watch where we're going.

"I'm not really sure, honestly. I just haven't really seen anyone else with eyes like yours before. Mar's eyes are more blue than gray." Though the physical differences between the sisters go far beyond their eyes.

Eve nods her head, "Yeah, she takes after our dad."

"Right, I always forget you're half sisters." Mar's mother died so long ago that it's hard to remember a time when Mar didn't live with Eve.

I point to the right as we switch paths again. The cave walls become more narrow the further we go into the city, forcing us to walk single file.

"Sometimes I do too. I've never felt like she is any less of a sister to me just because we don't share a mom, even when her mom was still alive. Besides, her brothers are like family too." Eve smiles at me over her shoulder.

I sigh, "I wish Finn and I were like that. Sometimes I wonder if we're even related. He's the complete opposite of me."

Eve laughs, "Finn is *exactly* like you."

I slap her arm lightly and she laughs again.

"What, it's true. You and Finn are more alike than you probably want to admit. Don't get me wrong, he still has a lot of growing up to do, but in some ways we all do." Her words fade away, leaving us in a weighted silence.

I frown, a feeling of dread creeping in. "I just hope that we're not too late. That he'll get to grow up after all this is over. He deserves a childhood." My heart begins to race as the fear and doubt creeps in. If I fail, I could lose everything. Including Finn's future.

Eve stops abruptly, spinning around to grab my arm firmly. "Look at me. I swear to you that your brother, your entire family, they're going to be okay. I won't let anything happen to them, or you." Her voice is strong, filled with an unwavering conviction that I can't help but doubt.

I shake my head, "You can't promise that. For all I know they could already be dead."

Eve places her hand over the center of my chest. "Do you still feel that pull? The one you told me about earlier."

I nod my head.

"There. As long as you feel that, as long as your magic can feel them, you don't need to worry. Just keep focusing on that." She raises her brows, waiting.

I smile at her and nod my head.

Eve walks forward, leading the way. The path becomes more familiar and I realize it's pretty much a straight shot from here so I don't worry about giving her any further directions. No, instead I listen to what Eve said, focusing on the magic, the pull of my parents ahead of us.

The pulse of my mother's magic echoes through me. As I reach for it I can hear her singing me to sleep. Feel her hand smoothing my hair and brushing through the waves. I can picture her swimming beside me, her beautiful emerald green tail shimmering in the water. I feel the warmth of her hands over mine the first time she taught me healing magic. With each memory my nerves relax and breathing becomes easier.

Next I focus on my father's magic. His is stronger, almost like a drum beating in my chest. A warrior's anthem before battle. I let it draw me into more memories. Him and I racing around the kitchen, throwing flour at each other. My first magic lesson where he showed me how to make a water jet. How he would squeeze my hand when I was scared. Then more recent memories. The day he pulled me into his office and told me it was time to learn more about ruling. Spending hours going over maps and talking about court politics. Lessons on the different cultures of all the other realms and kingdoms. The day he taught me to summon a portal, *just in case* I ever needed to get far away.

I never thought I would need to use it to get home. Not for something like this. In my darkest nights I could have never imagined my kingdom empty and quiet, with enemies prowling the halls. Shadows that snuff out any light, any sign of life, leaving an overwhelming hollowness in their wake. In some ways I always imagined our biggest struggles to be the sirens. Their craving for chaos is something we would always have to manage.

Then again, no one could have expected this. There hasn't been anything close to war in nearly a thousand years, since the dark kingdom tried to murder other rulers and steal their land. No, since then we have had nothing but peace. Sure there might be some internal strife but that is inevitable. A full on attack like this is something outside of the realm of possibility I was ever willing to think of. That any of us were willing to think of.

Letting my mind focus on my parents' magic again, I feel my father's waver for a second. My heart stops in my chest. For just one second it dips, like something has weakened him. Rushing forward, I push past Eve without thinking, racing down the hall as fast as I can. I hear Eve curse from behind me but I can't stop. I need to know he is okay, that whatever I felt was nothing. I *need* to know.

A sliver of light appears ahead of me, slipping through the cracks in the door that leads straight into the throne room. Just as I'm about to push it open and rush out, Eve grabs my wrist, yanking me backwards with a grunt.

"I know you want to go out there. But please, just think for a second. Whatever is out there, it could be bad. I know you don't want to hear that but it's the truth. And as much as it might hurt, we have to be smart about this. Rushing into things is an easy way to get ourselves killed and we're no good to anyone dead."

I open my mouth to argue but the words fail to make it past my lips. Because she's right. For once, Eve is actually thinking about the next steps, about what the *smart* decision would be. Convenient for her to lose her impulsivity now when I need it most. I nod slowly, not trusting my voice to speak.

Eve stares into my eyes, looking for any sign that I might lose it again. Seemingly happy with whatever she finds there, she turns to the door, giving it a once over. "Alright, I'm going to peek my head out and take a look. If it's clear then we'll go in together. Okay?"

"Fine. But please, do it fast," I beg, my hands balling into fists at my sides.

She hesitates for only another moment before nodding and slowly pushing the door open, peeking her head out, and looking around. My heart is racing so hard it feels like it will burst from my chest. The drum is so strong that I can't concentrate on my parent's magic. My breathing is uneven as panic starts to swirl inside me uncontrollably. Eve has one minute- max- before I lose it again.

Turning back to me and pulling the door shut she lets out a long sigh. "Okay, just outside the door is a set of chairs that we can hide behind once we go out there."

"Did you see my parents?" I cry. Fear and anticipation war inside of me, fighting for dominance. For control. If there is one thing I know it's that fear can't win. I can't afford to let it.

"There's a thick fog in there making it really hard to see. I think if we keep low to the ground and stay silent we might be able to get close enough to actually see something." Eve runs her hands over her legs, checking that her daggers are still in place.

"I can use my water magic to dispel the fog," I offer. In reality, I have no idea if that would even work, but at this point I would do *anything* to ensure my parents are okay.

Eve seems to think about it for a moment before shaking her head. "No, it will draw too much attention. We should let the fog be until we have a better idea of whatever is going on in there." She runs a hand over the back of her neck, wiping away sweat as the heat of the enclosed space rises.

"Okay, let's go." I rush forward but Eve blocks the door. Sweat drips down my back but I ignore it, frustration building along with anger at Eve's stubbornness.

"Before we go out there, I need you to promise me that you won't do anything stupid. That you won't rush into things." Her eyes search my own, desperate for something that I can't give her.

"I can't promise that. If my parents are- if they need me- I just can't, Eve. I won't." I swallow a lump in my throat.

She nods her head knowingly, letting out a deep sigh. "Alright, fair enough. I had to at least ask. Let's do this." Eve pushes open the door slowly, crouching low to the ground and gesturing for me to follow her.

I follow behind, keeping low and trying to be as silent as possible. We move along the backs of chairs all lined up in a row, facing the center of the room. Eve stops just before the chairs split into an aisle. I poke my head up over the chairs and have to cover my mouth to stop the sob from escaping.

There, at the foot to his throne is my father on his knees. His tunic is torn, his face covered in blood and his eye swollen shut. Dark hair clings to his forehead, damp and dripping. My mother is beside him, her hands are tied behind her back and long hair falls forward over her chest in wet clumps. She otherwise seems fine while my father struggles to breathe. His breaths come out harsh, each inhale accompanied by a wince.

Standing before him is a cloaked figure, similar to the ones we saw in the hall. It towers over him, shrouded in darkness as power ripples from it in waves.

"Let's try this again, shall we? Tell me where it is and we'll be on our way," the figure offers, arms extended outward like they might hug my father. The voice is light, not quite feminine or masculine, it slithers over my skin and sends a chill down my spine. *What have my parents done to lead to all this?*

My father spits a mouthful of blood at their feet, a storm brewing in his eyes. "I told you. I have no idea what you're talking about."

The figure laughs, the sound makes my stomach roll with nausea, threatening my composure with each passing second. "Do you take me for a fool? I know that you know, so how about you cut the bullshit and just tell me what I want to know so I can go home. I tire of this kingdom already."

My mother is shaking her head, "We don't know what you're looking for. Please. Let my husband go."

The figure turns to my mother, head cocked. "Cute, how you would beg for him and not yourself. Tell me, if I offered you your freedom in exchange for his life would you take it?"

My heart skips a beat as the air in my lungs gets stuck in my chest. For a moment all I see is black. Then I feel something grab my arm. I look down and find Eve's hand there. When I look up to her face she is staring back at me, pleading with me silently, her eyes begging me to not react. I have to fight every part of me that screams to go to them, to *save* them. But I manage it-this time-and force myself to take a deep breath, turning back to the exchange unfolding before us.

"Never. I would rather die," my mother bellows. Her lips curl into a cruel smile even as her eyes swell with unshed tears.

The figure shrugs, "Suit yourself. Although I can promise you, death is not so kind to those who lie. And I've had enough lies to last me a lifetime."

"Why are you doing this?" my father demands.

I search for his magic and find the steady pulse of it humming, comforting me even now as I watch.

The figure pulls back the hood on their cloak, revealing long black hair and pale skin. There is something beautiful and terrifying about their face, the carved cheekbones and firm, pointed, jaw. "We've been over this and I do *hate* repeating myself." The figure turns their back on my father and a cloud of mist appears before him. The mist takes shape in the form of a person and extends an arm.

Before I can process what is happening, shadows shoot from their hand and attack my father. He collapses to the ground and writhes, twisting and contorting in on himself. A painful groan slips past his lips and echoes off the marble walls. The shadows seep into him and I feel his magic waver inside me again.

I grab Eve's hand in a death grip and she lets me squeeze so hard I know it has to hurt.

My mother screams and shouts to release him but they ignore her. The shadows continue to ravage my father's body until he is left panting and bleeding all over from wounds I can't even see. Everything inside me screams to heal him. To go to him and help. But then it hits me.

His magic is strong again. The moment the shadows remove themselves from him, I can feel his magic in full force, almost like he was hiding it from them. Realization dawns on me. If he wanted to, he could heal himself. But he doesn't. Beyond that, he hides his magic from the shadows. The realization settles my racing heart ever so slightly.

"Right, well, I am getting awfully bored of all of this nonsense so please, do us all a favor and just tell me where the magic is so we can be done." The figure groans, playing with the ends of their hair. They pace lazily back and forth, not even sparing my parents a glance.

I look to Eve in confusion but find her gaze is locked on the person torturing my parents. Her eyes are glazed over and her mouth is hanging slightly open, like it was frozen mid gasp. I wave my hand in front of her eye and she blinks rapidly. She turns to me with her pupils fully dilated and a sort of dazed look on her face. I want to ask her if she is okay but can't risk calling attention to us so I squeeze her hand instead. Turning back to my parents, I watch as my father forces himself to sit upright, his knees digging into the cold marble floor.

When my gaze moves to my mother's I suck in a breath, finding her eyes locked on my own. They widen as she realizes who I am and what this means. I watch as a silent *no* slips past her lips and tears begin to fall across her cheeks. I can't take my eyes off my mother as the shock and fear is written plainly across her face. My mother's eyes cut to my father for a moment before returning back to me. Her gaze turns to one of complete determination and she sits up straighter. She turns away from me and I already miss the comfort of her turquoise eyes.

"Fine. I'll tell you. But you must swear to leave here immediately and do no further harm," my mother commands, her voice filled with the power of a true queen.

I almost stand at her words, begging her to reconsider. Whatever magic this person is looking for, I know we can't give it to them. My father groans again and I can't help but stare at him. I've never seen him look so weak. Nearly folded in on himself, he looks centuries older than he is.

Without thinking, I send a small burst of my magic his way. The moment it reaches him, his head shoots up as he looks around the room frantically. The moment he finds me I feel his magic beat stronger, comforting me even now. Though his expression mirrors that of my mother, panic and fear.

The figure approaches my mother slowly, gliding across the floor with a trail of mist following behind them. "Interesting. Although, I'm not at liberty to make promises like that. After all, those who draw first blood are not so easily forgiven."

"I don't know what that means and truthfully, I don't care," she says with a broken chuckle, "just promise me that you will leave here, and I will tell you what it is you want to know."

The figure traces my mother's jawline with a long finger, "Tell me what I want and we'll see what happens."

My mother shakes her head, "No. Swear first or no deal." Her teeth grind together as she stares her captor down, challenging him with her eyes.

"Need I remind you that you aren't exactly in a bargaining position here?" The figure stands, circling my mother. Their calculating gaze takes her in from head to toe. They search for any sign of weakness, any crack in the facade.

With every step they take I see how this will unfold. I watch it happen over and over again in my mind. Helpless to stop it. But I can't just sit here, not anymore. The fog is thick around the room and creeps closer to the center with each passing moment. I reach out to it with my magic tentatively, testing its response. When the figure doesn't react I grab hold of it, willing it to do as I want.

Putting all my energy into controlling the fog I draw it closer. I form a wall of mist around myself and crawl closer to the aisle, surprised when Eve doesn't try to stop me. I sneak up the path until I am almost at my father's side.

My mother's eyes meet my own while the figure's back is to her and she pleads with me silently, begging me to leave with a subtle shake of her head. But she doesn't know that that's impossible. Because the moment I stepped into this room I knew exactly what I was going to do.

Eve might hate me later but there's only ever been one choice, one path forward. Unfortunately, that path might just be the death of me.

Chapter 39

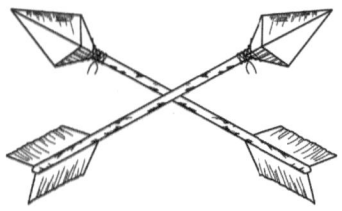

Oak

Time moves slowly as we make our way to the city. Finally, Regan announces that we are close, sensing the magical barrier surrounding Tepis.

Oliver's magic is, remarkably, still holding strong. In fact, his magic never wavered, not even for a moment. Something about that makes me uncomfortable. Oliver draws his power from the earth just like the rest of our family, the rest of our realm. Yet for some odd reason he doesn't seem to be the least bit affected being so far from home.

I watch his back as he leads our small group forward, Rian at his side saying something that makes my cousin tense. Calling on my fae hearing, I focus on their forms, listening intently.

"... and another thing, I'm nearly twice your age. You should show *me* some respect," Rian continues.

"I owe you nothing, least of all respect," Oliver mutters.

"How do you figure that?" Rian scoffs.

"Simple. I'm more powerful than you, more important, and generally better in every way," Oliver answers with a shrug. Prick.

"You just love to hear the sound of your own voice don't you?" Rian mocks, shaking his head. The vampire falls back a bit so he walks beside Nat as she fiddles with her sword, turning it over in her hands and inspecting the long blade.

"Report," Rian says sternly.

Nat's head whips up as she quickly sheaths her blade. "Um, what would you like me to report on? *Sir*," she tacks on as an afterthought, the slightest hint of sarcasm lacing the word.

Rian lets out a sigh that seems to come from his soul. "Remind me to give your brother a good punch to the gut for recommending you the next time I see him."

"Regretting your choices so soon?" Nat questions with a laugh.

"Every moment since we left Vulca, and don't even get me started on whatever is going on between you and the heir. Don't think I didn't notice," Rian groans.

The two of them fall into an easy banter and I decide to focus on my role in all this. We aren't sure what to expect when we make it inside the city but one thing is clear, we'll all need to be on our guard and ready for anything. Amongst our group we have a strong mix of creatures. Two fae, a vampire, dragon, nymph, gorgon, mermaid, and even a hydra. The power levels are practically off the chart, even with half our group being cut off from their realms and kingdoms.

"We're here," Oliver announces.

Regan steps forward and looks over all of us, determination burning in her eyes. This next part won't be fun. There isn't an easy way to pass through the barrier without leaving the safety of our stone dome. Oliver will have to release his magic just as Regan pushes hers in, granting us passage. In that moment we'll have to hold our breaths- literally- and hope that this plan works.

We each take up position, pairing one water elemental with one earth or fire, ensuring that if this doesn't work, those of us who can't breathe down here don't drown. Regan steps up beside Oliver, Nat smiles at the nymph, and Rian takes his place beside the mermaid. I am left standing beside the hydra, his hulking form towering over me.

With one final look, Oliver releases his magic and the water crashes over us all. I fight the urge to release all the air in my lungs as the pressure of the ocean pushes in around me. My head feels like it's going to explode as Regan pushes her hands into the magical barrier, willing it to let us in.

My lungs burn as the magic ripples beneath her palms and just as I'm about to lose consciousness we stumble through and the barrier snaps back into place behind us. I immediately collapse to the ground, gulping in air and find Rian and Nat in similar states. Oliver, of course, looks completely unphased. Asshole.

Once we have all regained our composure we take in the city around us. We're on the far edge, on the opposite side of the main palace according to Regan. The small courtyard we entered into is empty aside from a cracked marble statue. I walk closer to it and let my hands run over the smooth surface until it meets the rough edges where it split in two. The king's proud face stares back at me with concrete eyes.

The entire ground beneath our feet begins to rumble and shake, the entire city seeming to follow suit. The dome above us flickers and small streams of water begin to fall. Regan calls everyone's attention to her, taking the lead. "Whatever that was, it wasn't good. Now, we need to get control of the situation, find out what's happening, and find the king and queen."

"And the princess," my partner offers.

"And Mar," Rian chimes in.

"And Eve," Nat says with a shy smile.

"And my cousin," I add finally.

Oliver rolls his eyes, clearly unimpressed. Though something tells me a certain mermaid is at the forefront of his mind.

"We'll need to split up to cover more ground. You three," Regan commands, pointing to her guards, "you're with Nat and sir full of himself over there." They nod their heads and step up beside my cousin who glares at Regan. She ignores him. "You two are with us," Regan gestures to Rian and I, forming a small group with the remaining guards.

Once we've all split up, we establish an easy signal to each other. If we find an enemy, send one blast of magic shooting straight into the air. If we find a friend, send two. If we need help... don't need help. That one comes from Oliver.

Regan is giving further orders to her guards as Rian checks in with Nat, whispering quietly into her ear. Her expression shifts to one of shock and then quickly resolves into one of determination.

My brows pinch at the change. Shaking it off I step up beside Oliver and punch him straight in his side. He doesn't even flinch. I stare up into his hazel eyes, his freckles dancing across the bridge of his wide nose, his loose curls sweeping across his forehead. I silently commit the details to memory. Asshole or not, if he goes and dies on me I'll miss his arrogant ass. Though I suppose if I really start to forget what he looks like I can always take a peek at his brother.

Just as I open my mouth to say something Oliver slaps his hands over it. "Save it. I don't do sappy goodbyes."

I roll my eyes and pull his hand from my face, "Whatever. Just don't die, okay? That would be a real pain in the ass for me, and your mother might kill me."

Oliver leans in close, "Your *aunt* would *absolutely* kill you. After all, I'm her favorite child." His smile is smug and absolutely infuriates me.

A laugh tumbles out of me before I can stop it. Oliver shoots daggers at me with his eyes and moves to turn away but I grab his arm and whip him back around. "I love you," I say quickly. The words feel foreign on my tongue. It's never been easy for me to show affection but the last time I hesitated to say those words, I never got the chance again.

Before he can respond I jog over to Regan and Rian, ready to do what needs to be done. Our two groups break off without further delay and head in opposite directions. My group heads to the south of the city, sneaking through the halls as Regan takes point.

When the attacks began, most of the guards would have been in the training rooms so that's where we'll go first. As we move through the halls an eerie sense of being watched falls over me and I look around. Nothing looks out of place to me so I push the feeling aside to follow after our group. Rian sticks close to my side, letting the water elementals lead the way. We might not be from the same realm but there is a degree of camaraderie in being the outsiders.

We turn down a corridor and come to a dead stop, finding a whole horde of cloaked figures standing in the middle of the hall, waiting for us. Regan curses as she draws her sword, the rest of our group following her lead.

I quickly pull the bow from my back and notch an arrow, taking aim at one of the figures. The urge to release the arrow is strong but I can't act recklessly. For a moment, no one moves, then Rian sends the signal shooting in the sky and complete chaos breaks out around us.

The figures rush forward, pouring some sort of fog or mist from their hands as they race to meet us in battle.

I guess now we know where the fog was coming from. The moment they make a move I let the arrow fly. It cuts through the air and finds its home in the center of a chest that promptly evaporates before me, leaving not a drop of blood or gore behind.

Before I can even begin to question what in Vana's name that means, a figure appears before me, shroud in darkness and promising an early grave if I don't focus. I don't have time to use my bow so I opt for magic instead. I summon a wooden spear into my hands and drive it home in the center of its chest. Just like before, the figure bursts into a cloud of darkness and then is gone. There one second and gone the next.

"What the fuck are these things?" Rian grunts as he fights two off, alternating between his fire magic and his sword, both of his opponents evaporate.

I quickly notch an arrow and send it into a third sneaking up on him just as cold hands grab me from behind and I am dragged backwards down the hall. Chills rush over me and bile burns the back of my throat. A million dark thoughts enter my mind at once, stealing a gasp from my lips before I can even register what is happening. My vision is completely back as I am pulled away from the others.

"Oak!" Rian screams.

The sound of my name calls me back and my vision clears. What happened? I try to call on my magic but for some reason the place where it lives inside me feels distant. Not entirely gone but like it is hidden beneath piles and piles of packed dirt.

With a grunt of effort I rip my bow off my back, tossing it aside temporarily so I can reach backwards. My hands grab onto whatever they can and yank forward. The figure is thrown over my head and hits the ground with a puff of smoke that invades my throat and sends me into a coughing fit. It reforms as I fight to catch my breath.

Something is not right about whatever these things are. The figure recovers quickly, turning back to me as its hood slips back. The blood drains from my face at what lies beneath it.

A nearly translucent creature unlike any I have ever seen before, its skin - if that's even what it is- is pulled taught over jutting bones, carving out a face with empty pits staring back at me where eyes should have been. The hollowness of this creature has my skin crawling and my heart shriveling. It's like the soul has been sucked straight out of the body and left this husk behind, fueled only by the darkness and mist that pours from beneath its shroud.

I really wish Regan had given us a bit more warning about what exactly we would be fighting *before* we got here. Maybe a heads up that these things were barely even alive, yeah that would have been appreciated.

Although, nothing could really prepare me for the unnatural thing that now stalks me across the cold marble floor. I scramble backwards until my back presses against something cold. I tilt my head back to loop up and find another one standing above me.

Muttering a curse I roll to the side as the two send mist into the exact spot I had been. I quickly get back to my feet and race back down the hall, sliding on my knees and grabbing my bow along the way, notching two more arrows at once. I send them flying in the next breath, not bothering to wait to see if they stuck.

If there is one thing I am damn good at, it's my bow. Spinning around I find the rest of my group fighting off the last few remaining creatures as they burst into clouds of mist. Rian appears behind the final enemy with his vampire speed and shoots fire directly at it.

As the fighting stops, our collective breathing comes out in pants. We take a moment to collect ourselves and check for injuries while mentally working on processing whatever creatures those *things* were. I feel a sharp burn against my shoulder and press healing magic into it without really looking at whatever caused it. Rian steps up beside Regan looking more angry than I have ever seen him, and that's saying something, he's always angry.

"What the *fuck* was that? You led us in here blind," he practically growls.

A harsh grunt follows as Regan delivers a wicked cross, catching him in the jaw. Rian's head whips to the side with the force of it.

I hold my breath waiting to see what he does but surprisingly he doesn't react beside the snarl that tears from his throat.

"Are you done?" Regan asks deadly calm. She shakes out her fist casually, barely paying it any attention.

Rian's jaw ticks but he stays his tongue, nodding instead.

I take this as my chance to ask my own questions. Only maybe just a tad bit nicer. "Regan, what were those things? They looked half dead."

She shakes her head, looking around at the empty hall, not a single body left behind, theirs or ours. "I don't know. They aren't the same as what we fought in the beginning. For starters, the magic is completely different than what we fought before. I'm not even sure that I could call that *mist* magic in the first place."

My brows crease. "What do you mean? There's something else out there?"

"I can't be sure but I know that when the enemy first arrived they used all kinds of magic, fire, earth, air, even water. I've never seen so many elements used at once."

"Did they look like the creatures that attacked us here?" Rian asks.

Regan glares at him for a moment before letting out a deep sigh, "Yes... and no. They were also cloaked. But the ones we fought had veils over their faces, we couldn't see them. Also, there weren't many of them, less than a half dozen, not that that mattered in the end."

Images of the creatures haunt my mind every time I close my eyes and I desperately wish I could unsee whatever the hell I did. Something about them left a stain on my soul, one that no amount of power or magic will ever be able to erase.

"Yeah well these ones aren't exactly winning any beauty contests," Rian scoffs.

"Agreed," I echo, a shudder rolling through me.

"The one thing I will say is that they both seem to have whatever that mist is. The ones here were much weaker and didn't seem to be able to summon quite as much but if we find ourselves fighting the others, I worry it won't be a fight so easily won."

My pulse picks up at the idea of fighting another unknown enemy. I mean honestly, who invades and attacks a kingdom and doesn't even announce who they are? The least they could do is own their actions.

"Alright, no use standing around here talking about what could or might happen. We need to keep moving," Rian commands all of us.

As if his words summoned it, the ground begins to rumble beneath our feet. None of us move until it stops a minute later. Small bits of dust and debris fall from the stone ceilings but not enough to do any serious damage. Though the look on Rian and Regan's faces speaks to how delicate this safety is. Without further discussion we all take off back down the hall in the direction we had been going. Regan once again takes the lead but this time Rian stays by her side.

My fae ears are listening out for any sign of voices as we race through the halls. For a while there is nothing beyond the growing cracks and creaks of the city falling apart but then I hear it. The rumble of words not entirely discernible, yet words nonetheless.

"Wait. We need to go that way," I call out, pointing down a hallway to our left.

"We should keep going this way, we're almost to the training rooms," Regan argues. She's standing to the side, heading in the opposite direction of the voices.

I shake my head. "No, I can't hear anything coming from over there. But this way? I hear voices."

Rian steps forward and stares down at me, "Can you make out what they're saying? Anything about who they might be?"

"No," I admit, "but something is better than nothing."

Rian pushes a hand through his ashy hair, mulling it over. His expression shifts and he seems to have made a decision. "Alright, let's split up again. Even if they're unfriendlies, it will at least give us something."

Regan blanches at the idea, "Are you insane? This group is small enough as is. If we split up any further we are putting ourselves at serious risk."

"Yeah well this city is pretty damn big and it's going to take forever to search everywhere we need to like this," Rian counters, letting out a frustrated groan.

"I don't like it. But fine. You two go that way and the rest of us will continue on towards the training room," Regan agrees reluctantly. The other guards murmur their agreements, ready to follow their lieutenant wherever she commands.

The ground rumbles again and this time a whole chunk of ceiling drops down not even 10 feet from us. "If you find the other guards, get them out. I don't like this rumbling," Rian demands, holding onto the wall to steady himself as the ground continues to shake beneath our feet. They're becoming more intense with less time between them.

"I make no promises. I will do whatever is best for my kingdom. I trust you to do the same," Regan says as the rumbling ceases. She nods to her guards and as soon as the others regain their balance they take off, leaving Rian and I alone.

He turns his back to me and crouches down as I give him my best *what the fuck* look. He rolls his eyes at me and pats his lower back with his hand. "Jump on. We'll cover more ground this way."

I consider fighting him on this but aside from the fact that he is nearly as stubborn as Oliver, he is also right. With his vampire speed we can move much quicker and likely even avoid more run-ins like the one from earlier.

Setting aside my dignity, I climb onto his back, wrapping my short legs around his torso and crossing my ankles over his belly button.

He takes a moment to check that I feel secure and then we're shooting through the halls in a blur.

Chapter 40

Rose

Mar and I race side by side through the halls as the rumbling continues to roar through the city. We're still a decent way away from the throne room but we're making good time. Luckily, other than Alma and the other servants, we haven't had any run-ins. As odd as that might be, we aren't going to question a blessing like that. Vana knows we need all the luck we can get.

When we first talked about coming here and fighting, I thought it would be different. I thought there would be battle and bloodshed around every corner. I spent hours mentally preparing myself for the level of gore that my brothers have described to me. Yet nothing could have prepared me for the silence that awaited us. Each empty hall sends another trill of anxiety through me, nausea builds in my stomach as we wait for *something* to happen. Whatever happened here, it left nothing behind. No *one*. The emptiness of the halls makes it feel more like a ghost land than a bustling city.

A large chunk of ceiling breaks off and crashes down in front of us as Mar grabs my hand, pulling me back before it can crush me, her vampire reflexes a true saving grace.

"Thanks," I breathe. My heart continues to pound in my chest, the drum echoing in my ears deafening.

"We need to find a better way to do this. We can't just keep running around." Mar pushes at her hair, smoothing down the golden strands that have come loose from her braid. Her pupils are blown, wide and frenzied looking.

I step forward and extend my arm to her. "Here. Drink."

Mar shakes her head, taking a step back and slapping a hand over her mouth. "No. I can't, I won't weaken you." Her throat bobs as she swallows, clearly far more hungry than she would ever let on. We might not have encountered any enemies but Mar has been using her vamp speed to get us through the halls quicker.

"I'm fine," I assure her, "I've barely used any magic. If anything I need to get rid of some of it and you need to drink."

Her eyes lock on my neck where my pulse thumps wildly and before I can urge her on any further, Mar pounces on me. One hand shoves my head to the side while the other locks down on my wrist. The moment her sharp fangs bite into my neck I tense.

Being bitten by a vampire isn't exactly an unpleasant feeling. It's more like a sharp bite of pain and this odd heat. The place where the vampire's mouth meets the skin practically burns while the rest of you slowly grows colder as the blood is drained from your body. I've actually heard some people enjoy the bite, though, I would imagine that comes mostly from fellow vampires.

Over the years we've all let Mar have a taste so it's not exactly a foreign experience to any of us. Yet for some reason no matter how many times I find myself in this situation I can't seem to let myself relax. I know that if I did I might even enjoy it. But the unfamiliar feeling of another person's lips on my skin makes me unusually tense. Even now, after all these years, I can't figure out why.

My fingertips start to go numb as Mar continues to drink from me greedily. I rub my fingers together as they tingle, feeling the odd pin pricks of the friction. Mar's grip on me loosens as she notices the movement, pulling back and practically shoving me away from her.

"That's enough. I probably shouldn't have even taken that much." Her tongue sweeps across her lips, collecting the last bits of blood that stain them. Her blue-gray eyes are wide, her pupils blown with the fading bloodlust. The tips of her fangs peek out through the seam of her lips.

"I've still got plenty of magic left and my throwing daggers work just fine without it anyways." I shake my head, causing small starbursts to cloud my vision. Slowly, blood returns to my hands and I feel myself steadying. Mar reaches out and quickly heals the two puncture wounds resting just below my ear.

She smirks at me, grabbing the small weapon strapped to her thigh and pressing a button on one end so that a large staff shoots out, standing taller than her by half a foot. It's thin, slowly narrowing from one end to the other. She spins the staff above her head and behind her back, stomping it down again at her side. "True, but I've got my staff and plenty of fighting experience so I've got us covered no matter what."

I roll my eyes at her casual boasting. For a moment I'm reminded of my brother and a part of me wonders if he is here somewhere. Oliver has this sort of cockiness to him that makes people want to punch him in the face. Mar on the other hand, just breathes confidence. Even when she might seem arrogant you can't help but respect her. Respect the work she put in to back up her claims. Even when she acts spontaneously, maybe even recklessly, she will find a justification before anyone finishes reprimanding her.

There are parts of me that will always wonder if I will ever be good enough. For my mother, my realm, myself even. The constant internal battle to live up to the expectations put on me. In those moments I wish I could be half as self-assured as Mar or Eve. The two wild sisters, equal parts crazy and kick ass. For once I just want to dive headfirst into something and know, without any doubt, that I am doing the right thing.

Mar continues to twirl her staff around her, delivering quick blows into the air as I watch with rapt attention. Why she chose a weapon like that I will never understand. "You know, for a vampire, you chose a weapon that doesn't draw any blood, isn't that a bit odd?"

She clicks the button on the staff, collapsing it back down into a small tube and reattaching it to her thigh. "Not at all. If I want to draw blood I have my fangs to help me. No need for fancy blades." She winks at me and I can't help but roll my eyes. Sometimes she is the complete opposite of her sister, other times it's like they're one person, a reflection staring back at each other from either side of a mirror.

Twisting around at the waist, I throw a dagger into the wall 10 feet or so ahead of us. It lodges itself perfectly in the center of a mural depicting a bunch of nymphs playing in a pond. "I guess. But there is just something so satisfying about the way the blade glints as it flies through the air," I sigh, summoning my blade back to me with my magic.

Mar laughs, "You and my sister, the two of you just love sharp and pointy things don't you?"

I shake my head fervently. "I like to *throw* my blades. You know, keep some distance. Eve on the other hand is a complete psycho. Why she feels the need to get all up in her opponent's personal space is beyond me."

Eve has a small boundary issue, never afraid to get up close and personal.

"I could spend a lifetime trying to understand the decisions of my sister. But, it's not worth trying. I'm not even sure she really knows herself." Mar scoffs.

We both laugh as the ground begins to tremble again. This one is more intense, throwing both of us off balance as reality comes crashing back in and we remember what we're supposed to be doing here.

"We need to keep moving," we say at the same time.

A small smile tugs at the corner of Mar's lips and I can't help but share one of my own. She gives me a nod and then I'm following behind her, moving quickly and dodging falling debris.

The more the ground shakes the harder it becomes to stay on my feet. Even with the added agility of being fae, I continue to stumble. A large rumble knocks me completely off my feet and I tumble through the air before landing on my side. My shoulder aches as Mar rushes over to me, pulling me up into a sitting position.

"You okay? That looked like it hurt." She winces at my shoulder as blood begins trickling from a small puncture wound.

"Yeah," I say, rubbing my aching arm as I push healing magic into it. The pain fades quickly and then I'm back on my feet shooting down the hall alongside Mar. I continue to direct us through the many winding corridors as we make our way through the city. A shiver of awareness creeps up my spine and I look over my shoulder, half expecting to find someone standing there, watching.

I push the feeling away, focusing instead on staying on my feet. As much as I knew Mar needed that little energy boost, I can certainly feel the effects of it lingering in my head. My vision occasionally goes a bit black from lack of blood. I continue to subtly heal myself while Mar continues to race just slightly in front of me.

Part of me recognizes that she could go so much faster if it wasn't for me but the reality is that carrying me took up far too much of her energy. Maybe I should just tell her to go on ahead? The second the thought crosses my mind a feeling of foreboding enters my mind and I immediately dismiss the idea.

The last thing we need is to split up further. It's bad enough as it is with just the two of us, I really don't want to find out what would happen if I was left completely on my own. Although I have a feeling we would learn once and for all what's better, staff or knives. The feeling of awareness presses in on me again and I give it the slightest bit of attention.

As soon as my mind shifts I can feel just what my senses were trying to warn me about. Two very distinct energy signatures are moving towards us, quickly. I open my mouth to warn Mar as we cut past another hallway but before I can get a word out she is sent crashing to the floor. I rush to her side in an instant and pull her up.

Her eyes are wild as she searches for the threat, already releasing her staff from her waist, and then widens further when they land on her attackers. "Rian?" Mar asks, her voice thick with confusion. She stands up from her crouch, silently hiding her weapon once again.

Focusing on the new additions, I look the guard up and down. His ashy blond hair is disheveled and his breaths are coming out in heavy pants. A head pokes out from behind him and a choked sob breaks free from me before I can stop it.

"Oak!" I cry, shooting forward as my cousin races to meet my outstretched arms.

Her face buries against my chest as I squeeze as hard as possible, my arms wrapping around her small frame easily. Oak claws at my back and I pull away so she can breathe. It's barely been a few days but the sight of her before me has my eyes welling with tears.

Her green eyes roam over me, looking everywhere as she checks for injuries. "Vana, I forgot how tall you were. How is that even possible I *just* saw you."

I smile at my cousin, looking her over in turn and then doubling back just to be sure. Other than a few bumps and bruises she appears completely fine. "I know what you mean. It feels like a lifetime since you left but it's barely been a few *days*."

Oak smiles at me and then turns to Mar, giving her a quick once over and checking for any obvious injuries. Mar's smile is tense but I think that has more to do with the angry male in front of her than my cousin. Wait. That reminds me. I'm supposed to be pissed at her.

I take a small step back and clear my throat. "Well, I'm glad you're both alright. How did you end up together?" I ask Rian, ignoring Oak as she opens her mouth to answer. Her eyes narrow suspiciously but she doesn't say anything about my sudden change in mood.

"Long story, but Nat is with your brother," Rian answers with a groan, like even mentioning Oliver warranted some degree of annoyance.

I have to agree. Although a small part of me wishes I could have checked on him as I had Oak. Asshole or not, he is my brother.

"That's good to know. Did you get separated?" Mar asks, a breath of relief leaving her.

"Sort of. We found a few of the Rayan guards and opted to divide and concur, what about you? Do you know where the others are?" Oak answers. Her voice holds the smallest hint of fear that sends a sharp pain into my chest.

I spare her the briefest of glances and try to remind myself that I have every right to be pissed off. Even if it isn't exactly the best time for a family argument. Fuck it. I'll make time. If I die I want her to know she was in the wrong here. Petty, sure, but justified nonetheless. I've spent more than enough time biting my tongue when it comes to my family's secrets. Not anymore.

"Rose and I ended up here together after the spell. We aren't sure about Cay or Eve. Although my guess is they are together," Mar supplies by way of explanation. Her eyes are fixated on Rian and it's obvious there is more she wants to say. It's rare for Mar to hold back so I don't push her on it. Whatever her reasoning is, I trust it.

We spare a few more minutes quickly recapping what we know. Rian explains the fight that they had with the misty creatures and my skin crawls just thinking about it. When Oak describes how she was almost captured I feel that same, sharp, pain in my chest and it draws a small gasp from my lips. Mar gives me a look out of the corner of my eyes but I shake my head, not wanting to get into it. She respects that choice and turns back to Rian.

He is staring at her with a mixture of anger and relief written plainly across his face. I can only hope he's a better guard than he is at hiding his feelings. Once we're all caught up, Mar and I make the suggestion that we continue on towards the throne room. I give my simple reasoning and explain how to get there. I even suggest letting Mar and Rian carry us so we can get there faster, even though it would likely drain a lot of their magic to do so.

Oak looks inclined to agree but Rian seems to be weighing his options. He rubs a hand against the shadow of hair that has crept up his neck and covers his jawline. Mar shifts beside me and I lean over to whisper in her ear but Rian grabs her before I can. Smirking to myself I watch as he drags Mar to his side, his mind seemingly made up.

She doesn't immediately rip it from his grip, which is only somewhat surprising, but her posture tenses all the same. "I know what you're going to say," she growls, her eyes narrowing on her guard.

"If you know then don't make me say it," he growls back. Their eyes are locked on one another, neither willing to yield or break their harsh stare.

"No, I want to hear the stupid come from your own lips." Mar tilts her chin up at him, even though he's not all that much taller than her.

I look back and forth between the two of them and can't help but smile at the tension, so thick in the air you could almost choke on it. Mar has been, and always will be, the definition of *hard to get*. Not that I blame her. No matter who it is, she *always* makes her partners work for it which is a complete badass move if you ask me. Now, whether she knows it or not, she's got that same challenging look in her eyes as she stares down her guard.

Rian considers her, thinking through his response rather than just rushing in and answering through anger alone. It's a lose-lose situation for him either way but gotta give him credit for at least thinking things through first. This half of the wild sisters might be younger, but she isn't any less stubborn. This staredown would last all day if he let it, and Mar would never back down. "Don't be difficult," Rian groans, shoving a hand through his short hair and rolling his eyes.

Mar smiles to herself, victoriously.

Oak looks between them, hesitant to interrupt so instead I step forward, "Okay, care to fill the rest of us in on what exactly you're *not* talking about?"

Rian throws his hands up in the air and paces back and forth before getting all up in my face. I fight the urge to take a step back. I won't be backing down today. Never again, the days of hiding and turning a blind eye are *done*.

"Look at the barrier surrounding the city. Do you see those ripples?" he asks, pointing to a few different places along the dome surrounding us. The light moves across it and like he says, small ripples occasionally cascade across the dome.

"Sure. What about them?" I question, watching the ripples dance across the reflective barrier.

"The barrier is weakening, it's what's causing all those rumbles and shakes. We need to be long gone before that thing breaks unless we want to see how long we can really hold our breath," Rian gives me a cruel smile.

Mar opens her mouth, ready to fight him on it but Oak interrupts. "I think technically if that much water filled the space all at once, with us all down here, we would probably just be crushed or at the very least our eardrums would explode from the pressure," Oak offers oh so helpfully.

I fight back a gag as I am accosted by the mental image of my friends all swollen from drowning, their eyes staring out into space unseeing. I shake my head to dispel the unsettling image.

"I don't care, I'm not leaving her until we find my sister and fix things. We came here to help. We can't just tuck tail and run. There are people counting on us," Mar states matter of factly. Her voice is so full of conviction that even I can't argue against it. Not that I would, not when I saw Finn and spoke to Alma myself, no, this is too important to give up on.

Though truthfully, he has a valid point as well. Not that I would ever admit that. I couldn't bear to just leave now, not when we've barely done anything to really help. Cay deserves answers, she deserves to know that her brother is okay and that he is waiting for her outside. If we can help even the tiniest bit then I want to stay. Burst eardrums or not.

Rian whirls on Mar, stepping so close to her that their chests brush against each other. "It's my job to protect you. I've let you get your way long enough, now please, listen to me for once and we can-"

"Not going to happen," Mar cuts him off, "I will not be leaving here until the issue is resolved and we have my sister. Understand?"

For a moment I think he might fight her on it. Brave male if he does. Then he angles his head to the sky and mutters under his breath, something like a curse or a prayer, maybe both. "Fine. Then let's find the future queen and we can all be on our way, deal?" Rian offers.

Mar extends her hand and grabs it hesitantly, shaking it once. "Why am I getting the strangest sense of deja vu here?"

Before we can indulge that thought further the ground begins to quake violently beneath us. Oak and I are knocked off our feet and onto our backs. We land side by side on the ground and we can only stare up in horror as we see it coming.

A large chunk of the ceiling breaks away, crashing down as we scream our warnings at the same time. My voice matches Oak's as we shout to move out of the way, but even with their vampire reflexes we aren't fast enough. It hits the ground with a thundering boom and a plume of dust explodes around it, blinding me for a moment. Oak and I lay on the ground as the dust settles and reveals the mountain of rubble before us, cutting off our path and leaving no sign of Rian or Mar.

Chapter 41

Eve

My eyes are locked firmly on the figure torturing Cay's parents. I can hear her mother pleading quietly but I don't see her. I can't see anything except *them*. Their long black hair falls well past their waist, how it doesn't get all tangled is a mystery to me. I watch their face unblinkingly, taking in all of the details without really trying. Skin paler than I have ever seen yet a subtle undertone there that gives it a dewy glow. Almost porcelain like.

There's something about their face that seems so familiar yet strange all the same. They turn their back on the king and snap their fingers. Two more figures, identical to the ones Cay and I fought, appear beside them.

"These are my friends," the figure says, circling the more mist-like forms. Their hand caresses one of the heads and for a moment it becomes nothing more than a cloud of smoke with no real form to it.

My heart pounds inside my chest and my magic is going haywire inside of me, demanding to be used. My skin practically burns from the inside out. I take a few steadying breaths and try to calm the fire beneath my skin but it barely helps, so I opt to create a small fire in my palm, releasing the energy. The heat is almost painful in the freezing room. How Cay lives in a place this cold I will never understand. I turn to look at her and my fire immediately dies out in my hand when I find her spot beside me empty.

Shit.

Whipping around I spy her creeping closer to the figure in a shroud of mist and silently curse myself for becoming so distracted. I look back to the last place I saw the hooded figure but they're gone. My eyes search the room and panic builds in my chest when I can't find them. The two mistlike figures march up to the king and start pouring more and more magic into him. His screams echo off of the large room and back to me. I watch in horror as his skin begins to pale and take on a sort of grayish tinge. Cay's mother watches on in abject horror.

What are they doing to him? I raise my hand, ready to send a blast of fire their way and hoping that I don't end up killing Cay's father in the process, but then she is there. Leaping through the mist like some sort of warrior and landing in a crouch behind one of the mist creatures. She lifts her hands above her head with a fierce battle cry and drives down the point of her trident straight through its chest. Just like the ones from the hall, it vanishes in a cloud of smoke.

I jump up, ready to join the fight but then the air is stolen from me and I immediately start the fight to breathe. I spin around with my hands clawing at my throat, hunting for whatever is denying my lungs the breath they so desperately need. A shadow moves in my periphery and I send an uncontrolled blast of fire in the direction, hoping my instincts were right.

My fire collides with a wall of mist but whatever magic holds me vanishes and I gulp down air as my lungs scream and burn. Lifting my palms up I quickly compose myself and prepare for a battle of my own while Cay works to free her parents.

"Interesting. What do we have here?" a voice whispers against my ear and I shriek.

363

A long arm grabs me from behind, wrapping around my waist and tugging me against a cold body. Everything in me recoils at the contact but then I hear the whisper of a word in my ear. "*Relax*," the voice demands of me and I feel the fight leave my body.

An undeniable feeling of calm washes over me yet my magic is going wild in my chest. I have to fight to keep it from growing out of control, unsure that I could really stop it if it did. I try to look back at the person holding me but cold fingers press against my cheek, forcing my gaze back to Cay. Their cold grip bites into my chin as they force me to watch as more and more of those mist figures keep appearing and Cay is fighting wildly against them. Completely overwhelmed.

Her father is half slumped over as they continue to pour that mist into him. Every time Cay gets rid of one, another appears, then two more. The room is full of them as a thick cloud of mist begins to invade the space. Cay's mother is begging her to stop, to run, but I can see even from here that she is lost in her mind. A kind of fight in her eyes that I know to be the most basic of our survival instincts.

A scream cuts through the air and her mother's eyes widen in shock as the same mist begins to pour into her. I am forced to watch as Cay spins on her heels and starts fighting off her mother's attackers too, bouncing back and forth between her parents against a seemingly endless stream of enemies. All while I'm being held completely immobile and unable to help. One appears behind Cay as she fights off two more, and I shout a warning just as its magic rips into her back. She drops to one knee with a gasp as I continue to scream her name.

I fight wildly against the person holding me but for some reason I can't seem to break free of them. Another scream is tearing through my throat as Cay begins to whimper, still fighting against the magic. I lose sight of her for a moment as the fog becomes too thick to see through and my heart freezes. Then, the lot of them are thrown backwards and away from not only Cay, but her parents too.

A small opening shows me just how bad her parents are doing. Her mother is lying face first on the ground, and for a moment I fear the worst. Then I spy the slightest movement of her chest rising and falling, and I can breathe again.

Cay spares a glance at each of her parents before using her trident to create a whirlpool around her, forcing the creatures back and giving her a wide space to fight. More creatures burst into existence in front of her but Cay has the upper hand now, casting streams of water into the center of their chests and sending them back to wherever it is they came from.

I smile at her, pride filling me at the warrior she has become without me even realizing. For so long Cay has been this delicate, fragile girl but not anymore. I can see the wildness that has been waiting to burst free and it calls to my own. I know that if Mar were here she would feel it too. She might be born of water but there is a fire in her heart that will burn through everything in its path to protect her family and her kingdom. This is a future *queen*.

"Alright, that's enough I suppose," the voice says from behind me and I stiffen, having momentarily forgotten the predicament I have found myself in.

The world goes black around me for a split second and when I can see again, I am standing before Cay in the center of the room. Her palm is outstretched between us like she was ready to send another blast but stopped. Her breath is coming out in uneven pants and I can tell her magic is nearing its limitations.

"Right, well, as entertaining as that was, I'm going to have to ask you to step aside so I can get the answers I came for," the figure behind me demands, grabbing my face tight enough to make me bite down on my lip and draw blood. Their unyielding grips tightens further and I can't help the yelp that slips through my lips. I tilt my head back to look into my captor's eyes but they grab my face roughly and force me to look back at my friend.

A storm is brewing in her gaze, her seagreen eyes swirling with a promise for retribution, and I can't help but smile as I know who will be the one walking out of this fight. I might not be any help, but Cay knows how to take care of herself. When it's clear that she doesn't intend to yield I am yanked against my captor's chest, a blade presses firmly against my throat, digging in ever so slightly. Hot blood trails down the column of my throat.

"So, this is how it's going to go. You're going to tell me what I want to know or little miss fire fists here will find herself choking on her own blood. Got it?" the voice growls, the sound rumbling through their chest and into my body. Their voice isn't deep yet it holds this power that I can't seem to ignore. My magic continues to writhe inside of me.

Cay makes a move towards us but the blade pushes in even deeper, making her freeze. Blood continues to drip down my neck and splash against the marble floor. I force my body to relax into the blade, letting it dig in a little deeper and focusing instead on calming my heart. If I can just get my magic under control I can be of some real help to Cay.

The figure behind me doesn't move, waiting to see what Cay will do or say next. "Well?" they prod.

"Let her go. Release her now and I won't kill you," Cay demands, her voice surprisingly even, though her eyes betray her. She keeps looking at my neck, my blood. If she were a vampire I might think she is just thirsty but no, she clearly is scared. Her hands are wrapped firmly around her trident as she holds it out beside her.

I really want to tell her how badass she looks right now but figure it's probably not the smartest move given our current situation.

The silence stretches on while the figure decides what to say. *Seriously could they make their mind up a bit faster, all this waiting is making it difficult to stay calm.* Which I imagine is exactly what they want.

"I'll tell you what. You drop that weapon and *I* won't kill *you*. No promises about the king and queen though. They've had this coming for centuries," my captor scoffs.

Looking between Cay's parents, it's hard to tell which is worse off. On the one hand, Cay's mother is entirely unconscious, on the other, her father has that gray tint to him that can't mean anything good. Given the blade pressed to my throat I'm not really doing all that well myself. My heart starts to thump as my anxiety builds but I force it back down, focusing on filling my lungs and releasing it slowly. Centering myself so when the time comes, I can go crazy without killing everyone by accident.

Cay weighs her options, looking between myself and her parents and knowing there is no winning choice. Either way someone isn't leaving this room. You can practically taste death in the air. Actually, I *can* taste it. It's tart and burns the back of my throat. A warmth builds beneath my skin and an idea starts to form before I even realize what I'm doing.

I press myself back into the figure firmly and hope that this idea works. My ass grinds against them and a smug smile tugs at the corner of my lips. Sometimes being a succubus can be extremely helpful. I wiggle again, this time pushing my hand back so it rests against their thigh behind me, slowly dragging it up their leg.

They grab my wrist and yank my hand away painfully. A ripple of shock goes through me. That was rude.

"Stop that. It's fucking weird," they admonish. Leaning back I angle my head to get a better look at them but they continue to force me to look away.

Alright, time to switch things up then. I pull against them but they don't budge, one of their hands is wrapped completely around my wrist in an unyielding grip, the other grips the knife at my throat. Taking a deep breath I call on my fire. My skin begins to heat as I force as much magic as I can into the exact spot on my body where their cold skin meets my own.

They release my arm with a curse and I quickly force the blade from their hand, turning it on them and slicing down their side. Blood splatters against the ground around them as they continue to shout curses, jumping back from me and trying to put more distance between us as I continue to slash at them. My borrowed blade carves through the empty air and meets flesh again and again. Each slice has my confidence building and them cowering away.

They step back just outside my reach but then Cay is there, leaping forward and jabbing with her trident. The long spear at the center lodges in their side and a blast of magic knocks Cay off her feet, sending her sliding across the ground until she knocks into her unconscious mother.

"Heal her!" I cry as I quickly unsheath my own dagger, wielding a blade in each hand.

Cay immediately reaches for her mother and starts pouring healing magic into her still form. Her father is panting heavily, struggling to hold himself upright. If we don't heal him too, and soon, I worry what might happen. We don't have time to play games anymore.

I shoot forward, ready to engage our enemy again but they are quick to dodge everything I throw at them with nothing more than a grunt of annoyance. Their lithe body glides around the room, a trail of mist following them. Moving the blades to one hand I form a fireball in the other and send it shooting forward. They counter with a wall of mist so thick I can't see through it.

My magic hums beneath my skin as I continue to draw on its power, forcing my own wall of fire to push against the mist. It breaks through with a flash of light and I take a moment to celebrate the small win. Only the figure is no longer standing on the other side. I whirl around, searching for them in the room and find them creeping up on Cay as she leans over her mother.

"No!" I scream, sending a blast of pure energy slamming into their chest.

The moment it connects their narrow eyes widen in shock but they don't falter on their path. Terror seizes me as their magic knocks into Cay and she gasps, her eyes glazing over. Her entire body starts to jerk violently, her hands falling limp at her sides. Her mouth is open on a silent scream and all of my senses sharpen at once.

I rush across the room but they quickly direct a blast of their power into me. The first blast does nothing so they send another, and another. The third stuns me and for a moment I am paralyzed, waiting for its full effects to take hold of me. But it never comes. Whatever this power was meant to do to me, it didn't work. A shiver of awareness dances across my skin but beyond that slight tingling, *nothing*. I continue to race across the room as they send more blasts straight at me, focusing the bulk of their attention on stopping my advances.

Another blast hits me square in the chest but I barely feel it. Nothing more than a brush of cold air against my otherwise burning skin. They seem to realize that whatever they are trying to do isn't working so instead they whisper something imperceptible and 50 more of those mist like creatures appear. I am immediately swarmed by them. The bite of their cold hands grabbing me all over and dragging me away from Cay as a scream finally breaks through and my chest tightens in response. I fight desperately to get free of them but it's no use.

A bright light blinds me followed by a rush of water that fills the room and quickly steals my breath. The water reaches the ceiling in a wild wave and then quickly washes away, like it had never been there to begin with. I'm left sputtering on the floor and trying to understand what happened. Looking up I find that most of the figures have vanished.

Standing in the center of the room is Cay's father, locked in a battle of magic and strength as the enemy attacks on all sides. My eyes find the one who is different, the one with the long hair and moves about like a dancer. They have one hand stretched towards Cay, continuing to pour that mist like magic into her as she writhes on the floor, her skin turning that terrifying shade of gray that her father's had been before. Their other hand is casting a barrier between them and the king but it is clear they can't maintain both. Can't torture and defend at the same time.

My legs are moving before I have a clear plan formed in my mind but I know what I need to do first.

Get Cay away from them as quickly as possible.

I use my fire to carve a path forward and jump straight over Cay's body, landing right in the line of fire. The moment I block their path the magic shifts to me and everything goes black.

Chapter 42

Mar

I hear the crack above us a heartbeat before Oak and Rose's screams. The sound of the ceiling breaking off with the force of the rumble that shakes the entire city. I throw my hands up above me in reflex, even knowing that my fire will do little to protect me. It feels as though time stops as I watch my friend's faces contort in fear and I can do nothing to force myself to move.

Arms encircle me from behind, pulling me backwards and towards the ground, forming a shield around my body just as the concrete crashes down. The force of the impact sends a large cloud of dust into the air and fills my lungs. I immediately begin to cough and sputter, my eyes burning and unseeing in the haze. My front is pressed into the cold ground as the body behind me shifts.

The arms that saved me squeeze tighter for a moment before I hear his voice in my ear, "are you alright?"

My heart pounds within my chest and echoes in my ear, making it difficult to hear anything else other than its frantic beat. I can just barely make out Rose and Oak's voices on the other side of the rubble, calling our names. I turn my head and try to blink away the debris so I can get a clearer look at him. Rian's face is covered in a thick layer of dust and there is a slash above his brow, coated in blood. His usually light hair is covered in a layer of dirt turning it a darker gray. His icy blue eyes search mine for something as I stare at him.

He pulls one arm out from under me with a wince. "Mar, are you alright?" he asks again, his calloused fingers tracing the lines of my face and looking for any cut or bruise. I am left staring up at him, his face so close I can feel his warm breath on my cheeks, the frantic rise and fall of his chest as he catches his breath. My entire body is left aware of the places our skin touches and every hard ridge of-

A hand cracks across my face with a sting. Heat builds in me as I lift my hand to my burning cheek, narrowing my eyes at Rian. "Did you just fucking slap me?" I growl. Heat pools in my stomach as anger flares behind my eyes.

"Yes, now are you alright?" he demands, pushing himself off of me and standing. He leaves his hand outstretched to help me up but I knock it away, jumping to my feet.

"What the hell did you do that for?" I shove him in his chest, pushing him back half a step. I do it again, shoving him hard enough to knock off his balance. He bares his fangs in warning before moving forward but that only makes me angrier. Rian grabs my wrists in each hand and holds them away from him as I fight against his grip. I yank my arms back trying to free them but he forces them behind my back, holding them at the base of my spine with one hand.

He tilts his head at me expectantly. "Can you stop acting like some rabid animal for ten seconds and just answer my question?" He raises a brow and winces when it pulls at the fresh cut.

"I'm fine. Which brings me back to why the hell you thought it was appropriate to *slap* me." I try to free my hands again but his grip is firm. Each attempt to remove his hands pushes me further up against him.

He crowds my space becoming impossibly closer, tightening his grip further, his rough palms rubbing against the sensitive skin there. His eyes flare with a challenge that I am entirely too ready to win.

"Mar! Rian!" Rose cries from the other side of the rubble. Her voice is shaky, full of fear and uncertainty.

A pang hits my heart as I realize I hadn't even thought about her since the ceiling crashed down. Seriously, bad friend moment. Not trusting my own voice to answer her, I raise my brows at Rian, to which he rolls his eyes.

"We're fine," he calls back to her. His eyes roam over me lazily, waiting to see how I might respond. I flash him a sardonic smile and he just chuckles. The deep rumble of the laugh vibrates through me.

"Thank Vana, alright don't do anything. We're going to use our magic to move this stuff and get you out of there," Rose says in relief. The sound of small rocks shifting on the other side lets me know they've already begun.

I could probably just use my fire magic to blast a hole in the thing but it might not be the safest option, especially with how unstable things are already. Faster sure, but better to just let the earth elementals take care of it this time.

"Got it," Rian answers, staring down at me like he expects me to contradict him. Every look is a challenge, baiting me with his every breath. It infuriates me. He begins walking us back, my legs stumbling as I try to match his steps, until my back is pressed up against the wall and pinning my arms so I truly have nowhere left to go. His body presses into mine again, a shiver of awareness moves over my skin as I feel the heat rolling off of him. His hands tighten around my wrists even more, to the point of pain as I try not to wince.

"Care to explain to me what the hell you thought you were doing?" he asks, his voice low, commanding. The edge of dominance is so new to me that for a moment I can only stare at him. Then he pushes me further into the wall and I can already see the game clearly. He wants me to play, I'll play.

"What?" I spit, tilting my chin up so I can stare him down. He might only be a few inches taller than me but that somehow doesn't stop him from looking down on me. Bastard.

"We're in the middle of a warzone and you thought what exactly? You could just stand there looking pretty?" his eyes narrow on me. His free hand pushes back a strand of hair that has escaped my braid, sending shivers down my spine. "I'm not sure I know what exactly you're so pissed off about given the fact *you* were the one to slap *me*. Something that I am still wondering about actually." I cock my head at him.

Rian laughs in my face. "Don't give me that shit. You don't care that I slapped you. Fuck you probably liked it," he says the last bit more to himself than me.

My mouth drops open, denial burning my tongue yet never escaping past my lips. Where the fuck did that come from? He has zero right to speak to me that way. Besides, why does he even care? "And what would you know about that, Rian? Hm? Or are you just looking for me to confirm it?" I scoff. I won't admit it, even knowing the way my body heated when he did it.

His jaw ticks in annoyance, his eyes burning with that same challenge. I've never shied away from a fight and Rian doesn't seem like the type to either. "Believe me, I have no desire, or interest, in what you *like* or not. No, I am only concerned with keeping your annoying ass alive. A difficult feat as I am learning, given the fact you can't even seem to maintain awareness of your surroundings."

I roll my eyes, "I saw it coming."

"Then why didn't you move?" he questions, his brows raised.

My pulse quickens at his question. I know I should have. Probably could have even. Yet my body did nothing to avoid the death that had been waiting for me, always waiting. If he hadn't pulled me out of the way I would be buried beneath the pile of rubble Rose and Oak now work to remove. "I was about to," I lie. My heart quickens.

Rian smiles, confirming that my heart betrayed me. "Bullshit."

I consider denying it but there's no point. He'll know when I'm lying whether I want him to or not and that's not really a conversation I am in the mood for at this moment. I pull against his grip on my wrists uncomfortably, his eyes tracking the movement.

He loosens his grip on me slightly, before letting go of one wrist entirely. He keeps the other firmly against the small of my back, still pinned between my body and the wall. "If I was hurting you you should have said something," he mutters. He shifts on his feet uncomfortably, turning to look away from me.

The new position shows me the red staining his hair and I can't help but bring my free hand up to his face, tilting his head to get a better look at the cut on his forehead. It's not deep but blood still leaks from it steadily. "You're bleeding."

"And?"

"And you should heal yourself. There's no reason to leave yourself injured" I press my fingers against the cut and push healing magic into them.

He rips my hand away and presses my wrist back to my side. "Don't waste your magic."

"How about you stop telling me what to do? Hm? I don't do well with demands, you should know that by now," I bite, laying down a challenge of my own.

Rian laughs in my face, leaning forward to whisper in my ear, his hot breath fanning my sensitive skin, "Keep telling yourself that. You're getting awfully good at lying to yourself. But you can't lie to me. How about you put more energy into watching where you're going so I won't have to save your fine ass again?" He pulls back yet remains close enough that I can feel his rough stubble grazing along my jaw.

I turn my face, brushing my cheek against his own. "I've never asked you to save me."

"Maybe, but then again it would be a shame to let something so mesmerizing get hurt," he whispers, licking his lips and letting his eyes drop to my own, his gaze becoming heated.

A tidal wave of emotions builds inside me, heating my blood with a mix of rage and something else. His condescending tone, the way his lips tug into an arrogant smirk, the way his tongue traces his lips makes my core tighten in response. I focus on my anger as my hand aches with the desire to punch the arrogance off of his face. To hit him so hard he would never talk to me like this again. Yet another part of me hopes that he'll never stop.

I twist my wrist, testing his grip. It's loose, loose enough that I could do it. Without giving it a second thought I yank my hand free. My arm shoots out in a vicious jab to the nose while my other hand shoves him away from me. Rian's head whips back from the force of it, the sound of his nose breaking sending a wave of satisfaction through me. I can't help the smile that splits my lips as I watch blood pour from his nose as a growl tears from his throat.

He's on me in a second, slamming my back into the wall as he wraps a hand around my throat, squeezing lightly on the sides. Not enough to cut off my air but enough for me to know that he's in control.

I don't fight it, I even tilt my head back and push my neck further into the palm of his large hand. Rian's chest pushes into my own as I take deep, controlled breaths. Letting my lungs expand fully and making sure my chest rises against his. He pushes one of his thighs between my own and pins my free hand between us against my stomach and his carved abdominal muscles.

I spread my fingers, letting them rest against the hard plane of his stomach as my body becomes very aware of the contact. Heat spreads over my body, a warmth settling deep in the pit of my stomach as my pulse spikes in anticipation. Of what I'm not really sure. A second pulse throbs and I say a silent prayer to the goddess that he can't feel it against his leg.

He wipes a hand under his nose, smearing the blood there and subtly healing the break to stop the bleeding. "Try that shit again and see what happens," he growls against my ear. Before I can respond he bites down hard on my lobe and sends electricity skittering over my sensitive skin. A gasp escapes me and my body pushes into his involuntarily. Rian moves to pull away but the hand trapped between us grabs onto his shirt, having a mind of its own. "Something you want to say?" he asks teasingly. His leg moves higher and presses firmly against my heat.

Fuck, I hope he can't feel how wet I am. This is so messed up. I try to move away from him but with my back against the literal wall and his hulking frame pinning me there I don't have many options. I refuse to turn my head, even as my cheeks begin to burn. No, I look into his eyes and let him see everything I am feeling inside me. He tilts his head so he can stare down at me, a low chuckle falling from his lips.

"Let me go," I insist, my voice coming out breathy, betraying me. There is absolutely no heat behind the words and we both know it.

Rian licks his lips slowly, my eyes tracking the movement. He leans forward, our noses almost touching, "No, I don't think that's what you want to say at all."

I pull against his hold on me but he doesn't let me move more than a fraction of an inch. My body is completely immobilized beneath him. His hand is still firmly wrapped around my neck as my heart races and I fight to keep my breaths even.

"I mean it, Rian. Let. Me. Go," I practically pant.

"Make me," Rian challenges.

My creature stirs within me, my fangs snapping out and piercing my own skin. Two dots of blood form on my lower lip and Rian's eyes watch them hungrily. I suck my lip in and drink down my own blood for a moment, not that it does anything to restore my power. Still, his gaze darkens as my lip pops free and the blood begins to pool again. "Feeling a bit hungry, Rian?" I mock.

I turn my head but his hand between us moves to my jaw and forces my head to look at him. One hand remains on my throat while the other holds my face. He shoots forward, crashing his lips to mine fiercely. My lips part on a gasp and he takes advantage, plunging his tongue inside with a growl.

I fist his shirt, pulling him against me until there is no space left between us. I move my hand from my side and tangle my fingers in the hair at the nape of his neck, tugging on it harshly. Rian groans against my lips and tightens his hold on my neck. I whimper and pull him even closer.

This hand on my jaw moves to my hip, and then lower to my thigh. He grips one leg and tugs it up so it wraps around his waist, my heel digging into his ass as I practically grind against him. The hard length of his cock presses firmly against my center and I can't help the needy moan that escapes me.

My thoughts are scattered, anger and everything else lost to the lust that has built inside me and is now commanding all my attention. I push the hand between us under his shirt and over his defined abs, up to his chest. I let my nails rake back down painfully as he digs his fingers into my thigh hard enough to leave a mark.

He releases my neck in favor of lifting me so that both my legs are wrapped around his waist and the hardest part of him grinds against the part of me that needs him the most. There is no sense in our movements, our hands roam over each other greedily, pulling and scratching, demanding more. His hand finds my breast and squeezes firmly, making me whimper and press into him. Our mouths clash in a battle for dominance and control, our tongues sweeping over each other and tasting all of the wildness that we have been trying to lock away.

This defies all sense or reason. We don't have time for this. Yet even Rian, the perpetually rational guard that he is, doesn't seem to care. The heat that has been building between us is now a raging fire that we can't seem to snuff out. My body is aching for him, no matter how hard I try to deny it.

"Rian," I moan. Arching my back so that I am pressed more firmly against him.

He growls in approval, moving his mouth to my throat and leaving wet kisses down to my chest. I hiss at the sharp prick of his fangs against my collarbone, his bite sending a wave of pleasure through my body. He doesn't drink from me, just presses his fangs in and digs that pain in deeper. He moans against my chest before pulling his fangs free and trailing kisses down even further. Rian tugs on the neckline of my blouse, exposing my breasts fully as I had opted to skip the undergarments. He mutters a curse as his tongue traces my nipple.

I arch into him, eyes closing tightly as his lips close around the hardened peak. My hips roll, grinding into his hard cock and bringing the smallest bit of relief to the throbbing need building in my core. He sucks and nips as I writhe against him, his large hands gripping my waist and holding my weight up effortlessly. I move my hands to his waistband, my fingers fumbling to remove his belt.

The walls and ground begin to shake violently. My eyes snap open as Rian's head whips up. He quickly tugs up my blouse and eases me down so I am standing on my own, my legs a bit shaky. Smaller bits of the ceiling begin to break off as Rian pushes me back into the wall, using his body to shield me.

I stare into his eyes as we wait for the shaking to stop. When it does, we stand there in silence, our breathing uneven. Rian's pupils are blown with lust, his hair is streaked gray and a complete disaster from my hands. I want to reach out and touch him, to pull him closer, but his eyes shift and I can see that he is back to his usual serious self.

I harden my face, creating a mask of indifference before turning away. I force my hands into fists at my side, neither of us acknowledging what just happened. The weight of it hanging heavily in the air along with the silence.

Chapter 43

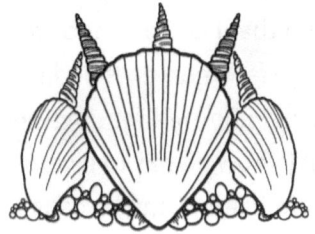

Cay

Agony. Pure agony is all that finds me in the darkness. Shrill screams echo in my mind as my body jerks violently against the cold, stone floor. A monster is carving through my mind, searching for something, the slice of magic tearing into my very soul and ripping it apart. Bits of who I am fracture away. My magic thrashes within me, desperate to fight off the intruder in my mind.

My body feels like it has been pulled apart into tiny pieces, my mind and heart existing on a separate plane than my physical self. I try to speak but my voice is lost to the screams and I somehow know that they belong to me. Whether anyone else can hear them is a mystery. Stinging tears threaten to spill from my eyes and I am helpless to stop them. Each drop a silent plea to end the pain, to just make it stop.

And then it does. All of the pain, the suffering, it falls away. I can feel my soul stitching itself back together piece by piece as my vision is returned to me. The darkness gives way to a blinding light as I blink through the wetness of my tears. My body feels spent, used and discarded. My throat raw yet feeling entirely unused at the same time. Sitting up takes a great deal of effort, my body moving languidly, practically refusing to do as I command.

The room appears before me, shock and fear crashing over my body and chilling my blood. My father stands on quivering legs, a torrent of magic spilling from his hands as he pours every bit of it at the cloaked figure. His face is contorted in a pain that I know all too well. The deepest pits of my magic were drained by the few moments of darkness that had consumed me. Yet my father, my king, endured for *days* and now stands before his enemy giving more than I know he has to give. I can feel it.

His magic calls to mine like the moon calls to the sea, the beat of it familiar beneath my skin. But now, what used to be a steady hum is no more than a weak thump. He can't hold out much longer, his magic already running on fumes. I turn to see how our enemy is faring, to search for hope, but despair is all that meets me.

Eve is locked in the grip of the shadows. She sits on her knees, back bowed and arms stretched out wide beside her, almost in offering. Her mouth hangs open, not a sound slipping free, her eyes are completely black, consumed by the shadows that now invade her mind. Her dark hair cascades down her back in waves, blowing on a breeze that no one else can feel. Something black slithers beneath her skin, spreading out in a weblike pattern.

The mist continues to pour from my enemy, their eyes locked on Eve and a look of shock filling their gaze. They hardly notice my father anymore. The shield between them is solid, not a crack in sight as my father's magic bounces off of it. They lick their lips and take a step towards Eve, making my heart rate spike.

This is bad. Very bad. Worse than I could have ever imagined. My father has barely any magic left, my mother is still unconscious beside me, and Eve seems to be consumed by the shadows. Her mischievous smile flashes in my mind and my magic flares inside me. No. I won't let this go any further, won't let them harm my friends, my family, for another moment.

"Hey!" I scream, standing on shaking legs.

Their eyes don't move from Eve so I do the only thing I can think of. I send a blast of water magic into my friend and send her sliding across the room, the connection to the shadows broken. There's no time to see if she stirs, to check if she is alright, because the darkness turns right back on me but this time I am ready.

I form a wall of ice six inches thick between us as I look to my father. His eyes find me and I can see the plea in them. The same thing that my mother said. To run and hide, to save myself. But I am no coward, I will not run away anymore. No one is here to save me but myself.

A million ideas rush through my mind and I can picture them perfectly, playing out like a movie in my head. All the different paths I could take and things I could do, how they might play out. I might not be able to take down this shadowy fucker on my own but I just need to get to my father so I can lend him a bit of magic. If I can do that then he'll be able to break through their shield and end this. I can see it. I can practically feel his large arms wrapping around me and drawing me into a fierce hug.

Before I can second guess myself I shoot out from behind the wall and race across the room towards my father. Dark magic shoots towards me but I dodge it, moving left and right and ducking right before it crashes into my head and snares me again. I let my gaze cut to Eve for a moment and relief spills through me as I see her pushing herself upright. Determination burns within me and I up my pace, making it to my father's side and skidding to a halt at his back.

"Daughter, what are you doing? Go. Get your friend and leave," he commands, his voice resolute. A sheen of sweat coats his grayish skin.

"I'm not leaving you until this is finished. We can do it together." I place my hand on his shoulder, casting a bit of healing magic before offering my magic to him entirely.

He shakes his head at me, "Minnow, I don't have much magic left. You need to save yours so you can get out of here." His hand caresses my cheek, his thumb swiping away the lingering tears there.

The ground beneath our feet begins to rumble and shake, far more intense than it had earlier. Small bits of debris cascades down from the ceiling as I search for my mother where she lies on the floor. Her chest continues to rise and fall with her labored breaths. I cast a subtle shield around her and hope that it is enough to protect her. Eve is slumped against the wall, staring at her hands with a look of utter confusion plastered across her face. "It's now or never, father, let me help you," I beg.

He stares down at me, his cerulean blue eyes so full of love and adoration that I know he won't deny me this. My father reaches his arm out and offers me his hand, squeezing mine tightly the second I place it in his palm. I let my magic begin to flow freely towards him but it pushes back into me, this time feeling full of power. "Father," I whisper fearfully but he just squeezes my hand.

"Don't fight it, let my magic in," he breathes. He gives me a reassuring smile.

Trusting him I do as he says, dropping the thin barrier that kept the magic flowing from me and immediately feeling the difference. Magic beats within me in time with my heart as I accept his power, drawing it in and tangling with my own. Raising my hand out in front of us I take a single steadying breath and then let it all go. Water pulses from the palm of my hand in a singular jet stream, the force of it smacking into the enemy's shield and forcing them back. The combined force of our magic sends cracks in their defenses and my father laughs.

"You thought you could come into my kingdom, destroy my home, and hurt my people and family?" he bellows, sending more and more of his magic into me, strengthening our attack.

"What would you know of home? Of family!" the figure demands. Their power is concentrated in blocking our attack, a force of pure energy that ripples in the light emitting a soft glow.

Their voice echoes off the marble walls and back to me, sending a chill down my back. My father removes his hand from mine, placing it lightly on my shoulder. I bring my second hand out in front of me and push everything that I have into my attack, commanding my magic to break through their shield and end this already.

"You monsters walk about acting like the heroes when we all know what you did. What you stole! Don't preach to me about my misdeeds, first look only to yourself," the figure adds with a sneer.

"Monsters?" I cry, "The only monster here is you!"

They laugh mirthlessly. "Princess Cay, is it? Oh yes, don't look so shocked, we do like to know our enemies before eradicating them." Their face contorts into a mask of barely restrained disgust.

My magic wavers for a moment and I let my eyes slip to my father, his face a mask of rage and fury. "I could say the same of you. What is your name, where do you come from?" my father pries.

"I am Teru, and I come from the land forgotten, the darkness, the mist itself. My king sends his regards," Teru says, sending a blast of magic towards us. Their own shield shatters and darkness whips at my father and I, sending us flying backwards.

Pain ricochets down my spine as my back slams into the wall on the opposite side of the room. I slump forward, my hand going to my back and finding wetness there. Looking at my hand I find it covered in red as a pained sob escapes me. I look up expecting to see my father beside me but he stands in the middle of the room, his back to Teru and his eyes locked on mine.

My father looks at his hands, a mixture of fear and utter confusion crossing his face before his arms go limp at his sides. He drops to his knees and I push upright, forcing my body to half crawl across the floor to get to him. A sad sort of smile spreads across his face as blood begins to leak from his nose and eyes.

Fear grips my heart and I scream, dragging myself across the room. My father mouths something to me and then his entire body goes slack. He lays in a crumpled heap with red streaked across his cheeks. My magic searches for his. Panic consumes me as it fails to find a whisper, a single thread of power. I finally make it to his limp form and cradle his head in my lap, looking into his cerulean eyes, desperate for any sign of the love and life I have always found there. Instead I find them unseeing, glazed and utterly *empty*.

The entire room is cast in a while light as I feel myself begin to rise up off the floor. Magic swells inside me fueled by the pain that threatens to consume me. I decide to let it. My skin becomes heated with rage, my arms and legs burning so intensely I just might be on fire. My head pounds with the echo of loss that I feel deep within my soul, and my heart cracks and splinters with the knowledge that my father is gone. Stolen from me. I embrace the very thing that I have feared for so long and let it become all that I am.

I open my mouth and let the song rip from my throat without any hesitation.

Chapter 44

Rose

My powers are already beginning to wane as Oak and I work to shift the rubble and clear a path to Mar and Rian. We work in silence, taking turns to move the rocks without making the whole thing topple over. I can feel Oak's eyes on me when I turn my back to her. The weight of her stare heavier than any boulder.

Magic flows freely from my hands as I lift another large section and set it down off to the side. There is still so much left to move and I wonder if this is even worth it. We could probably find another way around and catch up with Mar and Rian later. I try to voice this idea to Oak but she is having none of it. So now we work in silence.

Whenever I open my mouth to say something I remember the lies that my cousin has been feeding me for Vana knows how long. Not just her, my entire family, my mother, my brothers. Maybe even Reed if I am to assume he is as close with his sister as I think. Then again, what do I even know at this point. How can I trust anything they say?

There is a price to pay for being an heir, even a second born son or daughter has responsibilities tied to their role. Oliver has acted as emissary to this very kingdom for years now. He might act as though he wants to do so but everyone knows he has little choice.

I always thought that my role, my purpose, as the third in line would be made more clear as time went on. Now I see I was wrong. My mother might have called on me for *guidance* over the years but thinking back on it now, how often did she truly heed my advice? For how long have I wasted my days studying over politics and strategy only for it to be completely and utterly wasted? What value do I hold to my family?

Terran and Oliver have their parts, Oak her own and even Reed has been studying under the apothecary for a while now. Me. I'm just here. Destined to follow in their footsteps, forever cast in their shadow as I fight to achieve even a sliver of their greatness. A laugh escapes me as I realize the absurdity of it all. This is not new, not unimaginable. The truth of my position has been made clear from the moment that my father passed. I have simply been refusing to see it. Now the true mystery is why it took my cousin's betrayal to open my eyes.

"Are you going to talk to me about whatever is bothering you or are you just going to keep chucking those rocks?" Oak says with a grunt. She is using her magic to lift a boulder twice her size completely overhead. The stone floats above her with ease and is set gently on the ground behind us.

"I have no idea what you're talking about." I throw another boulder behind us and it crashes into the one she just moved, shattering it into tiny little pebbles.

Oak raises her brows at me and then shakes her head, turning back to the concrete. "Whatever this mood is, get over it. We're on foreign soil, battling unknown enemies, and for all we know we could drown at any second. So less of whatever that," she says gesturing to all of me, "is and more focus on the task at hand."

"Excuse me? I know exactly the situation we are in. Don't lecture me about danger when you're the one who rushed off here without any backup." Another boulder goes soaring over my shoulder.

"Is that what this is about? You wanted to tag along?" Oak snorts. She rolls her eyes in indignation.

"No." My magic pulses as I continue moving rocks.

"Really? Then tell me, Rose, why are you so angry?" Oak continues to work, pushing her magic far beyond what I am capable of. We've hardly made a dent in this mountain of rubble and I'm already feeling the effects of using so much magic.

I wipe my hand along my brow, catching the sweat before it can slide down my face. "I'm not angry."

She stops moving things, turning to look at me expectantly. "Liar."

"What?" I yell, whirling on my cousin.

Her green eyes widen at the outburst and she opens her mouth but I don't let her speak.

"You're calling me the liar? Seriously? How dare you after everything that you've done," I snarl.

"Whoa, back up. What are you talking about?" Oak's eyes shift to the rubble, narrow, and then widen on me again. "You talked to Mar." It's not a question, she knows I did.

A mirthless laugh leaves me. "About your lies? Yeah. We *talked*. Do you have any idea how it feels to learn that you have been made a fool of by your *entire* family. For *years*."

"What? How are you getting that?" Oak asks, the surprise clear in her voice.

"Oh please, am I to believe that my mother and brothers were not *aware* of what you were really doing out in those woods? Hm?" Knowing that the secrets of our realm have been hidden for me my entire life only fuels the rage at my entire family.

Oak takes a deep breath, letting it out slowly. "Listen, Rose, I didn't enjoy hiding things from you. But you have to know that it is part of my job to-""Your job? Please Oak, you and I both know that you are a shit spy. My mother only keeps you around because it is convenient for her." I regret the words the moment they leave my mouth yet I can't find it in me to apologize.

Hurt flashes in Oak's eyes. She turns her back to me continuing to work, her magic more uncontrolled now. The boulders tossed around rather than gliding.

"So that's it? You're just going to turn your back to me? Nothing to say about your betrayal?" I scoff. What was I really expecting her to do, own up to it?

Oak whips around, and hands balled into fists at her side. "Betrayal? Honestly, Rose, can you be *any more dramatic*?" she says, emphasizing each word individually.

"Don't belittle me," I warn.

She laughs, the sound grating against my ears. "I'm not. I'm simply calling it as it is. You're upset because you didn't know everything for once in your life. You're mad because you feel left out. Well I'm sorry, but sometimes these things happen. It's not my fault if your mother doesn't trust you. I am doing my *job*, if you have a problem with what that entails then take it up with her."

My mouth hangs open in astonishment as I stare at her back. When I don't say anything for a while she glances over her shoulder. Barely looking long enough to see the anger brewing behind my eyes. Words are lost to me as the rage builds beneath my skin, my magic swelling along with it as the intensity grows until it is difficult to hold it in.

Oak looks back to me again and curses. She drops the pile of rocks and rushes to my side. I'm staring down at her, my magic coiling and writhing beneath my skin, waiting to be released on whatever and whoever is waiting in its path.

"Shit, Rose. Look at me. You need to calm down. Okay? You need to get your magic under control before you hurt someone, hurt yourself," her tone is soothing, but her eyes show the concern she so obviously feels.

Oak grabs hold of my wrists and tries to draw my magic into her but it retaliates. Oak jumps back with a yelp as my magic becomes a living beast inside me.

A thousand thoughts race through my mind. Oakley, lying to me. Oliver, laughing at me. Terran, pitying me. My mother overlooking me. No matter how hard I try to push the images away I can see them all as if they stand here in front of me. How dare they treat me like this? To push me aside until it is convenient for them. To use me as nothing more than a face, a name, another part of *the royal image*. My mother's constant posturing and expectations for me.

"Rose, focus. I know you're upset. I understand why. But whatever it is you're thinking, I need you to let it go. This rage will consume you if you let it. Magic is delicate. It feeds off of emotions and yours right now, they're all over the place. If you don't get control of it you're going to do something that you'll regret." Oak' voice is far away.

The ground beneath my feet begins to tremble and fear begins to penetrate that rage burning inside me. I try to get control of my magic, to make it stop, but I realize, it's not me that is causing it. Oak looks around anxiously, using her magic to cast a shield above us in case another hunk of the ceiling decides to break off.

Focusing on containing my own magic, I draw in long breaths, letting them out slowly until I feel more in control of things. The anger begins to fade and I can actually think again. I grab Oak's hand and add my magic to hers with ease, reinforcing the shield protecting us. Oak looks up at me with a question in her eyes but I shake my head. No matter how pissed I might be, there are more important things to worry about right now.

The ground begins to shake more violently and I can't help but look towards the spot in the dome where Rian noticed the ripples before. Shock and horror tears through me as I find a gaping hole in the barrier, a flood of water rushing in like a waterfall.

Oak curses as she sees it too. "We need to move."

I nod my head. The path ahead of us is still blocked by the concrete and we don't have the time to move it. My cousin seems to realize the same thing and starts to look for other ways around. "Mar! Rian! Can you hear me?" I yell through the rubble.

"Yep," Mar answers, her voice unusually high pitched.

"Is everything okay over there?" I call back.

"Yep," Rian answers, his voice extra gruff.

"Okay, listen, things are getting bad over here. The barrier is already starting to collapse and it's going to take too long to move all this. You two go on ahead and we'll find another way around."

"Do you want me to blast it with a fireball?" Mar offers.

"You can't," Rian chastises, "this whole place is already falling apart, a blast like that could bring the whole thing down."

An enormous explosion of power booms from the direction of the throne room and my heart nearly stops. I can feel the magic radiating from that area, even from here. If Rian is worried about a small fireball bringing this place down, Vana only knows what something of that magnitude could do. Whatever caused that, I hope Cay and Eve -even Oliver- are nowhere near it.

"We're going towards whatever that sound is. You two be careful," Mar announces, her voice more even this time.

"You too," I call after her.

"Rose, this way, I found a way around," Oak shouts from around the corner, back the way we came.

I race to her side and follow her lead as she takes off down the hall.

"This whole place is unstable. If we aren't out of here before that barrier crumbles, we're going to have a much bigger problem on our hands," Oak says breathlessly.

Another rumble nearly knocks me off my feet but Oak grabs my hand, keeping me upright and practically dragging me after her. Once I regain my footing I snatch my hand back. Impending death aside, I'm still angry as hell about all the lying and I'm not going to just forget about it or pretend it didn't happen. Actions have consequences and it's time my family learned that.

We race through the halls as the walls continue to rumble and shake around us. Our hands are extended above our heads casting a continuous shield there and making sure we aren't going to be caught by surprise by some falling debris. All we have to do is make it to the throne room, find the others, and get out of here before the entire castle comes crumbling down on top of us. Easy enough. Only one nagging thought keeps entering my head. How the hell are we getting out of here?

Chapter 45

Eve

Something tears me from the darkness. I'm not sure what but when I look down I see tendrils of smoke seeping through my fingertips. I stare at them, trying desperately to make them go away but the little wisps are still there no matter how many times I blink. My entire body seems light, like I could float away on a gust of wind and no one would know better.

Magic hums beneath my skin but not like it usually does. No, the fire inside me burns but this, this new magic or whatever it is, it's more like a *caress*. Something about it soothes me, calming my heart and letting me breathe deeper, for what feels like the first time I take a breath and I feel it *everywhere*. It's intoxicating. And terrifying.

Somewhere in that darkness I could hear, could feel everything that was going on around me. Teru, as I learned their name is, kept some kind of link on this plane of existence while their magic invaded my mind. Yet in doing so they didn't just let themselves exist in both worlds, I did too. Part of me wonders if I had followed that magic back, if I might be able to glimpse inside their own mind. I can't remember what they were looking for in my head, something to do with magic.

Power. Of course, it's always about power.

Music fills the air, sweeping over me and snaring me in its grasp. An angel-like voice calls me to her and I go willingly. Everything feels warm, and well. Peaceful. My body begins to twirl and dance and glide across the floor. I stand up on one foot as I spin, spin, spin, spin until I nearly fall over. Hands glide over my thighs and then caress my neck. Mine. My hands. They feel so distant, like another person's. A laugh escapes me before I can stop it. Oh how I wish someone else would touch me.

If only Nat were here, she would dance with me all night long and then hold me until morning. Her fiery red hair would feel so soft against my skin, her long fingers would feel wonderful. Another laugh escapes me as my hands glide all over my body. I twirl again, my arms going up over my head. I trail my hand down the opposite arm and let my fingers press against my wrist. The sharp sting of the blade slicing open my skin gives me a moment of clarity and I drop to my knees, panting heavily.

A scream brings me back to the moment fully. The sound of pure, absolute grief, shatters my thoughts and echoes through the room, bouncing off the marble walls and back to the center. I stare down at my arm and find that I have slit my own wrist.

Shit. I quickly heal it before I lose too much blood. Searching for the source of the scream, I find Cay hovering over her father's lifeless body. My heart stops, words of denial choking me. But it's impossible to refuse what is so clearly laid out before me. I look back to my friend and find her screaming at the top of her lungs, yet all I can hear is a song so beautiful I want to listen to it for the rest of my life.

Fuck. I slice my palm open and let the pain linger, grounding me in the moment. I push back to my feet, a wave of dizziness making my vision blur for a moment. My body is covered in small cuts and slashes from my own blade as I just willingly carved myself apart, entranced by Cay's song.

The back of my head is pounding, I press my hand there and it comes away covered in blood. I make quick work of healing it and the pounding stops but the dizziness doesn't go away. I don't bother healing the rest, letting the pain keep me here and focused on getting control of the situation.

Taking a few hesitant steps forward I watch as Cay begins to rise further off the ground, magic swelling inside her. It grows into something wild, fierce, and completely destructive. Cay lets out another scream, mangled and broken, filled with the heartbreak over the loss of her father. Memories of the two of them flood my brain and for a second I just stand there, shocked.

Cay as a baby balanced upon her father's knee. Cay as a toddler, learning how to walk and then only weeks later, run. I watch as she grows into the woman I know now. How her magic scared her so much when she first began to use it. Thousands of moments between her and her father, all the way up until his final moments. How his eyes swelled with pride at the image of his little girl, even as fear tore apart his heart as he knew he was leaving her. More fear for the fate of his wife, his son.

So much fear that I nearly throw up, the feeling so overwhelming that I have to pinch myself to clear it away. The sharp pain brings me back to the here and now. Whatever that was, it has never happened to me before. My heart aches for my friend knowing what this loss will do to her, to her entire kingdom. I can't help but search for her mother and pray to the goddess that there is some bit of hope for my friend.

My eyes search the room, roaming over the floor and looking into every nook and cranny for any sign of her. My breath catches in my throat as I see Teru, slumped against the wall with blood pooling around them. Their midnight black hair spills over their shoulder and hides their face from me. I let my gaze move past them, still searching for the queen. I find her sprawled out on her side, her body so still that for a moment I can only feel dread. But then she takes a shuddering breath, barely deep enough to move her chest yet all that I need.

Cay's magic is out of control, a large sphere of water begins to form around her, her eyes a raging storm. Her dark hair whips around her face, torn free from its braid. I'm not even sure that Cay is aware of what's happening, she is so lost in herself, in this magic. I take another step towards her, holding my hands out in front of me, prepared to shield if needed.

A pang of fear ricochets through me as I realize I have no idea if my magic will work like it's supposed to. Whatever dark magic Teru let into me, it might take control. Still, whatever risk it might be, I have to get through to Cay, bring her back to this reality, as painful as it might be.

The closer I get to the storm that is Cay, the harder it becomes to move forward, the force of her magic driving back against me. It becomes too much and I only have one option unless I want to be torn apart. I have to use my magic. Taking a steadying breath I place both hands out in front of me, mist still seeping out, and I call on my magic.

A gasp escapes me as I feel the complete euphoria of using my magic. It starts as a burn, the fire blazing beneath my skin and to the surface as I begin to cast the spell. Then it changes, it becomes cooler until the chill sends tingles shooting down my back. The combination of hot and cold so foreign yet entirely familiar at the same time.

Casting my magic, I continue to march forward, my steps coming with ease as the shield rests firmly in place before me. Somehow it feels stronger, more sure now. Like my magic is *easier* to control, not harder. There's no time to consider what that means as I breach the outer layer of Cay's cyclone. My clothes are completely drenched and I can barely see through the water lining my lashes. I could wipe it away but it would be pointless; Cay's magic is unceasing.

I spot my friend at the eye of the storm, floating above the ground, the tips of her toes barely brushing the floor as her hands are extended out on either side of her, palms up as water shoots out of them like geysers. I've never seen anything like it. So much raw power. All of the royals have an absurd amount of magic, more than any commoner at least, but this is next level.

The taste of jealousy is bitter on my tongue. Never have I felt magic like this before. Although maybe this new dark magic will change that. A terrifying yet exhilarating idea. Pushing the thoughts away I focus on Cay. I get as close as I can before calling out to her, "Cay! You have to calm down! This magic, it's too strong. Okay? Listen, I'm sorry about your dad."

Cay's magic flares and I'm shoved back a few feet. Reinforcing my shield I move closer again. Damn she is really not making this easy. "I know how much he meant to you. But think of all of the other people who you love, who love you! Think of Rose, Mar, think of your brother! Cay, think of me! I love you, you are my sister, maybe not by blood but in every way that counts. Please, Cay, don't do this to yourself."

Tears flow freely down my cheek as Cay's magic continues to grow and it becomes harder to resist the force of it. Black dots appear in the corners of my eyes and I blink them away. "Your mother is still alive. She needs you! I don't know how to help her, it has to be you. Please, come back to us, okay? We'll get through this together. What am I supposed to do without you? I need you," my voice cracks on the last part.

Cay's magic dims for a moment and hope swells inside my chest. An explosion of power rips from Cay and ripples through the entire kingdom, sending me flying backwards yet again as I am thrown into the wall. The power continues to ravage my body as it forces its way free from Cay. My vision is growing blurrier with each passing second and somewhere in the back of my mind I am reminded that it has been days since I last took my tonic. It's a miracle that I've even lasted this long. Stupid mistake. And now what will it cost me? My life? Cay's life? It already cost her her father.

Forcing myself to stand, I watch as the magic begins to fade, drawn back into Cay as she lowers to the ground. My vision is practically black now as I fight to remain conscious. Maybe I should sit back down? Prop my feet up? I try to press healing magic into my head, hoping it will provide some sort of relief yet knowing it won't.

There are things that I have come to recognize as meaning I am too far gone for any healing magic. The way my heart begins to race. How my fingers go numb and my arms become heavy. All well under way by now. Next is the nausea. It builds in my stomach as everything begins to grow colder. That's it, the final sign. I can feel the depths of nothingness calling to me like an old friend and I am helpless to stop it.

My knees buckle as the world is ripped out from beneath me, the ground waiting for me yet again. Only it's not the ground that catches me. No. Instead, I find myself in the arms of someone cold, and so thin that I swear I can feel their every bone as they lift me to their chest. I am curled against them, my eyes barely able to remain open, unable to even lift a finger or say a word. And in the moment before darkness claims me again I hear them.

"My king is going to be very intrigued to meet you."

Chapter 46

Cay

The song rips through me, bursting free and filling the air like an uncontrolled storm. I don't stop it. I let it become everything that I am. My magic purrs excitedly beneath my skin, finally set free from the prison it has been kept in for so long. I let it build until it reaches a crescendo and blasts through the pain in my chest, becoming all that I feel. I'll tear it all down and wash it away. I'll destroy every trace of the shadows that dared to darken the halls of my home; that stole my father from me.

I pour every ounce of my magic into it. Letting it tear through the world like my father's death tore through my heart. I feed the pain and agony living inside me until it grows into a beast, so entirely feral that I'm not sure I might ever contain it again. I let my fear evaporate and anger fill the void that it leaves. I shove aside all of the warnings and prophecies that were told to me and just give in to this monster that lives inside me. Starved for the chaos I have denied it.

Until now. But never again. The room disappears around me and my vision becomes clouded. It's only for a moment and then I see them.

Images of war and bloodshed, the world painted red. Brother turning on brother. Mother on son. Lover against lover. There is something so mesmerizing about the way they turn on each other. The way they rip each other to shreds. If not for my song I might be laughing.

I watch as magic clashes on an open field. Voices call out to me from everywhere. Their cries are like a symphony in my head. Some of them are begging. For what I can't discern. Nor do I care. I spy a land shrouded in mist so thick it is like a wall. Screams fill my ears and turn my blood ice cold. I bask in it all. So much pain and heartache invade my mind that I am lost to it, a heady feeling enters my chest.

The delicious misery, so like my own. My song builds and builds until I can't hear anything else. Beneath the sounds of the pained and dying, I hear whispers. Calling to me and showing me the sweetest kind of relief, one that I am so ready to accept. To be free of my own pain and bathe in the bloodshed they so willingly offer me. To lay waste to the world. I feel the tears flowing freely down my cheeks. Tears for my father. For myself.

But as I embrace this magic, give in to it and let the whispers draw me closer, I hear a voice. One that sounds so familiar and yet I am sure I have never heard it before.

Don't let them in.

As if a switch has been flipped I see thousands of people whose bodies lay crumpled and broken. Most of them are strangers. Others are my friends. I see Rose, lying on her back, a blackened hole at the center of her chest. I see Mar ripped in two, right down the center. I see my brother's head speared atop a spike driven into the ground. I see Terran and Oliver, their bodies twisted and broken, bent in a dozen different directions. I see Oak's green eyes unblinking, glazed over like my father's, blood leaking from them. Then I see Eve, the image so grotesque it takes everything in me to not throw up.

These visions offer nothing but horror and with each face that I see, I feel myself breaking apart. Shattering to a million tiny pieces that might never be put back together again. The fragments so small they could be carried away by the wind. A small part of me is still tempted to let it, just to be free of these nightmares. To let the magic consume me. When I welcomed it in I thought the pain was over, but this is anything but the peace I sought.

Then a new voice breaks through the storm. One I know almost better than my own.

I need you.

I hear it as though it is spoken directly into my mind. A sob so broken that I feel it echo in my own heart. Despite the pain I know waits for me, I fight back. I push against the magic, the whispers, with everything I have. I draw in every ounce of power that I can and drive the magic from my body with such force that it explodes out of me and back into the universe.

Ripples of magic flow throughout the entire kingdom, shaking the very foundation. The barrier surrounding the city cracks under the force of it and for a second a new fear seizes me. Will *I* be the destruction of my home? Not some enemy or some disaster, but me? I always knew that I would be my own ruin, and now, everything that I love.

As the magic leaves my body I feel myself lowering to the ground. I fall to my knees and the visions fade away. My eyes find my father's body and uncontrolled sobs break free. Tears flow freely from me, clouding my vision. The overwhelming grief that washes over me threatens to rip me apart, just as fiercely as the magic might have. I fall forward, curling in on myself as the world goes numb around me. I squeeze my eyes shut against it all.

I lay like that for what feels like an eternity. When hands grab me I don't bother to fight against them. My body is feeling weaker than it has ever felt before. The hands pull me upright, my eyes still shut, shielding me against the world around me. Against the crumpled form of my once great father. His dark hair and kind eyes. But more than that I am shielding the *world* from *me*.

"Cay, look at me," a male voice begs of me. Deep and kind. Soft hands smooth my hair back from where it clings to my face. "Please, princess, show me those beautiful eyes of yours," the voice begs.

I'm gathered into strong arms and pulled against a warm chest. There's something so comforting, so gentle about the way the male holds me that I let a single eye crack open. Daring to face the world. Hazel eyes beneath a mess of chestnut curls stare down at me.

"I've got you. You're safe."

I open both my eyes wide, taking in his wide nose, his full lips, not a smirk in sight.

Oliver.

I throw my arms around his neck, burying my face there and letting him pull me closer as I fall apart all over again.

He traces soothing circles over my back with one hand, the other presses into the crown of my head. He drops his mouth close to my ear and whispers to me over and over again. *You're safe. You're safe.*

I pull back enough to look into his eyes as they survey every inch of me. The warmth of healing magic spreads over me and I let out a sigh as all of the physical pain washes away. It does nothing to heal the aching in my heart. Tears swell in my eyes again and I do nothing to stop them as they slip free.

Oliver brushes them away with his rough thumb. His face is covered in some sort of black goo that smells positively rancid.

"You smell terrible."

He smirks, the shadow of a dimple in his right cheek, "Of course the first thing you say to me is an insult."

Hurried footsteps sound from behind me and my entire body tenses up. I don't dare look at whoever or whatever approaches.

Oliver notices the change and he looks over my shoulder, his brows pinching together. "Are they…"

"The king…" the female voice trails off. Sharp pain radiates through my chest, knowing what they dare not speak.

Oliver nods, eyes glancing down at me. "And the queen?" he asks, his voice surprisingly even.

"Unconscious, but alive. Though she doesn't look good," she answers.

Everything inside me freezes. Alive. I tear free of Oliver's grip and turn to face my mother. Nat stands above her where she is laid out on her side. Her body is so still but as I look closely I can see the subtle rise and fall of her chest. I crawl towards her, too weak to stand. Nat and Oliver try to protest but I ignore them, dragging myself across the room until I am close enough to touch my mother's face.

Her skin is cold, colder than it should be. Fear threatens to seize me again as I take in how shallow her breaths really are. How it shudders out of her. I press my hand to her chest and try to heal her but my magic is completely empty. I lift my head with frantic eyes and find Oliver there, already healing her.

Nat kneels down beside me and looks between us. "What happened?" she asks hesitantly.

It is all I can do to shake my head. I'm not even sure how much time has passed since I first saw my parents at the mercy of Teru's shadows. Since I watched my father fall before me. Since I banished the magic from inside me, leaving nothing but this emptiness.

"Cay, I know that you're grieving but I need to know. Where's Eve?" Nat asks, her face entirely serious.

I turn to look around the room. Searching for any sign of her. Willing her to appear before me. "She was here, I don't- she was here and then- the magic," I struggle to find the words, to think of the last time I saw her. How long has it been? What happened to her? I continue to search the room and then it hits me. Eve is not the only one missing.

"Teru. They're gone," I breathe. My words barely above a whisper.

"Who?" Oliver asks, his jaw set in a firm line.

"Teru, they- they said 'they come from the land forgotten, the darkness, the mist itself'. They were responsible for the attack on the kingdom. But what does that even mean?" I ask no one in particular.

"Did you see where they went?" Nat demands.

"I- I don't..." I struggle to form words, my eyes swelling with tears.

Oliver spares me from answering. "Nat, she's in shock, give her a moment."

"What about Eve? Where is she?" Nat seethes.

Oliver sighs, "I don't know. But if what Cay said is right then-"

"I'm going after her." Before either of us can stop her, Nat takes off running.

Oliver continues to heal my mother, not even acknowledging that Nat just went chasing after the enemy all on her own.

"Oliver, where did they take Eve?" I beg.

He doesn't look at me.

"Tell me. What did they mean by that? What is this 'land forgotten'? I don't understand."

He continues to ignore me.

"Answer me!" I scream.

His hazel eyes meet mine and they are filled with so many emotions that I can't place just one. Oliver continues to stare at me as my heart begins to race.

If I had a single drop of magic left in me I know it would be going wild yet again. "Tell. Me. Where. They. Took. Her," I say each word pointedly.

His answer is flat, devoid of all emotion. "Cansu."

My mind whirls as years of history lessons come rushing back to me. "That's not possible. Cansu and all its people haven't existed in over a millennium. Our ancestors made sure of that."

"Cay, you need to focus on you right now. On your mother. She needs help and much as it pains me to admit this, I'm not a good enough healer for whatever is wrong with her."

I stare at him, a ringing in my ears. My father is dead. My mother lays here dying. Eve is gone, taken to a land that we thought eradicated long ago. I retreat into myself. Locking out the world around me, the death and despair. I dig deep into my own mind and tuck myself away there, where nothing else can hurt me. The world ceases to exist. I cut off my senses and let myself leave my physical body. Even as Oliver tries to force me to stay.

Chapter 47

Eve

I blink my eyes open against the pounding in my head. Bright light surrounds me, sending a flare of pain straight through my skull and I immediately close them again. My heart feels sluggish as my body fights to regulate itself after the episode. The moments before passing out send my heart racing. Followed by a dramatic drop that sends me plunging into darkness. I focus on my breathing knowing it is the only thing that I really can do at this point.

Sensation returns to my toes first. Tingling at first and then somewhat painful as I try to wiggle them in my boots. My legs feel leaden, my arms are still relatively numb where they hang at my sides. Nausea builds in my stomach just like it always does after. Someone is carrying me, that much I know. The movement of their hurried steps churns the acid in my stomach, adding to my queasiness. Bile rises in the back of my throat and I force it back down.

No matter how many times it happens, or however I try to prevent it, waking up feels an awful lot like getting run over by a carriage. All of the muscles in my body ache along with the lingering metallic taste in my mouth. I try not to think about it as I take deep, steadying breaths. My pulse grows stronger with each passing moment yet my magic remains completely drained. Whatever little bit of it was left after using it earlier has surely depleted, my episode burning through it entirely.

Feeling returns to my fingertips and I try to subtly move my hand to my thigh. Brushing my hand over the spot where my daggers should be, I find them missing. Rage builds in me followed by a moment of fear. I am without magic or weapons, barely conscious, and in the arms of who I am guessing is my enemy. Though I suppose there is a slim chance that the strong arms that hold me actually belong to a friend.

Forcing my eyes open I look up at whoever holds me in their arms. Blinking though the light, my vision swims with black dots and bright bursts of color. Staring straight ahead is Teru, their face so close to mine that I can see details I hadn't noticed before. The graceful slope of their jaw, the carved cheekbones and high brow. The bridge of their nose is relatively flat between their narrow eyes. Eyes that shift to mine and have my own widening.

The color is so familiar. Like I have stared into them a thousand times before never knowing who they belong to.

"Stop staring at me," they chastise.

Using whatever strength I can muster, I twist in their arms, attempting to roll out of their grip and break free. I barely move an inch. Their slender arms clamping down on me and refusing to budge. They're surprisingly strong. "Release me at once," I demand.

They snort, "And why would I do that? You're going to be my gift to my king, after all, he'll be very interested to meet you."

"Oh? And why is that?" I continue to yank against their hold, ripping one arm free only for them to snare it again with their shadows. The moment the dark mist touches my skin I suck in a breath.

Cold bites down to the bone, chilling my entire body and searching for the well of magic inside me. Teru seems irritated to find it empty, drawing their shadows back as soon as my arm is pinned to my side again.

"I deserve an answer." I growl.

Teru raises their brow, "Oh? Is that so? Captives feel entitled in your kingdom do they?"

I narrow my eyes at them. "Is that what I am, a captive? And here I thought I was some fancy gift," I snort.

"You are both. Now shut your mouth before I knock you out again," Teru bites.

"For that to be possible that would mean you knocked me out the first time, which you didn't, so how about you answer some of my questions. Oh and while you're at it, put me down." I thrash in their arms, hoping to loosen their grip enough to fight back, weak as I am.

Teru ignores me, marching forward without a hint of hesitation.

Looking around I find us shrouded in mist, a fog so thick I can hardly see through it. Panic seizes me as I realize I have no idea where I am. Not only that, I have no clue what happened to the others. We got separated from Mar and Rose so long ago, who knows where they ended up. Besides that, Cay was… unwell the last I saw her.

Reaching deep down inside me, I search desperately for any shred of power. Something to give me an advantage. At the least to free myself so I might fight with fists if not magic. I look Teru up and down surveying their lithe body. Their hooded cloak hides much of them from me, but even still, they move with the elegance of a dancer, or perhaps an assassin. Judging by our current circumstances I'm willing to put money on the latter.

"Where are we?" I ask. My heart is already racing inside me as the fear begins to rise.

They don't even acknowledge I spoke. Not a blink or a twitch of the mouth. They pull the shadows around us tighter and a thought forms in my head before I think to stop it. I dip back into that well again but this time, instead of searching for my fire, I search for shadows. Hiding deep

406

within me they curl and twist, waiting for me to notice them. I call out tentatively, inviting them to wake and asking for their help at the same moment. They curl around my hand and then up my arm. I let them build up around my entire body silently then force them away from me in a blast that has me thrown from Teru's arms.

They hit the ground in a crouch, a mixture of shock and excitement plastered across their face as a smile splits their lips. "I knew it," they whisper.

I don't ask what that means or wait to find out. I take off running, practically blind as I try to navigate through the thick fog. Their haunting laugh follows me but I don't look back. Something snags my foot and I go tumbling forward. I curl my body into a ball at the last second, rolling forward and quickly standing again.

Shadowy arms reach through the void in front of me and wrap me in their hold. I gasp at the coolness of their touch, freezing me to my bones instantly. I fight against their hold to no avail. Switching up my approach I try to get control over them, to *make* them release me.

"These shadows are mine. They only listen to me," Teru's voice whispers in my ear from behind me. A shiver snakes down my body. The shadows dissolve into real, solid arms, snaring me in their grip and forcing my arms to my sides.

"Fuck you," I spit.

"Ew. No thanks," Teru sneers.

Ignoring their blatant disrespect -I mean seriously that was rude- I search for my own shadows.

"Nope, not letting you get away with that twice," Teru grunts, their own shadows slipping under my skin.

I wait for the darkness to consume me, to drag me into their inky depths and steal any chance I have at saving myself. But instead of being consumed I feel them feeding me. Magic swells inside me, not just shadows but fire as well. "Oh it's on fucker," I say with a laugh. I throw my head back, driving it into Teru's face.

They curse but don't release their hold on me. Not that it matters. I let my skin heat until it is unbearable, my fire burning across my flesh yet leaving it unscathed. A new kind of hope burns in my heart as I get reconnected with my elemental magic.

Teru's hands begin to burn, the flesh turning an angry shade of pink. "*Stop*," Teru grunts against the pain.

Something in their voice forces me to cut my magic off. The fire dies in me as suddenly as it was there and with it, that small bit of hope. A scream of rage leaves me as I begin to thrash against Teru.

"Stop," Teru says again but this time without that added lilt to their voice that demands to be followed.

"I'll fucking kill you!" I snarl, slamming an elbow into Teru's stomach. Their grip on me loosens and I am able to wrench an arm free. I call the shadows to my fist and pull my arm back before delivering a wicked punch to their jaw.

"Bitch," they sputter, spitting blood from their split lips.

A ball of bright red light cuts through the shadows over their shoulder and I duck at the last second as a ball of fire hits them straight in their back.

Teru lands on their face as the shadows evaporate around us and we are left in an open field. Teru groans where they lay on the ground and I take the opportunity to look at our surroundings. The castle is just behind us, in the direction the fire came from.

Emerging from a cloud of dark smoke, fiery hair blazing behind her, is Nat.

My heart squeezes at the sight of her, my feet moving instantly.

Nat's eyes are locked on mine as she sprints through the open field. Her face is a mixture of anger and relief. She's covered in some sort of black sludge but it doesn't seem to phase her.

I can practically feel her warmth, her soft skin, as I race towards her. I don't take my eyes off her face, forcing my legs to move as fast as I can even as they scream at me. The exhaustion of my episode still weighs me down but I ignore it. Fighting against the darkness that rings my vision and makes my limbs go numb.

Nat looks over my shoulder at something and throws another ball of fire at whatever creeps up on me but it's too late.

Cold arms grab me and yank me backwards, pressing me firmly against their chest. I don't have the energy to fight them off as they immobilize me, the shadows slipping under my skin again only this time my magic doesn't stir. My vision darkens but I use my remaining strength to stay awake, focusing on my breathing in an attempt to get control over my racing heart.

Teru's hand clamps down on my throat, cutting off my breathing and making my heart beat wildly again. Their magic seeps into the depths of my soul and wraps around it tightly, like a snake coiling around its prey.

I watch Nat as she makes it the final distance between us until she is standing a mere 10 feet in front of me.

Her eyes are locked on Teru's hand at my throat, then lower, where they press one of my own blades into the spot just between two ribs. Perfectly poised to puncture a lung.

"That's far enough," Teru says with a dark chuckle.

"Release her or the next fireball will be aimed at your head," Nat demands. Her voice is steady, even as her hands shake where they are outstretched in front of her.

"Try it, I dare you. Let's see who's faster, you, or my blade," Teru taunts.

"I don't need to try. When it comes to the woman in your arms, I'll be whatever she needs me to be," Nat states boldly.

All I can do is stare at her. To try and memorize her freckles, the fiery curls that frame her delicate face. Looking at her now I see so much more than the warrior I have come to know over the past week. There is still so much I want to know about her, about her life and family, her dreams. Still, the one thing I want more is for her to have the chance to make them happen.

"Oh look, you've got a girlfriend," Teru patronizes.

"The woman in your hands means far more to me than that. She is my-"

"Yes. She is my girlfriend. So please, just let her go. Take me and let her leave here in peace," I beg, cutting Nat off before she exposes who I am on the off chance that Teru doesn't realize they hold the heir to the Vulca throne. Better they think us a couple madly in love than a knight protecting her future queen.

Nat opens her mouth to argue but then the ground begins to rumble and shake.

I look to the sky as ripples in the barrier grow and expand until they cover the entire dome. Recognition flares in me as I realize what that means and know it is only a matter of time before that barrier breaks. "Nat, find the others. Get them out," I say hurriedly.

"If you think I'm just going to leave you here, abandon you to this-"

"That's an order," I command. My tone is firm despite the lump forming in my throat.

Nat seems to consider challenging me for a moment before cursing. She shifts in the next breath and takes to the sky in her brilliant dragon form. Her black wings cast a dark shadow over us. She flies close to the barrier and then disappears from view over the crest of the castle walls.

"I didn't take you for someone so dominant," Teru sneers.

"I'm just full of surprises," I deadpan.

"That you are," their voice is thick with desire, yet not for my body, "my king will be more than willing to help you discover all of them."

I watch in silence as the barrier fails and magic washes over me. The same magic that exploded from Cay. There is a comfort in knowing that she is with me now, even if not in the physical sense.

"Right, time to go," Teru says, yanking me back against them.

Before I can question how exactly they plan to do that, a cloud of mist surrounds us and pulls us through the very fabric of reality.

Chapter 48

Mar

R ian races alongside me as we use our enhanced speed to weave through the castle, dodging falling debris. His eyes keep glancing up at the barrier and I know he is waiting for the inevitable. My heart beats wildly with the mere thought of what happens when the dome breaks, when all that water comes crashing in. We haven't spoken, not even a word, about what happened back there.

A wealth of emotions swirl inside me, turning my stomach. What we did was idiotic, yes. But did I regret it? No. Not if I'm being honest with myself. Something draws me to him. Part of me wants to chalk it up to simple lust mixed with general curiosity about my reserved guard. Yet another part of me sees how his eyes flare when I challenge him, when I push back. I very well could be the first person in his life to do so.

Being the daughter of the king isn't something I've thought about too often, even back home. Eve is the heir, taking away any pressure or expectations off of my shoulder before I even know they exist. Yes there were things I've had to do, a role I have to perform as second in line.

Especially recently. But for the most part I have been granted the freedom to be who I want, to choose my way in life. Even when it comes to who I take to bed.

I let my eyes roam over Rian again, assessing. His broad shoulders are stiff, his defined jaw locked in a scowl. My gaze catches on his hair and I have to stifle a laugh as I look at the mess of it. Strands poke up at odd angles giving it a just fucked appearance, even if we hadn't gotten that far. It's not a bad look on him, though that anger painted across his face tells me all I need to know about thoughts like those.

Rian might be content to ignore whatever happened between us, but I'm not. I don't hide from my feelings and I certainly won't pretend nothing happened. As soon as things are settled and everyone is home safe, we *will* be having a conversation. Maybe a little fighting. If I'm lucky, I might just push the right buttons until he has me pinned to another wall. Preferably one that wasn't on the verge of total collapse. My thoughts drift back to those moments where our bodies were pressed firmly together, heating my blood. I stumble over a crack in the floor, catching myself before I completely faceplant.

"Focus," Rian growls from beside me.

I bite down on the inside of my cheek, holding back for now. We turn down another corridor, driven purely by instinct. I can feel a powerful source of magic drawing me towards it. My own magic hums in approval the closer we get. Whatever, or whoever, caused that blast must hold an immense well of magic inside them. Hopefully, they're on our side. I don't even want to think about what it means for us if they're not. If we're right and Eve and Cay really are in this room... I drive the thoughts away.

Eve has been trained practically her entire life. Her skill with a blade far above my own, of anyone I have ever seen. So long as she can use her blade, her enemies don't stand a chance. Aside from that, her magic is strong, rivaling even our father's when it comes to pure power alone. Though she might struggle to control it at times, it might be exactly what she needs.

Cay on the other hand, I do worry about. This is her kingdom, her *family* under attack. That brings the added layer of emotions that can so easily cloud a person's mind. As was already shown when her spell that brought us here cracked under the mere sight of her city's destruction. One slip in concentration, one moment of distraction and she could be in serious trouble. I hesitate to think what she might do should something happen to her parents.

Things start to look familiar and I realize that I have been here before, a few years ago during some kind of ball. Blood begins to pump steadily through my veins as I push my body to move faster. We approach the large double doors that open into the open throne room and I immediately turn into the room, not giving a moment of hesitation.

I nearly run straight into someone. I'm saved by Rian who grabs my arm and yanks me to the side at the last second. This is the second time he has saved me now, damn him. Rian steadies me beside him and I look back to see who was walking out of the room.

Oliver half carries Cay, her arm wrapped around his waist and leaning into him for support.

"Cay! Fuck, are you okay? What happened?" I throw myself on my friend, my arms going around her neck and squeezing tightly. Taking a step back I look her over from head to toe, searching for any sign of injury.

There are a few spots of dried blood and she is completely drenched, her cotton dress clinging to the curve of her hips and the dip in her waist, otherwise she appears unscathed, or at least already healed.

Oliver whispers something to Rian and he shoots off into the room.

I watch as he kneels down beside Cay's mother and begins pressing healing magic into her. Fear grips me as I strain to hear the thump of her heart, the dull beat barely there even as Rian pushes everything he has into healing her. My gaze roams across the rest of the room and a harsh gasp escapes me as I find king Callan, Cay's father, lying in a heap.

His eyes are still open, glazed over with streams of blood dried over his cheeks like tears. I take a moment to say a silent prayer to the goddess on

413

his behalf. I might not have known the man well but he was a good king, a good father too. My own spoke highly of him often enough to know. Not to mention the many stories Cay has told us over the years.

I force myself to continue looking over the rest of the room. My eyes sweep over the vast space once, then twice, then a third time. Each time finding it noticeably empty. No other bodies, no enemies, no one at all. Living or dead. Dread clogs my throat, cutting over the question I am desperate to ask yet fearing the answer all the same. I look at Cay, studying her face and trying to find the words written there so she doesn't have to say them.

The only thing that stares back at me is emptiness. Not relief, not happiness, or sadness, not even grief. Just emptiness. The bright and smiling friend I know and love is completely absent from this shell of a person standing before me. I take her hands in mine, my grip firm yet weak at the same time. I stare into Cay's eyes willing her to see me but she seems lost to her own thoughts.

I turn to Oliver, meeting his hazel eyes, the mirror to his sister's. They're full of emotion, only it is not the smug, teasing gaze I have come to expect. "Oliver, do you know what happened?" I ask, my voice barely a whisper.

Oliver nods slowly. He gives no teasing remarks, no snide comments, nothing but that one loaded gesture.

I look past him for a moment to see Rian staring at us. His gaze tells me he is listening, even if he can't be there beside me. It gives me the strength to ask the next question. "Where is Eve? Where is my *sister*?" my voice breaks on the last word.

Oliver doesn't wait to shatter my world. Doesn't hesitate or draw out the pain that he knows his answer will inflect. "She's gone. They took her."

My heart skips a beat. I look past him again, searching for Rian's eyes. His lips move on a silent word. *Breathe.* I suck in a sharp breath, letting it out slowly. It does nothing to steady me. "Who?"

Thundering footsteps interrupt, drawing our attention back down the hall. Rose and Oak charge forward. They rush into the room, stopping beside us with a thousand questions already pouring from their lips. I don't hear them. Their mouths open and close but no sound comes out. None that I can hear. Rose is looking over at Cay, trying to get her to talk, to move, to do something other than stare into space. She turns to me and I force myself to focus on what she is saying. "Mar, what the hell is going on?" Rose asks, her voice laced with fear.

I ignore that question, turning back to Oliver. "I need to know who took my sister," I state plainly.

Rose and Oak go deathly still. The former letting out an immediate denial that nearly has my heart cracking in two. Oak blanches, her bronzed skin leeched of color.

Oliver looks between the three of us, then down at Cay. His arm around her shoulder seems to tighten, like he might protect her from this even though it is clear, she isn't here. Not really. Not in the way that counts. "From what I understand, the enemy was Cansu. Someone named Teru seems to have taken Eve. I believe they are also responsible for the murder of King Callan," he says, voice gravelly.

Rose's head turns to the room and tears begin to flow freely down her cheeks.

Rian lifts his head from the dying queen and calls for help, "She's fading fast. I don't have enough magic or skill in healing to keep her alive."

"I can help. I've been studying up on healing magic. Reed has been helping me along with the healers," Rose looks at me, a question in her eyes.

Will I be okay if she leaves now? I look back to Rian, his expression grim and give Rose a nod. "Go. Do whatever you can. We can't let Cay lose her mother too."

Rose rushes off to help Rian, even as her eyes say she wants to remain right where she is.

Oak steps forward, nearly half his height yet she still manages to crowd Oliver's space. Her face is determined, her eyes flaring with wild intent. "When? When did they take her, we might be able to-"

"The dragon went after her. It is unclear when she was taken but by the time we made it to the room there was no sign of her, or her captor. Not even a *trace* of magic was left behind," Oliver growls.

"That's *impossible*, there must be something. We have to find her, to track her, something! I refuse to believe that she just vanished, people don't just go *poof*," Oak says, making a popping sound with her mouth.

"They do when they're made of shadows, *cousin*. The people of Cansu were the most dangerous, most deadly, because it's like they were never there. They could appear in a cloud of smoke, eradicate entire cities, and then vanish like they were never even there. Or as you say, *poof*," Oliver says, with a mirthless laugh. The sound grates my ears and makes me want to rip his throat out.

"You say that like they are dead and gone yet you *also* claim them to be the enemy responsible for this attack," Oak challenges.

"Correct. Everything our history tells us is that we locked the kingdom of darkness away over a millennium ago. Practically signing their death warrant. How the hell they are back is a mystery to me," Oliver snarls in his cousin's face. Whatever sympathy or reserve he had shown me, clearly lost on his own kin.

"Why? Why did we lock them away?" I ask. I'm not sure why but the question feels important. Like somehow it will make things make sense, even when everything in me is screaming that nothing ever will again. Not while Eve is gone.

"Ask your history teacher. We don't have time for this right now." Oliver's answer is clipped.

A rumble builds beneath us. All of us turn to watch helplessly as a ripple cascades across the dome surrounding the city. Time seems to freeze for a moment. Then we feel it, the flood of magic as the barrier fails and the city begins to crumble around us. There is nothing we can do as water crashes down and seals our fates.

416

Chapter 49

Rose

Rian looks up and curses. "We need to move, now." He gathers up Cay's mother, Queen Mira, into his arms and runs towards the rest of our group. I follow on shaking legs.

Eve is gone.

The words keep playing through my mind in an endless loop. A million questions burn the tip of my tongue, all silenced by the same intrusive thought. I'll never see her again. Never hear her laugh as she and Mar execute one of their horrible pranks. Never feel her arms wrap around me in a hug that heals my soul. I'll never crack jokes with her as we take turns throwing our blades at targets in the woods.

Eve is gone.

If what Oliver says is right then she has been taken by an enemy that we know so little about, one that we thought was long gone.

We make it to the others just as the barrier fails completely. Rian must have sensed it because his eyes are locked on the exact space where large ripples form along the dome. The ground shakes violently, the entire city feeling the shocks as buildings start to crumble around us. Thankfully the ceiling of the throne room holds overhead.

A crack sounds at the end of the hallway and we all watch in silence as water rushes in around us in a powerful wave. It quickly fills the hall and washes into the throne room. There are gaping holes throughout the length of the dome barrier where water pours in. If I had to guess, it will only be a matter of minutes before it consumes the entire castle, the stone walls will do little to protect us when the force of it well and truly descends upon us.

A shower of dust falls around us and Oak quickly throws up a shield using her earth magic. Oliver tries to do the same but he is having some difficulty when he only has one arm available. Thankfully dust is all that falls. I move forward and try to take Cay from his grip but he tightens his hold on her with a growl, his eyes flashing a warning at me to back the fuck off.

I open my mouth to fight him but Mar grabs my hand. I meet her stare and she gives me a silent plea. Setting aside my anger at my brother for whatever *that* was, I step up beside Mar. Her hand is shaking in mine but I don't think she notices. My thumb moves over the back of it in soothing circles. Mar turns back to watch the sky as more and more water comes flooding in.

A heavy weight settles in my chest as we stand in silence, waiting to see what will happen next. The tension is so thick in the air that I'm tempted to try for a joke. I'm saved from doing so as a black spot appears in the sky. My breath stalls in my chest as a large dragon soars around streams of water, its large wings casting a shadow over the castle as a fierce roar tears through the air.

Mar squeezes my hand and I return the gesture. We shift on our feet, the water up to our calves already.

The dragon swoops down, avoiding the gaping holes in the barrier where water rushes in. It banks right and dives toward a small opening at the top of an archway, tucking its wings close to its body and shifting as it passes through the narrow hole.

We all wait as the now shifted dragon rises up with Nat's familiar head of red hair curtaining her face and hiding her expression from us all. Not that we need to see it to know the truth. When Nat came diving in the way she did it was enough to know. She didn't find Eve. Or at the very least didn't bring her back.

I'm not sure which is worse.

Mar drags me forward as she wades through the now knee deep water. She steps up in front of Nat, whose head is still hung low, avoiding our gaze. "Where is she? Nat, tell me you know where Eve is," Mar practically begs. Her voice is hard but the waver there is indication enough that she teeters on the edge of breaking.

I look back over my shoulder and find Rian's face stone cold and devoid of all emotion. His already pale skin blanches leaving him looking positively ghostlike. I might not have known the guard long but if his clenched fists and grinding teeth are any indication, he is not happy with his second. For a moment I worry about what he might do to Nat but thankfully he seems willing to hear her out.

Oak is focused solely on Nat, her eyes locked on her drooping head. I don't need to use my enhanced hearing to know that her heart is racing as fast as my own. Her large round eyes are brimmed with tears before Nat utters a word.

My gaze shifts to Oliver and finds him deep in thought, his eyes distant as he formulates some plan or idea in his mind. Cay is still looking wholly vacant, like she has removed herself from this moment entirely. Not that I can blame her.

Time moves slowly now, everyone fighting back the emotions warring inside them while the water continues to rise steadily, reaching my mid thigh. I turn back just as Nat lifts her head slowly, my breath stalling in my chest.

Her pale blue eyes are glossy yet she fights to restrain her emotions, maintaining a guard's composure even as she croaks, "/they took her. I- I found her and I was trying to fight but she wouldn't let me."

Mar lets go of my hand and grabs Nat by her shoulders, "What? What happened?" There is an edge to her, a bite in her words and the slight flash of her fangs which have me taking a step closer. Ready to intervene if she -or Nat- needs me to.

Nat shakes her head, "She told me to leave. To get you all out. I- I wanted to stay but she- she ordered me to leave her." Nat seems to crumble in on herself, her shoulders fall forward, her chin hits her chest. Whatever resolve she had was shattered the moment Mar confronted her.

Mar sucks in a breath and shares an agonized look with me. Her bright eyes are brimmed with tears though her anger at Nat seems to be holding them at bay.

Nat takes a deep breath, lifting her head to face her princess with whatever strength she has left. "Mar, I am so sorry. I should have done more, should have fought harder. I let her down, I let everyone down, I am so-"

"No, you don't blame yourself for this. My sister is responsible for her own actions. Idiotic as they might be. You did the right thing," Mar seems to struggle to get the words out. She wipes at her eyes hurriedly and stares up at the ceiling.

We all know that as her guard, Nat had no choice but to listen to her future queen. No matter how much we may want it to be different, Nat did everything that she could. That Eve would *allow*. Little self-sacrificing asshole she is.

When we get her back I'm going to kill her myself for pulling this shit. I don't care if she is the heir to the Vulca throne or not, had I been the one to find her I would have dragged her by her dark hair to keep her out of Cansu's grip.

Realization dawns on me that it is very possible Eve doesn't even know who exactly has taken her. Vana knows she has never paid any attention in her history lessons. She'll have no idea the sheer gravity of her situation. Prior to Oliver figuring it out we all just assumed we were dealing with rogues from one of the other kingdoms, maybe even Rayan itself. Even the mortal lands seemed more likely.

Still, Eve might be an idiot but she's not dumb. Surely she will realize when they get wherever they are taking her. Although there is a high likelihood that her mouth will get her into far more trouble than she already is before long. If that is even possible anymore.

The water continues to rise up, already reaching my waist. A glance back at Oak and Cay shows the water is almost covering their breast. Oak's arms move back and forth along the surface of the water absentmindedly. Oliver looks entirely ready to help Cay should the water cause her any issues, not that it ever could.

"We need to move, before the water gets any higher and we can't get out of here," I announce.

"That sounds great but how do you suppose we do that?" Oak asks, tossing her arms up and letting them smack against the water.

Irritation flares at her yet again, our argument far from over.

"We fly out," Rian and Oliver answer at the same time. The two men share a disgruntled glance and then look at Nat. Whether they like it or not, the pair of them think the same way. Not to mention, Rian is the only person I have ever seen with a level of arrogance that rivals that of my brother.

Rian turns to Nat, "you need to shift and fly us all out of here. It's our best shot if we want to avoid drowning or being crushed by the pressure."

Nat nods her head without question, resolved to her new role. She takes a few steps back from our group and then shifts, landing on all fours before us. She stands well above the water as she extends a wing for us to climb up.

For a second we all stand there. No one moving forward or climbing up first. It's not exactly every day that a dragon allows you to ride on their back.

Rian shoots forward, getting as close to Mar as possible with Cay's mother still in his arms. "This time, it's not up for debate. Get on the dragon, now," he says pointedly.

Surprisingly, Mar doesn't fight him. Doesn't even get on him for his tone or the fact he just demanded she do something. Instead, she goes first. Using her vamp speed to easily shoot up and onto Nat's back. She leans over the edge to watch as I climb up next.

I grab onto a few spikes on the edge of Nat's wing and try to pull myself up. I struggle for a moment before Mar extends her hand down to me, the ghost of a smile on her lips. I return it as I take her hand in mind, letting her haul me up beside her.

She immediately pulls me into a tight embrace that I return. We pull apart and both reach down and help Oak up, her short legs dangling beneath her as we do. Oak mutters a curse and then uses a little magic to push herself the rest of the way up.

Rian adjusts his hold on Queen Mira and then shoots up, similar to how Mar did it. He lays the queen down on her back, placed delicately at the center between Nat's large wings. "Rose, I need you to continue healing her. Whatever magic they used on her doesn't seem to be letting go any time soon," Rian says, running a hand through his messy hair anxiously.

"Sure. I can do that." I walk over to Queen Mira and sit down at her head, pulling it into my lap. I instantly start to push my healing magic into her, watching Nat's wing closely, my brother appears.

Oliver holds Cay in his arms effortlessly, not bothering to make a show of it as he usually would. He moves over to me and guides Cay down beside her mother, whispering something in her ear. Cay is still wrapped tightly under this arm, his hand makes smooth circles over the exposed skin on her shoulder and I can't help but follow the movement.

It is so unlike Oliver, to show such *comfort* to another. I never got to see him as a child but Terran once told me that he used to laugh when others would fall down or get hurt. He would mock them for it endlessly until eventually all of his friends abandoned him.

Yet this Oliver, the Oliver with arms wrapped around my friend so delicately like he is scared he might break her, this Oliver is not the brother that I know. I can only hope that this recent development of a heart and compassion actually sticks around. Vana knows we're going to need all the kindness we can get when we get home.

The thought pulls my gaze from my brother and back to Rian. He's hovering at Mar's back where she sits close to Oak, the two of them staring silently at the ground below us. His eyes are locked on Mar, a fire blazing behind them that almost has me rethinking my question.

But the truth still stands, someone has to ask. "Where exactly are we going?"

Nat huffs out in agreement beneath us.

Rian turns to me like he knows my question was directed at him. "Our first priority is to get to land. We'll go to Atran and figure out our next steps from there. I'm sure we *all* have somewhere we need to be right now." His gaze wanders back to Mar before sitting down with his eyes squeezed shut.

Nat doesn't waste time before moving under us. She does her best not to jostle us around too much as she prepares to take off. She stalks towards the end of the hall and seems to wait there for something.

Oliver lifts his gaze from Cay to investigate why we stopped and he rolls his eyes when he sees the wall before us. Without so much as a word he uses his magic to blast a hole in the concrete. Water rushes in but atop Nat's back we don't need to worry too much.

Nat moves forward and through the narrow archway that has opened up, turning to exit into the courtyard on our right. The moment we are outside-or at least outside of the castle walls- she extends her wings and takes off into the air.

I stifle a scream as we shoot through the sky, dodging the raging waterfalls around us, and pushing higher and higher. Once we reach the edge of the dome Nat begins to circle. There's still at least another couple hundred feet of water before we reach the surface. The pressure outside the dome alone could be enough to burst our brains. "What now?" I ask, hesitantly.

Rian opens his eyes and stands. His feet planted firmly at the center of Nat's back. He takes a deep breath and then channels some sort of spell into a bubble that surrounds us. Rian calls out to Nat to tell her we are good to go and fear rushes over me.

I've never seen a spell like this and it brings a new fear to the forefront of my mind. What is this spell? Is it even strong enough to do this? What if the second we go beyond what's left of the barrier we end up going *pop*?

"Relax, sister, the spell is strong. Can't you feel the magic surrounding us?" Oliver asks with a roll of his eyes.

Note to self, this new Oliver is still an asshole to everyone else, just not Cay it seems. Ignoring my brother, I focus on what he said instead. I nearly gasp when I feel what he's talking about. The heavy weight of the magic surrounding us and pushing the water away as we finally break free of the protective barrier.

The world around us is dark, but the further Nat flies, the brighter the light grows, until we're breaking the surface and Rian releases his magic with a grunt. He falls to his knees and takes in ragged breaths before turning onto his back and seeming to pass out, or maybe he just closes his eyes, I'm not really sure nor do I care. No, the only thing I care about right now is the sun cresting the horizon behind us as we fly towards land.

I look around and take in everyone here. Queen Mira is still unconscious, no matter how much magic I pump into her. Oliver is solely focused on Cay who still hasn't said a word since we met up with her. Rian is, again, either sleeping or passed out. As my eyes roam over to my cousin and Mar I let my heightened hearing listen in on what they're saying.

"We'll get her back. I swear," Oak says, grabbing Mar's arm.

The conviction of my cousin's voice has me swallowing back a sob because she's right. There is no future where we don't get Eve back. I won't allow it.

Chapter 50

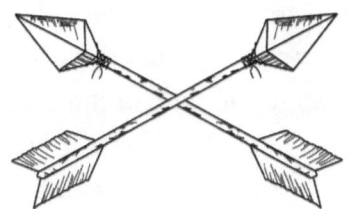

Oak

Nat carves a path through the sky with the seven of us upon her back. Silent aside from the air whipping around us. Each pump of Nat's wings brings us closer to the shore and farther away from the destruction of Tepis. From above, the water appears calm, undisturbed. Yet deep below, along the ocean floor, an entire kingdom has been uprooted.

There are still so many questions left unanswered. None more important to me than wherever Eve has been taken. Everything stopped when I heard those words. A million thoughts filled my mind and then emptied, leaving this hollowness behind.

Mar sits beside me, staring off into the distance. Her hands are balled into tight fists beside her. Every part of her appears tense, like she is poised to strike out at anything that dare comes her way. In all the years of knowing Mar, of watching her fierce anger, I've never seen her so silently deadly.

I let my eyes drift past her to my cousins. Oliver has an arm draped around Cay's shoulders protectively. Something that has not gone unnoticed by his sister. Rose's eyes flick between her friend and brother with a degree of mistrust in them, yet for some reason she seems to bite her tongue. No. Not just *some* reason. *Eve.*

Rose has always observed the world around her with keen eyes, always searching for answers and discovering things hidden from her. Yet it has always seemed like she is blind to our family's lies and secrets. I have to wonder if her eyes are seeing Oliver with a new sort of clarity, if they might find something that he does not wish to be known.

Nat starts to dive forward, the sand of the beach growing closer and closer with each passing moment until we land softly.

Rian bolts upright and instructs us all to wait while he surveys the area, jumping down and racing around using his vamp speed. It only takes a minute before he is back to us and helping people down off of Nat's back.

Mar jumps down first, landing beside her guard without even sparing him a glance.

I slide down next, not bothering to wait for someone to help me make the jump. The impact sends spikes of pain up through my legs but they're gone as quickly as they came.

Rose appears beside me and then we're all helping ease Queen Mira down next. Once we have lowered her off Nat's back, we place her on the soft sand, her head in Rose's lap as she continues to pump healing magic into her.

Last to jump off are Oliver and Cay, the two of them still pressed to each other's side. Oliver's arm moves from Cay's shoulder to her waist, earning a scowl from Rose.

Nat shifts back into her mortal form and stretches her arms above her head and then across her chest. "What's next?"

"I need to go home," Mar says, her voice gravelly, "someone has to tell my father what happened. He needs to know about Eve."

Rian nods his head silently beside her.

Nat crosses our small group until she stands before Mar, her chin held high. "I can do it. I am responsible for what happened, I should be-"

Mar cuts her off, "No. It has to be me. I'm her sister. If anyone is going to tell our father that she is missing it should be me." The three Vulcans step to the side to discuss.

I turn to my cousins and find them locked in an epic stare down. "Alright, what's our plan then?" I ask, drawing their attention to me.

Rose looks up to the sky with a sigh. "I guess we will head home. Not much else we can do at this point."

"Mother will want to know what happened. To prepare," Oliver adds.

"To prepare for what?" Rose asks with a snort.

"The enemy," Oliver bites, "we have no real understanding of why they chose to attack Rayan. We should use this time wisely and assemble our people."

"And what good would that do? Hm?" Rose looks up at her brother with fury burning in her eyes. "How exactly do we *prepare* for something like this?"

Oliver sneers at her. "Maybe if you spent less time reading you-"

"Enough," I bark, "the two of you going at it isn't helping. If we're going home then fine, but that doesn't answer the question."

"What question is that, cousin?" Oliver asks indignantly.

"Many actually. Starting with how we plan to transport Cay and her mother when they are..." I raise my brows, casting my eyes in the direction of the pair.

"Are what?" Oliver growls.

"I merely mean to point out that the queen is in no condition to travel. Nor is Cay. She looks on the verge of passing out." I nod towards them, forcing my cousin to acknowledge what we both already know.

Oliver looks down at Cay, his jaw snapping shut at what he finds.

Her already pale skin is completely leached of color. Her eyes are glassy and her pupils blown wide. I'm not entirely convinced that if Oliver wasn't holding her that she could even stand on her own, let alone walk anywhere.

"Oak has a point," Rose says almost reluctantly. Her eyes cut to my own for a brief moment and a mixture of mistrust and anger are waiting for me in their depths.

I should probably add 'talk to Rose' to my list of things to do, right behind keeping everyone alive and finding Eve. Her name forms a lump in my throat and sends pain to my chest. Images of her being tortured torment me and I have to force myself to think positively.

Eve is smart. She's strong. She knows how to fight, especially when she is pissed off. She'll be fine, we just have to figure out a plan to find her and get her back. As soon as things are sorted out at home I'll meet up with Mar and we'll start our search. First, we have to make it back to Sena and get things sorted. Oliver and I will surely have to answer for our disobedience.

"We should take some time to rest, let Cay and her mother recover a bit before we try to do anything else," Rose says, her voice thick with concern.

"The village on the edge of the border should be safe. If we make it there before the sun starts to set we can rest overnight and leave first thing in the morning tomorrow," I suggest. The village wouldn't be too far from where we are now and offers a level of protection that we don't have here on the beach. We're only a few miles from the edge of Atran and there is no real way of knowing whether or not more of the mist creatures are there, unless we want to go check it out and I for one, would rather not.

Oliver seems to mull it over before agreeing. He and Rose start talking about plans to move the queen while I make my way over to Mar.

Rian and Nat are deep in discussion a few steps away from where Mar sits in the sand, her long legs stretched out casually. The water just nearly touches her toes before pulling back out with the tide. If the circumstances were different this day might even be beautiful. The sounds of the waves, the gentle breeze blowing the salty air against our skin, the sun creating the perfect orange glow.

I plop down beside her and pull my knees to my chest, hugging myself and taking a moment to enjoy the peacefulness. "What's your plan?" I ask, breaking the silence.

Mar takes in a deep breath and lets it out slowly, closing her eyes before she answers. "We'll fly back on Nat's back. She says she can get us there before the sun sets this evening."

"That fast? Isn't she tired from flying us here and you know, everything else?" I draw an outline of a dragon in the sand absentmindedly.

Mar looks over her shoulder to her two guards, a flash of something in her eyes as she takes in Rian's grim expression. "She said she should be fine. She's not really taking no for an answer. Not that I am inclined to argue anyways."

I nod in understanding, letting the silence envelope us for a moment more.

Mar breaks it first, "You know, I've never wanted the crown. Not even for a moment."

I watch her from the corner of my eyes, her gaze locked on the water searching for something that we both know she won't find.

"Eve always used to joke about it. How it should be me not her. That I was meant to be queen or something like that. I always laughed her off." She takes a long, shuddering breath, letting it out slowly.

Reaching my arm out I grab Mar's wrist. Her light blue eyes meet mine, full of one question. "We're going to find her, Mar. This is *Eve* we're talking about. Okay? She's clever, and strong. She knows how to fight," I say, telling her the same thing I needed to tell myself, "All she needs is a blade. Fuck, she'll probably save herself before we even get the chance."

Mar cracks a smile, small but there nonetheless.

"I swear to you that no matter what it takes we will bring her home." My voice is unwavering, strong despite the tears that burn my eyes and threaten to spill. I am so sick of crying. Arms grab me and pull me into a tight embrace. Mar squeezes me in a fierce hug that we both needed, maybe more than either of us were willing to let on. When we pull back our expressions share the same resolve.

"We've got to go if we want to make it back to Vulca before sundown," Rian calls from behind us.

Mar nods and I grab her hands. "I have to go back to Sena." My heart begins to race, already dreading what awaits me back at the castle.Mar gives me a tight smile. "I understand, go. We'll figure out our next move soon enough. I'm sure there will be lots of questions when I get home myself."

"Let's make a plan to meet in three days. At the village in the north, right as you cross the border." I search her eyes, praying to the goddess that she can trust me again. That she knows I would do anything for Eve. For any of them.

"I'll be there," Mar agrees.

The two of us stand and brush the sand off of our hands. Then, we turn and walk back to our respective groups. Nat waves to us before shifting. As soon as she does, Rian and Mar jump on her back and the three of them take off, becoming nothing but a black dot in the sky before vanishing altogether in the distance.

I take point for our group, my bow and arrow notched and ready should anyone decide to try their luck in attacking us. Rose has to pry Cay from Oliver's side but once she lets go she clings to her friend instead. Her feet move in more of a shuffle than a walk but it's better than the alternative.

Oliver uses his earth magic to make a sort of cart covered in thick moss, and lays the queen down in it gently. Once she is settled he grabs the cart and starts pushing from the rear. We move almost painfully slow. Stopping multiple times to take a break so Rose can press more healing magic into Queen Mira. The unconscious queen never stirs, never moves more than the subtle rise and fall of her chest. It's unclear what is wrong with her but at the very least Rose is able to keep her stable for now.

~~~

By the time we make it to the outskirts of the village the sun is nearly gone. Oliver instructs Rose to wait with the queen and Cay, just outside the village's boundaries. The two of us head in to scope the place out.

"Shoot first, ask questions later." Oliver instructs from beside me.

"That was my plan." An arrow already at the ready.

"Well I'm just reminding you. Don't want a repeat of last time." Oliver gives me a scathing look, staring down his nose at me.

I roll my eyes at him, "I don't know what you're talking about."

Cool metal bites into the skin of my neck. "You should really pay more attention to your surroundings," a familiar voice says from behind me.

I push the blade away from my neck and turn to look at her. Dark brown hair sticks up at all sorts of angles, dirt covers her face and a shadow of a bruise darkens her temple.

"Regan, thank Vana you're alright," I say, relief flooding through me. There was no time to consider anyone else as we had been fleeing the city but a part of me still feels guilty that we left Regan and the other guards behind. "Is everyone alright? Where are the others?" I ask, looking around.

Oliver seems bored although his eyes continue to scan the woods, searching for any potential threats.

"We found almost 60 soldiers unconscious in the training rooms. None of them have any memory of what happened but if I had to guess I would say they were ambushed during training. Luckily there were no major injuries among them," Regan says, sheathing her blade.

"Wow, 60? That's incredible. When the barrier failed..." shame cuts my words off.

Regan seems to notice and slaps a hand on my shoulder. "We got lucky, this group's got some strong magic between them. I'm glad you made it out. "

I give her a hesitant smile. Strong magic is always an asset but it's not always enough to save people. Cay and Eve both have incredible power, more so than either of them probably even realizes. Yet Cay couldn't save her father. Eve couldn't save herself.

Oliver appears beside me. "Alright, we need to keep moving. Where are all those guards you found?" he asks Regan.

She points towards the center of the village, "That way. After we escaped we holed up there. I figured if you lot got out you might head this way."

Oliver narrows his eyes at her but I jab him in the rib with my elbow. His eyes promise vengeance but I ignore him. "I'm glad you did. Why don't you come with us? There are- well just come see." I start back towards Rose and Cay.

Regan hesitates for a moment before following after me, Oliver a few steps behind. As we turn a corner they come into full view. Rose helping hold Cay up, the queen still asleep in the cart. Looking over my shoulder I watch as Regan sees them for the first time. Her eyes widen and she inhales a sharp breath. She walks beside me, dropping to one knee the moment we reach the others.

Oliver and I look away, giving them a moment.

"My princess. I am so glad you are alright. I had feared…" Regan trails off.

Rose clears her throat and the guard looks up at her in confusion. "I'm sorry. Cay isn't really up for speaking just yet." Rose says sheepishly.

"Of course. I didn't mean to-" Regan stands quickly, coming to attention.

"No! No, not at all. She's just been through a lot, is all," Rose says placatingly.

Regan nods, her eyes roaming to the queen. "And the queen?" Her voice is remarkably even.

"We aren't sure what happened. We weren't there and Cay- well, anyways. She just seems to be in some sort of deep sleep. I've been using healing magic to keep her stable but no matter what I try, she doesn't wake."

"Thank you, for taking care of them. It is my duty to protect the crown and I failed them," Regan says with a hint of defeat.

Before I know what he is doing Oliver approaches the guard. His hand lands on her shoulder, much as hers did mine. "You can't blame yourself for this. There was no way to know that Cansu was still *around*. Let alone how to fight them." Shock washes over me as I take in my cousin *comforting* someone. Well, someone other than Cay. Which was a shock in itself honestly.

"Cansu? The land of mist and darkness? What do they have to do with this?" Regan demands, her voice turning hard.

It's Rose that answers, "We learned that Cansu were the ones who attacked. They took our friend and," she shares a hesitant look with Oliver, "killed the king."

Regan drops to her knees. She punches the dirt for a full minute before Oliver stops her. Tears stream down her face as she screams in frustration. The weight of Rose's words seem to settle on her as she composes herself.

Oliver helps her to her feet as Regan wipes at her face. "I'm sorry. I shouldn't have reacted like that. I just..."

"We know. It's okay," I say, stepping forward.

Regan stares at me for a moment before her face changes to one of determination rather than defeat. "Right, well. We don't have much of a camp but it's better than just standing out here in the open. Follow me." She leads the way back through the village. Rose and Cay a few steps behind her while I walk alongside Oliver as he pushes the cart.

"That was nice of you. What you did for her." I nudge against his side.

Oliver snorts, shoving me away, *hard*. "I'm not nice."

A small smile tugs at the corner of my lips. "Keep telling yourself that."

~~~

Regan leads us to the center of the town where a large building holds most of the guards. A few of the ones who were with her before stand outside keeping watch. They nod to us as we enter. The moment that the doors close behind us, all eyes turn our way. A hush goes over the room and a path appears before us. Split down the center of the crowd gathered there and leading us towards the front of the room.

Regan takes point as we pass by the many beaten and bruised faces. Whispers grow louder as people start to realize their princess and queen are among them. Once at the front of the room, Regan steps onto a small platform, lifting her just slightly above the audience so she can be seen by everyone. The rest of us shuffle off to the side, so that we aren't in her way.

"Soldiers!" Regan yells, commanding attention her way, "I have returned to you with news and friends. First, our queen and princess are here, safe from the enemies that sought to destroy us!"

A rumble builds through the room.

"Our enemies are those who we thought long gone, Cansu! The creatures of the mist and darkness have returned!" Regan shouts, her voice echoing through the room and back to us.

I turn to Oliver and find his jaw set. Rose seems to be holding her breath, waiting for what we all know will come next.

"Not only have they destroyed our home, stolen our friends and family, they have taken the life of our beloved king!" Regan riots. A chorus of denial and outrage sings from every corner of the room.

Oliver and I take a step back, disappearing into the shadows at the corner of the room as Regan continues to rally her forces. "What do you make of all this?" I ask him, my voice low even though no one would be able to hear us over the shouting.

"I'm still deciding," he answers.

I watch his face, waiting for a smirk or a hint of whatever he may be thinking. When I find nothing but cool indifference I sigh. "I think it's a good thing we found them. We could use all the allies we can get."

"Maybe. Although I want to know more about how they miraculously made it out before that barrier failed." Oliver watches Regan's speech with rapt attention, analyzing every word, every call to action made.

My brows pinch together, "What do you mean? Regan said they had someone with strong magic. We made it in, why wouldn't they be able to make it out?"

Oliver laughs mirthlessly, "When we did it, we had me. That's extremely different."

"Wow, okay, good to know asshole Oliver is still in there."

"I'm serious. No one here should have power levels even remotely close to mine," Oliver declares with complete conviction, not a singular doubt to be heard.

"And why is that, Oliver? What makes you so special?" I ask, looking up at my cousin.

His eyes are locked on Regan who seems to be finishing up her speech. His jaw ticks.

Before I can press him for an answer, Regan appears before us. "We found a secure place for you all to rest for the night, if you'll follow me I can show you the way to your rooms," she offers with a smile.

"Room. We'll only be needing one," Oliver counters.

I glare at him but don't contradict. The idea of being separated from the others makes the fear spike in my chest.

"Of course, follow me," Regan says, gesturing towards a back door.

Rose and Cay go first, followed by Oliver pushing the cart. I hang back for a moment and let my eyes sweep over the large room. There are dozens of guards in here, most of them looking pretty much unscathed. A shadow creeps along the back corner of the room, catching my eye. I start towards it but in a blink, it's gone. I stare at the spot where I saw it for a few moments longer before hurrying after the others.

Chapter 51

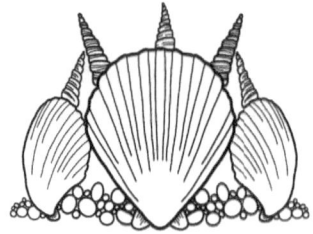

Cay

Once again the sound of screaming fills my mind. The sound is a sort of broken cry that speaks of pain and mourning, something that I now know all too well. It echoes around inside my head, over, and over, and over again. Constant.

Strong arms grab me by my shoulders and I am startled awake. My eyes shoot open but everything is still black. I instantly begin thrashing around, kicking and clawing at whatever, or whoever, has me.

"Shh, Cay, stop, you're alright. Calm down, breathe," a deep, soothing voice speaks through the darkness, belonging to whoever is holding me.

I force my eyes to adjust and his face becomes clear. Warm, hazel eyes, a strong defined jaw and cheekbones. All beneath a head of chestnut curls. Recognition seeps in and everything eases.

Oliver traces easy circles against the curve of my shoulders, his rough, calloused, thumbs scraping against the smooth skin. His hands are warm, comforting, tension eases from my body as I let myself relax.

I let my eyes roam around the room but it's too dark to make out many details. I'm half laid out on a bed barely wide enough for one person. Oliver sits beside the bed, his eyes locked on my face like he is searching for something. "Someone was screaming," I croak, my voice unusually hoarse, raw.

"That was you. I think you had a nightmare." His eyes are kind as they sweep over me, he pulls a blanket up higher so it covers most of me.

I nod my head in understanding, balling my hands into fists and relishing the small bite of pain as my nails dig into my palms.

"Are you alright?" Oliver asks, his voice barely above a whisper.

I consider his question. Am I? My heart is racing, my body is covered in a thick sheen of sweat, and my mouth tastes like dirt. My head is pounding with a fierce headache and my entire body aches. But none of that compares to the cold, piercing, pain in my chest. In my heart. "He's dead." The words slip past my lips before I even know I'm going to say them.

"I know," he confirms gently.

My eyes squeeze shut, trying to force back burning tears. It doesn't work. The hot droplets splash onto my cheeks. After so much crying I would have thought my eyes to be completely dried out, yet here I am, sobbing, *again*.

Oliver moves his hands slowly, brushing away the tears with his thumbs before they have a chance to roll down my face. The gesture is so soft, so gentle, so completely at odds with the Oliver I have known most of my life, that for a moment I am frozen. Unable to say or think anything at all. He pulls back, placing his hands at his side and creating a small bit of distance between us.

I instantly miss the warmth of his hands on my skin. I take in a deep breath, focusing on letting my lungs expand fully before letting it out slowly. I repeat the steps until my heart has calmed down and the fear that threatened to rip me apart fades to a more manageable level.

"Feeling better?" Oliver asks, eyebrows raised.

"A little. I can breathe now." I suck in another breath for emphasis.

"That's probably good, I've heard that breathing is sort of important," Oliver says with a playful smile.

A smile tugs at my lips but it's more forced than I would have liked. "Where are we?"

"Technically still in Rayan. We're in a village right on the border between realms. What's the last thing you remember?" he asks cautiously.

The tone of his voice threatens to make my heart race again; like he is trying to approach a wounded animal. "I remember my father. And my magic, it got out of control. I remember you. But nothing after that. What happened?"

Oliver's eyes are filled with pain as nods his head, his jaw becoming more tense. "After we found you, everything went to shit. The barrier fell and we had to get out."

"We?" I croak.

"Yeah. Oak, Rose," he gestures to the other side of the room where I notice the two of them curled up on their side for the first time, "Mar, the dragon, and that other vampire." He waves his hands through the air disdainfully.

I take a moment to process what he said. The barrier fell which means… Rayan is lost. My home and anyone left inside, *gone*. Like my father. The reminder of his death brings another thought rushing to the surface and I sit up fully, getting far too close to Oliver in the process. "Wait, what about my mother? What happened to her?" I beg, my voice coming out in a frantic rush.

"She's here. She's okay. Well, technically she is in a coma but otherwise she seems fine." He rubs a hand along the back of his neck. For the most part he looks fine, maybe a bit tired but otherwise, completely unscathed. A part of me does wonder what that black goo was that covered him when he found me but not enough to outweigh thoughts of my mother.

My shoulders sag in relief but a part of me still believes it's too good to be true. "Can I see her?" As terrified as I am to see her *asleep*, I also know that it's the only thing that will calm the rising panic in me. She has to be alright and until I see her, I won't be able to think of anything else. He nods and I'm jumping to my feet in the next breath. The quick movement makes my vision swim and my head pound. I have to grab the bed to steady myself and keep from falling over.

"Easy. You haven't eaten or had any water for who knows how long," Oliver warns as he reaches out to steady me.

I let him grab my elbow and lead me out of the room. He shuts the door behind us gently, and then continues to lead the way through the next small room. It seems like we're in someone's house based off of the set of couches and chairs all facing the center of the room. A small kitchen area is off to the side, along with a round table.

Oliver leads me through the front door and outside. The air is cool, making small bumps rise across my bare skin. It's still fairly dark outside so it must be pretty late in the evening. Oliver leads us past a few other houses, identical to the one we emerged from on the outside. There is not another soul in sight which makes me wonder where the inhabitants of this village have gone. He walks up to a much larger building with two men on either side of the door.

My entire body freezes at the sight of them, my muscles locking up and refusing to move another inch. It's not until one of them turns to face me that I realize, I recognize them both. They're castle guards. Ivan and Mort are their names if I remember correctly. I used to watch them train from the rafters of the training halls, studying their movements when they sparred with one another.

Ivan is tall, almost taller than Oliver's impressive height, and huge. His shoulders are broad and stacked with corded muscles. His head is bald and is carved down the center with a jagged scar. I asked my father about it once and he told me Ivan had been injured during an attack decades ago. If it wasn't for the helmet he had been wearing it likely would have split his skull in half. I meet his eyes and find a warmth in them that I wasn't expecting.

Looking at Mort, I find a similar expression on his face. He's slightly smaller than Ivan, his shoulder more narrow and less muscular. He also has a full head of wavy black hair, slicked back from his face. His eyes are a warm chocolate brown, his prominent nose sits perfectly between them. There is something comforting about having two familiar faces here. I smile at them hesitantly and the two of them seem to light up from the inside.

Oliver clears his throat and their attention shifts back to him. "The princess would like to see her mother," his voice is firm, demanding.

I expect my guards to tell him to buzz off, but they step aside without a second thought and allow us to pass through the large double doors. I'm not sure what I expect to find inside but a makeshift infirmary is certainly not it. There are rows upon rows of beds lined side by side throughout the large, open, room. Most of the people are asleep in their beds although a few are sitting up, talking to one another. Oliver steps forward and I trail behind him, trying to walk as silently as possible so that I don't disturb those trying to rest.

I expect us to stop somewhere amid the many soldiers, out in the open, but Oliver walks right past them all and into a room in the back. He steps to the side as soon as we are through the door and I immediately see her. She's laid out on a thin mattress set atop a table. Oliver places a gentle hand on my lower back and I realize that I haven't moved since we entered the room.

Rushing to my mother's side I drop to my knees and pull her hand in my own. Her body is so still, barely rising and falling with each breath, for a moment I fear that Oliver was wrong and that she too is lost. Still, when I grab her hand I feel it, the warmth yes, but also her magic. The thread tying us together pulses deep inside me. My magic reaches out to hers and merges gently. I push healing magic into her and after a few minutes her breaths seem more steady.

"Wow," Oliver says from above me. He moved closer at some point but I didn't notice.

I look up at him and find his eyes wide. "What is it?"

"Nothing, just, that's the most reaction I've seen from her since we got here. We've had healers coming in every half hour since the moment they put her in this room, but for the most part it doesn't seem like anything has helped." His brow creases as he tries to work out the reasoning.

"I didn't do anything special, I just pushed a little bit of healing magic her way," I say, my nose scrunching up. I study my mother's face, searching for any sign that she might wake up. Just in case I send more power flowing into her yet she still doesn't blink.

"Maybe it's your magic. Maybe hers recognizes you and is letting you help," Oliver suggests, leaning over to watch my mother's face closely. His chest is pressed against my back slightly, the warmth seeping through our clothing and heating my skin.

There are reasons why I should put distance between us. Reasons that Oliver must know himself, yet neither of us move. We sit in silence for a while, simply allowing the other to exist in this shared space. Eventually a healer comes in but when she offers to help I send her away, opting to use my own magic instead. I watch my mother's chest as she sleeps, studying the rise and fall and searching for any small change. After what feels like hours, the sun begins to rise and peek through the glass windows at the far side of the room.

Oliver clears his throat, "We'll be leaving soon. Heading back to the castle. I should gather the others."

"The others?" I mumble, barely aware of my own words, exhaustion and fear for my mother making it difficult to concentrate.

"Yes, there are a few dozen guards from Rayan here, along with Rose and Oak. They've all asked to travel with us." Oliver groans like it's a huge burden, yet when I look up at him I can't help but notice he doesn't look all that upset.

I know that for me at least it's a comfort, knowing that more people managed to escape the city before the barrier fell and that they'll be with us along the way. Still, there is this nagging feeling weighing on me. Like

441

something is sitting at the back of my mind, waiting for me to remember. "Oliver, where did you say the others went?" I ask.

"Hmm?"

"Mar and the others. Where are they at? It doesn't seem like they are here from what you've said." I watch him closely, studying his eyes and lips and focusing on his reaction. He notices this and quickly turns around so his back is to me, hands balled into fists at his side. Nothing about that comforts me. I stare at the back of his head as dread builds in my chest. "What's going on? Where are they?" I push.

So much happened so quickly and no matter how hard I try, my memory keeps getting stuck on my father's face. The blood that poured from his eyes. I stand up with a gasping breath, almost like I could force the memory away if I physically ran.

He whips back around, his eyes filled with raw emotion that I am not used to seeing in him. Whatever he is about to say, it *pains* him. He crosses the small space till he stands right in front of me. Gently, he pushes on my shoulders until I am sitting back down. "Mar went back to Vulca. She and her guard rode on the dragon's back."

I nod my head, processing the information. Yet something sticks out to me as odd. "What about Eve?" The sound of her name in the air sends memories crashing back in on me.

Eve. The mist. Everything. Oliver's words from before hit me all over again.

Eve was taken by Cansu.

And I let it happen.

~~~

My body shakes violently from the sobs that have been non-stop since I remembered Eve's fate. Almost an hour of crying and begging Oliver to tell me I was wrong. Only he wouldn't lie to me. He confirmed that she was gone and that it was my fault. Well, technically he didn't say that part but I know it's true. I was the one who lost control. If I had just kept my head clear, not let my emotions get the better of me, maybe I could have done something. Fought them off before they could take her.

No. This is entirely my fault. My father's death, Eve's capture, my mother's situation. All of it can be traced back to one person and that person is *me*. Guilt weighs on my chest making it hard to breathe. Every bit of air I take in feels like shards of glass, ripping at my insides. All of the warmth inside me has been replaced by an unrelenting cold. I shiver and pull the blanket that Oliver wrapped around my shoulders tighter. It doesn't help.

The door to my mother's room creeps open and Rose pokes her head in. The moment her eyes lock on my own we are both running. We crash into each other, my arms wrapping around her waist as she pulls me into a fierce embrace. Just like when we were reunited only a few days ago. So much has changed in such a short amount of time yet the love I feel for my friends, the relief at her being safe, that hasn't changed at all. The two of us stay like that for what feels like a long time, both of us refusing to be the first to let go. In the end, it's me.

I pull back and stare up into my friend's hazel eyes, the same as her brother's, and I break all over again. "What are we going to do? Eve is gone, Rose." My voice cracks on Eve's name. Something about the way it sounds sends a very physical pain barreling into me.

"I don't know. But we'll figure this out. We'll get her back. Mar and Oak will help. We'll do this *together*." Rose grips my shoulders tightly, determination burning behind her eyes.

"Everything is so messed up. My parents, my kingdom. I don't even know what happened to Finn. Vana, Rose, if something happened to him..." I trail off, refusing to even entertain the thought of something bad happening to my little brother.

Rose smiles down at me, "Let me ease your mind of that. Finn is fine, or at least he was the last time I saw him."

"What- what do you mean?" My chest swells with hope at her words. Images of my little brother flash through my mind in rapid succession. His constant teasing and pranks. Him practicing his magic on the guards. The most annoying yet utterly adorable half laugh half snort he makes when someone does something he thinks is funny.

"Mar and I saw him in the city. He was with a bunch of the servants. They got him out, Cay, I watched them escape. We told them to go to Sena. He's probably already there," Rose says, her voice filled with the same hope that I feel in my chest. Her eyes search my own, making sure that this has truly sunk in.

"He got out? He's okay?" I ask. A part of me is still hesitant to accept this small gift.

"Yes. And he'll be wanting you to join him as soon as possible. Your mother too," Rose says, nodding to my mother beside us.

I know she's right. That this is the thing we need to do next, but still, a part of me feels like the moment we leave, it means they're really gone. Left behind like they were never here. Eve and my father, two people who mean the world to me.

"We'll get her back," Rose states adamantly, like she knows exactly where my mind has gone. I can't help but smile at her conviction. Rose has never backed down from a challenge and I can see now that this will be no different.

Looking down at my mother's serene face, I try to push aside all of the fear and regret and guilt eating away at me from the inside. Once I'm certain I can get the words out I turn to Rose. "Let's go."

~~~

Everyone is ready remarkably fast. Within an hour all of the guards, including the injured, are ready to move out. I meet Regan quickly after the decision is made to leave and I instantly love the older guard. I may not recognize her from inside the castle but she commands respect from all those around her and they follow her willingly. A sign of a great leader. Something I fear I will never be.

I stay glued to my mother's side, Rose never more than a few steps away. Her presence soothes some of the anxiety inside me as I watch the organized chaos work around us. My eyes search through the throng of people for something that I can't quite discern.

My gaze catches on Oliver as he issues out orders in between arguing with Oak who seems to feel very strongly about something. His eyes shift to mine for a moment and my breath catches in my throat. For a moment, everything stops and it's just him and I. There have been so many chances for me to thank him. To tell him how much his simply being there has meant to me. But there is just so much tension, so much bad blood between us, I can't force the words past my lips. By the time I blink he is back to work and the moment is gone.

Everything moves quickly and before I know it we're all on our way. I offered to portal us there but given how that worked out last time and the sheer size of our group, it was determined to not be the best option. I had to agree. The walk back to Sena is long, at least a few days minimum, and with how many injured people we have it will take even longer. So as soon as we are ready we move out, leaving the village behind.

Each step feels like the sharp slice of a blade. One by one a piece of me is carved away as we get further and further away from my home. From the last place I heard my father's voice and saw him alive. The halls are full of memories that are now tainted with the image of him as he took his final breaths, words whispered that I never got to hear.

The knowledge that I will be the one who has to tell my mother and brother that he is gone is something that haunts my every waking thought. No matter how hard I try, the words never sound right, never feel *real*. Lucky for me, I have plenty of time to figure it out. Let's just hope that when I do, I don't screw it up like I did everything else.

Chapter 52

Mar

Cool air whips through my hair and across my skin, leaving small bumps in its wake. I wrap my arms around myself, pull my knees up closer to my chest resting my cheek on one of them and staring out over the horizon.

Nat flies close to the tree line, her large black wings flapping steadily on either side of where Rian and I sit on her back. She's been flying for hours, determined to prove herself and to get us home. But not all of us.

I've felt Rian's eyes glued to me for the last hour. Watching. Waiting to see if I'll fall apart. At first it pissed me off, I just wanted him to leave me alone and mind his own business, but over time it began to feel more comforting. Knowing that he was watching me, prepared to step in if I needed him, I wouldn't turn that away anymore. Not with how close we are to home. To my father.

The scenery changes as we fly closer to the center of the kingdom. The air becomes hotter, the leaves on the trees shift to a mix of vibrant white and yellow flowers, their scent wafting through their air and reminding me of summers spent with my brothers. With Eve.

My sister's name sends a sharp pain through my chest, followed by nauseating dread. In the hours it has taken us to fly back to Vulca, I still haven't thought about what to say. How to tell my father and Eve's mother that she is gone. Instead, I've been focused on trying to remember the last thing I said to her. How I should have hugged her longer. How I should have never let us run into the mess that we barely escaped from. That she *didn't* escape from.

Fuck this. Pushing aside the thoughts that threaten to drag me down to a dark place, I focus on what to do next. There is no use in wallowing in self pity or thinking about all the things I wish I had done differently. We can't change the past, we can only embrace our failures and make sure they never happen again.

Nat banks to the right and cuts through an invisible barrier that conceals our home from anyone that we don't want to see it. The moment we cross through, the large volcano appears, towering before us. From the outside, one might think it is just another crop of the northern mountains. What they don't realize is that inside the heart of that living volcano is an entire city, Izal, the heart of Vulca.

The entrance to the city is a large, cave-like opening carved into the base of the volcano by magic. It's giant. Large enough to accommodate Nat's broad wings as she flies straight through with ease. My eye's fight to adjust to the immediate darkness that greets us.

Weaving through a long tunnel, Nat guides us towards the expansive landing platform specifically designed to accommodate a dragon. The pale blue light of iridescent algae covers the tunnel's ceiling, the same as the interior city. As we fly deeper into the tunnels, my eyes adjust to the soft light so I can see better, and take note that Rian has slowly crept closer to where I sit.

His chiseled jawline is tight with tension, his brows furrowed in deep thought. I can practically *see* the wheels turning in his head as he works out some puzzle or question. One hand is placed casually on the hilt of his sword where it is sheathed against his hip, always ready for battle, even now that we are home. Though I suppose his adrenaline must still be pumping after escaping the collapse of Tepis.

Pushing to my feet I walk hesitantly-careful not to fall off Nat's back- and stand beside him, staring off into the darkness as he is.

"How are you?" he asks from beside me, his voice echoes off the tunnel walls.

I humph out a laugh. "How am I? Really? Is that what you've been working so hard to think up?" When he doesn't answer I turn to look at him and find his brows raise at me in question. "What? I could see you searching your brain for something from all the way over there," I say, gesturing back to where I was sitting before.

"I wasn't aware that I had an audience." His jaw tics.

"Don't let it all go to your head." My words are left hanging in a consuming silence between us. I shift on my feet right as Nat starts to take the final turn towards the landing platform. The motion pushes me off balance and I fall to my right, knocking into Rian.

His large hands grip my upper arms firmly to steady me. The moment he seems sure I'm not about to plunge off Nat's back, he lets go. Heat lingers where his palms pressed against my bare skin, sending a shiver up my spine. Memories of that heat pressed against my chest send a deep flush to my cheeks.

Nat lands gracefully on the landing platform, tucking her wings back in as Rian and I jump off and step to the side. Within a few seconds she has shifted back into her mortal form again. Her arms reach high above her head as she stretches them out, turning at the waist and bending over, reacquainting herself with the feeling of this version of her body.

"Thank you, for flying us home," I say, stepping forward and wrapping my arms around her without thinking. Her entire body freezes, her arms never moving to return the hug. I pull back quickly, putting a bit of distance between us. "I'm sorry."

"Oh! No, don't be. I just wasn't expecting it," Nat explains, her hands raised up between us as if to soothe the nonexistent hurt her rejection left.

A smile tugs at my lips but I force it away, knowing that this next part is going to be hard. "I need to see my father. The king needs to know what happened immediately." Our father deserves the truth. But that doesn't make me any more excited to have to face reality. Especially when I know the blame will be placed on me, if not by him than by myself. Eve and I promised to always look out for one another but I failed her. I won't let anyone else take responsibility for her *absence*, not when I had the power to prevent it.

Nat plays with the ends of her bright red curls, twirling them around her finger anxiously. "Right, so, what now?" It is disarming to see the many sides of her. The strong, fearless guard. The sweet, shy girl, whose eyes always seem to seek my sister out in a room. In the small amount of time I have gotten to know her, she already feels like an important part of my life. Perhaps it's all the new things we have in common.

Rian steps forward. "Now, we go see our king and pray to the goddess that we live through what happens next."

"The king would never kill us," I bite, my voice coming out harsher than I intended.

"No. Your *father* would never kill *you*. Nat and I on the other hand are mere guards who were given one job to do. A job that we failed at. It would be within his every right to punish us for what I allowed to happen in Tepis. I would expect no less." Rian holds his chin up high, his shoulder pulling back in a show of resolve. The mask of the perfect soldier slips back on seamlessly.

Nat's already pale skin seems to blanch at the reality that Rian laid bare to us. She's still so new, she likely hadn't even thought about punishment for failing to protect the heir.

I wish that I could comfort her, tell her that he is wrong. Only I know that he isn't. If my father wanted to he could have both of their heads before the day is done. I will have very little, truthfully no power, to stop it if he gives the order. I just hope that I am right and he wouldn't blame them for this. "He won't," I say, maybe more to myself than them. "My father is kind, and fair. He wouldn't do that to you for my own mistake."

Nat's mouth drops open. "What? This isn't your mistake, I was the one-"

I cut Nat's words off with a raise of my hand. "I knew what she was going to do. I could have told my sister no at any point in time, could have forced her to stay where it was safe. I could have done so many things at every step of the way to ensure that we would never end up exactly where we are right now. So yes, it is my fault. And you *must* let me tell the king and queen exactly that. It's the only way to be certain that you are protected. I owe it to my sister."

"I can't let you take the blame for this," Nat exclaims, her hands balling into fits at her side.

Rian is notably silent beside us.

"You can and you will. Now, let's go. No point in waiting around any longer." The quicker we tell my father the quicker I can start searching for Eve.

~~~

We walk in a single file line through the many tunnels and caves until we enter the main part of the city. Rian goes first, followed by myself, and Nat takes up the rear. I tried to fight them on it but the look in Rian's eyes told me it wasn't an argument worth having. We weave through the streets, passing familiar buildings and feeling the ghost of my sister in every alleyway. When we pass Oz's bar I can't help but think of her dancing, how carefree she was in that moment. We continue on until another building comes into view.

My steps falter as we approach the entrance to my towering home. The large building looms in front of us and reminds me of a night that feels so long ago. Eve and I sat together, eating and laughing about what book I was reading and what antics my brothers had gotten up to recently. The memory settles like a weight on my chest and makes it difficult to breathe.

Rian leads us through the doors and walks past all of the guards stationed in the lobby area. He moves straight to the lift and summons it down to us. I watch the numbers count down until it hits number one and the three of us file inside.

It's evening, which means the king and queen are likely eating dinner together in the dining hall. The doors open and we walk through the halls leading towards the dining room, except a noise draws my attention from down the opposite way and I turn. The door at the end of the hall is cracked open and voices can be heard on the other side. Without second guessing myself I walk straight up to the door and push it open, revealing my father and the queen standing over a desk in the war room.

My father's head shoots up as the door creaks open. His auburn hair is disheveled, like he has been running his hands through it frequently. The lower half of his face is covered in a thick beard that is begging to be trimmed. Blue eyes, the same as my own, stare back at me. "Mar?" My name slips past his lips, so filled with hope and relief that I nearly buckle from the sound alone.

Before I make the decision, my body is crossing the room and launching myself into his arms. He gathers me against him as I wrap around his waist and press my forehead into his chest. My father crushes me to him, his large hands so familiar as they trace soothing circles against my back. At this moment I feel like a child again. Like I have fallen and scraped my knee and need my dad to make it all better. I barely notice the tears slipping over my cheeks until he pulls me back and wipes them away with the pads of his thumbs.

"What's wrong? What happened? Tell me everything. Where is your sister? I heard about the attacks in Rayan and was worried that they might reach you both in Sena. Thank Vana that you're alright." His questions come out as one continuous stream of thought. Not a breath between them and no room for me to give him a single answer.

Queen Elani, Eve's mother, takes a step closer to us. "Mar, what is it? Where is Eve?" Her eyes cut to the door like she expects her daughter to come bounding into the room any moment. After a second she turns back to me, looking me over from head to toe, concern clear in her eyes.

I push away from my father and begin pacing. A nervous habit I haven't turned to in some years. So many thoughts race through my mind all at once, threatening to push me over the edge and send me spiraling into the darkest depths. What happens next, what I say, will determine more than just the course of this conversation. It will be the deciding factor to Rian, Nat, and even my own fate.

Taking a steadying breath I force myself to plant my feet and turn to face my father and his queen. Something in my eyes must tell them the severity of what I am about to say because the queen grabs onto her king like he is a lifeline. I have to do this. No more stalling. "Eve is gone." The words come out as a broken sob. I have to will myself not to lose it completely.

"What do you mean *'gone'*?" my father asks, his voice firm. A king's command.

"When they attacked Rayan we went to help. All of us. When we arrived we became separated and Eve was alone with Cay. I'm not sure the full extent of what happened with them but they were there when Cay's father was killed." I fight the urge to throw up, the panic rising in me churning my stomach.

Their eyes widen as I reveal another piece of the heartbreak. "Callan is dead?" my father asks in disbelief.

"What of Mira?" The queen presses, wrapping her slender arms around herself, holding her elbows.

"The queen was in some sort of deep sleep the last time I saw her. But yes, King Callan was killed." I try to detach myself from the words, from the pain they bring. I have to get through this and I can't do that if I'm crying.

"Poor Mira, she must be devastated. What about her son, Finn?" The question comes from my father. His eyes are full of emotion, and I am grateful that I at least know this one piece of good news.

"I'm not sure if she knows yet but I am sure she will be once she awakens. Finn is fine, he was sent to Sena for his own safety," I answer.

Reminders of Finn have me desperate to go to my own brothers, to wrap them all up in a tight hug and not let go for days.

"Good, but what does this have to do with Eve? You said she was there but that doesn't answer why she is not *here* now," my father says, his words hanging in the air between us.

"Like I said before, Eve and Cay were there. From what I understand they were fighting alongside Callan when he was killed." I wish Cay had been able to tell us more, to explain what happened from her own point of view, not just broken snippets and inferences.

Elani marches up to me, staring me dead in the eyes. "Where is she? What happened to my daughter?" the Queen demands. The way she says daughter is like a slap against my face, reminding me that *this* is not my mother. No matter how much she has felt like one since my real mother's death.

I turn away, putting a bit of distance between us and refusing to meet her eyes as I force the words out. "She's gone. Taken."

For a moment, no one speaks, no one makes a sound. I glance over my shoulder to see their reactions just as the queen walks straight up to me and delivers a harsh slap against my face. Her palm connects with my cheek and makes a cracking sound as it whips my head to the side. I squeeze my eyes tightly closed, fighting back the burning tears.

"Elani!" my father shouts.

A warm hand grips my chin delicately and tilts my head to get a better view of my stinging cheek. I open my eyes and suck in a breath at how close Rian's face is to my own. I had forgotten he and Nat were even here. A silent presence by the door. An audience to the worst moment of my life, aside from the day my mother died.

Rian leans forward and blows cool air against the aching skin, sending another shiver down my spine. His pale blue eyes slide to my own and search for something. Content with whatever he finds he releases my chin and takes a step between the queen and I. "This was not her fault. I was their guard, I was the one responsible for their safety. I should be the one to bare-"

"Leave us," my father commands, baring his fangs, "I'll deal with you and all of the guards who failed this kingdom later."

Rian's muscles tense at the challenge but he doesn't engage. Instead he leans in close to my ear and whispers against it, "I'll wait for you outside." With a nod to my father Rian leaves the room, grabbing Nat's arm and practically dragging her out behind him.

I stare after them even as they close the door shut behind them. Hopefully whatever punishment my father sees fit for them both, won't be so bad. At the very least, not death.

"Mar, tell me absolutely everything. No detail is too small. Start with who took her," my father says, bringing my attention back to him. He approaches me slowly, looking between his wife and I.

I nod my head. "Of course. I never saw who exactly took her but I know where they're from; Cansu."

Glass shatters. I turn to face the queen who has gone ghostly pale. Her hands tremble and broken glass lies at her feet from where she dropped it. "What did you say?" she croaks.

"Mar, that is impossible. Cansu has been gone for a millennium. You must be mistaken." my father says with a sigh.

The queen crosses the room again hurriedly. Coming to stand a mere inch away from my face. Her gray eyes are frantic. "How *exactly* did they take her?" she commands.

I look at my father with concern plainly etched across my face and he gives me a small nod. "They grabbed her and vanished just as quickly as they appeared, in a cloud of mist."

Queen Elani gasps and then she is falling. My arms shoot out to catch her as she collapses in on herself. I stare up into my father's eyes as he appears beside us. He screams for the guards and Rian and Nat come rushing in, more guards piling in behind them. My father gasps and looking back at the queen I see why.

Thin streaks of blood begin to pour from the queen's eyes, nose, and ears.

Chapter 53

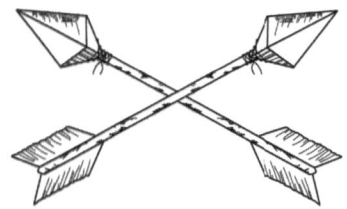

Oak

Three days. Three agonizing days of walking from the village on the border of Rayan, back to the castle in Sena. With so many injured and minimal supplies we've had to stop regularly. For the most part, no one complained. The guards who had escaped walked silently, side by side, following every order given to them. Even when it came from Oliver.

I watched how he interacted with them. Noting the comfort that they felt when he spoke, when he sat beside them in the evenings. I mentioned it to Rose and she brushed it off, saying something about his time in Rayan as emissary. It made sense, enough to drop it. But the closer we get to home the more aware I become of someone watching us, all of us.

I've felt a presence lurking in the shadows as we trudge through the forest. I continue to find myself searching the darkness and coming up empty. Each time making me more on edge. Between this presence and the way that Oliver so seamlessly blends in with the Rayan guards, I can't help but feel the dread slowly bubbling up inside me.

And now, as we approach the entrance to the castle grounds, I send a silent prayer to the goddess that we aren't about to walk an enemy right into the center of our home. Guilt and fear war against one another inside my mind. Guilt over assuming the worst of the people who just lost everything. Yet at the same time not wanting to be next. I've already lost everything once before, I won't let it happen again.

We make our way up the path with the many guards trailing behind us. Rose and Oliver walk side by side, whispering back and forth to my left. Cay is off to my other side, walking beside her mother as Regan pushes the small cart carrying her. Hey eyes are wholly fixed on the shallow rise and fall of the queen's breath. Dark shadows take up residence beneath her sea-green eyes, the color unusually dull. I turn my gaze back ahead of us in time to see the grand double doors burst open.

Terran comes rushing out, eyes burning with mixed emotions as he runs full speed down the path until he is right in front of his siblings and I. "What the hell happened?" he demands, "Mother is furious." His eyes roam over all of us from head to toe. No doubt searching for any sign of injury. Once he is sure that we are all in one piece-at least physically- he looks past us and takes in our large entourage.

"I'm sure she'll get over it," Oliver says with a roll of his eyes.

Terran looks back to his brother, mouth hanging slightly agape like he can't believe his flippancy.

Rose groans from beside him, wiping a hand down her face. "Listen, we've been walking for days. Can we just settle in and deal with this all later?"

Terran turns to his sister, giving her a look that questions whether she has lost her mind too. Clearly, however he had *expected* this conversation to go, it wasn't like this. "Oh sure, go ahead, take a bath, relax, I'm sure mother will be patient after two of her children went running off to fight in a battle that was not theirs. Against direct orders if I remember correctly," Terran says, voice dripping acerbically. He clenches his hands into fists at his side in a rare show of rage.

The gesture is enough for me to step in. "Just let us get the others taken care of first and then we'll deal with the high lady. Okay?"

Terran's furious eyes land on me, "don't think you're getting off so easy."

"I don't. But there are more important matters at hand," I say placatingly.

His eyes roam past me again and he sighs. "Fine." Terran steps to the side and immediately begins directing people what to do. Sena guards appear out of nowhere, starting by helping carry wounded and leading people to the medics. Terran's gaze lands on Cay where she remains beside her mother, a deep sort of longing swirling in the depths of his eyes.

Terran stands there frozen for a moment, just watching Cay as she strokes her mother's hair. He blinks a few times, coming out of his momentary daze and crossing the short distance to stand by her side. "Cay. I am so happy to see you are safe. And your mother. I want you to know that Finn arrived two days ago, unscathed. The servants that brought him here made sure he was well taken care of," Terran says soothingly.

Cay merely nods, her gaze locked on her mother.

Regan steps over to Terran and extends a hand. "My name is Lieutenant Regan Auger, but please just call me Regan, everyone else does. I want to thank you for your hospitality and for letting my soldiers into your home. They have been through an ordeal." She gives a grim smile.

Terran takes her hand with a tight smile, giving it a firm shake. "Nice to meet you, all Rayan refugees are welcome in Sena. People have been showing up over the last few days and we have a better understanding of the situation but I would love to get your perspective whenever you are feeling up to it."

"Of course, I would be happy to help. I am grateful to know we are not among the only survivors," Regan breaths in relief. She turns back to look at the queen, her body looking more relaxed than I have seen it since she learned of her king's fate.

"Far from it," Terran offers with a more genuine smile. His eyes continue to roam back and forth between Regan and Cay, warring between his duty to act as heir and his blatant desire to go to Cay.

Oliver on the other hand, doesn't seem to have any hesitation as to what he wants at this moment. He creeps around Rose and I until he is at Cay's shoulder, whispering in her ear about something. Cay seems to visibly relax, her shoulders drooping and head falling to the side so it presses against Oliver's arm.

I swear my eyes almost bulge out of my head as Oliver shifts his arm to wrap loosely around her waist. Which is nothing in comparison to the seething glare that Terran sends his brother's way. His eyes heat as they remain fixated on the point of contact between Cay and his brother, shifting between her head and his hand.

Rose clears her throat, getting her eldest brother's attention. "Queen Mira needs immediate attention. Cay and I have been healing her as much as we can but she has hardly shown any signs of improvement and I'm not even sure if my magic is helping at this point. I'm not sure what to do from here." Rose holds her head up high but I don't miss the way her shoulders fight not to sag, or how she continues to sway a little on her feet, exhaustion clearly pulling at her.

"I see. Regan, why don't you take your queen and princess inside and meet up with the other medics." Terran calls a guard over to lead the way. "They'll get your men settled and see what they can do for the injured, including the queen," Terran suggests, his eyes lingering on Cay despite his words.

"That would be much appreciated," Regan says, walking over and grabbing the queen's cart. She doesn't wait to head inside, gently lifting and wheeling it forward after the guards leading the way.

Surprisingly, Cay doesn't immediately follow. Instead she turns to Oliver, her eyes looking up at him as he stares down at her. Neither of them speaking a word. Something passes between them and I can't help but watch, transfixed in the way they stare like they're seeing each other for the first time.

Rose shifts uncomfortably beside me, clearly also noticing this little exchange, though we both do our best not to address it. Whether that's for our sake, Cay's, or maybe even Oliver's, is a mystery to me.

The moment passes and Cay turns to walk off after her mother. Oliver sticks by her side, a looming shadow barely a step behind her. As he moves to pass Terran, his older brother's arm shoots out, grabbing him by the bicep. "Where do you think you're going? You three, need to go see the high lady. *Now*. That is not up for discussion," Terran commands, looking between his siblings and I.

Oliver jerks his arm out of Terran's grasp and gets up in his face. "Where she goes I go." There's no reason to ask who *she* is. After what we just saw I think we can all see things very clearly. Tension is thick in the air as the two brothers become locked in a staredown, neither one willing to yield.

Cay pauses, looking back over her shoulder and seeming to wait to see what will happen next. Her eyes are glazed over, becoming more distant and unavailable by the second.

Rose shares a look with me that tells me she also noticed the change in her friend.

Terran takes another step forward leaving no space between him and his brother. "What the fuck is that supposed to mean?" he practically growls.

"Wouldn't you like to know?" Oliver mocks, his familiar smirk spreading across his face.

Rose steps forward, pushing the two of them apart, and staring up at her eldest brother.. "Alright, enough. Terran, leave it alone will you? We've all been through a lot, we don't need you two fighting. *Cay*, doesn't need this," her voice drops to a whisper at the end, barely loud enough for me to hear.

"There is absolutely no way that I am allowing him to go with her," Terran scoffs, shifting ever so slightly so he is more in Oliver's path. The two are so evenly matched that I'm sure if Oliver truly wanted to get by, he would.

"I want him to. Please," Cay pleads from her spot a few feet ahead of us. It's the first time I've heard her voice in days. The rare moments she spoke were all whispers shared between her and Oliver, no one else, not even Rose.

Terran seems taken aback by her request, looking between them like some answer will magically appear. It takes him a moment before he recovers, clearing his throat and taking a step away from Oliver and towards Cay. "Of-of course. If that's what you want." He coughs.

Oliver gives Terran another mocking smirk and walks off after Cay, making sure to shove his shoulder into his brother as he goes.

The two of them disappear inside the castle walls before Terran turns back to Rose and I. "You two aren't getting out of this. Go see the high lady. Now."

My stomach drops. Still, I nod my head and head inside, Rose following closely behind me. We walk in silence, nodding to guards as we pass them by. There is an eerie quiet throughout the halls, not nearly as bad as in Tepis, but enough to make the hair on the back of my neck stand up. We turn down another hallway and find it entirely empty, sending a burst of anxiety through me. The image of gaunt cheeks and empty eyes flashes in my mind.

Rose grabs my arm and pulls me to a stop. "We need to talk about what's been going on with you. *Before* we see my mother."

I sigh, shaking my head. "Please, Rose, I'm tired, you're tired. Can we just get through today and talk later?"

Her grip on my arm tightens, almost to the point of pain. "No. That's just an excuse to avoid the conversation. I deserve answers and I'm going to get them. *Now*."

Pulling my arm free from her ironclad grip I continue walking down the corridor. Not even bothering to answer.

"Seriously? You're just going to walk away? Why am I not surprised?" Rose scoffs from behind me.

I whirl around, tossing my hands in the air as I do. "What would you like me to say, Rose? I'm sorry? Is that what you want to hear? Well get over it. There is way too much shit happening right now for me to worry about your *feelings*. So suck it up, and let's go face the consequences of our actions."

Rose's eyes burn with a fury. The temperature drops around us and a chill snakes its way over my skin. My eyes catch on the slow moving vines that start to creep across the floor, moving from Rose towards me as if they are stalking a prey.

My magic tingles beneath my skin and at the tips of my fingers, ready to defend myself if necessary. For a moment I think she's really about to attack, but then Rose takes a deep breath, letting it out slowly, and her magic fades. The small bit of warmth left in the air grows.

"Fine. But after we talk to my mother, you and I are having a conversation. No more secrets, no more lies," she demands.

"Agreed." The lie burns my throat. We're not far from the high lady's office. Within a few minutes the two of us are standing outside her doors, neither of us raising our hands to knock. Just as I am about to, the doors are pulled open from the inside and two of the high lady's guards usher us inside.

High Lady Ayana is sitting behind her desk, her eyes squeezed shut and a perfectly manicured finger working the space between her brows. The guards quickly make their way out of the room once we have been deposited inside, pulling the large doors shut behind them. The moment the door is firmly closed behind us, the high lady stands. She points the same long, elegant finger straight at my chest. "How *dare* you go against direct orders." Her words are clipped, each one said with a bite that could have lesser people cowering in fear.

I hold my head high, taking a step forward. "Let me first begin by saying that I am sorry for disobeying your orders. I know how wrong that is. But,

I wouldn't change my actions. I stand by what I did. Helping those people was the *right* thing to do, even if how I went about it was not."

Ayana slams her hand down on her desk, making me jump. "You *know how wrong that is,* do you? If that were true then you would have never done it in the first place. And now, now you sit here lecturing to me about right and wrong. You. Know. Nothing!" she bellows.

Rose steps forward. "Mother, please. Cay is our friend. We had to help her kingdom. If you would only let us-"

"Silence! I will deal with you in a moment, *daughter,*" the high lady spits, "right now, I am dealing with your insolent cousin here."

"I take whatever punishment you have for me willingly," I state proudly.

"Oh yes you will. Because that is what you *deserve.* You are a soldier, a spy. I think it is time that I started to treat you as such. You went against direct orders and so you clearly need a reminder of what is expected of you," she says with a clap of her hand.

The door opens behind us, drawing Rose and I's attention.

A tall, lithe figure walks in dressed head to toe in black. I allow my gaze to roam over their unfamiliar attire. The pants are made of a thick material, various blades tucked into straps up and down the sides of their legs. A fitted tunic wraps around their chest, held tightly together by a series of corded leather straps, adorned with more blades. The sleeves go all the way down to their hands which are covered with leather gloves. Most of their face and head are hidden by a head wrap. Only a thin gap is left for their eyes to peek through, surrounded by smooth tawny skin.

The figure crosses the room and stands with their hands pressed firmly to their sides. "High Lady Ayana. I am here, as requested," they say, voice smooth and feminine.

The high lady smirks, looking so much like her son at that moment. "Good. Rose, Oakley, this is Aine."

"Hello," Rose offers hesitantly, clearly as confused by this new addition as I am.

"Aine here is one of my Ghosts," Ayana beams, looking over the girl with such pride that I feel the bitter taste of jealousy on my tongue. In all my years of serving as her spy, she has never praised me for my work. Not genuinely, not with that look in her eyes.

"What's a Ghost?" Rose asks from beside me.

"The Ghosts are a group of women who have trained their entire lives to become the most elite spies. Their skills are unmatched by any other kingdom. They always remain undetected, slipping in and out without a trace." The high lady laughs, turning to look at me. "Aine here has been following you since the moment you left the castle."

Shock ripples through me. "I'm sorry, what?"

"You heard correctly. I sent Aine to watch you after our little meeting, knowing that you would defy me. Of course I had hoped I was wrong."

"You were spying on me?" I ask, the words coming out shakier than I would have liked.

"Aine was, but yes," Ayana says with a shrug.

"Why?" What have I done to lose her trust? What, except keeping her secrets, telling lies to everyone that I care about, and distancing myself from anything good in my life. How could she do this to me?

"Because clearly it is necessary. Now, enough questions." The high lady motions to Aine who steps forward and begins to pat me down.

"Mother, what are you doing?" Rose practically shouts. She finally seems to have realized the gravity of our situation. Or mine at least.

Aine removes all weapons from my person, tucking them into various open slots throughout her uniform.

"Aine is here to collect Oakley, daughter. She will be sent to train with the Ghosts until she learns what it means to truly be one of my spies. Maybe then she will learn to respect the orders given to her."

I am left speechless and frozen, arms hanging out beside me awkwardly.

Rose looks at her mother frantically. "What? You can't do that, you can't just send her away! I-"

"Do you, daughter, need a reminder of your place as well?" She pauses, waiting for Rose to reply. When she is met with nothing but silence she continues, "Oakley is going. That is final. She will leave immediately."

Those words bring me back to the moment. "Wait! Please, I need to search for Eve. I swore that I would find her." If anything would make me defy my aunt, it's my friends. It's the reason I left for Tepis, to help Cay, and if I have to fight day and night to keep my promise to Mar-to bring Eve back- then that's what I'll do.

"I do not know what happened to the Vulca heir, but let this be your first lesson, niece." Ayana walks forward, placing a gentle hand on my cheek and staring down into my eyes. "Do not make promises that you cannot keep."

Aine steps forward, grabbing me by the arm and dragging me from the room.

Chapter 54

Rose

I'm forced to watch as Aine drags my cousin from the room. Oak's eyes meet mine in the second before they leave the room and I see the plea written in them.

I whip back around to my mother as she sits back down in her seat, unbothered by what she just allowed to happen. What she *did*. "You can't do this. Oak is family, she is more than just some spy. Her place is here, with us." I refuse to shout, refuse to raise my voice and show her just how enraged I truly am.

"I can and I just did. Oakley needs to learn her place. And apparently so do you." My mother rubs a hand along the back of her neck, seemingly exhausted with this conversation.

"What does that even mean?" I ask with a shake of my head, already struggling to hold back the emotions warring inside me.

"It means that it has not escaped me that you also disobeyed me. You put yourself and all of those other girls at risk. You are no soldier, Rose. You had no business running off like that," my mother accuses me.

I begin to pace, my hands opening and closing into fists by my side. Magic is pooling beneath my skin, taking up an incessant hum that leaves me feeling itchy and on edge. The ground begins to tremble beneath my feet as my breaths become ragged, the rage taking over what little control I had.

"Sit down before you cause an earthquake," my mother commands.

The trembling only grows stronger as I force myself to sit across from her.

She raises her brows at me. "Now take a breath. Calm yourself."

I force myself to breathe in, it's shaky and doesn't quite reach my lungs. Still, I repeat the process until it feels like I have a better grip on things. On my magic.

"Good, now, are you ready to have a rational conversation or are you going to throw another temper tantrum?" my mother mocks.

"That's not what I was doing." I fight to maintain my control.

"Really?" she asks, head cocked, "then what *were* you doing? Explain it to me."

My hands curl into fists again as I bite my cheek, trying to remain calm despite the rise that my mother is trying to force from me.

"Listen to me now, Rose. We each have a role in this family, it is time that you start taking yours seriously," she says, her words are so similar to what Oak said in Rayan that it feels like being splashed with cold water. Everything becomes numb as my mother begins to berate me. "I understand that you have some *training*. However, that is in no way comparable to that of your brothers, or any of the guards. You could have *died* in Rayan, and all because of what? Stubbornness?" She shakes her head.

I open my mouth to defend myself but she raises a hand.

"I will tell you when it is your turn to speak," my mother snaps. She takes a few deep breaths of her own before smoothing her hands down the front of her simple gown. "There are things that we each must do, Rose. A duty to our realm and our people. I am the high lady before I am anything else, including your mother."

Her words cut deep, pain blossoms in my chest. I have always known that her duty-*our* duty- was to the people. I have never doubted that for a moment in my life. But to hear her say it so plainly, to know that she values her role as high lady above that of my mother? It hurts more than I thought it ever could. The pain fuels me to speak up, to challenge where I might not have before.

"You speak of my duty, my role, yet you have cut me out of every conversation that truly matters. You let me think that you cared about my opinions, that you valued what I had to offer. Yet you keep so many secrets and tell so many lies that I don't even know what to believe anymore."

She sighs. "I do not have to explain my decisions to you. You will know what I want you to know and when."

I push to my feet, my arms thrust out beside me. "Do you not trust me? Am I not a part of this family? Have I not proven myself to be a good daughter time and time again? I am owed some answers, I have a right to know about these things." My mother sends a burst of her magic my way, forcing me to sit back down.

The small attack is so unexpected that I don't even have room left for the shock of her laugh as it echoes through the room. "You are entitled to *nothing*. Do I make myself clear? Trust is earned, family or not. This conversation has done nothing but further show me how little you understand your place in this family, in this realm. Clearly you have spent too much time around your cousin," she says with a roll of her eyes.

The sound of the door opening draws my mother's attention while mine stays fixed on her. I have always adored my mother. Our relationship has been strong. But now it feels like nothing more than a lie. A story told to keep me from asking too many questions. It makes me question every interaction that we have had. Someone sits down in the seat beside mine and I let my eyes sneak a glance. I am unsurprised to find Terran settling down beside me.

"Now, Rose, I need you to walk me through everything that happened. No detail is too small. We need to be prepared for anything." my mother demands, waving her hand in a way that tells me to begin.

"Oh so *now* you care what I think?" I say with a roll of my eyes.

"Rose!" Terran chastises, clearly taken aback by my blatant disrespect. He's never seen me act this way towards our mother, because I never *have.*

"It's fine, Terran, your sister is feeling a bit frustrated with me at the moment. She does not agree with many of my choices, least of all sending Oakley away," my mother says with a groan.

Terran stiffens beside me. "Where did you send Oak?"

"To train with the Ghosts," our mother says flippantly.

If Terran is shocked he does not show it. He simply nods his head. "Who is going to oversee her training?" he asks, showing the slightest bit of hesitation that has my gut churning.

"Aine will be overseeing it. She has become familiar with Oakley's shortcomings since I first assigned her to watch," my mother answers.

I sit up straighter. "Wait, how long was Aine watching Oak? I thought you said she started following her when she left the castle?"

Terran turns to me, ready to scold me again but my mother-surprisingly-answers my question.

"Aine has been watching Oakley on and off for the last few years. Since I first enlisted your cousin as one of my spies," she says matter of factly.

My mouth is left hanging half open. She's been watching her for *years.* And for what? None of this makes any sense. A thousand questions burn at the tip of my tongue but before I can even think to ask them my mother is moving on.

"Tell us what happened, no more dawdling." Her long nails tap against the table impatiently.

"Is Terran going to be privy to this information then?" I ask with a hint of mocking in my voice.

My tone sets her off and my mother stands again. "Yes, because Terran is the *heir*. He is the one who has a *right* to know these things. He is the one who knows where his *duty* lies, where his *place* is. And he at least is willing to do what is necessary for *this* realm."

Terran says nothing, just stares at some random spot on the desk between our mother and us.

I push to my feet, ready to have this fight if that's what she wants. "That is so unfair. Terran might be the heir but I am still your child, still the *high lord's* child. His blood runs through *my* veins. He would have never treated me like this," I throw the words out like they're my blades, my mother's heart is the target hung against the tree.

"Life is unfair. Losing your father was unfair. You need to learn to live with disappointment. I will not continue to allow you to speak with such entitlement. You will learn your place, no matter what it takes to teach it to you." She stands, placing her hands down on the table and staring me down.

"Are you going to send me away next? Where to this time, mother? Will I go to the Ghosts as well or is there somewhere even farther away from you that you would like me to go?" A frustrated scream escapes me.

Terran cuts me off before I can continue my tirade. He grabs my wrist and forces me to look at him. His eyes are wide, a mixture of emotions swirling in the greens and brown of his iris. "This is a conversation for another time. No one is sending you anywhere, Rose. Right, mother?"

I turn to study our mother's response but she just gives a small wave of her hand, as if that is answer enough.

"Rose, we need to know what happened in Rayan. Please, walk us through what you saw. Do you know who attacked the kingdom?" Terran asks, this time focusing only on me.

I fight the urge to continue the fight, biting the inside of my cheek until the metallic taste of blood coats my tongue. I know that they're right, we need to be prepared in case they decide to come here next. Still, how do we fight an enemy we know nothing about? "Yes, but you're probably not going to believe me," I say with a mirthless laugh.

"Of course we will, just tell us everything you know and we'll go from there, okay?" Terran says, offering me a reassuring smile.

"Fine. It was Cansu. They're the ones who attacked Rayan. They destroyed the barrier, murdered King Callan, and took Eve." I leave it all out on the table, letting them take however long they would like to process things.

"What? I'm not sure I heard you correctly. Who did it?" Terran pushes.

I take a deep breath and repeat myself, making sure my words come out slow and clear so that there is no mistaking it.

"That's not possible," my mother denies. Her entire body seems to have gone rigid in her seat. Her jaw tense, shoulders tight, even her eyes seem to have grown colder.

"It is the *truth*," I emphasize.

"It *can't* be. What makes you believe that Cansu, a realm long dead, has anything to do with this?" my mother challenges.

"The way they move and fight for one. Oak told me it is as though they are made of mist. When you cut them they don't bleed, they don't die, they simply vanish in a cloud of smoke. Not to mention that they *told* Cay exactly who they are," I explain.

"Well then we must speak to her, Terran, summon the girl and have her meet us here immediately," my mother commands.

"You can't just summon her here. She isn't your subject, she is an heir of her own right and she *just lost her father*. Her mother is sick, possibly dying. Show a little empathy," I scoff, staring at my mother like I am seeing her for the first time. How can she be so cold, so heartless? This isn't the woman who I have known all my life. I refuse to believe it.

"She's right about that mother, we should allow her time to grieve, to heal. She lost not only her father but her entire kingdom," Terran adds, for once in what feels like a long time, actually agreeing with me.

"Yes of course, I shouldn't have suggested it. Of course she should be given time. Still, time is of the essence, who knows when or where this mysterious enemy will attack next," she says with a deep sigh.

471

"It's not a mystery. It's Cansu," I reply, refusing to allow her to brush this truth off.

"Yes, well, moving on. What else do you know?" she prompts.

I open my mouth to push her further but Terran gives me a look that practically begs me to drop it for now. I give him a slight, nearly imperceptible nod, and walk them both through everything that I know.

For the most part they listen quietly, only nodding occasionally. Once I have gone through everything I can remember I let them ask their questions.

"You said that the creatures disappeared in a cloud of mist? That they didn't bleed or die just vanished, can you explain that further?" Terran asks, giving me an encouraging smile.

I shake my head, "Not really. The others were the ones who truly fought them."

Terran nods like he expected as much from my answer.

Meanwhile my mother groans. "That will be all Rose, go find Oliver and see to it that he comes here, *immediately*."

"That's it? You don't have any other questions?" I ask looking between my mother and brother. The latter gives me a pained smile.

"Yes, it doesn't seem as though you have much to add to the matter. Unless of course you are forgetting to tell me something?" she taunts.

My teeth grind together as I force myself to stand. "No, mother. I have told you absolutely *everything* that I know." With that I turn away from her and make my way from the room. Slamming the door closed behind me it almost immediately reopens.

I expect my mother to come chasing after me, scolding me for being disrespectful in slamming the door like that. Only it's Terran who emerges from the room, jogging a few paces until he walks alongside me. "What can I do for you, brother? More questions? Or perhaps mother changed her mind and I am being sent away?"

Terran pulls me to a stop, one hand on each shoulder as he stares down at me. "I will never allow that to happen."

I turn my head away from him but he forces it back, holding my cheek with one of his rough, calloused palms. "I am so proud of you. What you did. Even if I don't agree with how you went about doing it. You might not have fought those creatures directly but you did something even more important, you protected the people who needed help. You made sure that those servants and Finn got out while they could. There is no shame in that."

"I am not ashamed of what we did. The *only* regret that I have is that Eve did not get to come home." My heart squeezes as I think of Eve. Captured and possibly being tortured at this very moment. If the other leaders, like my mother, refuse to acknowledge that Cansu is responsible, how can we even begin to think of a way to get her back?

"I understand that you are upset about Eve. I am too. But right now, we have to do what's best for Sena, for our home. I am sure that Mar and her father will work diligently to bring her home. Have faith in them."

"What if that's not enough? What if they can't bring her back alone? Mother refuses to even consider the idea that our enemy is from a land we know nearly nothing about," I counter.

Terran sighs, pulling me forward until I am buried against his chest. His large arms wrap around me in a firm hug. His chin rests on the top of my head. "She's scared. There hasn't been an attack like this in her lifetime. We were lucky enough to be raised in an era of peace but that peace is fragile. A threat like this, it's terrifying. Sometimes it is easier to search for something that makes sense, rather than confront the unknown."

"Cansu is back. We can't hide from this. The longer that we pretend, the worse it becomes." Something builds inside me, a bitterness that tangles with fear and anger, a mess of emotions that threaten to consume me if I let it slip even the smallest bit.

Terran pushes me back, placing a single kiss on the top of my head. "I admire your passion, your willingness to help others. But we have to take care of ourselves before we can take care of someone else."

I take a step away from him, holding back the tears burning in my eyes. "What if she sends me away next? What if I'm not of use anymore?"

"She won't. I swear it," Terran vows, before turning back to the room.

My mother's words echo in my mind. *Do not make promises that you cannot keep.* I turn away intending to search for Oliver. As I pass by the library, I pause. Looking inside at the rows and rows of books. Ancient tomes full of knowledge dating back eons.

Without giving it a second thought I decide that if my mother wants to find her son, she can do it herself. I, on the other hand, have something more important to do. And it starts right here in this library.

Chapter 55

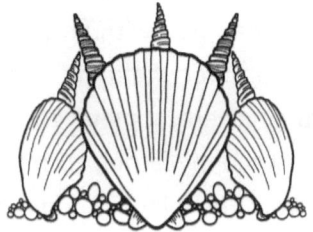

Cay

"Leave us. I'll take it from here," Oliver orders the guard Terran had assigned to lead us. The guard gives him a quick nod before rushing off down another hallway. "You can follow me, the medics are this way," Oliver says, turning on his heels and walking down the corridor.

Regan pushes my mother in her cart, working to keep it steady and not jostle her around too much. I can see the older guard's muscles strain with the weight. Sweat beads along her hairline despite the chill in the air. She does nothing to stop the drops as they stream down the side of her face.

I look up, hoping to get Oliver's attention to see if we might take a break but he is already there, pushing Regan aside. "Let me, you've been carrying her for hours."

"She is my queen, I would gladly carry her until my body gives out," Regan replies, wiping the back of her hand across her brow. Still, she lets Oliver take over, pulling the corner of her tunic up to wipe the rest of her face. Her bright green eyes are shining against her flushed skin.

"Please, it is my home, let me at least pretend to be a gentleman," Oliver says with a playful smile and wink.

Regan shakes her head at him with her own smile. Gratitude is written over her features and I feel it echoed throughout every piece of me. Even if I cannot find the words to express it at this moment. Or any moment it seems.

Since waking up I have grappled with an agonizing mix of emotions, guilt, fear, grief, anger, and an overwhelming sense of relief. I feel thankful to be alive, that my brother is here, somewhere within these castle walls. But when I close my eyes I see my father, crumbled and bleeding before me and I hear the same words echoing around in my mind. Over and over again.

I come from the land forgotten, the darkness, the mist itself. My king sends his regards.

Those words have consumed both my waking and sleeping mind, refusing to allow me even a moment of rest from their torment.

Oliver leads the way through the castle halls, pushing my mother's cart with ease.

I walk alongside them, my hand reaching out to smooth her hair back from her face every once in a while. Her chest rises and falls ever so slightly but even that small movement propels me forward. The weight of my own body is nearly crushing as I force myself to move. Exhaustion threatens to consume me before we even make it to the medics, yet somehow, when I focus on my mother instead, I can take the next step.

We round a corner and the familiar doors to the med room looms before us. The large stone archways are covered in thick moss and vines, swirling around the intricate designs carved into them. Oliver leads us through them and then immediately stops, placing the back of the cart down gently. "I'll be right back, I need to find Florence," Oliver says to us before heading off into the large med bay.

There are cots lining the walls with a large open walkway up the middle. Many of the beds are filled with Rayan soldiers in various states of health.

A dozen Sena healers bustle about the room, caring for each of them. Tending wounds, fetching water, even just keeping them company. If I look to the far left wall I will find the bed that I myself occupied only mere days ago.

"Princess, if it is alright with you, I would like to check in on the guards here," Regan asks, her gaze wandering between my mother and the rest of the beds.

I give her the best smile I can muster. "Of course. We'll be fine. Take some time to be with them and then make sure *you* rest. You're of no use to them exhausted."

"It will take more than a few days' journey to knock me out, still, I appreciate the kindness." With that Regan gives me a deep bow and hurries off to help the others.

I wait by my mother until Oliver comes back, a woman dressed in healer robes by his side. Her hair is completely white in its tight bun atop her head. Wrinkles cover her entire face and frail body, giving away just how old she must really be. She looks to be at least 100 which means, by my guess, she would have to be at least 800 years old.

Oliver holds her elbow as she hobbles forward, stopping just in front of the cart. "Is this the queen?" Her voice is as brittle as her bones appear to be.

"Cay, this is Florence, she has been the royal healer for generations. Florence, this is Cay, crown princess to the Rayan throne, and this," he says gesturing to my mother, "is her beautiful mother, Queen Mira."

Florence steps forward and places a hand on my mother's ankle where a bit of skin is exposed. Her eyes close as she holds onto her, whispering to herself. Minutes go by and I'm about to say something when Oliver gives me a shake of his head. I have to bite my tongue to keep from speaking out. The last thing I want to do is offend the old woman.

"It's been a long time since I felt magic like this," Florence says finally, her small eyes opening and revealing white irises.

My eyes find Oliver's, wide with fear, but he just mouths *later*.

"I know you're talking about me boy, I can sense it," she says, smacking Oliver in the chest. "Now, young lady, you come here so I can get a feel for you."

I take a hesitant step forward.

Florence tsks, "don't be shy now, get a move on."

Moving quicker I close the gap between us until I am standing right in front of her. She reaches out with her shaky hands and I take hold of it with my own. She turns my hand over and runs her papery thin fingers over my skin. "Ah, yes. I can sense very powerful magic in you. Strong, just like your father's. Though not as strong as I would have thought. You said her father passed, correct?" The question is directed at Oliver.

My breath catches in my throat at the reminder of my father.

Oliver answers for me, "Yes. King Callan was lost a few days ago."

"Hmm, interesting. And dear, did you feel the power transfer to you at the time of his passing?" Florence asks, squeezing my hand.

I clear my throat, trying to dislodge the lump that seems to be stuck there, making it difficult to breathe right. "Um, no. Not exactly. My magic seemed to react, but it was only for a moment. I haven't felt the transfer happen yet. Is that bad?"

"It's certainly abnormal. When a ruler dies, their power transfers directly to their heir. If you truly are your father's first child, it should have passed to you immediately."

My blood turns to ice in my veins. Fear bubbles up inside me and I can't help but look at Oliver. Seeking out the comfort that he has come to provide me since the moment my world fell apart. Never in my life would I have thought Rose's arrogant, obnoxious, infuriating older brother would be the one to calm my heart and clear my mind.

His hazel eyes are narrowed, working something out in his mind. "What could that mean, Florence?" he asks, his eyes searching my face for something.

"Boy you know well and good to call me Flora, I will have none of your nonsense today. You too, darling," Flora says to me with a smile.

Oliver blushes, actually blushes, at her words.

"There are a number of things it could mean. Though I fear that it might have something to do with the magic that seems to be infecting the queen," Flora continues.

"Infecting? What does that mean? How can magic infect someone?" I ask, my hand reaching for my mother instinctively.

Flora leans in closer, pulling Oliver down too so that we are all in a tight circle. "Not here, let us speak somewhere more private. Bring the queen." She takes a step forward, releasing Oliver and clinging to my arm instead.

Oliver grabs my mother's cart and follows behind us as Flora leads the way to the very back of the med room. She turns down a narrow hallway, barely wide enough for two people. "Leave the cart, Olli boy will you? You're big and strong, you can carry the queen from here," Flora commands.

I fight back the snicker at her nickname for him, hearing *Olli* grumble from behind us.

He lifts my mother with ease, following down the narrow path until we enter a small work room. He sets my mother down gently on the cot in the corner of the room, then starts gathering chairs.

Flora takes the cushioned one in the center of the room. I have to help lower her down into it but once she is there she shoos me away. I take the chair offered to me next, a small wooden thing with a square back, not exactly comfortable but my legs are still grateful for the break.

Oliver is left with a small stool, so low to the ground that his long legs are pushed into a near squat, knees pressed against his chest. I fight off another giggle as it threatens to burst free from my lips. Somewhere deep inside me, I fear what the sound of my own laughter will do to me.

"What did you mean by infecting the queen, Flora?" Oliver asks, adjusting in his seat awkwardly.

"That is a complicated answer. You see, magic is a living, breathing piece of us. It flows through our body as much as our blood, it breathes through our lungs and beats in our hearts. Our magic is like a piece of our souls. It makes us who we are and connects us to one another," Flora says whimsically.

I think about that power drawing me to my parents, how it led me straight to them and let me fight by my father's side even if it couldn't save him. Our souls knew each other and connected. "I know what you mean, I can feel my power connect to my family. It made sharing magic that much easier between us."

"Exactly, dear girl. Because your magic is one in the same. It comes from the same place," Flora leans over, patting my knee.

Oliver shifts uncomfortably. Flora notices the movement but chooses to leave him be. The stool groans beneath him.

"So what does all this mean about my mother? Do you know what is wrong with her?" I ask, bringing the conversation back into focus.

Flora sighs, her thin lips set in a deep frown. "When I sense your mother's magic, it is as though it has been cut off from her. Trapped, deep inside the well that lives inside her, inside all of us. Being cut off from her magic like that has made it impossible for her body or mind to heal."

"Heal from what?" Oliver asks, leaning forward.

"I sense more than one kind of magic inside your mother. There is darkness, a poison if you will. It seems to have crept inside her and is being awfully stubborn. I fear that we might not ever be able to remove it. Not without the knowledge to do so."

"What does that mean for my mother?" Panic creeps up inside me steadily.

"From what I can gather, your mother's magic is doing everything it can to protect her from this darkness. Which is why she is in a deep sleep. It is not that she is hurt, but like she is conserving power, fighting with every tiny piece that she can to stay in this world."

My heart beats wildly in my chest. Panic begins to set in as I picture my mother, forever locked in this comatose state, never waking up. She'll never get to see Finn grow. She'll never see me become queen or get married, have children. She'll miss it all until she isn't strong enough anymore and she simply *fades away.* It is a fate worse than death. And I refuse to accept it.

"How do we save her? What can I do to bring her back?" I practically beg.

Oliver leans towards me and wipes away hot tears that I hadn't noticed spill onto my cheeks.

"Olli told me that your healing magic helped?" Flora asks.

I nod my head. "Yes, or at least it seemed like it did. She seemed to breathe better, deeper, though it only really seemed to help as I was actively healing her. The moment I stopped, the effects seemed to stop too."

Flora nods like it as she expected. "If I had to guess, it worked because you and your mother share a thread of power together. Her magic recognized yours and responded. It might not be a true solution, but I believe we should begin by having your mother under constant healing."

"Constant healing? By who?" Oliver asks.

"We'll need to have my girls rotate. Never ceasing their work. The queen must be under constant supervision until we know how stable her condition is," Flora states firmly.

I shake my head, "Rose tried to heal her but it barely did anything. How do you know that my mother will respond to your girl's magic?"

Flora seems to consider that for a minute before clapping her hands in front of her. "Perhaps it is not a matter of who, but what."

"Come again?" Oliver says.

"Maybe it is not about *who* does the healing, but rather the *source* of their magic. Do you have healers here with you? Ones with water magic?" She directs the question at me.

My mind catches up with where she is going and I sit up straighter, filled with the smallest sliver of hope. "I'm not sure about those trained in healing but at the very least all soldiers learn basic spells. I'm sure that some of them would be adept at healing with a bit of practice."

"Good, good. I will have my girls begin checking for the gift among those gathered here. With luck, we'll be able to form a small collection of healers and your mother will respond to their water magic," Flora says with a toothy grin.

I let out a deep breath, letting the tension go with it. Up until this moment it felt like we were chasing after something that wasn't there. But now, we have a path. A way forward. Even if it isn't *the* solution, it's a step in the right direction.

"I hate to be the downer here but, how does this help with the infection, as Flora called it," Oliver says, bringing me back to the larger problem at hand.

"Do you know the source of this darkness, the magic that consumes your mother's?" Flora asks, shifting so she is facing me.

A shudder rolls through me. The phrase flashes through my skull again, just as it has for days now. "*I come from the land forgotten, the darkness, the mist itself,*" I repeat the phrase back to Flora.

Her entire body seems to recoil. She spits over her shoulder and mutters something under her breath. "Cansu," she sneers, "I haven't felt their oily powers in a millennium."

"Wait, you were alive all this time? You saw *them*?" I ask, mouth hanging agape in shock.

Flora chokes on a laugh. "My dear, I am nearly 1,200 years old. I have seen a great deal of things. Even if I can't any more," she says, confirming my suspicion that her eyes are no longer functional.

"But, what does this mean? I don't understand why they are back, or how. What purpose do they have in attacking my kingdom? Of *killing* my father?" I ask, tears now flowing freely down my cheeks. Rage is simmering just beneath my grief, threatening to make an appearance with every passing second.

Flora reaches out a hand and I take it, she pulls me towards her until I am crouched on my knees in front of her chair. "Sweet child. I do not know why they did what they did, only that they have been monsters since the moment they were created."

"Created? What does that mean?" Oliver asks.

Flora shudders. "*That* is a story for another day. Now, I need my rest so you two run along, I'll see to it that the queen is taken care of."

I hesitate to leave my mother, ice cold fear racing through my veins.

"Don't you worry, I'll take care of her. You take care of yourself. Run along now," Flora says, pushing me to my feet. For someone so frail she pushes hard enough to knock me off balance.

I stumble into Oliver who stands barely a step behind me. I look up at him and he gives me a small smile, the hint of a dimple appearing in his right cheek. "I've got her, Flora, thank you for all of your help. I'll be back to check on you tomorrow." Oliver leads us back through the narrow walkway and out of the med room.

The sun is setting outside the castle walls, stealing the small bit of warmth with it. The cold reminds me of home and the craving for my own bed sets in. My feet have begun to ache, the tension in my muscles finally setting in. It's like my body has finally caught up with the fact that we're safe and we can actually relax.

I follow behind Oliver, lost in thought, and hardly realize where he is taking me until I am back in the rooms given to me for Rose's party. The blue gown that I wore that night hangs by the window. It feels like years since I was poisoned, since I woke to the news that my home was under attack. Now, staring at the large bed off to the side of the room, all I want is to crawl in.

"I can get you a bath setup if you'd like, we've been traveling for a while," Oliver offers, moving towards the small bathing chamber.

I shake my head. "No, it's fine. I would rather just lay down."

"Your things are still here, would you like something to change into?" he asks, moving to the trunk at the foot of the bed instead.

"Yes, actually, that would be divine." I can suddenly feel all of the grime sticking to my skin and clinging to my dress.

He opens the lid and searches through it, briefly pausing with a smirk on his face and one of my silk nightgowns in his hands. I expect him to tease me about it, to crack some sort of joke or act as he usually would. Only he doesn't. He folds the nightgown back up delicately and places it back inside the trunk, pulling out an oversized cotton gown in its place. He even grabs the matching shorts and hands them both to me.

"Give me a moment to get changed, I'll be right back." I move to the bathroom and immediately begin shucking off the filthy dress I have been traveling in for days. I look at the clean clothes stacked against the vanity and pause for a moment before using my magic to rinse off the layer of grime coating my skin. Once I feel a bit more clean I pull the shorts on and the dress over my head quickly, and head back out into the main room.

Oliver is standing by the window, staring out as the final rays of sun disappear and we are cast in darkness.

I move over to the bed and hesitate before crawling in.

"Go on, I'm going to tuck you in," Oliver says, nodding towards the bed.

I roll my eyes but do as he asks. "Is this for you or me?"

Oliver shrugs, pulling the covers up over my neck and making sure I am comfortable. "Why not a bit of both?" He stays there for a moment, our eyes staring into one another as my words of gratitude burn in my throat. He squeezes his eyes shut and when they open he feels more distant. Clearing his throat he moves to leave but I grab his arm.

"Stay."

His head whips back around to look at me, eyes wide.

"Stay," I say again when it seems like he is completely frozen.

His throat bobs as he swallows thickly, running his free hand through his loose curls. He pulls back so I grab on tighter but he just laughs. "I'm not going anywhere. But if I'm staying then I'm getting comfortable."

I narrow my eyes at him in confusion but quickly catch up as he rips his tunic off over his head, exposing his bare chest to me. Light brown skin covers corded muscles. His chest is firm, his abs stacked in a way that makes me want to trace each defined square. A deep V is carved into his hips and a small trail of hair leads up from beneath his trousers and to his belly button. His large hands work to unbuckle his trousers before dropping them to the floor.

My eyes snap shut immediately, cheeks burning, as I slap my hands over my eyes.

"Relax, I have on undergarments," Oliver says with a laugh.

I peek out from behind my hands and find that he isn't lying. He wears a fitted pair of shorts beneath his pants, the fabric clings to the muscles of his thighs and… other things. I avert my gaze again, opting to stare at the ceiling instead.

"If you've changed your mind I can go." Oliver offers, his tone serious.

"No, no, you're fine. I just want to give you some privacy." I feel the bed dip on my left as he crawls in beside me. I lay flat on my back, continuing to stare up at the ceiling as Oliver makes himself comfortable beside me. Once he is settled I turn to face him, my eyes searching his face. "Oliver…"

He turns to lay on his side so he is facing me. "Yes?"

"Can I ask you something?"

"Anything," he breathes.

I take a deep breath. "Was my father's death my fault?"

"No," he says without a moment of hesitation.

I nod my head, already feeling the tears that seem to keep sneaking their way past my defenses. "Is my mother going to be okay?"

He pauses this time. "I'm not sure."

A choked sob escapes me at his words. It's not that I expected him to answer differently but I had hoped he might.

"But," he continues, "we're going to do everything in our power to help her. Flora is the best healer in all of Estarynn. She'll figure this out."

I squeeze my eyes shut before blinking away the tears. We lay there in silence for what feels like hours before I ask the question that continues to eat at me. "Oliver, was Eve being taken my fault?"

"Do you really want to know the answer to that?" he replies.

I force my head to nod.

"No," He says, reaching out to brush away the lingering wetness on my cheeks, "but that isn't going to stop you from blaming yourself."

His words fracture whatever self control I have held on to and I break apart. The sobs come fast and hard. My entire body shakes with the force of them and my breaths are nothing more than ragged gasps.

Oliver pulls me forward until I am buried against his chest, tears and snot coating his smooth skin. He holds me like that until I stop crying, until I drift off and hear the words that promise to haunt me for everyday moving forward. And somehow I know, he'll be gone when I wake.

Chapter 56

Mar

My father disappeared behind these closed doors only moments after his wife, Queen Elani, was ushered inside after collapsing. Nat and Rian were among the first to respond to my father's and I's panicked shouts. Yet the moment the queen was behind these doors, they were sent away, told to return to their barracks and wait for further instructions. Part of me is relieved that at least they are safe, for now anyway.

I turn on my toes again, spinning around in place and walking the same 10 steps that I've been pacing for hours. No one will tell me anything. Every time I ask they tell me to be patient or have faith. That Vana will protect her. Both of which are becoming increasingly difficult as my anxiety rises. So instead, I've paced back and forth, just beyond the infirmary, waiting. Sending prayers to the goddess for good news.

The fear that I found in my father's eyes after everything first happened told me just how severe this is. The queen's condition has been deteriorating for quite some time now but something about what I said seemed to have made it worse. Be it the news of her daughter or the mere mention of her captors, something triggered the queen. Somehow, I've found myself responsible for her deterioration.

The door opens slowly behind me and my father emerges, looking completely worn down. His auburn hair is sticking up at odd angles, like he has run his hand through it a few too many times. His pale eyes are distant, unseeing, even as he comes to stand before me. My father's arms open wide and I rush into them, wrapping my own arms around his waist and squeezing into his chest. He crushes me to him in a fierce hug. The familiar scent of cinnamon surrounds me. When we pull apart he gives me a sad smile and places a gentle kiss on the top of my head.

"How is she? Do they know what's wrong with her?" I ask frantically.

He shakes his head, "No. The medics are at a loss for what to do next. They're not sure if it is her condition or if the shock triggered something else entirely." My father lets out a deep sigh.

"Is there anything I can do? Anything at all. I want to help," I push, determined to do everything within my power.

My father shakes his head, "The only thing that I need you to do is take care of yourself. Get cleaned up. Rest. We can talk more in the morning."

I stare up at him, the shadows under his eyes worse than when he entered that room. The scruff lining his jaw is getting a bit unruly, giving him this sort of wild look. That paired with the hollowness in his cheeks, there is more going on that he isn't telling me. "You would tell me if you knew more, right?"

My father's eyes widen. "Of course I would. What would make you even question that?"

I shrug my shoulders, "I don't know. Maybe you thought it would be better that way. That if I didn't know you could protect me. It seems to be a trend amongst the other rulers at least."

He pulls me back in for another hug, talking into the crook of my neck. "Darling daughter, I would never keep secrets from you. I will tell you as soon as I know anything more. You and your sister are my world. No matter how dark the world around me is, with you by my side, I see light."

I nod, my face pressed against his chest. I take a moment to listen to the sound of his heart beating against my cheek. To feel the thread of our magic calling out to one another. Everything about my father screams home, safety, love. The only other people in this world who I feel this with are my siblings and the girls. Rose, Cay, and even Oak have become a new kind of sister. A bond chosen of love, not blood.

"What are we going to do about Eve? We have to find her, we can't just leave her in their hands," I whisper, thoughts of my sister's disappearance always at the forefront of my mind.

"We will get her back. But we have to be rational, we can't just rush into things like your sister does," he says with a forced laugh. The sound rumbles through his chest and makes my heart squeeze.

"What do we do first? I need a plan, I need to know that we aren't just doing nothing," I practically beg. My hands fist into the back of his tunic. "Thinking things through and making a plan is not doing nothing. We have to be strategic, think about what is best for everyone. So, give me time. I will think about where to go from here and as soon as I know, you'll know too. Deal?" he says, pushing me back so he can stare down at me.

I consider what he said, thinking through what the smartest move going forward really is. And even in the few moments I dedicate to formulating a plan, I know that he is right. We can't rush into this. We're going to need a lot of help. Thankfully, I know that our friends will be there no matter what. I nod my head to him in agreement.

"One last thing, it's a big request, Mar, but completely necessary." His tone is serious.

"What do you need?" My pulse spikes.

He looks around the room, searching the shadows for anyone who might be lurking there. Once he is sure that we are truly alone he leans forward and whispers in my ear, "You can't tell anyone else about Eve. The people mustn't know that she was taken from us. Nor can you mention the queen's condition. As far as our people are aware, all is well and good. Eve decided to go off on another adventure and will be back after some time. The queen has decided to relax in her absence."

The shock of his request ripples through me. The words clang around in my mind, foreign and almost too much to even think. If we keep this a secret it means that we can't ask for help, we can't send our soldiers out there to find her. It means that we're on our own.

I can understand the need for secrecy. We cannot appear weak lest we want new enemies to seize this as an opportunity. With both the heir and queen gone, all one would need to do to assume power is kill the king. My stomach flips just thinking about it, which is exactly why I give my father a forced smile and nod my head. "Of course, whatever is best." Even if my heart is screaming at me.

He gives me one final squeeze before disappearing back behind the infirmary doors, leaving me alone in the empty hallway once again.

Too many emotions to name war inside of me. But one sticks out above the rest, anger. Without putting much thought into my plan, I make my way down to the training room. At first, I think the room is empty. The dummies are all tucked away in their spots and no weapons are missing from the wall. Yet something or someone has the hair on the back of my neck rising. I take a hesitant step inside, listening closely for any sound of a potential attacker.

A loud stomp sounds from behind me as someone drops down from above. I fight the instinct to whirl around, recognizing him from the magic I can feel tingling in the air around us and the faint scent of cedarwood.

"Hiding out in the rafters, Rian?" I ask, refusing to turn around.

"If I was hiding, you wouldn't know I was here." His words come out gravelly, his warm breath brushing against my ear. The sensation sends heat racing over my skin.

I spin around, finding barely an inch between us, our chests brushing with each deep breath that we take. "I wouldn't be so sure about that." I haven't seen him since they sent him away. Now, we stand in silence, neither one of us moving. Then, Rian closes his eyes and takes a deliberate step back, putting distance between us.

His eyes follow me as I begin to walk around the room leisurely, trailing my hands along the walls of weapons feeling the cool blades against my heated skin. The sight of my sister's daggers sitting untouched has an ache building in my chest. "How's Nat doing?" I ask, my back to Rian.

"Not handling things well truthfully. She is still so young, so new to all of this. She blames herself for what happened," he answers, his voice seeming to follow me as I walk the length of the room in circles.

"Is there anything I can do to help? Maybe I could talk to her again," I offer.

"Nat was granted a temporary leave at her own request. She left an hour ago for her own home, said she wants to visit her mother. Although, I'm not sure what good it would have done even if she were still here. Nat is stubborn. She will bear this guilt likely for the rest of her life, warranted or not." Rian sighs.

Nat left. Which means there is one less person to help find Eve. Still, we have Rian and Oak and the others. Though, I'm not sure what help Cay will be while her mother is still so sick. My thoughts shift to the queen only a few floors above us. I can hardly blame Cay for wanting to be with her mother, if I had the chance I would give anything for a moment with my own. I suppose I can hardly fault Nat for making the same decision then.

"I'm glad Nat left then, she deserves a break. Besides, it might be safer for her to spend some time away for a while."

Rian's voice is closer when he speaks next, only a step behind me. "Should I be worried? Maybe I should arrange a visit of my own?" The small hint of Rian having a family sends an unwanted flare of jealousy through me.

I freeze mid step. Pain flaring in my chest at the thought of him leaving too. That I would have to search for Eve on my own, at least for now. Which is why I decide to tell him the truth, he deserves as much. "I don't know. Possibly. My father thinks it is best if we don't tell the kingdom about

Eve. To protect us all. If people perceive us as being weak they could take advantage of the situation. It's smart, strategic."

"But?" Rian says, so close now that I can feel his breath against the back of my neck.

"If we do this, if we keep this secret, then that means no one is really looking for Eve. It means that she is alone out there and everyone who *should* be looking for her doesn't even know." It means I'm alone. I keep that part to myself even if the words are true. There is no reason to place that burden on Rian too.

His large hands grab me by my shoulders and spin me around so that we are nearly chest to chest once again. His eyes bore into mine with a fierceness I have never seen before. "Do you agree with this? With hiding it from your people?"

I'm left momentarily speechless by his words. It was certainly not the response I had imagined he would have. "It's the right thing to do. The *smart* decision."

"That's not what I asked. I said, do you *agree* with this?" Rian pushes, his hands tightening their hold on me.

My next breath comes out more of a sigh. "It's not about what I want. It's about doing what's best for the kingdom. Besides, it's not my choice." I look up at him and search his face. Looking for any sign that he understands this decision. Even if I don't myself. Rian is a soldier, a guard, someone who has lived long enough and fought in enough battles to know when to wait and when to attack.

He stares down at me but my eyes are locked on the tips of his fangs as they graze his lower lip, peeking out ever so slightly. As if aware of where my gaze caught, he lets his tongue sweep over the seam of his lips, wetting them.

I am momentarily transfixed by the simple action. My mind going to all sorts of places it shouldn't. Of all the things he can do with that tongue. The things I would let him do to *me* with that tongue. My entire body heats with the images pouring into my brain. It takes a conscious effort to meet his eyes.

When I do, I find his pupils nearly consuming the blue of his irises. His breathing is coming out as short pants. Making direct eye contact, I sweep my own tongue across my full lips. The action brings a growl from the back of his throat that has my own fangs snapping to attention. Never willing to back down from a challenge.

Rian's hands slide down my arms and shift to my waist, tugging me against him. I'm not sure he is even aware that he is doing so. It's more like a subconscious decision, his body moving on its own without much thought. His cedarwood scent fills the air between us again. The intoxicating sweet and warm scent makes me want nothing more than to taste him.

I lean forward and push up on my toes ever so slightly. Moving slower than I normally would, giving plenty of time for him to push me away. My lips brush against his softly, barely a touch let alone a kiss. He remains frozen for a moment before his hands squeeze my waist.

Then he is crushing his lips against mine as we battle and war. Fighting for control. It's a clash of tongues and teeth, his fangs graze over my lower lip and draw a small bead of blood to the surface. A guttural groan releases from the back of his throat.

I can taste my blood on the tip of my tongue as his dances with mine, knowing he can taste it too. My hands make their way to his ashy blond hair, my fingers threading in the short locks at the base of his neck, tugging roughly.

He growls his approval into my mouth and I feel warmth shoot into the pit of my stomach. His hands move to my ass and squeeze. Rian lifts me and my legs go around his waist automatically. I feel his hard length press against my throbbing center. He rolls his hips and I gasp into his mouth pressing my chest against his.

Our kisses become frantic. Messy. Our hearts beat wildly, each pounding uncontrollably inside our chests. Everything about this moment is driven by passion and need and frustration. I can taste it on his lips. I can feel it in the hard grip he has on my ass, firm and teetering on the edge of painful. "It's becoming a real habit for you to abandon your job around me isn't it?" I tease between kisses.

Rian goes still against me. His head pulls back and anger is burning in his eyes.

I unravel my legs at his expression and let them fall back to the floor. The second I do so, Rian is releasing me and putting a solid three feet of distance between us. "What just happened?" I ask, confusion overwriting the lust filling my brain.

Rian refuses to meet my eyes. His hands balled into fists at his side.

"What, you're just going to ignore me now? What the fuck is that about?" I demand, my own anger rising to the surface.

He whirls on me, getting up in my face for an entirely different reason than before. He bares his fangs to me and I can't help but bare my own in return. Rian shakes his head and takes a step back. "You don't get to do that."

"Do what? What is going on right now?"

"I tried to stop you from going. The moment you told me that idiotic plan of yours, I wanted to drag you both back to Vulca, but you refused. You commanded me to ignore my duty and instincts and now look where that got us."

My mouth drops open and my vision goes wholly red for a moment. I rush forward and shove my hands against his chest. Hard. The attack barely moves him half a step. "I am not responsible for ensuring that you do your job correctly. You make your own choices."

"Do not lecture me about my own shortcomings. I know and accept my role in what happened. I am taking responsibility. Can you say the same?"

"What the fuck is that supposed to mean?" I growl. Magic bubbles just beneath the surface of my skin. The air crackles with the power as Rian's does the same. A sort of static energy charges across the space between us, wild and explosive.

"It means that while you might *pretend* that you did not have a hand in the choices I made, I know the truth. You are a member of the royal family, your word, your command as I recall, is as good as law," Rian spits. Turning so that his back is to me.

A mirthless laugh escapes me. "Is that what this is about? You believe I forced your hand?"

Rian doesn't bother to look back at me as he answers. "I am a male who takes responsibility for his own failures. I know what hand I had in your sister's capture. If you would rather place all the blame on me than I will bear it, as is my *duty*. But beyond that, I have nothing more to say to you. Goodnight, princess." And with that Rian leaves, not even sparing a glance back over his shoulder.

Rage consumes me as I watch him disappear from the room. I immediately get to work setting up the training dummies and collecting weapons. I pull my staff off of its clip at my hip and click the button that expands the long metal rod into my staff. Then, I work my body until it is screaming in agony. Until the fire in my veins cools and the power tingling at my fingertips fades. I work out all of the aggression inside of me, all the while thinking and planning what my next steps are.

Starting tomorrow, I will search for my sister and I *will* bring her home. If I have to do that alone then I will.

Epilogue

Eve

Darkness envelops us for a moment and then vanishes in a cloud of mist. My knees buckle beneath me and I collapse to the cold ground. Nausea churns in my stomach and I fight to hold it back but the burning hot contents of my stomach still force their way out.

Positioned on all fours, I empty the contents of my stomach out with tears burning my eyes and violent shakes wracking my body. When nothing else is left, my body continues to dry heave, my stomach contracting painfully.

Hands grip my arms harshly and pull me to my feet. Blinking past the tears in my eyes I wait for my eyes to adjust to the darkness surrounding us. The sky is nearly wholly black, the ground barren and cracked. A thick cloud of mist permeates the air. Something about it looks oddly familiar and I can't seem to shake the sense that I have been here before.

"Move," Teru demands. Something in their voice has me moving forward without complaint.

I try to fight it, reaching deep into the well of power inside of me and searching for anything that would help me. But that well is empty. Not a speck of power or magic left behind. That feeling of emptiness is likely responsible for losing what small bit of food I had left in me. My entire body shakes, not from the cold but from the lack of magic, the weakness of my body as it fights to stay standing.

Teru keeps a firm grip on my arm, their long fingers wrapping around my bicep and digging in painfully. Their steps are nearly twice as long as my own as they drag me along beside them. Occasionally, they release a noise of frustration and pull my arm harder.

"Can you slow down?" I ask regrettably. My lungs burn and my entire body aches.

"No," they say with a laugh. As if in punishment, they walk even faster.

My foot catches on something and I stumble forward. Teru lets go of my arm and I fall flat on my face with a curse. I push up onto my elbows and try to catch my breath.

Teru crouches down in front of me and places a single finger under my chin, tilting my face till I am looking up at them. "Have you always been so graceful?"

"Fuck. You," I grind out, stumbling to my feet.

"As I've said before, ew," Teru says with a grimace.

"What is your problem?" I demand, wiping my hands against my pants.

"You," they grumble.

I just stare at them, bewildered. "If I'm such a problem then why bother with me at all? Why take me? You could have just left me behind and we both would have been better off."

Teru steps forward, pinching my chin between two of their fingers painfully. "That is where you are wrong."

"Care to elaborate?"

Teru laughs, the sound cold and callous. "I don't think I will. Now, *move*." They turn on their heels and stalk forward. Leaving me behind this time.

I look around the barren land, barely able to see farther than my hand outstretched before me. I could make a run for it. Just take off and disappear.

"I wouldn't do that if I were you," Teru calls from ahead of me.

"Do what?" I bite.

"Run."

Before I can ask how they knew I was thinking of running, they appear in front of me in a cloud of smoke, or mist, maybe both.

"A little advice? Do as you're told or face the consequences," Teru whispers against my ear.

I wish I had some magic left to blast them away from me. But since I don't I'll just stick with one of my other favorite weapons of choice. "Fuck. You."

Teru groans. "Can you stop saying that? It's truly disgusting," Teru sighs, swiping a hand down their face, "I am looking forward to the king taming that mouth of yours."

"Oh? And what king would that be. Because as far as I'm aware there are only two. You murdered one and the other is King Basc of Vulca, who I happen to know is not an evil maniac," I mock. I'm careful not to let it slip how close I am to the king, you know, my father.

Teru's eyes turn deadly and before I can process their movement they have me pinned on the ground, a fist full of my hair in their grip. "Watch your fucking mouth."

"Or what?" I challenge. My entire body recoils as Teru's magic slips beneath my skin, stealing my vision and plunging me into a pit of nothingness. Then, there is pain. A searing, blistering pain that burns from the inside out, as though my entire body has been set on fire.

Then, in the next breath, the magic is gone and Teru is standing at least 10 feet away. Their eyes are wide, their mouth set in a hard line. "Get up. We need to keep moving." Without waiting to see if I listen they once again turn away from me and walk off through the thick mist.

I fight to control my ragged breathing as I force myself back to my feet. "If we're in such a rush, why don't you just do that little poof thing again."

They hmph a laugh. "Poof thing? It's called evanesce. And no, I can't evanesce where we're going."

I consider the answer. Evanesce. I've never heard of such a power before. Still, they seem to be willing to answer my questions, maybe I can get more out of them. "And where is it that we're going?"

"To my home," Teru answers vaguely.

Okay so maybe they won't answer all of my questions. I stumble behind them as they lead the way through the mist, contemplating my next move. I need to think. I can't act rashly anymore. "If it's your home then why can't you *evanesce* there?"

"There are spells and wards preventing anyone from entering the main city using that kind of magic. So, we get as close as we can and we walk the rest of the way. Something that would be made much easier if you would just use that heightened eyesight of yours."

As if on queue, I trip again, somehow remaining standing. "I am."

Teru laughs, "No. You're not."

"Yes I am," I grumble, "do you really think that I enjoy stumbling around practically blind in this darkness?"

"Perhaps. Though still a lie."

I throw my hands up in the air. "And how, pray tell, would you know that?"

"Because, if you were using your true eyes then you would be able to see just as well as I can. Also you would be able to see that hole you're about to fall into."

I stop dead in my tracks, searching the darkness for any sign of a deadly hole waiting to trap me. Teru laughs ahead of me and I shoot daggers at the back of their head with my eyes. "Very funny," I say dripping with sarcasm.

"I could show you if you'd let me," Teru offers mockingly.

"No thanks, I'd rather fall on my face."

Teru shrugs, the motion barely perceptible from their place ahead of me. They come to a stop and I walk up beside them.

"What?" I ask, narrowing my eyes at the nothingness ahead of us.

Teru shakes their head and holds out their hands in front of them, then pushes them away from one another and seems to split the fog. As the fog dissipates a sprawling city is revealed, complete with a towering castle at the very center. The sky is varying shades of blues and purples, full of clouds. A thinner layer of the fog layers the ground leading into the city but it's not nearly as thick or dark as the barren lands we have been walking through for hours. It's absolutely beautiful.

"What. The. Fuck," I exclaim, taking a step forward. Teru grabs my arm.

"Wouldn't do that if I were you. There's magic surrounding the city and if you walk through there without casting the right spells first, it will tear you to shreds."

"Ummm, okay then. After you," I say, extending my hand.

Teru steps forward and lifts their hands, casting another sort of spell that leaves small wisps of black smoke swirling in the air. Both beautiful and terrifying at the same time. Content with their work, they turn back at me and motion for me to follow them through.

I expect to feel the magic as I cross over the boundary into the city but aside from the slight dip in temperature, it feels completely normal. I watch the back of Teru's head as they lead us forward, grateful for the extra light. The mist seems to curl at their fingertips, wrapping around their arms and legs, almost in welcome, like it's alive.

"Can I ask, what is your magic? It's unlike anything I have ever seen before," I ask, not bothering to hide the bit of wonder in my voice.

"No," Teru sneers, "you can't ask."

Rolling my eyes I catch up to them and walk side by side, looking all around us as we get closer and closer to the large stone walls surrounding the city. The walls tower high above us, covered in various flowers of the deepest blues and purples, almost identical to the color of the sky.

"What are those flowers?" I ask, pointing them out as we get closer.

"Do I look like someone who knows the name of every plant that grows?"

I narrow my eyes at them, "You're really a horrible guide."

Teru whips around to face me, snapping a hand out so that it wraps around my throat in a vicelike hold. They press down on the sides of my neck, not quite heard enough to cut off my air but enough to let me know they could. "I am not a *guide*. I am your captor. At least until we make it to the castle. So can you please just *be quiet*."

I raise my brows at them, waiting for them to release me. When they don't I roll my eyes, bringing my hand up to wrap around their wrist. "Fine. But only because you said please."

"Vana help me," Teru groans, releasing my throat and grabbing onto my arm instead.

We walk side by side up to the main gates of the city. A singular thought eating away at me. "So, you believe in Vana then?" I ask, unable to hold back the question any longer.

"Of course. Why wouldn't I?" Teru asks, raising a brow.

I shrug, "I just assumed that you wouldn't."

Teru snorts, "Of course you did. Your people are always just assuming things about everyone else now aren't they." The words are said with complete and utter disdain and loathing. So much so that I decide it is probably best to just keep my questions to myself for the time being.

As we approach the gates, Teru once again uses their magic to cast some sort of spell. The large gates open and I step forward to walk through them. The moment I do, my vision once again goes black. Fear seizes my heart. Panic threatens to consume me as I am once again left defenseless. *Vulnerable.* My heart beats wildly in my chest as the rest of me remains frozen. Hands grab me from behind and I choke back the scream threatening to tear free.

"Let's go," Teru mutters. Pulling me forward.

"I can't see," I breathe. My words coming out shakier than I want.

"I know. Move."

I shuffle my feet forward cautiously. After what feels like only a few steps Teru curses and then I feel arms grab me around my waist and at the back of my knees. I am lifted off the ground and this time, I do scream.

"Enough. Stop thrashing about," Teru grumbles.

"Put me down. Right now. Give me back my eyesight," I command, my heart ready to burst.

"No. Now relax before I drop your ass." Teru's grip on me tightens and I am forced to still. My entire body is shaking but Teru doesn't say anything. They just march forward, stealing my vision and leaving me completely at their mercy.

I can barely hear the sounds of the city as we move. People are talking, that much is for sure, yet I can't hear what they say. It's like they're a thousand miles away, like someone stuffed cotton into my ears and muffled their words.

Despite my fear and general state of discomfort, Teru keeps me relatively steady. They don't jerk me around unnecessarily and they don't make fun of me as they take me to wherever they intend to hold me prisoner no doubt.

My mind races with all the possibilities awaiting me. I've never been tortured before. At least not in the bad sense of the word. Would I break easily? Would I betray everyone that I know and love? Pause. There is no way that they know who I am, right? I made sure that Nat didn't say anything. For all they know I'm nobody. Just another random girl who happened to be in the city that they chose to destroy.

Yeah, I'll stick with that. I'll just feign ignorance. Tell them I know nothing and pray to the goddess that they believe me. Then, as soon as my magic is restored, I can fight my way out of here and get back home. That's my plan here. Just bide my time until someone comes to save me. My father, sister, friends, anyone. They'll come for me. All I have to do is be patient and be ready for when they come.

And in the meantime, I'll learn everything I can about who these people are and why they did what they did. Someone will answer for the death of

Cay's father. It should be by her hand, she is owed as much, but if it comes down to it, I'll be sure that justice is served. You fucked with the wrong girl if you thought I would play prisoner gladly.

The arms holding me suddenly vanish and I fall through the air, landing on the ground, hard. My tailbone hits the stone floor, pain shoots up my back and across my ass. I wince but otherwise hold back any reaction. I roll over so that I am on my knees and just as I am about to stand I am forced back to the ground with a punch to my gut. The force of it has me doubling over clutching my stomach and trying to breathe through the intense pain.

Bright light nearly blinds me as my vision is restored and my eyes struggle to adjust. Once they do I immediately search my surroundings. The floor is made of dark concrete, the walls black stone, carved with intricate designs. The walls stretch up and up and then begin to slope, coming together to form a singular pointed ceiling. There are lanterns placed throughout the room, hanging from the walls and ceilings and casting a faint glow over the entire space.

I turn my head and find Teru leaning against the far wall, a smug smile on their face. I glare at them as I continue to search the room. As I do, I realize that Teru isn't alone. There are three others standing opposite to them, dressed exactly the same and standing side by side in a line.

The first person is tall and broad with a shaved head and a thick mustache covering their top lip. A jagged scar carves its way down the center of their face, nearly dividing it in half.

The next is petite, probably my height if not shorter. Their frame is thin, with a small, round face, and narrow eyes. Their lips are painted black and their skin is leached of all color, though it could possibly be paint covering their face rather than the skin itself.

I let my eyes roam to the last in the group and do a double take. This person is nearly identical to Teru. Their faces are a mirror image. The only difference is that where Teru wears their hair long and pulled back from their face, this person keeps it in short waves cropped close to their head.

They also are glaring at me like they are ready to rip my throat out at first chance.

Tilting my head, I flash the trio a bright smile that has the big one muffling a laugh. The small one rolls their eyes and the Teru duplicate only glares harder. I turn my back to them, looking towards the center of the room where a singular throne sits upon a raised dais. The air seems to ripple around the chair and I narrow my eyes when suddenly, a cloud of mist appears and vanishes before I can blink.

My breath gets caught in my throat as I take in the male left behind.

He's dressed in linen pants with a thick waist band slung across his hips, and a floor length robe that opens in the middle, revealing flawless golden skin. His hair falls in dark waves around his face, framing narrow eyes of the most beautiful brown. A rich color, flecked with gold and framed by dark lashes and thick brows. His jaw is carved in a straight line leading to a squared chin beneath wide, full lips of pale pink.

The male rises, stalking towards me. His long legs carry him gracefully down the small steps until he stands just before me.

Every part of my body becomes aware of his proximity. A mixture of the powerful magic pulsing from him and the complete beauty of his body. My stomach warms and my body clenches, betraying me. One of the downsides of being a succubus is that we respond to physical attraction like a drug, and right now, my body wants a hit. The empty well of magic inside me yearns to fill it with pleasure stolen from the male standing before me.

"Well, what do we have here?" His voice is lyrical, enchanting.

I wonder what my name might sound like spilling from his lips. Clearing my throat, I set that thought aside. "Where am I?" I demand, my voice is surprisingly firm.

The male laughs, the sound doing funny things to my chest. "Allow me to welcome you to the land of mist and darkness." He stops just in front of me, crouching down so we are at eye level. "This is Cansu, and I am its king."

Before I can respond, mist surrounds me and I realize a second too late that while we might not have been able to evanesce *into* the city, that doesn't mean they can't use the magic once inside. I can do nothing to stop him as he sends me tumbling through the darkness.

To Be Continued in Book Two of the Sovereign Sisters Series:
REALMS OF SECRETS

Acknowledgements

There are so many people who I would like to thank. First and foremost, I want to thank my best friends, Ali, Delilah, and Kaitie, for inspiring this series and being an endless source of support. From the very beginning you have been there for me and I am so lucky to have you by my side. Thank you for putting up with my constant complaining, bouts of self-doubt, and plenty of tears. You were the first people to read this story and your unwavering faith in this book is truly what got me here today. I am so grateful to all of you.

I want to thank a few people for their contributions to this book. I want to thank Nora for being my editor and helping take the jumbled mess that was the first draft and get it to something remotely legible. Your patience with me and ability to meet the crazy deadlines I set are both much appreciated and a warning because it is only going to get worse from here.

I also want to thank Delilah Cay specifically for not only designing the cover art (which is a feat in itself) but also designing the chapter art, merchandise, social media posts, and always helping with any kind of creative project surrounding this book.

I would like to acknowledge and thank my incredible beta readers including my sister, Sharity, who never shied away from telling me just how much she hates Oliver. You all were such an invaluable part of this process and I am so glad to have had you on this team. Truly, this book would have never been possible without the support and feedback you all provided. Between complications with technology, the MANY typos and grammatical errors, and the somewhat rigorous timeline, you pushed through and gave me such valuable insight. For many of you, this won't be the last Sovereign Sisters beta rad that you do, and for that you have my eternal gratitude. I am so unbelievable blessed to have so many people who love this world, it's characters, and the story as much as I love it myself.

I want to share a special note that as a reader, I am not often discouraged by grammatical errors and typos in writing, but also recognize that this is not the case for many readers. I do my best to manage my dyslexia and catch any of those issues throughout the writing and editing process, but I am human and it is entirely possible that you may find them throughout current and future writing. I hope that despite the distraction they may cause, that you continue to enjoy my work and support me in the future.

A very special shout out to my dog, Vera, who was always down for the cuddle sessions before, during, and usually after an intense writing session. Rest in peace my sweet girl, I hope you know how much you are loved and missed.

About the author

Teanna Lynne grew up in Orlando, Florida where she spent her childhood surrounded by stories. She is the youngest of three girls, and an adoring aunt to her nephew. Teanna graduated from Florida Gulf Coast University with a B.A. in Communication and a minor in Creative Writing. She then went on to receive a M.A. in Communication from the University of Central Florida. Teanna is a proud member of the LGBTQ+ and works closely with Diversity, Equity, and Inclusion in her work.